FORWARD

CLARE DOWLING

POOLBEG

Published 2000 by
Poolbeg Press Ltd,
123 Baldoyle Industrial Estate,
Dublin 13, Ireland

©Clare Dowling

The moral right of the author has been asserted.

A catalogue record for this book is available from the British Library.

ISBN 1 85371 981 1

Cover design by Slatter-Anderson
Set by Pat Hope
Printed and bound in Great Britain by
Caledonian International Book Manufacturing Ltd, Glasgow

Acknowledgements

Thanks to Caroline Williams and Siân Quill for their ideas, endless encouragement and for letting me burn up their phone lines. Thanks to Marie Thérèse Duggan for introducing me to the world of film back in 1992, to my father for sharing his knowledge of the world of politics and to my mother for knowing when to ask how it was going and when to say nothing at all. Thanks to Philip McDermott and Gaye Shortland of Poolbeg for reading the only four chapters that existed and deciding that there just might be something in it, and to Paula Campbell for falling in love with Peter Fisher. Special thanks to Stewart for his patience, belief and the constant supply of Heineken in the fridge, and to Seán, whose birth in the middle of it all restored my faith that there was a deadline I could actually stick to.

For Stewart and Seán

Biography

Clare Dowling was born in Kilkenny in 1968. She trained as an actress and has worked in theatre, film and radio. She began writing for theatre in 1992 and has had five stage plays produced in Dublin. Her award-winning half-hour film *The Big O* was produced in 1995, and she is the co-author of a second half-hour film, *The Very Stuff*, produced in 1996. She has had drama and children's fiction published, and her play *The Marlboro Man* is included in an anthology of new Irish writers. She co-writes a weekly children's fiction series on the Internet and she is currently a scriptwriter on Ireland's top soap *Fair City*. She lives in Dublin and is married with a son.

Chapter One

Cathy Conroy looked like a boy.

Now, she wasn't a fool. She had known all along that she had not been gifted with a heart-shaped face or bouncing blonde curls. And as for curves? Forget it. She had a long, thinnish, narrow-hipped body, topped by a head of cropped brown hair. Nobody could accuse her of looking like Pamela Anderson. But nobody had accused her of looking like a boy before, either. It was just the latest in a long line of insults.

"Excuse me!" A woman was leaning over the checkout desk aggressively. "It's two cabbages for a pound."

"Sorry?" Cathy said, startled.

The woman plucked two fat cabbages from her shopping bag and waved them under Cathy's nose.

"It says over there that it's *two* cabbages for a *pound*. And it says *here* on my receipt that you've charged me sixty pence *each*." She spoke as though Cathy were rather slow.

"Terribly sorry," Cathy mumbled, taking the receipt and scrutinising it.

A *boy!* It still rankled, even though the audition had been yesterday morning. Cathy had given it her all; never before had Juliet died with so much pain, anguish and conviction. The producer had murmured to the director, "Fantastic". *I've got the part,* Cathy sang to herself as she sailed out of the room, *I've finally landed a part in this town.* That was when she heard the producer add, "But don't you think she looks like a boy?"

"I haven't got all day!" The blasted woman was still on about her cabbages.

Cathy tried to be apologetic. "There does appear to be a mistake on your receipt all right. Sometimes the computer system gets it wrong . . . "

"I don't want your excuses! You're always over-charging in here!" The woman was outraged. "I'm seriously considering taking my business elsewhere!"

Take it then, you old bag. For a horrified moment, Cathy thought she'd spoken aloud.

She offered the woman a sickly smile. "I'll refund you the difference." Fingers fumbling, she punched keys on the till to open it.

A *boy.* It was incredible really. If they'd had any problem with her, surely it should have been with her accent? She was Irish, after all. This was London. Usually, she was typecast as a fresh-faced colleen who spoke in a charming lilt and who probably ate potatoes for breakfast. Even with the walk-on part in the detective series *2 by 2,* the pinnacle of her acting career in London, she had played the hard-drinking moll of an IRA hitman, required only to say "God bless" and "Feck off". But to have all her talent and effort dismissed on the basis that she looked like a boy? Things were obviously worse than she'd thought.

"Do I have to call the manager?" the woman demanded, waving the cabbages dangerously.

"If you'd just bear with me," Cathy said, desperately wrestling with the till. The damned thing was jammed. The queue at her checkout was getting longer by the second, everybody craning their necks to see what the commotion was about. "Cabbages," one customer helpfully explained to another. This caught the attention of the queue at the next checkout. More eyes fell on Cathy. Sweating, she looked around wildly for help. But, as usual, Sarah and Amanda had legged it out the door the minute the shift was over, uncaring of the mayhem they left behind. Job dedication was something the employees of *Discount Shopping* didn't suffer from.

The fuck-off letter had arrived in the post this morning. *Thank you for coming in to meet us, blah-de-blah, unfortunately we are unable to offer you a part this time, blah-de-blah, but we'll keep your CV on file . . .* In the Actor or Actress filing cabinet, Cathy wondered savagely? She'd keep their letter too – in the file that held all the other fuck-off letters she'd received in her five long, hopeless years in London.

She had another file too – a thick, dusty file full of yellowed press clippings that she never looked at any more.

Simply divine! . . . Cathy Conroy is outstanding as Alison . . . if you see only one show this year, see this one . . . Cathy

3

Conroy is a new talent whom we will undoubtedly see much of in the future . . . Exhilarating! . . . Cathy Conroy steals the show . . .

Back then, she had been a Somebody. Feck it, in Ireland Cathy Conroy had been a star.

The play they'd raved about had been called *Outsiders.* But Cathy had been in no position to enjoy her success. She had jumped on a plane to London less than a week later and had never gone back.

"For heaven's sake, let me have a go!" The woman with the cabbages reached for the till.

"No, it's fine, I've got it . . ." Cathy punched in another code, but the till resolutely remained closed.

"This is ridiculous!" The woman roundly belted the till with one of the cabbages. Immediately, the supermarket's central alarm system was activated. A red light flashed merrily over Cathy's head, accompanied by a deafening bell. Oh *Christ.*

"Here!" Cathy said, digging deep into her blue-checked overall. She counted out a fist-full of coppers. "I'll pay for the damned cabbages myself!"

She thrust one pound twenty into the astonished woman's fist. And, heedless of the approaching manager, the startled security guards, the flashing lights and the ringing bell, Cathy Conroy got up from her seat.

"This checkout is closed!"

"I hope she chokes on the fucking things," Tracy declared, never one to mince her words.

Thank God for Tracy, the only Londoner who

regularly acknowledged Cathy's existence, even if the sight of her gorgeous, curvy, girlish little body was enough to make Cathy puke.

"Honestly!" she went on, puffing furiously on a Superkings. "Some people have no fucking lives!"

Cathy slumped in a chair by the door of the four-by-eight box which had the cheek to masquerade as a staffroom. As always, a dense blue fog of cigarette smoke hung evilly in the air. Visibility was zero.

"Are you saying *we* have?"

"What?" Tracy didn't like this. Tracy was cool. Tracy was *hip*.

Cathy went on bravely. "Well, look at us! Working in this dump for four pounds an hour!"

"Four-twenty."

"Whatever! But we said we'd only stay for six months, didn't we? To pay the bills until our careers took off? Me as an actress and you as a . . . what was it you wanted to be again?"

"Oh, I can't remember." Tracy languidly flicked a hand.

"Anyway, that was five years ago, Tracy! Five years!"

Tracy was now in full-blown denial. "What's got you in such a bad mood?"

Cathy shrugged, defeated. "Sandra didn't show up again today."

"Drugs," Tracy murmured.

"No thanks."

"I meant Sandra. Didn't you know?"

"No, and I don't care."

At the venom in Cathy's voice, Tracy took a thoughtful drag of her cigarette and squinted at her through the clouds of smoke. "So you didn't get the audition then."

"What?"

"That's what's *really* upsetting you, isn't it?" Tracy said wisely. "So what was it this time? Too old? Too young? Too Irish?"

"They thought I looked like a boy," Cathy said heavily.

Tracy was outraged. "That's fucking discrimination! That's ... that's sexism!"

"It's not."

"Oh. Well, they're bastards anyway!" As always, Tracy got on her high-horse on Cathy's behalf. "They wouldn't recognise talent if it sat down beside them and said 'Hello'."

"Tracy – " Cathy didn't need this right now.

But Tracy was on a roll. "Some day you'll turn around and laugh in their faces," she went on heatedly. "You'll say, I'm a big swing now – I'm a *huge* fucking swing now – "

"Look . . ." Cathy again tried to head her off.

"And I don't get out of bed for less than a thousand pounds a week!" Tracy stabbed a finger wildly in the air. "No, *ten* thousand!"

"Tracy, shut up! They're not going to pay me ten thousand pounds! They're not going to pay me ten *pence*, okay? They don't bloody want me in this town!"

Silence. Tracy's cigarette landed with a damp hiss into the dregs of her coffee. A blue flame briefly illuminated the murky room as she fired up a fresh one. Cathy knew she was hurt by the wet smack of lipstick as she sucked on the cigarette three times in quick succession without exhaling.

"Sorry, Tracy," Cathy mumbled. "I'm just a bit fed up, that's all."

After a tense moment Tracy graciously exhaled, forgiving her. "Course you are," she said cheerfully. "But there's always the next audition."

"No."

"What?"

"It's over, Tracy. This acting lark."

Tracy was unimpressed. "You say that every week."

"I do not."

"My fanny."

"This time I mean it. What's the point? I'm either too tall, or not pretty enough, or I can't do the accent, or I look like a boy."

"That's ridiculous."

"Or maybe I'm just not good enough," Cathy finished quietly.

"Yes, you are," Tracy said with quiet conviction. "You're brilliant, Cathy. I've seen you act."

"Yeah – in fringe shows in dumps that nobody has ever heard of."

"You need to push yourself more," Tracy lectured.

Cathy's frustration came tumbling out. "I've pushed myself in London for five years, Tracy. And I've nothing to show for it except a poxy job in a supermarket! So why don't I just wake up and admit it – that it's time to call it a day and do something else, instead of fooling myself all my life!"

It felt good to get the words out, to voice what had been bugging her for months now. The letter this morning had only put the tin hat on it all.

"You know what you need?" Tracy said slowly.

"Yeah – a life."

"An agent."

Cathy tried to bite down her irritation. "I can't get a bloody agent! Do you think I haven't tried?"

Tracy suddenly sat up. "Why don't *I* be your agent?"

"What?" Please God may she be joking.

"We're friends, aren't we? We should help each other out," Tracy declared generously. "Besides, I think I'd be quite good at it."

"Tracy, thanks anyway, but I just don't think …"

"What?" Tracy said, affronted.

"Well, you don't know anything about the business," Cathy said, trying to let her down gently.

"I can learn," Tracy said brightly. "I can read that *Stage and Coach* magazine."

"Stage and Screen," Cathy corrected her.

"That's the one. They advertise for actors in that, don't they?"

"Tracy – "

"Come on, then," Tracy said briskly. "I know you have a copy in your bag, you carry it around everywhere with you. We'll go through it now."

Cathy hadn't the energy to protest. She handed the

magazine over; she'd bought it yesterday but hadn't had the heart to open it yet. Maybe Tracy would be sufficiently intimidated by the actory-jargon that she would hand in her resignation as Cathy's agent before Cathy was forced to fire her.

"With me behind you, we could be out of this kip and earning mega-bucks in a matter of weeks," Tracy said confidently, thumbing through the magazine. "What's an NSP?"

"A Non-Speaking Part," Cathy said through gritted teeth.

It would be easier, of course, if she had another career in mind. But ever since she could remember, she had wanted to act. The smell of the greasepaint and the roar of the crowd were her reasons for getting out of bed in the morning. How could anything else compare?

"Can you sing?" Tracy was busy with a red pen, circling what she considered to be possible job opportunities.

"What? No, look, forget about the musicals, Tracy."

It would be easier too if she liked London. Or if it liked her. But there was a mutual antipathy going on there, and the prospect of another five, ten or fifty years here in some mundane job didn't appeal.

"How about skate-boarding?" Tracy demanded.

"*What?* No!"

"Shame. Can you play the mandolin at all?"

"Oh, for God's sake, Tracy!"

"As your agent, I need to know these things," Tracy said regally. "And I'll also need some background information. You know, on what you did in Ireland."

Cathy started a little. "I acted."

"I *know* that. But in what?"

"Plays and things," she said blandly.

Tracy busily jotted it all down. "And what role brought you to London?"

"No role."

Tracy was getting exasperated now. "Why did you come then?"

"Directors don't need to know things like that."

Tracy flung down the pen. "Jesus, *I* don't even know! Why are you always so bloody secretive about Ireland? What did you do, rob a bank or something?"

Cathy met Tracy's eyes squarely. She had encountered all the same questions before. The thing was not to look defensive, not to seem as though she were hiding something.

"No," she said casually. "Anything else you want to know?"

As always, it worked. Tracy shrugged, not bothering with the interrogation further. Cathy relaxed a little. She was safe again.

"I'm late to start my shift," Tracy declared. "But let's meet up later and put together a strategy, okay?"

She presented Cathy with her pert behind and swanned out of the room.

Cathy felt jaded all of a sudden. It was all she could do to struggle out of her uniform and into street clothes. There would be no meeting later on. There would be a hot bath in her dingy flat in Brixton and a long session

10

of soul-searching on what she was going to do with her life from now on.

Steel slammed as she opened the communal locker in the corner of the room. The blue-checked overall was stuffed into her bag, along with her shoes. As an afterthought, she reached for the copy of *Stage & Screen* magazine. She could light the fire with it or something.

She froze as her eyes fell on the open page.

There he was. Smiling. Looking out at her from a black-and-white photo. *Smiling.* Looking for all the world like the successful author that he was. She had not laid eyes on him in five years.

The piece underneath was short and gushing.

Carl Tallon's smash-hit play Outsiders *will finally make it onto our screens next year. The talented playwright has turned his hand to screenwriting and the film adaptation of his period extravaganza is due to go into pre-production in Ireland in the autumn.*

Cathy slapped the magazine shut, blinking hard. *Outsiders.* His play. Her play too. Together they had ridden on the back of its success. Only he had gone on to bigger and better things, it seemed. While she had ended up selling cabbages in London.

Anger ignited in Cathy now as she looked again at his face. So well he might smile. He had not given anything up. She was the one who'd had to leave town.

And here she was, contemplating giving up even more; ending her acting ambitions because she was too frightened to go back and pick up the pieces of a career that had looked so promising five years ago.

A steely resolve gripped her now at the injustice of it all. It was time to stop running, she decided, and reclaim what was rightfully hers.

"I'll never live this one down," she muttered, as she went to find Tracy to tell her that she was going home.

Chapter Two

There wasn't a dry seat in the house.

They clustered around him like teenage groupies at a pop concert, eyes shining and hands outstretched. He was their hero. Their man. The one who had made it all the way to the top in this rotten game, but who had never forgotten his humble roots. The combination was devastating.

And you're not even aware of it, husband dear. Tess Fisher prudently sipped an excellent Rioja and allowed herself a grudging smile as she watched Peter Fisher wow the crowd. A quick glance to her left and right told her that she was not alone. Half the party wives surreptitiously charted his progress even as they clung possessively to the beefy arms of their husbands and struggled to keep their balance on the ludicrously high stilettos they dusted off once a year.

The other half were watching her. Tess registered envy, jealousy and a certain outraged astonishment that she, over any of them, had managed to pull it off. They smiled ingratiatingly at her now, the ones who caught her eye, but she knew that every last one of them was sick to her stomach that it was Tess Fisher who had landed Peter Fisher, Minister for Arts, Heritage, Gaeltacht and the Islands, and the best-looking Irish politician in living memory. The *only* good-looking one, some snidely remarked. What, the party wives furiously asked each other in the steamy secrecy of the ladies' room, did Tess Fisher have that they didn't?

It was as plain as day to Tess as she watched them analytically now, in their fussy Clery's frocks and eighties' shoes, up from the country for the day. Their hair all curled and cut and coiffed by the local hairdresser who had never heard of Jennifer Aniston from *Friends*. Faces shiny in the heat, blue frosted eye-shadow and jammy lipstick starting the downward slide. All clinging tightly to their too-large handbags and snatching quick puffs of each other's cigarettes when they thought nobody was looking. And they wondered what she had that they didn't?

Tess was well aware that she wasn't a conventionally beautiful woman but that was neither here nor there. Understated class and good taste shouted politely from her neat brown John Rocha suit and cream silk blouse. No high heels for her; her Bally shoes were square-toed and low and the height of fashion. Declan at Peter Mark in the Stephen's Green Shopping Centre had spent an hour this morning bullying her hair into a smooth, shiny cap. Her face was worth every minute of another hour spent at Make Up Forever. A pair of tiny pearl earrings

14

completed the effect. Tonight, like every other night of her life, she looked like a Minister's Wife. And image, Tess well knew, was what success was all about.

"He's moving well."

She turned to find Party Press Officer John Graham beside her.

"He's spending too much time with Pat Tynan's crowd," she replied shortly. Peter hadn't even greeted the local boys yet and seemed to be purposefully ignoring the reporter from the *Sunday Independent*.

"Tynan's an agitator. Better to diffuse him early in the evening," Graham returned noncommittally, his eyes never leaving the crowd. At a glance, Graham could expertly gauge the atmosphere at any gathering. The best spin doctor in the business, crowds were his speciality. His gift was neither complicated nor deep. Rather he assessed large numbers of people as he had once kept watch over the sheep on his father's farm as a boy. The principle was the same: both excitement and boredom were dangerously infectious and could either set off or kill a party stone dead in five minutes flat. So far, all was going well tonight.

A raucous laugh broke out across the room.

"They're half-cut already," Graham told Tess. "Nobody can resist your wine."

Tess feigned innocence. "Ah, but I had nothing to do with the wine."

The catering for this annual Ard Fheis was officially done by Howards, the top outfit in town. Unofficially, Tess Fisher had supervised every last sip and morsel that would pass the lips of the crowd. And nothing but the best would do.

Graham lifted one knowing eyebrow and Tess smiled. They understood each other perfectly.

"Mind you, I think most of them would have preferred Guinness," Tess observed a touch disparagingly.

"That'll come later. After dinner."

Of course. That was when the real fun started, once the official business and rhetoric of the annual Ard Fheis weekend was formally at an end; more importantly, once the last of the die-hard hacks from the *Times* and *Independent* had given up and gone home, shell-shocked by an entire day of political bullshit.

Then the big wooden doors to the ballroom would be securely shut and the kegs of porter hastily opened. Freed from the media spotlight, the politicians would spontaneously climb down off their pedestals and cross the great divide, that between the electorate and the elected. They would gratefully accept pints from tearful supporters and allow their cigars to be lit. Ties would be loosened and jackets discarded. As the night wore on, they would amble from group to group thanking, reassuring, reminiscing and getting blind drunk in the midst of the people – their people, the grass-roots supporters, the backbone of the party. When not a single common man or woman had gone ignored, the spontaneous speeches would begin: heart-stirring, emotional tributes to the people who had put the party where it was today 'which is in *Government*!' as if anyone were in any doubt. Then the tearful pleas for their continuing belief in the cause, followed quickly by the vitriolic and highly defamatory assaults on the opposition parties and leaders. And finally, when half the room was under the table and the other half clamouring for the last of the porter, the party song would spontaneously begin. Tears would stream down faces of TD and backroom boy alike as the last refrain died away. Shoulders would be slapped and grown men would shamelessly maul and kiss each other before drunken goodbyes were made. Then the grass-roots supporters would stumble upstairs to their rooms, hearts bursting with pride in their men, their party, their night, which surely had to be the most spontaneously brilliant Ard Fheis ever.

Tess Fisher and John Graham knew that there would be nothing spontaneous about any of it. It had all been planned for weeks, from the number of kegs of Guinness to which politician would sit at what table of commoners. Cynical, maybe, but it worked. Every single supporter would leave this room tonight feeling that they were a vital part of the machine that had propelled the party into Government after ten long years in the wilderness.

Tess eyed the rowdy crowd. "You'd never think that this time last year we were in opposition."

"The election was a great victory," Graham returned loftily.

Tess had never been one for self-congratulation. "A victory by a margin of one seat, John. We should never forget that."

He stiffened slightly. Tess was uncaring. She only spoke the truth. For all the bluster and guff tonight, the party was only one seat away from the bad old times.

"It was still a victory. And it was largely down to them," Graham defended the crowd.

"No, John. It was largely down to Peter," Tess corrected him nicely.

Two years ago, when Peter and the other party bosses had set about a New Labour-style overhaul of a party which had grown flabby and irrelevant, many of these very people here tonight had almost sounded the death-knell. They had doggedly fought every effort of Peter's to mould the party into the kind of organisation that was ready for the new millennium. Tess had seen him come home many a night in abject despair, to rant and rave about the small-mindedness and ignorance of these people, people who would almost prefer to see the party go to the wall than become something other than what it had been in their grandfather's time.

But none of them remembered that tonight. Instead they relished the war story of how Sandy O'Connor, God bless him, had romped home with seventeen votes to spare in the fifth count in Dublin South Central and saved them all.

Tess and Graham spotted the potential danger at once: it was Peter, of course. It was always Peter.

"I'd better go mingle," she said quickly.

"Perhaps you'd better," he replied even more quickly.

Tess set off briskly through the crowd. Her progress

was briefly slowed by Edel Kennedy, the Minister for Foreign Affairs' wife, and Geraldine Day. Day was the Minister for Employment and Enterprise and the first woman under thirty ever to be appointed to the cabinet.

"Toe-rag," Edel spat. "Aren't I right, Tess?"

"Who?" Tess enquired politely.

"That little creep from the council," Geraldine Day intoned in her usual grating whine. "Pissed drunk and trying to get a leg over anything with a heartbeat."

Tess pretended disgust and tried to edge away.

"Get him fired," Edel said indignantly. "She could, couldn't she, Tess?"

Tess dragged her attention from Peter and back to the conversation. "Absolutely. Girl Power and all that."

Geraldine smirked. "Or I could call his bluff."

"You could." *They don't call you Geraldine Lay for nothing, dear.* "Now, you'll really have to excuse me."

She could hear the raised voices as she pushed her way through the sea of apparently immovable bodies. Her heart rose into her mouth. Please don't let him spoil tonight. Please God.

She saw that Peter's face was red and his hands were sweeping the air furiously the way they did when he was on one of his soapboxes. Pat Tynan's jaw was bullishly set and the little cluster of people surrounding them was growing larger by the second, sensing confrontation.

"Bollocks," Tynan, the TD for Tipperary North, said.

"It's not bollocks," Peter heatedly replied, his Kilkenny accent more pronounced than usual. "If we don't go with it now we'll be left behind."

Tess knew immediately what the argument was about. The Taoiseach was determined to force through radical and expensive educational reforms in the area of information technology, despite considerable opposition from the likes of old-timers like Tynan.

Tynan shot sly glances left and right at his henchmen. "I thought you were already being left behind."

Zing. The dig hit Peter nicely between the eyes and Tess watched his face go black. In the past three months, two textile factories had closed in Kilkenny. Another two computer multinationals had pulled out of establishing major plants in the area due to lack of qualified IT staff. The county was still reeling.

"Precisely why we need to invest in the future now," Peter ground out. "Teach kids about computers in school. . ."

"Tell us now, Peter," Tynan interrupted, "Who's going to teach the teachers? So that they can teach the kids?"

"That has all to be worked out yet, there will have to be special training seminars . . ."

"More money!" Tynan cut in, an exaggerated look of horror on his face. "And this is after we give every school in the country a couple of thousand quid's worth of new computers! Computers that we all know they're going to piss away their time playing games on anyway."

Loud murmurs of support from the henchmen. Tess stepped forward, smiling brightly as though she'd just breezed up. "They've asked us to move into the ballroom." They hadn't, but they would now. Tynan was already

20

walking away, anxious for a feed of beef and Guinness. But Peter couldn't let it be.

"It'll go through, you know," he told Tynan's back. "And if it doesn't, it'll be the likes of you that will have added to the dole queues."

Tynan turned back, an ugly look on his face. "I don't see *you* subtracting from them yet. Or is employment up in the Kilkenny theatre community recently? *Minister?*"

He moved off, his followers stumbling eagerly in his wake.

"That backwards little bastard," Peter choked.

Tess laid a hand on his arm. "Peter." She was still smiling at the rapidly dispersing crowd but her voice was pure ice. "Can't you keep your opinions to yourself for just one evening?"

Peter angrily shook off her hand. "Did you hear him? Employment in the theatre sector? I'd like to see anyone with the arts portfolio succeed in taking a single person off the dole queue . . ."

"Michael D did." The sarcasm was out before she could stop it. But she was furious with him – him and his stupid ideals that he thought were worth making a scene over. Tonight, of all nights. Tonight was supposed to be a night of celebration and glory, an opportunity to pat themselves on the back for a job well done and an election well won. It was also supposed to be Tess's night; a vindication of all the work she'd done over the past fifteen years, work that had gone largely unnoticed and ignored by everyone, Peter included. Peter especially, she often thought.

No matter. Her hard graft was not meant to draw

attention to itself. In fact, it was a mark of her very success that it had *not* been noticed. After all, behind every politician is a crew of silent workers and campaigners, just as there is behind every party. And the most important of those silent and dedicated workers is The Wife. This Tess knew without a shadow of a doubt.

When Peter had first told her of his intention to run for election, Tess Fisher had suddenly found a purpose in her otherwise unfulfilling life. Married at nineteen, a mother at twenty and with a husband who even then spent four nights a week doing community and council work, she desperately needed a challenge. When she'd offered her services to Peter, he'd suggested that maybe they should think about having another child. Tess knew then that she would have to work behind the scenes if she was going to avoid being left out in the cold. So she went on the pill and went to work.

In the space of a month, she'd organised herself and her life around one goal – getting her husband elected. The baby, the bills, his consultancy business – Peter found he didn't have to worry about a thing. Sick relatives, sick children, sick *Tess* – she coped with it all efficiently, methodically and without complaint.

Then she set about subtly moulding Peter into the kind of man people would elect.

Out went the natty sports jackets and in came the stylish overcoats. Out went his John F Kennedy haircut and in came a smart crew cut. Peter drew the line when she tried to trade their lumpy family saloon for a muted black masculine number. He said that ordinary people might think that he was getting above himself. Tess countered that they wouldn't want someone who would let them down in Dublin either. When he accused her of meddling, she ceased all activities for a week and let things go back to the way they used to be. On the third night that Peter was forced to take his turn walking up and down the hall with his teething daughter, he finally had a glimmer of comprehension of what she was doing for him. The car was changed.

He won a seat in the election of 1987. He took her up onto the podium with him and thanked her in front of the crowd. He thanked his crotchety mother and his secretary in the same breath. Tess told herself she didn't mind. She knew that she was only The Wife. The difference now was that she was a TD's Wife.

She barely had time to enjoy her new status when the trouble began. Idealistic and outspoken already, Peter now had a platform. Not a week went by when he didn't make a passionate but naïve outburst on behalf of some group of unfortunates or other. The press loved him. The old-time party members began to have second thoughts.

Tess did the only thing she could: she packed her bags and went to Dublin, her lips tight with fury at watching her years of hard work being poured down the drain.

They'd spent a terse hour in Buswells' Hotel around the corner from the Dáil.

He'd explained sincerely to her that he was trying to make a difference. Tess brusquely cut him off. In no uncertain terms, she let him know that he was on the verge of jeopardising his entire career. What kind of a difference could he make then?

After that, Peter curbed his tongue. Or at least he made an effort. He still lost the run of himself on occasion, but Tess gradually came around to the view that this could actually work to their advantage. She was right. Over the years, he won for himself the reputation of being honest and incorruptible, which made a refreshing change in Irish politics. The common man and woman took a shine to him. The media adored him, and the party, by and large, admired and respected him. In the last election, he'd proportionately won the most votes of any TD in the country.

On the podium that night, he'd thanked the party, the people, the press. He got side-tracked into an attack on the hypocrisy of some elements of the media and forgot entirely to thank Tess. He was mortified afterwards, but the damage was done.

She'd accepted it now. Her reward was not his half-hearted praise but the fact that she was now, finally, a Minister's wife. And Tess Fisher would do anything to make sure that she remained a Minister's wife.

"Higgins made his mark only by virtue of TnaG," Peter said now, coldly.

Tess was silent. She could see that her dig about his predecessor had touched a nerve. Peter needed careful handling and she hadn't done it very well. Especially now. He had been very restless this past few months, since the hubbub of the election and the thrill of finally making it into Government had worn off. She knew that it stemmed from his dissatisfaction with his Ministerial portfolio. He didn't feel the arts gave him much scope to make that all-important difference. Doling out money to theatre groups and haggling with RTE over salaries didn't seem terribly important to him, especially when the very people who had elected him were staring unemployment in the face. No matter that he'd fought for and won a substantial increase in funding for the Arts in the last budget. What did people care about art when factories were closing all around them?

"You can outdo Michael D," Tess said soothingly. There was a long evening ahead and she wanted him focused and calm.

He laughed cynically. "How? By setting up a *French* language station?"

Tess laughed too, playing it light now. "Hardly. But maybe you need to think about making your mark in the Arts." *And that'd keep you out of other people's business and out of trouble.*

Peter looked irritated. "Making my mark in the Arts is not going to impress those queuing for the dole in Kilkenny every week, Tess. You've been away too long."

His barb hit its mark. Tess sighed. This was an old argument, stemming from the day Tess announced that she was upping and moving to Dublin with Peter, uncaring that Peter's constituents expected him to maintain a family home in Kilkenny.

"I go back often enough." She rarely accompanied him on his trips down the country. "Besides, Fiona is at school here. I'm not uprooting her."

Did he really expect her to rattle around Kilkenny on her own? What did he think she would do? Window-shop all day before cooking a meal for one?

She'd made the move three years ago and had never looked back. Tess Fisher was now a social lioness, centre stage right beside her husband. And she planned to stay right there.

Swiftly changing the subject, she said, "All I'm suggesting is that you can still do something for the people of Kilkenny."

"What, bring art to them?" he said flippantly.

That earned him a caustic look. Sometimes Peter treated her like an ignoramus.

"I'm serious," she said.

"How?" He was indulging her now. The little woman.

"Oh shut up," she said shortly.

But he wouldn't let it go. "What are you suggesting?"

"I don't know! But you got a great big lump of budget money two months ago. If you're so worried about the people of Kilkenny, why don't you use that money to help them instead of sitting around griping?"

"Well-spoken, Mum."

Tess and Peter turned around to find Fiona behind them.

"Is that alcohol?" Peter suspiciously eyed the glass in her hand.

"*God.*" Fiona tossed back her head and fixed him with a look. "There are enough piss-heads here tonight without me joining them."

Peter glowered. Fiona deliberately turned away.

26

Tess watched her fifteen-year-old daughter thoughtfully. She was the spit of Peter not only in looks but in temperament. Perhaps they were too alike, both outspoken and direct. At least *something* must account for the increasing hostility Fiona displayed towards her father. Or maybe it was simply an age thing, Tess mused. The terrible teens and all that. But still, she rarely treated Tess to her sharp tongue. If anything, she was the opposite, deliberately taking Tess's side in any small matter. She was doing it again now.

"I think Mum is right. Put your money where your mouth is."

Tess watched Peter swallow his aggravation. "If Michael D can set up a television station in the West, then what's stopping you in Kilkenny?" she suggested cautiously.

"Maybe," Peter said slowly.

Fiona favoured him with another pointed look. "Still, I suppose you won't want to be away from Dublin *too* long, will you?" She abruptly left them for Regina Burke, teenage daughter of Sheila and Harry Burke. Harry Burke was the Minister for Finance.

"Little madam," Peter bit out, but Tess saw that he was more hurt than angry. "What was that crack about Dublin supposed to mean?"

"Leave it, Peter," Tess murmured. She was wondering herself.

"Hanging around with that Regina one, that's what it is," Peter said disparagingly. "Those Burkes are poison."

Tess did not want to start him on a diatribe about the

27

Burkes. "So what do you think, Peter? About a project for Kilkenny?"

"I'll look into it," he said.

Tess realised that he was serious. "You'd really show them who was boss then."

Peter looked at her oddly. "I was thinking more along the lines of counteracting the factory closures, Tess."

"Of course," Tess said demurely. She could see the familiar zealot's light come into his eyes and felt a warm buzz in her stomach. If he could channel his energy into that, he would be too busy to do the sort of interfering which had given her many a sleepless night.

A cheer rose from the top of the room. Tess craned her neck to see.

"She's here," Peter said, a smile of genuine pleasure cracking his handsome face.

The crowd which had surged forward time and again tonight to greet the arrival of various TDs and Ministers was strangely aloof now. They were still unsure how to respond to their leader, the first female Taoiseach in the history of the State.

Carol Taylor, petite and pale, was not the sort you clapped heartily on the back. Rather, she inspired a quiet awe and respect amongst the grass-roots supporters tonight. Amongst certain hardened party members, Tess knew she inspired something altogether different. Carol Taylor embodied all that they detested about the new-style party. The very idea of a woman as party leader was alien and abhorrent to them and most of them had suffered from chronic indigestion since she'd been elected. The Deputy Prime Minister, an elderly and placid man put forward as her running mate to keep them happy, had proved no match for her and was firmly pushed to the sidelines. No one was in any doubt that Peter Fisher had stepped into his shoes.

Tess twirled her glass thoughtfully as the Taoiseach stepped onto the podium at the top of the room and motioned for quiet. Carol Taylor could build as many bridges as she liked between the old faction and the new, but a compromise candidate such as she could never hope to last a second term. And Peter, Tess knew, would be the obvious choice as her successor.

It was an interesting thought and one that Tess would not be sharing with Peter. A small laugh threatened to escape her as she imagined the look on his face. The laughter died in her throat as Carol Taylor announced quietly to the crowd that Tony Croft, elected deputy for Kilkenny, had suddenly passed away tonight.

Chapter Three

Peter Fisher woke with a pounding head and a residue of beery breath that threatened to knock even himself out. He eased open one bloodshot eye and peered at the alarm-clock on the night stand. Ten past seven. He'd had exactly two hours' sleep.

He looked down at the head which was bobbing enthusiastically beneath the bed-sheet somewhere around his crotch region.

"Love? Love, we don't have time."

The bobbing head continued undeterred. He felt the beginnings of an erection, which was a minor miracle considering the viciousness of his hangover. He shut his eyes again, fighting a wave of nausea. Images from the previous night struggled forth from his swollen brain like scenes from a surreal film that had turned nightmarish halfway through.

The beginning had been okay. He'd worked the room renewing acquaintances and securing support from all the right people for the Taoiseach's forthcoming plans for education, although Pat Hickey had slipped away early as usual and Vincent Ryan was so plastered that he'd have promised to support the Taoiseach's solo flight around the world in a hot-air balloon, if asked.

He'd touched base with all his Kilkenny people, accepting pints from Noreen and Willie O'Mara, neighbours and long-time friends of his from home. And Liam Downey, who'd taken two weeks off work to trudge door-to-door in the last election on his behalf. Peter had drunk with them all as he'd moved around the room chatting and gossiping, but mostly listening.

He'd heard how more funding was desperately needed to complete the new by-pass on the outskirts of the city. He was brought up to speed on the level of crime – not the clinical Garda statistics, but how people felt about it on the ground. He'd learned that there was growing opposition to a proposed council dumping-site that was necessary but that nobody wanted. Could he put in a word anywhere along the line…?

All across the huge ballroom, other TDs were doing exactly the same – listening to the same concerns of their supporters and being solicited for help. Most made wild promises of funding and influence which would be forgotten as soon as the hangover wore off and their supplicants were safely out of sight and out of mind down in some boghole in the midlands. But two years on, when the next election loomed, every last TD would race from Dublin to their constituencies like bats out of hell and work like madmen and women to make good on at least some of the reckless promises they'd made last night. And once elected, the same rigmarole of requests and promises would play itself out year after year until the next election loomed.

Peter found it wearying. Not only the behaviour of some of his colleagues, but the outrageousness of some of the requests.

"He's a good lad. Hard-working. Reliable."

Peter's face had tightened when a friendly conversation he'd been having with Michael Finn, a businessman from Kilkenny, had turned into a none-too-subtle request for assistance in finding his youngest son a job.

Peter's cold silence was lost on Finn, who leaned a little closer. The dried head of a pint of Guinness rimmed the man's fleshy lips. "There's a job coming up in the council . . ."

Peter cut in sharply. "Then I suggest he apply for it like anyone else."

"Peter?" Tess had miraculously materialised between them, smiling graciously at that weasel Finn. The woman had been born with an in-built trouble-sensor. "There are a couple of people waiting for a word. I'm sure Michael won't mind me stealing you away for a minute."

"Stop managing me," Peter said out of the side of his mouth as she tried to lead him away. Tess put on that martyred expression he hated so much, as if he were some kind of lapdog she had spent many years stoically training only to have him lift his leg against her best friend.

"Michael's a loyal supporter, Peter."

"He's a cute hoor and you know it."

Her lips drew themselves into the disapproving shape he privately called her duck's arse.

"Do you want another drink?" he asked.

She eyed the half-finished pint in his hand. He was well aware that she knew it was his fourth. "Let's go talk to Sheila Burke," she suggested instead.

He looked across the room to where the Minister for Finance's wife stood, a short little barrel of a woman with bright bird-eyes and a voracious appetite for gathering and dispersing gossip, often to carefully calculated and devastating effect. Peter loathed her and her kind. They had made careers out of their marriages, passing on embellished titbits of the loose talk their idiot spouses imparted in bed and before you knew it, truth and fiction had merged and found a prime slot in the gossip columns on the back pages of the Sunday newspapers.

"No," Peter said flatly.

Tess's eyes narrowed. "It would be nice if you could be civil to her, Peter. I can't do it for both of us."

No, but you try. It sickened Peter the way Tess humoured the old cow; the two of them always rushing off for four-hour lunches with the other cabinet wives. They were dangerous when they got together. Tess usually returned from these gatherings with more information on confidential Government business than Peter was in possession of himself.

"I said no," he repeated.

But it was too late. Tess had already waved to her; that affected, limp-wristed flap that she had acquired since moving to Dublin, along with her taste for designer clothes and expensive haircuts. Peter had nearly fainted one day when he saw a credit-card receipt for eighty-five pounds.

"Eighty-five quid for a *hairdo*?"

"We can afford it," she'd said breezily.

Looking at her now, you'd never guess that she had been born and reared in a two-bedroom draughty farmhouse and had taken bread-and-sugar sandwiches to school. Tess Fisher had reinvented herself as radically as the party had, and had done a better job of taking Dublin by storm.

"Tess!"

"Sheila!"

Kiss, kiss, both cheeks, skin never touching skin.

"Peter!"

"Sheila."

No kiss this time. Peter shook her plump, bejewelled hand quickly and let go.

"Us women aren't getting a look-in with you at all tonight, Peter!" A conspiratorial nudge in Tess's ribs and both women laughed politely. But those busy little eyes were keenly pecking at Peter's face, letting him know that she was in possession of all the latest gossip on his private life. She knew because Harry Burke couldn't keep his fat mouth shut.

"I could see that you were surrounded by admirers, Sheila," Peter said with a deliberate wolfish grin.

A chilly silence now. Sheila had been standing on her own and they all knew it. Furious, she was forced to draw in her claws a little.

"Harry's pissed," she sighed. This was an understatement at the very least. The esteemed Minister for Finance was at this moment wandering about with his fly half-down and singing along to the piped hotel music.

"Isn't he entitled?"Tess soothed, ever the diplomat. "You look *terrific*, Sheila."

"Oh stop! Just something I threw together."

Peter clenched his teeth and looked longingly into his empty pint glass.

"I'm thinking of throwing a little dinner party on Saturday," Tess confided. "I hope you'll be free."

"I'll check our diary," Sheila promised.

This, Peter knew, was a mere formality. Sheila would cancel her own funeral to be there. Tess Fisher was too big in this town to ignore.

"Look at them! Thick as thieves," Sheila said fondly, nodding towards Fiona and her own daughter Regina.

"It's in bed they should be," Peter said sourly. "This is no place for fifteen-year-olds."

Ignoring their startled looks, he left for the bar and ordered a pint. He stood there, looking over at Fiona. She had him rattled. He wracked his brains, wondering whether he had inadvertently slighted her in some way. Why else did she treat him with such disdain?

Deep down he knew that the explanation wasn't so easy. He just wasn't spending enough time with her. He never had, not since she was a child. But in this rat race there never seemed to be any room for such luxuries as family. He resolved to spend next weekend with her.

Then Carol Taylor's arrival, and the big ballroom

rendered so quiet by her announcement that when a pin had actually dropped from Geraldine Day's hat, people had jumped. Clumps of men and women standing around in stunned groups, waiting for someone to tell them what to do. Then the pints at the bar, people drinking fast without tasting or wanting it, just needing an escape from reality. The Kilkenny people had drifted together through instinct in a corner of the ballroom to pay fragmented tributes to Tony Croft, looking to Peter for reassurance. He had little to offer, as shocked as everyone else.

He'd left then for the fast drive across the city to another faceless hotel, the thirteen Cabinet Ministers staring at each other over coffee that nobody wanted while they waited for Carol Taylor to join them, the room deathly silent save for the unseemly sounds of a couple energetically making love in the room overhead. Peter remembered press officer John Graham murmuring calmly on the phone in the corner, expressing the party's shock and regret at the untimely death of one of their finest deputies. And no, he was unaware of any plans as yet for a by-election and frankly the question was premature and disrespectful to the bereaved family.

Peter had ignored him, lost in recollection of Tony Croft, a quiet man whom people had often written off as less than dynamic. But Croft had been a mover in his own way, eschewing the spotlight to work tirelessly behind the scenes for his constituents. He'd had little time for the shenanigans of many of his colleagues and had got on with the job, preferring to spend his spare time with his family rather than at the endless round of functions in Dublin. The Kilkenny people had responded by returning him five times in a row. He and Fisher had held the only two party seats in Kilkenny.

Gradually, Peter was dragged from his introspection by the realisation that all eyes were on him.

"It's your constituency," Geraldine Day said accusingly.

Peter glared at her. What did she expect him to do, go down and raise Tony from the dead?

Carol Taylor entered and took the head of the table. The bickering immediately ceased. "I've just spoken with the President and made her aware of the situation – that we are now a Government without a majority."

The Finance Minister Harry Burke looked as though he would cry. Just when he was about to get a great big whack of EU money too.

"This is no time to go to the wall," Carol snapped. "The President does not want a general election any more than the rest of us. And she agreed with me that with the summer recess coming up, we will not hold the by-election until the end of October."

That gave them five months to save their skins.

"Obviously we will not make any decisions on candidates until after Tony's funeral," Carol went on quietly. "But given the circumstances, we need to start coming up with names now."

Eyes darted back and forth across the table, everyone waiting for someone else to make the first suggestion. It was very slow in coming. Again, Peter felt eyes settling on him, this time in unspoken recrimination.

Geraldine Day, as always, was the first to get her size eight boot in. "Are the Kilkenny people aware of the existence of anyone other than Peter?"

Her smile was acid, her words largely truth. Peter was the Lion King in Kilkenny and while this had its advantages, it now posed a major problem in terms of the search for a candidate for the by-election. None of the young up-and-coming party members could hold a candle to him and had never been given the chance to try.

"There's always Gavin Williams," Peter said forcefully. "He'd get the youth vote, and he's strong on environment issues."

Phil Egan, the Minister for the Marine, sniffed sourly. "Forget it, he looks like a girl."

"Anne Duffey then," Peter replied testily. "She actually is a girl."

"Too young," Carol Taylor answered. "She's for the future sometime."

Peter wracked his brains. "Michael Lennon, how about him?"

"Who?" Harry Burke asked, swiftly scuppering that suggestion.

The night wore on. Lists were draw up and discarded and new lists begun. Names were tossed about like confetti and none of them inspired any confidence. They were facing a crucial by-election and they did not have a candidate.

It was John Graham who finally voiced what everybody else was thinking. "We have a profile problem in Kilkenny." His quiet voice always commanded attention. "We have a track record of two factory closures and two multinational pull-outs. No matter who we come up with, the people will not be inclined to vote for this party."

Geraldine Day got on her high-horse immediately. As Minister for Enterprise and Employment, the egg was firmly on her face. "We're doing our best, John. We can't drag industry to Kilkenny overnight."

"It's something we need to address," he returned blandly. "Otherwise we'll be throwing a candidate – any candidate – into the lion's den."

"Can you do anything at all?" Peter asked Geraldine.

"Oh sure!" she said, a slightly hysterical tinge to her voice. "You were the one who got the money in the last budget, Peter! Not me! Jesus, if we all had the cushy Arts portfolio, we'd be laughing!"

At this point, Carol prudently called a halt to proceedings and scheduled another emergency meeting for nine in the morning. Afterwards Peter would drive down to Kilkenny to pay his respects to the family.

He looked at the alarm clock again now. "Love? Love, we have to go."

The sheet was suddenly flung back. Helen Boyd, Carol Taylor's personal secretary, smiled up at him. A pink tongue darted out to flick around plump lips and down she went again.

Peter watched with a certain distraction. He liked Helen. He didn't love her. He found her honesty about sex refreshing, the way she enjoyed it as much as him. They had a lot of fun times with no commitment on either side. He had made that quite clear to her, he hadn't misled her in any way. With a wife and daughter, he wasn't in the market for anything else. She had agreed.

Peter knew perfectly well that he was selfish and dishonest. He was what women's magazines would nail as your typical bastard and he wasn't proud of himself. But he didn't stop either.

Often he wondered why he felt the need to hop from woman to woman in what was essentially a series of physical relationships. Was it because those rare sessions with Tess left him unsatisfied? But Peter knew that it would be easy to blame her and he refused to do so. He was inclined to think that it was his own capacity to separate sex from love and to feel no real link between the two that was to blame. He could have sex with a woman which lasted three long, sweaty hours and then get dressed and walk away without giving her another thought. Afterwards, he regarded himself with a deep distaste. What kind of man behaved in that fashion?

He had for the past ten years. Only now the thrill of those snatched moments in hotel rooms and secluded apartments was waning. It wasn't that he felt any guiltier about betraying Tess – he did all the time anyway, in a sort of objective, moralistic way – sometimes he just felt that it wasn't enough anymore. Recently he had started to doubt his own ability to forge or sustain any kind of emotional intimacy. Maybe it was too late. Certainly it was with Tess. They had been basically unsuited from the start and the distance had only grown over the years. For that too he blamed himself. Even if the love had gone, friendship and partnership might have carried them through. But he was putting so much into his career that he didn't seem to have anything left over for his marriage.

"What's wrong?" Helen murmured, raising her head of red curls for a moment.

"Ha? Oh, nothing. Tony, you know?"

This was partly the truth. After the meeting last night, Peter had not wanted to go back to the house in Dalkey where Tess would be sitting up in bed demanding to know in detail what had transpired. He had craved affection and warmth and sex and although he knew this was a common response to death, he had found his urges distasteful. But still, he was outside Helen's place in Donnybrook at half past four in the morning.

"Sorry for bursting in on you last night," he said apologetically now.

"You know I'm always glad to see you," Helen said. A long pause and then softly, "It's a shame we can't be together all the time."

Peter froze, his senses on red alert. "We manage," he said carefully.

During the week he usually spent two or three evenings in Donnybrook if it coincided with a late function. Often he would not arrive home to a sleeping Tess until well after midnight. But he never spent the night with Helen. That would be too much, too low.

"I just wish we could be open about it." Her eyes

held a hint of challenge. "I don't like all this sneaking around, the secrecy. It makes us a bit cheap, don't you think?"

Peter had heard it all before. Next she would be hinting that his marriage couldn't be very happy if he needed to have affairs. Sooner or later, they all started to put on the pressure, no matter how much they assured him at the start that they accepted his terms. He didn't blame them – after all, who wanted to stay forever in a relationship that was going nowhere? Unfortunately he couldn't help anyone out there.

"Let's get dressed, we're late," he said easily, swinging his legs out of bed. He added Helen to the list of worries that had to be sorted out sooner rather than later.

John Graham's official job description was Party Press Officer – a modest title for the man who had largely put the party where it was today, he often thought in his more humble moments. And entirely inadequate given that it would be up to him to save the Government's skin yet again. Certainly it couldn't be left to the Ministers, if last night's meeting was anything to go by.

Not that Graham ever left anything to the Ministers. They thought they ran the country but not a single thing happened that didn't go through John Graham's press office on the third floor first. In a way, he often mused, his cramped little office was where the real seat of power lay; he was the hot-line to the media, and it was all a media war at the end of the day. Never mind the pomp and ceremony of elected office – it was those behind the scenes who pulled the strings when all was said and done.

And Graham was a master string-puller. It gave him the kind of adrenaline rush that every other aspect of his life had thus far failed miserably to deliver.

The by-election promised to be exciting. Graham found that he was looking forward to it. Things had been too quiet for too long.

He crouched over his desk now like a lithe and alert monkey, chain-smoking Rothmans and listening to *Morning Ireland* on his battered old radio. A smile reluctantly twisted his neat features. He plucked up the phone and dialled an internal number. At the other end of Government buildings, Ulick Pearse, Party Press Officer for the opposition party, picked up.

"You sneaky bastard," Graham chuckled.

"John, my old flower," Ulick said. He too was trying to suppress a chuckle.

"A bit premature on your part, don't you think?" Graham said. "Croft isn't dead twelve hours yet."

"I have no idea where *Morning Ireland* got their information," Ulick said piously.

"A leak, I suppose," Graham said.

"Of course," Ulick demurred. This time the chuckle escaped him. Graham joined him until they were sniggering and laughing like two small boys. They would laugh some more when they met up for their usual game of poker on Saturday night.

"Seriously, though," Graham said, getting control of

himself. "You've persuaded Bill Mackey to run for you in the by-election?"

"Maybe," Ulick said, close-mouthed again.

"You bastard," Graham said again, filled with admiration.

Bill Mackey had until his retirement last year been a radio broadcasting star, the housewife's darling with his thrice-weekly radio chat-show almost exclusively devoted to women's affairs. The women adored him. The men he wouldn't have to bother with, having already won them over twenty years ago as a hurling legend, winning the McCarthy Cup three times for the Kilkenny Cats. On paper the man was unbeatable.

"All's fair in love and war," Ulick said, and they both laughed again.

They had played their game for years now, Graham at one end of Government Buildings and Ulick at the other. Trying to get one over on each other helped to pass the tedium of the day.

"I guess I'll have to raise you one," Graham said slowly, his formidable brain going into overdrive. It would be hard to come up with a candidate to better Bill Mackey, but Ulick's continued sniggering on the other end of the phone spurred him on.

"What's the bet?" Ulick said. There was always a small wager to add a little excitement to the game.

"Ten pounds," Graham said.

"Rubbish. I'm not going to bust a gut to win the by-election for ten quid."

"A hundred so."

A hundred pounds. Ulick knew that Graham meant serious business. "Done."

"May the best man win," Graham said loftily, hanging up.

Carol Taylor was standing motionless by the window when Peter finally made it into her office. Sharp blue eyes met his for a moment as he sank down into a chair with an apologetic grimace.

"Sorry, Carol. Traffic. Brutal."

"Peter, I don't give a tinker's damn what you do in your private life. But don't make my secretary late for work again. Understood?"

Peter was pulled up short. Sometimes he forgot how keenly observant Carol could be. And how caustic.

"Understood," he murmured.

Rank firmly established, they could afford to let their defences down.

"Christ, Peter, you look terrible."

"So do you."

Even today, after two hours' sleep, Carol Taylor looked anything but terrible. At forty-eight, she was slim and almost frail-looking, a feature she frequently employed to trick the opposition into underestimating her. Rather than trying to minimise her femininity in what was overwhelmingly a man's world, she embraced it, choosing soft powder-blue and burnt-orange suits over pinstripes, and sensual, flowing styles instead of military-style box jackets. Her make-up was bold and colourful and her fair hair so shiny that the Ceann

Comhairle swore that he could see his reflection in it. Carol Taylor had brought high fashion and glamour into the Dáil chambers fifteen years ago and most of the old-timers still weren't quite sure what had hit them. Some of them had been known to mutter that she belonged in a bedroom and not a boardroom – and certainly not in the Taoiseach's office.

Carol Taylor had smiled when she'd heard this. The next day she had worn a shocking pink trouser-suit and high heels into the Dáil and lambasted the gathering for poor attendance records and tardiness. She finished by reminding the males present that TV cameras had been in situ in the chambers for several years now and could they please review their wardrobe with this in mind and discard the many suit trousers with shiny bottoms that she had noticed of late. There were many red faces and no more comments about her dress.

The only indication of her fatigue now was a pinched look about her eyes.

"You've heard the latest?" she asked.

Newspapers were strewn across her desk, banner headlines screaming out: *TD Tony Croft Dies Suddenly At Home; Fledgling Government In Crisis At Death Of Deputy; Tony Croft's Death Could Signal General Election.*

The reporters had worked hard and fast last night. Right now thousands of people were digesting cornflakes and the news that the Government's one-seat majority was in jeopardy.

Peter pushed the papers away. He'd read most of them in the back seat of the Ministerial car on the way over. They had only added to his nausea. "Nothing we didn't anticipate last night," he said heavily.

Carol looked at him peculiarly. "You haven't heard the news then. They broke it on *Morning Ireland*."

Peter went cold as she told him how Frank Tavey, leader of the opposition, was dragging Bill Mackey out of retirement to run in the by-election.

"And they *announced* it on radio?" He was completely incredulous.

"Of course not," Carol said impatiently. "Too soon."

"Why the leak?" Peter asked. "It's an incredibly stupid move."

Carol lifted an eyebrow. "Is it? Think about it, Peter. Tavey's just wrong-footed us for starters. And he's also put his candidate right in the public eye at the start of the race. And what a candidate."

There was no argument there. Bill Mackey was quite possibly the most well-known man in Ireland. It was a stroke of genius.

Peter had to pour himself a glass of water. "Shit. We need to find someone, Carol. And fast."

Carol nodded slowly. "John Graham has made a suggestion."

"Really," Peter said dryly. It had come to his notice since the election that John Graham was never short of suggestions.

"Yes. Tony's son."

"Terry? I thought he was in London."

"The younger one. Roger."

Peter thought again but couldn't put a face to Roger.

Tony Croft had not mentioned him much, although he had proudly listed Terry's achievements in the construction industry in England.

"He must be quite young," he said doubtfully.

"Twenty-seven. Studied English and Politics in Trinity before leaving to work in the family business. Lives in Kilkenny, knows the people, he's presentable and he's smart."

John Graham had done a sell on him obviously. But he wasn't clutching at straws, Peter knew. Many a TD would never have got where they were now except that their father had served before them. Given that Tony's support was largely local-based, it made sense that a son would carry on the tradition. And people liked continuity, it made them feel safe.

"Maybe," Peter said, liking the idea more and more. "But he might not run."

"He's already agreed," John Graham said.

Peter looked around to find Graham sitting by the door. He had not heard him come in. It was a disconcerting habit of his and one that Peter didn't like.

"He didn't waste any time," Peter said.

Graham shrugged. "I ran the idea past him, strictly casually. And he said that given the circumstances, and his father's dedication to the party, he would have wanted him to run."

It smacked of insincerity. But Peter held his counsel.

"Will he be enough?" Peter asked. It seemed almost cruel to pit an inexperienced youngster against the might of Bill Mackey and Frank Tavey.

"Almost definitely not," Carol replied. "Which is where you come in."

"Well, of course I'll help him all I can. I'll canvass and do all that, but at the end of the day, it's Geraldine Day who needs to do something."

"She's back courting the computer multinationals," Carol said. "But those deals could take months. We need something concrete to bring industry to Kilkenny with our candidate as front man."

Peter was puzzled. "I was thinking of launching some kind of arts project down there, but that won't really do much to help."

Graham disagreed. "If Frank Tavey can pull out the showbiz tactics, then we need to too."

"Only we have to do it bigger and better," Carol added.

She was looking at Peter now in a way that usually made opposition members very nervous indeed.

"You mean I have to find this Roger Croft some pet project?" he asked.

"Exactly. Something that will wipe Tavey's eye and win over the voters."

Peter shook his head. "If we pull any kind of a stunt, they'll see right through it."

"And what exactly do you think Tavey's doing?" Carol exploded. "With a bloody chat-show host? If that isn't transparent, I don't know what is."

Peter needed an aspirin. She was laying it on the line to him. "You want me to save the Government," he said nicely. "That's a tall order."

"Somebody has to do it," Graham murmured. Peter

didn't know whether he was joking or not. You never knew with Graham.

Carol reached forward and punched the intercom. "Helen – we're ready now." She turned back to Peter. "Peter, this is your top priority. We've got five months to get this guy elected. Talk to him and see what you can come up with."

"I'll see him later at the wake."

"You'll see him now. I sent the helicopter for him this morning."

The door opened and a young man with a keen, good-looking face stepped into the room. Dark brown eyes quickly assessed the gathering before he came forward on polished shoes to shake Carol's hand, his demeanour properly respectful. Peter found that he disliked him on sight.

"Roger Croft," he said to Carol. "It's a great honour to meet you, Ma'am."

Peter had to bite his lip to stop a smile.

"I am not the Queen, Mr Croft," Carol said mildly. "Taoiseach or Ms Taylor will do nicely."

Roger's perfect skin coloured slightly. Peter got to his feet quickly and thrust out a hand; he could at least give the lad a chance. "Please accept my sympathies and extend them to your family."

Roger nodded. "Thank you, Minister."

Roger's handshake was a little stronger than necessary. Peter made sure to let go first.

"I need to speak with Helen. I'll leave you three to get acquainted," Carol said, and left.

"Sit down, Roger," Peter said, waving to a chair. "It looks like we've got quite a fight on our hands."

"Yes. But I have every confidence that I'll win."

Peter noted how neatly Roger brought it back to himself. Graham did too, he saw.

"This is no time to be counting chickens. The main thing is to get you working on something highly visible and preferably economically advantageous to Kilkenny."

Roger nodded briskly. "Yes. There's a lot of bad feeling on the ground about the party at the moment."

Peter swallowed his ire. Twenty-seven years old and Croft was already an expert, it seemed.

"We're going to have to work hard to counteract that," he said brusquely. "Any ideas?"

Croft hadn't. That much was clear. John Graham tentatively cleared his throat. "I have a suggestion."

Another one, Peter thought. "Well? What?"

Graham examined his hands. They were curiously delicate, like a girl's. "You mentioned earlier that you were thinking of bringing an arts project to Kilkenny."

"So?" Peter wished he would get to the point.

"So I was wondering whether you might consider a film?"

Chapter Four

"Holida-*ay*! Celebra-*ate*!"

Madonna belted out so loudly from the speakers that Cathy could no longer hear herself think. Heart pounding like a piston, she waited for the cue and, with a desperate lunge, kicked one long leg into the air as high as badly-toned muscles and gravity would allow. This was followed quickly by a twirl to the left, which she managed with all the grace of a baby giraffe.

"Number five. Number five!"

Cathy froze mid-twirl. That was her.

"Come here, please."

She looked to the bottom of the dance studio where the choreographer, the producer and the director sat. The choreographer, a bleached blond with a goatee to match, languidly waved a hand at her. Oh Christ, he wasn't going to make her do a solo piece, was he?

She stood rooted to the spot in terror. Her face was a blotchy red, her fringe plastered to her forehead in sweaty strings. And she had a horrible suspicion that half-moons of moisture had gathered under the armpits of her baggy sweatshirt and in the crotch of her faded leggings.

The choreographer was impatiently coming towards her now, crossing the dance studio in Digges Lane with impatient steps. Cathy watched his approach in the unforgiving wall-to-wall mirror with dread.

"Step out, please." He was bored.

"Step where?" Cathy asked foolishly.

"Out. You can leave now. Thank you."

Her heart took a bungee jump into her battered runners. Her audition was over.

"If you'd just give me one more chance…" She struggled to catch her breath. "That twirly bit is quite tricky, you know."

"*Thank* you," he repeated meaningfully.

"Please," Cathy blurted, hating herself. But she needed this part. She had only two pounds of this week's dole money left. "Give me one more chance," she said quietly.

The choreographer snapped his fingers loudly. Someone hit the stereo and Madonna went dead. The rest of the troupe stopped mid-kick and turned to stare. All were disgustingly toned and tanned and sporting skimpy leotards that revealed most of their impossibly rounded behinds. All of them were *tiny*. Curiosity turned to a savage amusement as they gathered around. The choreographer waited until Cathy thought she could bear the humiliation no longer.

"Listen, darling. We're looking for sylphs in the wood. And a sylph you are *not*."

Cathy's mouth opened and closed again. She thought

she would sink through the floor with shock, with shame. Her lip trembled and before she could make a bigger fool of herself, she turned on her heel and stumbled away. With every step, she felt those unforgiving eyes on her back. The door seemed miles away and she thought she would surely never reach it. She grabbed her rucksack from the pile by the wall and she could not look at the director and producer as she crept out.

Madonna started up again. Through the glass panel on the door, she watched the rest of the girls launch themselves back into the dance. Mops of luxuriant blonde, black and auburn hair swung as they turned this way and that, endless legs flicking seductively at the air. As the music speeded up, the girls flung themselves into a frenzy of spins and twirls, each trying to outdo the other until they were nothing more than a blur of hair and skin.

All this for the promise of a tiny part in the chorus of the Christmas panto at the Gaiety Theatre in December.

Cathy could not watch them any longer. They were everything she was not and never would be. What had she been thinking of, coming here today?

Her rent, for one; the astronomical sum her seedy landlord demanded for a one-bedroom hovel on the North Circular Road. A foothold into the business, for another; in her two weeks back in Dublin, she hadn't even had a sniff of a part. She would gladly have auditioned for a deaf, blind, hunch-backed mute if it would propel her onto the first step of the acting ladder.

Not that acting seemed to have much to do with it, if today was anything to go by. It was all looks – hair, height, curves, youth. Cathy seemed to have got the raw end of the stick on all four. There didn't seem to be much demand for tall, thin, brown-haired women who were long out of their teens.

Body aching with exertion and a deep-seated misery, Cathy hitched up her rucksack and trudged into the changing room. She was immediately sorry. The last batch of girls who had auditioned for the panto were standing around in various states of undress. They were even more beautiful and feminine than Cathy's group. They looked briefly at her as she entered and then away, lofty-eyed and dismissive. It was as if she did not exist. They reminded her of a gang of bitchy Barbie dolls.

She slunk past, head down. Damn. All the toilets were occupied. She'd have to change in front of them.

"Gerry said I'd be called back for the final round of auditions," a Blonde Barbie announced, clad in her birthday suit and a G-string. Gerry was obviously the choreographer. Cathy felt a fresh wave of hatred for him as she commandeered the darkest corner of the changing room.

"He said he wasn't making a decision today," a Brunette Barbie replied spitefully. "He said he'd let our agents know."

Blonde Barbie was triumphant. "I'm only telling you what he told me."

Cathy struggled out of her sweatshirt as fast as she could, hunching over to reveal as little as possible of her flat chest. She'd forgotten to shave under her arms too. Had anyone ever had a worse day?

"What about you?"

Cathy clutched the sweatshirt to her, startled. Someone was talking to her.

"Sorry?"

A small, graceful girl with short curly hair still wet from the showers dumped her stuff on the bench beside Cathy. "Did you get a call back? For the final audition next week?" She casually discarded her towel to stand there completely in the raw.

"You're hilarious," Cathy mumbled tightly.

The girl's eyes widened with hurt. "I was just asking. I didn't either."

Cathy bit her lip. She was so uptight today that she thought everyone was out to get her. "Sorry," she mumbled. "No, I definitely didn't get a call back."

The girl nodded towards Brunette Barbie across the room. "Maybe Barbara is right," she said hopefully.

A hysterical half-snort escaped Cathy. "She's really called Barbara?"

The girl looked at her strangely. "Yeh. But maybe she's right. Maybe Gerry *is* going to call our agents."

"He won't be calling mine," Cathy mumbled, flinging aside the sweatshirt and diving into a mansize T-shirt as fast as she could.

"They always do here. Even if it's a no," the girl said knowledgeably.

"I don't have an agent," Cathy said flatly.

The girl was mildly confused. "Then how did you get an audition this morning? It's agents only."

"I gate-crashed."

The girl looked appalled. "You what?"

"I just turned up and begged them to let me in," Cathy admitted, feeling as though she had just committed a crime.

The girl looked Cathy up and down doubtfully. "And you're a dancer?"

"What? No. Are you?"

"Of course. Everybody here is."

"Oh. I didn't know," Cathy said, feeling even more ridiculous that she'd gate-crashed an audition for professional dancers. No wonder she'd been thrown out on her ear.

"Just starting out?" the girl asked sympathetically. "Listen, I know what it's like. But you'll soon get the hang of it."

Cathy didn't bother explaining that she had been in the business for six gruelling years, five of them in London. Instead, she drank in the girl's kindness and managed a watery smile.

Sometimes coming home seemed like a dreadful mistake. She had left one alien city only to find another so changed that she hardly recognised it any more. Gone were the old familiar haunts, replaced by trendy coffee bars and themed pubs. Prices had risen astronomically, from food to clothes to drink. Traffic choked the streets, leaving a grey smog over the Liffey. Dublin's fair city had changed irrevocably, now a metropolis of high-rise car-parks, British department stores and a Spar on every corner.

But even more changed were the people. The Celtic Tiger had spawned a generation of the new rich –

twenty-four-year-old go-getters who were earning fifty grand a year playing with their computers. Josephine Public now walked down Moore Street in Prada shoes with a mobile phone glued to her ear. Ambition was rife; self-absorption pervaded the city and sometimes when Cathy closed her eyes, she could swear that she was back in London.

The new mentality had even permeated the acting profession where, for decades, actors and actresses had been happy – proud even – to promote their art in crumbling theatres to audiences mostly consisting of their parents. Now every last one of them was scrabbling to get into TV and film. They would sell their own grannies for a walk-on in *Ballykissangel* and you were nobody unless you had worked with Jordan at least once.

Had Cathy anticipated a home-coming party from her long-lost acting compatriots, she would have been sadly disappointed. Another competitor for the precious few TV and film roles going was about as welcome as a dose of the clap. They were not as rude as their counterparts in London, that was true. Some of them had even recognised Cathy and wished her luck, albeit not too heartily. But she had been gone too long and there were too many impenetrable cliques. While they went for pints in *The Flowing Tide*, Cathy went home to her bedsit to gulp down beans on toast and renew herself for another day.

And what days they were: pounding the pavements from dawn till dusk, hawking her CV and photo to any director who would give her the time of day; harassing agents, casting directors and producers; gate-crashing auditions and begging film production secretaries for five minutes of their bosses' time.

She quickly discovered that her fringe theatre work in London and her brief claim to fame in *2 by 2* elicited only mild interest and a half-hearted promise to give her a call should anything arise. Her newly installed phone was spectacular in its silence.

It seemed that the same rule applied in Dublin as anywhere else in the world: you were only as good as your last role. And it had been a long time since Cathy Conroy's last role.

"Want some?" The girl proffered a bottle of Lucozade Sport. Cathy shook her head. She needed more than a sugar-hit to lift her spirits today.

The girl took in her abject expression. "You know, you really need an agent to take you on."

"I know, I just can't make up my mind which one to go with," Cathy said sardonically. Every one she had approached had turned her down flat.

The girl hesitated, then reluctantly dipped into a leather-bound Filofax and extracted a card. "You could try her."

Cathy accepted the card. *Jean Orsmby. Theatrical and Film Agent.*

She knew how much it went against the grain for the girl to help out a competitor in this dog-eat-dog world. Her eyes threatened to well up.

"Listen – thanks, you know?"

The girl shrugged. "I don't know how good she is, to be honest. She hasn't been on the scene long."

Cathy was not put off. The salient fact was that Jean Ormsby was the only agent in town who had not yet turned her down.

The girl was looking at her peculiarly now.

"What?" Cathy asked, paranoid again.

The girl laughed. "Sorry. I just recognised you. You were in *Outsiders*, weren't you? Carl Tallon's play? About five years ago?"

"Yes," Cathy said in a clipped tone.

"You know it's going to be made into a film?"

"Yes," Cathy said again, her mouth tight.

"You'll have a headstart on the rest of us so. For the film auditions." The girl was envious.

"I won't be auditioning for the film." This time Cathy sounded loud and sharp.

A slow comprehension crept over the girl's face. "Sorry . . . of course, you and Carl . . . sorry." Embarrassed, she quickly gathered her things. "Try Jean," she babbled. "But I should warn you, she's not really taking on new clients. In fact, she's letting them go." She smiled crookedly. "She was my boyfriend's agent. He got the axe yesterday." She pulled on her coat, gave Cathy a brief thumbs-up, and left.

Cathy sat on the bench, fists clenched. She would *scream*, she thought, if just one more person in this town asked her whether she knew *Outsiders* was being made into a film. They could make a twelve-part mini-series out of it for all she cared, they could turn it into a fecking cartoon. It was nothing to do with her. *Nothing*.

They had long memories around here, she was

starting to realise that. And an insatiable interest in other people's business.

Well, let them. They were sad people if they were still dwelling on something that was dead in the water this past five years.

She was sad too. It was over. Finished. She had come back to Dublin to re-launch her acting career, not to take a trip down memory lane.

Resolutely, she turned her attention to the white business card in her hand. It was cheaply printed, with no frills. Whoever this Jean Orsmby was, she wasn't in the big league. Which meant that she couldn't afford to ignore talent, no matter how many people she was supposedly letting go. And Cathy didn't intend to be ignored.

With renewed determination, she gathered her sweat-sodden things and stuffed them into her rucksack. Purposefully, she pushed her way through the throng of semi-naked girls, now joined by the batch from Cathy's audition.

"Excuse me, Barbara," she said briskly to the brunette.

A small silence fell behind her as she made for the door.

"Who is *she*?" Barbara enquired with a sniff.

"Dunno. Cathy something-or-other. Never heard of her," another offered.

Cathy smiled to herself as she hauled open the door. *No, but you will, luvvie. You will.*

Chapter Five

A glossy photo of a big-breasted blonde wonder slid across the desk, stopping just short of Jean Ormsby's cup of coffee. A CV was attached. She didn't bother to pick it up.

"Experience?"

Patsy, her part-time secretary, screwed up her freckled nose in an attempt to remember.

"Um, she's done two voice-overs. Oh, and a dog-food commercial." No kidding. She *was* a dog.

"Send her an F.O.A.D.," Jean said automatically. A fuck-off-and-die. "Politely, of course," she sternly reminded Patsy, who last week had sent out a rejection letter saying just that in bald and simple terms. The recipient had rung Jean up apoplectic with fury. "Any more?"

"Seventeen," Patsy said painfully, indicating the large pile of unsolicited brown envelopes she had not got around to opening yet.

Jean eyed the envelopes with a growing despair. Seventeen actors and actresses, all begging to get on her

books. This might be flattering were it not for the fact
that Jean knew every other agent in town had turned
them down. "Leave them to me, Patsy. Any word back
on Leanne Potter's audition?"

"Yes."

That had been fast. Fierce hope ignited in Jean. "And?"

"And. . . they don't want her."

"I see. Did they give any reason?"

"They said she couldn't act."

Jean sighed inwardly. There was nothing for it. "Send
her an F.O.A.D."

Patsy was appalled. "But she's really nice!"

"Patsy, I know she's really nice. So is Tommy Butler
really nice, and so is Susan Murray. But the problem is
that they're not earning their keep and this agency is not a
charity!" Stress and fatigue made her voice sound sharper
that she had intended. "Sorry, Patsy. Why don't you take
a coffee break?"

Patsy lingered, her round face a picture of woe.
"There's something else."

There always was. "The landlord again, is it? Well, the
next time he comes looking for his money, tell him he has
a nerve charging rent for a building with a leaky roof and
a rat-infested basement. Better still, *I'll* tell him."

"It's not that. It's . . . I'm leaving, Jean."

Jean looked up, shocked.

"I've been offered a full-time job. It's more money."

"I see."

"I'm sorry, Jean. But you know how things are."

Jean did. The agency was sinking fast and Patsy was

bailing out while she had the chance. Who could blame her?

"All right, Patsy," she said quietly. "And if you need any references or anything, I'd be happy to give them."

Patsy seemed on the verge of tears. "Thanks. But what will you do? Who'll answer the phone and stuff?"

Jean forced herself to remain practical. "Maybe you'd put a notice in the window downstairs." She certainly couldn't shell out for an ad in *The Irish Times*. "Part-time, someone who can type. Okay?"

Patsy nodded. "Okay. And Jean, it's not that I don't believe in you or anything – "

Jean smiled brightly. "I know that, Patsy. I'll make something of this place yet."

Patsy managed a wan smile and left.

Alone, Jean's head fell into her hands. She stared at the chipped wood of her desk with blank eyes, head pounding. At times like this, she thought that she must have been completely deranged and insane when she made the decision a little over a year ago to open her own actors' agency.

Agency. What a joke. The entire staff of The Jean Ormsby Agency consisted of herself and Patsy who typed three mornings a week. Now it only consisted of her.

She would cope, she told herself. She could keep going on her own until the big jobs started to roll in. Which would be any day now, it had to be, she'd put in her time.

Stop fooling yourself. You're just not in the league, honey.

Several times recently, Jean had tried to face this

painful reality. The reality was that there would no big ones with the kind of clients she had on her books. The Jean Ormsby Agency proudly represented a handful of completely unknown actresses like Leanne Potter, one or two past-it stage actors and a fairly well-known character actress who only worked when the mood took her, which wasn't very often. And she had left the agency last week for more salubrious representation.

Jean remembered now the words of Bernice Gannon, a fellow-agent for whom Jean had once worked as an administration assistant: "You'll never poach the soapers from them, you know."

The "soapers" were the soap stars, the life-blood of most agencies in Dublin with their hefty weekly cheque. "Them" meant those three large agencies on leafy southside roads, the only players in Dublin who really counted. Between them, they had every successful actor, soap star and film actor on their books. There was little or no cross-over. It was a closed shop. But Jean had known this. She wasn't stupid. And she had no intention of trying to poach clients from other agents.

"I'm going for new people," she told Bernice. "I'm going to develop some young, fresh talent."

Bernice snorted. "Young *fresh* talent? Jesus, those poor sods can't scratch a living themselves, never mind their agents."

But Jean was adamant. And idealistic and naïve and foolish, she now saw. Her genuine enthusiasm for nurturing talent was no basis for a business. Instead, she had unwittingly become the target for every wannabe in this city who thought they could act, and whose unsolicited CVs arrived in frightening numbers in the post every morning. And she had put off most of those in positions to offer actors jobs – because who the hell of any note did Jean Ormsby represent anyway?

A year down the road, Jean was left with few illusions and less money. She could no longer afford the freeloaders, which was why she was letting most of the agency's clients go. And she was under no circumstances taking on a single other unknown.

It was sink or swim time. And the water was getting deeper.

To distract herself, Jean reached for the small pile of personal mail addressed to her. Patsy was under strict instructions never to open anything marked "private" or "confidential". For one thing, Jean didn't want her secretary knowing the dismal state of the agency's bank account. More importantly, she didn't want *anyone* to know how pathetic Ian had become in recent months.

It had been painful, the break. She supposed it was never easy to abandon someone you cared about when they were at their lowest. But Ian had been at his lowest for almost two years before Jean had finally thrown him out. She knew that if she let him stay any longer, she would be dragged down with him. In the end, it had been the lies and the deceit and the promises that he would change that had broken them up.

She opened a plain white envelope, her hands clammy.

My dearest Jean. I'm coming out in two weeks' time and would really like to meet you. Just for old times' sake. I feel so much better now and believe that I have finally got myself back on track . . .

She stopped reading and stuffed the letter back into the envelope. Of course he was better. A month of detox made even the worst addict better. But how many times now had he kicked it only to slide backwards three weeks later?

Cocaine. The recreational habit of the rich.

What a laugh. Try the addictive habit of the poor. Because at a gram a day, the money sure didn't last long.

"Square," he'd said teasingly when she'd first refused to try it. He'd controlled it for the first couple of years before it inevitably started to control him. The highs, the terrible lows, the temper tantrums, the empty joint bank account – she'd endured it all. And suffered with him, hardly able to credit what was happening to the love of her life, the man she'd been with for seven long years.

Cocaine. The drug that enhances your sex life.

Another scream. Ian had finally admitted that he was an addict the night he'd hit her after yet another failed attempt to make love to her.

Cocaine. The non-addictive drug.

That was the biggest joke of all. Ian had been in and out of treatment centres four times before she'd finally faced up to the fact that he was not going to change. She'd collected him from his last stint in the detox joint in the afternoon and by that evening, he was higher than Richard Branson ever got in *Challenger*. She'd packed his bags the following morning and told him to leave. Often she thought that she must have an extremely hard heart to throw out someone so desperate and vulnerable. But she simply couldn't stand it any more.

She also couldn't see him any more, no matter how many times he wrote. He was a time-bomb and she could not afford be in the vicinity when he finally exploded.

"Patsy, can you bring me in another coffee?" she said through the intercom, more to do something normal than because she actually wanted one. Ian's increasingly desperate letters always had that effect on her.

The next piece of post scarcely cheered her up. It was a job offer for one of her clients – the mildly famous character actress who only last week had upped and left the agency. The letter of offer came attached to a filmscript – they wanted her to play the second female lead.

"Beautiful," Jean said in resignation. "Just beautiful."

She felt sick as she thought about the handsome commission she'd just missed. Film was where it was at in this town. So when Patsy arrived in with the coffee pot, Jean asked for the third time, "Has Phyllis Harding got back to us yet?"

"No."

It had been in all the papers this morning. Jean's own copy of the *Times* was open on the desk.

Government Bankrolls Movie In Bid To Win Kilkenny By-election.

The piece was short on facts and long on speculation. There were no details of the proposed movie, and the reporter, Gobnait Purcell, had been forced to fill the article with the opposition party's scathing attack on what it called the Government's glitzy tactics. The Minister for Art's office, the article said, had refused to either confirm or deny any such plans for a film. A grainy photo of Peter Fisher hurrying to his car was all they could get. Next to the article was an obituary to Tony Croft TD, deceased.

Thankfully, Bernice Gannon had all the inside gossip when Jean had phoned her this morning.

"Oh, there's a film all right. At this stage nobody knows who's going to be in it or who's directing." She had paused heavily. "But rumour has it Phyllis Harding is casting."

"Who is she?" Jean had enquired innocently.

"Who is she? Christ, she's only the toughest, meanest bitch in town, that's who," Bernice had said sourly.

"But she's casting this film?"

"I know what you're thinking, Jean, and don't do it. Don't go chasing her. She's a barracuda."

"I like a challenge," Jean had said, and rang off.

Phyllis Harding might be tough and mean but Jean was resourceful and desperate. And if Harding was in a position to cast some of Jean's clients in this new film, then Jean was going after her. It was a last-ditch effort on many fronts.

So far, all five of Jean's phone calls to Phyllis Harding's office this morning had gone unreturned. How could she hope to break her down if the woman wouldn't even come to the phone? The last time she'd called, the receptionist had snootily asked Jean to spell the name of her agency. Phyllis Harding dealt only with the top agents and she was letting Jean know in the rudest terms that she wasn't a player in her book.

Maybe lunch had improved her mood. Jean reached for the phone again, trying not to betray her despair.

Ten minutes later, she was still on the phone and still on hold. Dogged determination and a growing dislike for Phyllis Harding made her refuse to be fobbed off this time.

"She's on that call still," Harding's receptionist told her again, irritated now. "Are you sure you wouldn't like to just leave a message?"

"I'll hold," Jean repeated calmly.

Idly, she doodled with a biro and tried not to think about Ian. She hoped that he would stay away from her this time. She didn't have the energy to play mother any more, and that was all she had been to him in the past few years. Forget a mature, adult relationship, with a bit of love and passion thrown in. Ian had been the wayward child and she his minder, cajoling, pleading and threatening him into staying clean.

Over the years, she had forgotten what a normal relationship was like. Sometimes she wondered whether she would ever have one again. She had fought too long and too hard on her own now to even contemplate what it would be like to have someone to share it all with.

She realised that she was doodling all over the filmscript that had come in the post. Hastily, she reached for the Tippex. Then first line of dialogue hit her between the eyes.

"Take her away and hang her."

By the time she'd reached the end of the page, the hair was standing on the back of her neck. The stuff was dynamite.

She forgot about the Tippex and the phone nestled in the crook of her neck; she was oblivious to the traffic on the busy street below. She was lost in the script, turning pages feverishly, eyes devouring the small black print. Time passed.

"Just what the hell are you doing, tying up my phone line?"

The voice exploded from the receiver by her ear. It belonged to one Phyllis Harding, who didn't bother to introduce herself.

Jean was flustered. "Oh. Thanks for speaking to me, Phyllis – "

"What do you want?"

"I was wondering about this new film the Government is making – "

"What film?"

"The one they're talking about in the newspaper – "

"What newspaper?"

"Eh, the *Times* . . . I heard that you were casting it, Phyllis."

Her hands were slippery on the phone now.

"I don't know where you got your information, Miss Ormsby," Harding said eventually. "Until I get a script, I am unaware of the existence of any such film."

Jean opened her mouth again but Phyllis wasn't finished yet.

"But if and when I *do* get a script, I will be contacting

all the agents I know in town." She paused. "And I don't know you, Miss Ormsby."

Slam. She put down the receiver so hard that Jean's eardrum tingled.

Jean found that she was shaking with humiliation. Phyllis Harding would never answer her phone calls again, she knew. She would never give a single one of her clients a job. Unless Jean managed to get Tom Cruise or Judi Dench on her books, of course. And the prospect of that was unlikely.

Jean massaged her temples wearily. What did it take to get a little respect in this town?

Her eye fell again on the script she had been reading. Phyllis Harding had said that there was no script yet.

Yet.

"Patsy. Hold all calls."

A noise out in reception caused Jean to lift her head reluctantly from the script. She blinked, startled to note that the afternoon was nearly gone. She was also parched and had the beginnings of a migraine.

But she didn't care. She was excited. Elated. High on adrenaline. God, was this script *good*! In the past three hours, it had dragged her back four hundred years into the world of the Butler family, a renegade, powerful Anglo-Irish family who had at one time ruled most of Leinster from their castle in Kilkenny. It was a period extravaganza, complete with heaving bosoms and tight trousers and oodles of sex.

The central characters were the fictitious Richard

Butler, the black sheep of the Butler family, and Alison, a servant girl who worked in the castle. Their forbidden love story had made Jean's heart sing. They were so real, so well-drawn, that they had made Jean rejoice, suffer, love, laugh and hate along with them. In the dying pages, when Alison was hanged for supposedly being a traitor to Ireland, Jean had even cried.

She couldn't remember the last time she'd seen a full Technicolor movie, never mind a dog-eared typescript, where she'd been on the edge of her seat aching to see what happened next. She was no script expert, but she would stake her life on the fact that this story was incredible.

There was more noise from reception. "But you don't have an appointment!" Patsy's voice was loud.

Now a muffled male voice, bristly and low. "It'll only take a minute."

"No, really, she's busy!" Patsy again, getting nearer.

The door to Jean's office was flung open and a young man stood there, all rough edges and black looks. Patsy flapped helplessly in his wake.

"I'm sorry . . . I did try to tell him . . . I said we weren't taking anyone on."

Jean looked at the stranger coolly. He stared back directly, dark eyes brooding and volatile. He had a slightly crooked nose in an otherwise fantastically handsome face and this lent him an even more ominous air. He reminded Jean of a young Heathcliff who had lost his way on the moors and had ended up in Dame Street.

For all his ill-concealed aggression, he did not advance

into her office and Jean knew that if she told him to leave right now, he would.

"Well, show the man in, Patsy," she said.

"Huh?"

"You can leave us now. And perhaps you'd get a coffee for Mr . . . ?"

"Tallon. My name is Carl Tallon."

"Ah." Jean smiled. "I've been expecting you."

But not so soon. She'd only left the message on his answering machine an hour ago. Obviously, she had been convincing.

"I'll bet you have," he said coldly.

'Two coffees then, Patsy," Jean said calmly.

Patsy retreated unhappily. The door shut and Jean and the intruder regarded each other in silence for a moment.

"Won't you have a seat?"

"I'll stand," he said roughly. Anger seemed to come off him in sparks. He was livid, Jean was delighted to note.

"So. What can I do for you, Mr Tallon?" she asked pleasantly.

"What can you *do* for me?" he spat incredulously. "You can keep your opinions to yourself for a start!"

Jean nodded agreeably. "Okay."

Tallon jabbed a finger at her. "Where did you even get my phone number?"

"It's on the front of your script," Jean said reasonably.

"My script? How did you get a copy of my script?"

"I just did." Jean smiled at him. "And I thought I'd let you know what I thought of it. I thought you might appreciate the feed-back."

74

He was almost spitting with rage now. "What, that I'd want to hear that my script was crap?"

Finally, he had got to the crux of what was really bugging him. What was *infuriating* him.

"I don't believe I said the word 'crap' on your answering machine," Jean corrected him evenly. "I said in my opinion it could do with more work."

"I don't care what you think! My script has nothing to do with you!"

"You're absolutely right," Jean said contritely. "I shouldn't have rung you at all." She grimaced apologetically. "I'm a perfectionist, you see. When I see that something could be better, I go rushing right on in there. Anyway. Terribly sorry. Patsy will show you out."

He couldn't bear to leave now, of course. He was a perfectionist too. She'd known that from the first page of his script. And she had just planted the first seed of doubt in his mind. She hid a smile as she pretended to look over some paperwork, ignoring him. Eventually he asked the question she was waiting for.

"So what was wrong with it? The script?"

"Hmm? Oh, nothing much."

The seed had just sprung up into a forest.

"The director thinks it's perfect," Carl Tallon blustered.

"And who's directing?" Jean asked, carefully casual.

"Jay Devaney," Tallon said loudly.

"Yes, well, Jay Devaney – I mean, he's a good director . . ." She let her voice trail off doubtfully.

Tallon was riddled with doubt now. He was almost hopping from foot to foot.

"He said I didn't need to make any more changes."

Jean knew when it was time to stop playing with Tallon. "Then he hasn't read the script properly," she said bluntly.

Tallon froze. "What?"

"It's fantastic, don't get me wrong. But there are huge holes in the material between Richard and Alison."

His anger abruptly dissipated. He seemed almost hurt. Jean had to suppress a smile.

"Holes?" he said.

"Yep. Nothing that a rewrite wouldn't take care of. But I didn't believe that Alison would give up her life for Richard. That she would actually die for him."

He was rattled, chewing on his lower lip and fidgeting at his tatty denim jacket.

"Because she loves him?" he suggested humbly.

"Ha!" Jean said. "You'll have to try harder than that."

He looked at her, waiting for her to go on, to explain to him what to do. She didn't.

"Are you a script consultant?" he asked eventually. "Because, you see, this script is important to me. I'll do a hundred rewrites if necessary."

"It'd be a lot of work."

"I don't care. I'll do it," he returned emphatically.

He was, she decided, the genuine article. The tortured artist who would rather burn his script on a bonfire than sell it short. He probably hung out in some rat-ridden writer's garret and starved as a matter of course. He was, she thought, really quite sweet.

"I'm not a consultant, Carl. I'm an agent."

"Oh. Well, I'd still be interested in hearing what you have to say," he said with a charming lack of tact.

Jean tried out a crocodile smile on him. "But I wouldn't want to step on Jay Devaney's toes, Carl. He *is* directing the film, after all."

"Nothing's signed yet," Tallon said quickly.

Jean felt relief washing over her. That had been the one huge gamble. And she had won.

"Really?" she said, admirably playing down her excitement. "But you have an agent?"

"No."

Alleluia.

"I suppose I could help you . . ." she said reluctantly.

His face lit up eagerly. "Would you?"

". . . but is there any reason why I should?"

He stiffened now.

Jean looked at him directly. "The Government is making a movie, Carl. Maybe we can help each other out here."

By the time Patsy sailed through the door, proud of the fact that she was able to balance two coffees, milk, sugar and a plate of fig rolls without dropping anything, they had struck a deal.

Her day didn't end until after eight. She was weary but optimistic for the first time in weeks. She had a client who would take her places.

She turned again to the open newspaper on her desk, which she had glanced at more times than she had wanted to today. Her eye kept falling on the photo of

Peter Fisher, in his expensive raincoat and his curiously shabby briefcase, running to his car. The camera had caught him unawares and he was looking straight out from the page, mildly startled by the intrusion. He had a dynamism and energy that transferred even to grainy black and white reproduction. The man was pure charisma and wild good looks.

Often, she had seen Fisher on TV, bursting onto the screen of the nine o'clock news with some vociferous argument or ardent outburst, stirring the feathers of the opposition party and the passions of Mńa na hEireann – Jean's mother had been known to comment that he was "*mmmm*!" and Jean suspected that at least two of her friends had voted for his party in the last election simply to insure a continuous eyeful of him.

She assured herself now that she was viewing him with a purely professional eye. He was making an Irish film. And he didn't have a script yet.

But she did. And he wanted it, then he could have it on the condition that her clients got several major parts in it.

If he wanted it. It was a big if. All she could do was try.

Patsy was long gone, but when Jean turned on the light in reception, she found that she was not alone.

"My God!" Her heart thudded unpleasantly. "Who the hell are you?"

A girl was hunched in the chair by Patsy's rubber plant. She looked almost as startled as Jean.

"I. . . I was waiting to see you," she mumbled.

Goddamn it. Jean had completely forgotten about the typing job they'd advertised in the window downstairs and the fact that Patsy had said that there was another candidate waiting. Jean had already briefly interviewed two no-hopers who were unable to spell the words "yours sincerely".

"Sorry for keeping you waiting," she said to the girl. "Time got away on me."

The girl lifted her head and smiled. For the first time, Jean got a good look at her. She was all angles and bones, big teeth and spiky brown hair. The combination was so unusual as to be startling. Like Peter Fisher, the girl possessed genuine charisma.

She was obviously unaware of it as she fumbled apologetically with a large brown envelope. "I didn't mind waiting. I have a CV for you to look at."

Jean waved it away. "Look, we can wrap this up quickly. Can you type?"

"What? Yes, a bit."

"And can you answer a phone clearly and politely?"

The girl looked confused. Please God, Jean implored, not another Patsy.

"Yes," the girl eventually answered, with a decisive nod.

She would do, Jean decided. Besides, anyone who had waited for hours for an interview without complaining deserved the job.

"Look, I can't pay you much yet," she stated.

"What? But I'm not – "

"I'll do a review in a month, okay?" Jean cut off any

complaints. "All you have to do is answer the phone and type letters. Oh, and keep away actors who don't have appointments – we're just not taking anybody else on. Period."

She said this strongly to get the message home.

The girl was silent. The hand holding the CV was slowly lowered. She looked anything but delighted at having just landed a job.

"Do you want it or not?" Jean snapped, her tiredness getting the better of her.

The girl hesitated, then nodded. "Yes. Thanks."

She stood then, and Jean blinked at the height of her. The girl saw this and immediately her shoulders stooped over and her chin dropped.

Don't do that, Jean wanted to tell her. How could someone look that amazing but have so little confidence?

The girl was halfway down the stairs when Jean went running after her.

"You never told me your name."

"Oh. Cathy. Cathy Conroy."

Jean smiled. "All right, Cathy. See you at nine in the morning."

Chapter Six

On the Aer Lingus flight from Dublin to Los Angeles International Airport, Roger Croft was stuck in economy class reading dross. His only consolation was that his travelling companion was an extremely attractive brunette with a substantial bust which she now carefully placed on her fold-down tray as she turned coyly to look at him. Not that Roger gave a fig about her bust. It was the boyfriend in the window seat who had captured his attention. He had the kind of dirty blond looks that spoke to Roger's soul. Or his pelvic region at any rate.

"I couldn't help noticing what you're reading," the brunette breathed. "Are you in the movie business?"

Roger allowed a suave half-smile to lift the corner of his mouth. "In a manner of speaking, yes."

His involvement with the movie business had begun in earnest an hour ago when Peter Fisher had appeared from business class, dumped twelve film scripts into his lap and told him to get reading.

"These are the cream of what the Film Board has at the moment. Pick out the best three."

He had told him no more – not even why they were going to LA or who they were meeting there. So much for them working side by side on *this* gig. In Roger's two weeks as Fisher's protégé, he had quickly learned that Fisher intended to lead and that Roger would be forced to crawl in his wake.

Roger had also learned that Fisher was an arrogant son of a bitch who treated him less like the Government's only chance of survival than a lowly secretary, sending him on coffee-making missions and photocopying errands. Last week, he'd dispatched him to the supermarket for a prawn sandwich and a packet of crisps. Roger had fumed at the checkout but was helpless to do anything about it. He couldn't even complain to Carol Taylor. Fisher was doing her a big favour and she wouldn't lift a finger.

Some favour. The surly bastard never let him near anything important, or invited him to attend any meetings in Dublin where he might actually learn something, setting him up instead at a desk in his constituency office in Kilkenny, where Roger spent his mornings meeting dreary members of the public and his evenings attending tedious community meetings. Then the whirlwind tours with Fisher, pressing flesh and visiting old folks' homes where the smell of steamed cod and incontinence made Roger's stomach turn. When Roger had finally mentioned that they might be better off

82

courting the media, Fisher had cut him off with the rejoinder that it was far too soon.

And as for the movie, the rabbit they were going to pull out of the hat, Fisher had completely cut him out. He had certain things to put in place first, he'd told Roger. It would all be hush-hush until they got the finance and key players in place and then there would be an announcement.

Roger was furious. The film was where it was at, not humouring old dears who would probably be dead by polling day anyhow. Roger had visions of himself on the front pages of the newspapers, alongside some American director and maybe a co-star or two, with the accompanying caption that he was the man who would breathe some life back into the Kilkenny economy and culture. What was the point in keeping it secret? There were less than a hundred and sixty days to the by-election and every one of them counted.

But Fisher held firm. There would be no media coverage until they were ready. And it was obvious that Roger would be told no more until *Fisher* was ready. To learn anything at all about the project, he was forced to go through Fisher's mail and computer disks when he was out of the office, and eavesdrop on his phone conversations on the other line. And thus he knew that they were going to meet some big industry swing in LA in the hopes of luring them on board.

Still, Fisher was some mover, Roger grudgingly had to admit. For a man of forty-something, his energy was astounding. Roger had tried to impress him on his first day by showing up at his Kilkenny office at eight in the morning. Fisher was already there. The next day, Roger made it in for seven thirty. Again, Fisher had beaten him to it. On the third day Roger was sitting triumphant, if bleary-eyed, outside the locked office at seven in the morning. But Fisher hadn't bothered to tell him that he would be holding open office for his constituents on the other side of town. Then he'd asked him to write menial follow-up letters to the various people he'd met.

"Couldn't your secretary do this?" Roger blurted, his frustration slipping out.

Fisher looked at him with interest. "Sit down, Roger."

Roger sat eagerly. Maybe the man had finally realised that Roger was due a little respect.

"You want to be a politician, Roger, is that correct?" Fisher asked gently.

"The public sector has always appealed to me," Roger said, voice dripping with sincerity. "Especially after seeing the satisfaction it gave my father – God rest his soul." He almost forgot to add that last bit. Fisher acknowledged it with a bow of his head.

"Perhaps even be a Minister yourself some day?" Fisher shot him a roguish grin.

Roger relaxed and gave a little self-effacing laugh. He'd obviously misread Fisher. He was one of the boys after all, despite his reputation for straight-talking and no compromise. "I don't know if I'd ever get that far." Certainly not under my own steam, Roger thought. But there was no reason at all why he shouldn't have higher aspirations once he'd sailed into office in the by-election on the coat tails of the great Peter Fisher.

Roger Croft got his first addictive taste of real power as a third-year student in Trinity College Dublin. That year he'd won the Presidency of the Student Union, arguably the most powerful Student Union in the country. The Union was a political force to be reckoned with in its own right and had in the past taken on the might of the Irish Pro-Life movement over the Abortion Information Act. The Union had taken them right to the Supreme Court.

Roger had intended to use his Presidency as a springboard into the Dáil, which should have been a natural progression, especially with the help of his father. But he hadn't reckoned on the unfortunate incident involving the allocation of Union funds in the sixth month of his Presidency. It had never been proven that Croft had been biased in their distribution; it was simply agreed all around that he would resign quietly, citing mental stress. It was the end of his glorious career in the Union and indeed in the college.

Ostracised, he'd failed to complete his degree and had crawled back to Kilkenny to face the wrath of a father who had built a career on honesty and integrity. It was clear that there would be no support from him when it came to the council nominations. Roger was forced to go to work in the family business and attempt to win back the affections of a father who no longer bothered to hide his dislike of his second-born son.

His father's untimely death was, therefore, a matter

of little regret to Roger. A major stumbling-block to a glorious political career had been removed. The icing on the cake was the one-seat majority that no longer was. With Fisher's help, it should be plain sailing.

The problem was that Fisher was a lone ranger. He didn't like hangers-on and aides. And no matter how helpful Roger had tried to make himself, Fisher didn't appear to take to him. But maybe today was the turning-point. Perhaps they could break a little ice together.

"It's a hard life, a politician's one," Fisher mused thoughtfully, resting his chin on his knuckles.

"Indeed it is," Roger agreed solemnly. "Pressure, commitments, the need to deliver – my father had little or no time to himself at all."

Fisher nodded sadly.

Having established intimacy, Roger leaned forward for the pitch. "That's why I want to learn all I can from you, Peter." It was a risk using the man's first name, but Fisher didn't appear to take offence. Good. "You can teach me what matters. The important things." Not typing letters to Joe Soaps in Kilkenny about noise pollution. More like election strategies and PR solutions to the voting patterns.

Peter nodded slowly. "Okay, Roger. If you're willing to learn, that is."

Roger rallied hard to conceal a triumphant grin. "I am. And thank you. I won't let you down."

Fisher acknowledged this with a bow of his head. He was a pushover really, Roger thought. Throw enough flattery their way and they're putty in your hands. He found he was disappointed with Fisher for having been taken in so easily. A man that gullible could hardly teach him very much. Still, he seemed to have won over the voters.

Fisher leaned in to him conspiratorially. Roger looked alert.

"Now, the first thing you have to learn, Roger – and learn right now, this minute – is the meaning of the word politician. Can you give me a definition?"

Roger was nonplussed. What was this – a trick question? But Fisher was smiling at him like a benign uncle, encouraging and kind. He supposed he'd have to humour the old fart.

"Well, it's someone who aspires to elected office . . . "

"Wrong." Fisher's voice cut across him like a blade. "Get a dictionary."

"What?"

"A dictionary, Roger." A small, loaded pause. "You must have learned how to use one in Trinity college, surely – or were you otherwise engaged?"

Roger's blood ran cold. The bastard knew. He knew about the Union funds. It was written all over him. Roger found he had to look away.

"You'll find one on the shelf there behind you, I believe, Roger."

Burning with suppressed rage, Roger was forced to look up the Oxford English Dictionary under Fisher's unforgiving gaze.

"Public servant," Roger read finally, throat tight and dry.

"That's right, Roger. Politics is not about scrabbling as high up that greasy ladder as you can, but public service." Fisher looked at him harshly and with contempt. "And that starts with writing letters to those people who might in the near future have the misfortune of you representing them. Please don't make your father turn in his grave."

Roger wasn't sure he had heard this last bit correctly. The roar in his ears was probably too loud in any case. For the rest of the afternoon, he crouched over a keyboard in the secretary's office, hate and loathing for the man in the next room emanating from his every pore.

After that, Roger made it his business to learn everything he could about Peter Fisher. He knew all about his cheating and his little dalliances but, then again, so did everybody else. He was familiar with the architectural consultancy work Fisher still did and knew that he didn't fiddle his tax. He knew what he paid for his rented luxury house in Dalkey and he knew that his daughter Fiona had been caught drinking at her private boarding-school.

Nothing terribly exciting yet and certainly nothing that could be used against him. But Roger could afford to wait. He had years yet.

In the meantime, it was time to run the by-election *his* way. So he phoned the newsdesks of the two main national newspapers with the tip that the Government was making a film in Kilkenny. It was unfortunate he couldn't give his name, but that would soon change. If

Fisher wouldn't use this film to Roger's advantage ASAP, then Roger would.

"Where are you staying in LA?" the brunette enquired, hungry eyes still fixed on the scripts.

Roger didn't want to admit that he was being shunted into some second-rate motel while Fisher and his wife were staying at the Regent Beverly Wilshire.

"I'm not sure what my secretary has organised," he said with the air of a man who went where his stretch limousine took him. "Why don't you tell me where you're staying? Maybe I can drop by later?"

He looked at the dirty blond boyfriend, who was not slow on the uptake. He, too, looked at the scripts with interest. With any luck, he was a down-and-out actor who would do pretty much anything once he heard the word "movie".

Roger settled back and ordered a gin and tonic. He'd give that slave-driver Fisher the low-down on these shitty scripts tonight and then he'd split. He was in LA after all and it was only fair and right to sample the local scenery.

The three stewardesses in business class were too well-trained to treat Peter Fisher to anything but the usual sterile smile. But in the privacy of the tiny kitchenette they huddled in a giggling clump.

"Christ, he's gorgeous."

"Mind you, the wife's not up to much, is she? I thought she'd be – like – *beautiful*."

"I wonder if he's giving any away."

Two minutes later they re-emerged and sashayed down the aisle, vacant smiles in place.

"Would you like anything to drink, Mrs Fisher?"

"Mineral water. Ice, no lemon," Tess rattled off.

The stewardess looked over at Peter enquiringly. He was absorbed in paperwork.

"Mr Fisher?"

"He's fine," Tess snapped, waving her away. The girl was practically drooling.

She sighed as she tried to re-cross her legs. Business class or not, there was never enough leg-room on charter planes.

"I don't see why we couldn't have taken the Government jet," she said for the second time.

Peter lowered the script and rubbed at his face. His eyes looked red and tired and Tess made a mental note to hunt out the eye-wash before dinner tonight.

"I don't want to announce to the whole world what I'm trying to do, Tess. Better that we keep this film under our hats for the moment."

"Bit late for that," Tess said tartly. "It's been all over the papers for a week."

"Not my doing," Peter snapped. The source of the leak was a mystery. "I've plenty more to be worrying about."

"Paramount is a no, then?" she asked casually. If Paramount had agreed to a meeting, there would be no charter flight. It would be all fanfare and ceremony, with the Government jet practically landing on their parking lot in a show of strength.

"Correct," Peter said in clipped tones.

So. Paramount had joined with Fox, Warner Bros, Universal and every other major Hollywood studio in politely rejecting Peter's overtures for an Irish-American co-production to be filmed on Irish soil.

Tess knew that Peter wasn't having much luck with the smaller studios either. She wasn't all that surprised. Even given the Irish tax breaks, what was there to tempt a studio to come to Ireland to do what they could accomplish on their own doorstep?

Peter didn't even have a script yet; he was still mowing his way through everything the Irish Film Board had received in the past six months.

"Who are we meeting for dinner then?" Tess asked, unable to conceal her curiosity any longer. Peter had been annoyingly secretive about the entire trip. Tess had been forced to fill three suitcases with an extensive wardrobe, as he hadn't been inclined to reveal anything about their itinerary. She didn't plan to be caught short.

He didn't answer her question, concentrating hard on the papers on his lap. They were covered in his untidy scrawl. Tess's irritation and curiosity grew. She stole a sideways glance.

Figures littered the top page. Film budgets, she guessed. One figure came to twenty million. Another thirty-five. Another fifty.

Fifty million pounds.

It was astounding, considering that most other films that came out of Ireland were made for less than a tenth of that. Scattered casually beside the budgets were lists of names; award-winning actors, producers, top Hollywood studios. Directors too – there was Spielberg, and Ron Howard and Jane Campion.

She studied his profile now, incredulous. Surely he couldn't possibly bring a film of that magnitude off? A fifty-million-pound production, and he didn't even have a script yet? It was insanity.

A clinical voice in the back of her head reminded her that Peter had never failed yet. She wouldn't put it past him to have half of Hollywood camped out on their back lawn, making the biggest film ever to come out of Ireland and possibly even Europe.

Peter looked up abruptly and caught her sneakily reading his notes. He smiled, amused.

"If you *must* know, Tess, we're meeting an actor."

"An actor?" Tess didn't bother to hide her chagrin. She thought they'd at least be meeting a top agent, maybe even someone from CAA. But an *actor*? What use were actors to anybody but themselves? Immediately she regretted that third suitcase.

"The studios are not biting, Tess," Peter replied edgily. "So I've had to look elsewhere."

Tess's mouth tightened. "What good is an actor to us when we don't have any money or any director or even a script?"

"Will you keep your voice down?" Peter cautioned. "That will work itself out. If we hook the actor, for example, then we have the director."

"What? You mean this person is big enough to lure a director on board?"

"He *is* the director, Tess. Or rather he will be, if he goes for it."

Tess looked at him, aghast. She'd known he was idealistic but she'd never have taken him for a complete fool. "Peter. You're not seriously considering a first-time actor/director."

Peter smiled. Actually smiled! "I am. Now before you hurl a load of statistics at me about failed movies by actors who think they can direct, let me tell you who it is."

"Surprise me," Tess said stonily.

"Jack Thornton."

Tess Fisher was nothing if not gracious in defeat. She smiled at her husband in admiration. "Okay. So you've surprised me."

Jack Thornton was one of the last of that rare Hollywood clichéd breed – a legend in his own time. A three-times Oscar winner, the last a Lifetime Achievement Award, he was the leader of that tiny pack of movie luminaries which included Paul Newman, Clint Eastwood and, some would argue, Jack Nicholson before he'd descended into a parody of himself.

Thornton had worked with most of the great directors of the old school and had starred in the kind of classics that were shown across networks world-wide on Christmas Day. Now fifty-eight, he worked only rarely because he refused point-blank to entertain the vast majority of directors in the business. He publicly branded most studio films as nothing more than "bubble-gum for the brain". His last Oscar acceptance speech – running almost ten minutes over the allotted forty-five-second slot – had been an embarrassment to the organisers and a delight to most of the audience present. In it, he'd lashed out at the state of the film industry in America, deploring its values of violence and sex and had urged directors to return to films with character, integrity and above all, "a frigging story, if it's not too much to ask". He got a standing ovation but didn't bother to hang around for it.

That was two years ago. Ever since, the whole of Hollywood had been avidly awaiting his expected announcement that he would direct a film himself. Thornton had blithely ignored them all and continued doing cameo character roles in films that took his fancy. Naturally, this had only increased speculation and interest. Could Peter be the one to persuade him to take the plunge?

Still, after fifteen years in the political rat race, Tess was cautious. "Okay. Suppose you get him. Then what?"

"Then I leave it up to him. He's got every studio in LA on the starting blocks, all waiting to be the first to fund his directorial debut. We get him, we get the money. Simple as that."

Too simple, maybe. "Why would he? If he'd wanted to direct before, surely he'd have done it already. What's he waiting for?"

Peter shrugged. "I don't know. I got a call from him out of the blue. He'd got wind of the project and asked me to meet him. I suppose we'll find out soon enough."

To Tess's annoyance, he resolutely settled back in his

seat and closed his eyes. He wasn't going to talk about it any more.

Tess was left to sip her mineral water and mentally go through her suitcases, trying to decide what to wear tonight. If it was dinner with Jack Thornton, then it was bound to be the biggest, poshest, swankiest restaurant in town.

It wasn't.

But Tess wasn't disappointed when the limousine Thornton had sent for them climbed high into the Hollywood Hills and into the drive of his house. *Mansion*, she corrected herself. It was hard to be blasé as she stepped out of the car into the playground of a very rich man. Thornton obviously had no truck with the low-key casualness most stars had adopted in the late 90s – his house and grounds were gloriously vulgar and ostentatious. You couldn't turn around without being confronted with heart-shaped swimming-pools and impossibly tall palm-trees. And was that an ostrich glaring at them from a clump of bushes?

"My God," she whispered in Peter's ear as she negotiated the crazy paving to a huge front door which was larger than the door to their double-garage back home. A surly Mexican maid left them to cool their heels in a huge marble hall, the focus of which was a chandelier the size of a fridge. While Tess marvelled, Peter seemed distinctly ill at ease. Glamour and money had never been his bag, worse luck.

"Are we early?" he said.

"Stop acting like a country bumpkin, Peter," Tess said. "Just remember – with the cutlery, you work your way in."

She had meant it as a joke but his eyebrows snapped together in irritation. She sighed. He had a short fuse these days and she seemed to bear the brunt of it.

She looked up at the clatter of high-heeled shoes across marble.

"Hi! I'm Lucy!"

Thornton exercised little restraint when it came to his lady friends either. His latest girlfriend was a twenty-two-year-old with startling breasts and a diamond stud in her belly-button. A large Irish wolfhound on a lead snuffled eagerly at her crotch.

Tess didn't so much as blink as she shook Lucy's hand. "Hello! Lovely to meet you."

"I'm an actress," Lucy stated, though nobody had asked. "Get *down*, Timmy!"

"Get that frigging dog out of here," a gravelly voice boomed.

Tess recognised the voice from the movies she'd snuck off to see with her very first boyfriend. And now here was Jack Thornton – legend, icon, luminary. He patted Lucy paternally on the bottom before courteously shaking hands with Peter and then Tess. No smarmy false kisses or paternal pats for her, she was glad to note.

"Come on through. Dinner's just up. We can talk afterwards."

Two hours later, Tess was stunned into silence by the sheer depth of Lucy's stupidity.

"*Baywatch*, I said! Jesus, I said to him, you've been my agent for two years now and all you can get me is a walk-on part in *Baywatch*? Can you believe it?" Whether Tess could or not was a matter of supreme indifference to Lucy. "It's watched by millions and millions of people, he says to me. Yeah, I said, but is a single one of those people an American? Jesus, I said. I mean, I'm not looking down on the British or anything – "

"I'm Irish," Tess managed to interject.

"Oops! Sorry. By the way, I absolutely adored your movie *The Full Monty*."

"That was British."

"Huh?" Lucy was hopelessly confused. Tess caught Jack Thornton's eye. He was embarrassed, she suddenly realised. And so well he should be. What on earth was he doing with a half-wit like Lucy?

"Honey?" he said quickly to Lucy. "Go see about the coffee. We need to talk about this project."

"Oh yeah. The film," Lucy said, her blue eyes immediately less vacant. "I hope there's a good part in it for me!"

Tess watched as Thornton's embarrassment mutated into annoyance.

"The coffee, Lucy."

"You promised me a part if you got to direct, remember?" Lucy said lightly, but there was a certain edge to her voice. She turned to Tess and Peter. "What kind of female parts are in the script?"

"We haven't got a script yet," Peter said diplomatically.

Thornton was mortified now. "We'll talk about it

97

later," he said coldly. Lucy knew when to let it drop. She obediently wriggled her way out of the room, the wolfhound padding in her wake. Tess knew with a quiet certainty that Lucy would be dispatched from Thornton's mansion tonight, never to be seen again.

She felt an angry flush stain her cheeks when Peter raised an eyebrow meaningfully in her direction. He actually expected her to meekly follow the moronic Lucy while The Men Got Down To Business. Bastard.

Thornton wasn't slow – he had picked up on it. "Maybe you'd like to stay, Tess? Can always use an extra perspective."

"Thank you," she said quietly, biting down hard on her anger. This was no time to score points off Peter.

"You got the fax I sent you this morning?" Peter began. "Those are just some starting points for us to work from."

"I like the idea," Thornton drawled, leaning lazily back in his chair. "I'm up for it."

Silence for a moment as this sank in.

"You mean you'll consider going to the studios for backing," Peter said carefully, doing an admirable job of concealing his excitement.

"No, I mean I *will* go to the studios. They'll jump, they're dying for me." A sly grin belied the arrogance of the statement.

Tess caught his eye again and her lips twitched. He was a hell of a lot smarter than his taste in girlfriends led one to believe.

Peter had his poker politician's face on. "That's great, I'm pleased."

Tess knew he would wait a while before asking the question Thornton expected them to ask. Well, she wouldn't. Thornton had to lay his cards on the table before this thing went one step further.

"Why? Why exactly do you want to shoot a film in Ireland if every major studio is dying for you?" She allowed a hint of sarcasm to colour her words and totally ignored Peter's knee knocking sharply against hers under the table.

Thornton laced his fingers together and carefully examined his hands. "You think I have some ulterior motive?"

"Not at all," Tess returned sweetly. "But now that you mention it, have you?"

Thornton laughed. After a tense moment, Peter did too. Tess didn't.

"Yes. And it's control," he said simply. 'If I make a studio-backed movie here, I'll have every one of their frigging accountants and tea-boys breathing down my neck and reporting back to Big Daddy. They'll tell me what to shoot and how. They'll dictate what actors I get to use and, frankly, I'm not standing for any of that."

"What makes you think it'll be any different if they give you money to shoot it in Ireland?" Peter asked. At last he'd weighed in, Tess thought.

"Oh, they'll send in the producers and the money-men all right. But there're six thousand miles between here and Ireland. I reckon that's far enough to keep some of the goons off my back."

"You'll still be answerable," Peter said bluntly.

"You mean I can't run riot in Ireland?" He put on the little-boy expression that Tess had always found unamusing in grown men. With a quick glance at Peter, she answered Thornton.

"Hardly. Actors, location, budget – all that will obviously be a consensus." Her voice was sharp. Thornton was quiet now and Peter was letting her go with it. She sensed him sitting back a little in his chair. It was a smart move. Let her, as his associate, ask the hard questions and take any flak that might come from Thornton. Then Peter could step in as conciliator, the man on Thornton's side. It was a classic political move and she'd seen him do it before. But this time, he was trusting her to bring it off.

"I get to say who's in it," Thornton shot.

"We need at least one big name," Tess shot back.

"I still get to say who's in it."

"Within reason. And budget," Peter murmured.

"That goes without saying," Thornton said testily, answering Tess. The ruse was working. "What about the script?"

"Peter's looking at them," Tess told him. "But so far, nothing's jumping out."

"I pick the script."

"Again, within reason."

"No. I'll compromise on everything else, actors and all that. But I've been in this shitty business long enough to know that the most important thing – and I mean *the* most important thing – is script. I pick the script. *Okay*?"

Tess knew that they would either win or lose him on

this. Peter knew it too. It was time for her to sit back and let Peter be the big generous buddy on Thornton's side.

"Of course," Peter said smoothly. "If you're not happy with the script, Jack, then there's no point."

The two beamed at each other and Tess had to restrain herself from rolling her eyes.

"One last thing," Peter added casually. "We'd like it to be shot in Kilkenny."

Thornton leaned back in his chair. One eyebrow lifted sardonically. "No kidding."

He'd known all along. Tess wasn't at all surprised.

Neither was Peter. "You're aware of the situation then."

"I know that fifty million dollars would be a welcome boost to the Kilkenny economy," Thornton said with an artful smile. "Especially when you're trying to get an unknown elected." Peter said nothing. Thornton eyeballed him. "And I think it's a bit sneaky of you not to have mentioned it upfront."

They were losing him. Tess could see it happen before her eyes. Then, to her astonishment, Thornton threw his head back and laughed uproariously.

"But I'll overlook it. My great-grandmother was from Kilkenny, how's that for a kick? Hell, I can go and look up my roots!"

A chuckle bubbled forth from Peter's throat. Thornton laughed harder. Tess merely smiled. She sensed the meeting wasn't over yet.

She was right. Thornton suddenly stopped laughing and pitched forward in his chair.

"Maybe I haven't entirely been upfront myself," he said. He looked to Tess. "You wondered whether I had an ulterior motive. Maybe I do."

Tess held her breath. Thornton smiled again, and it was pure, cut-throat LA.

"Let's talk again about the script."

Chapter Seven

Richard's face is shuttered: he's been hurt too many times to leave himself open again. "Your services are not needed any more."

Alison freezes. "My services were never yours to begin with, sir."

She picks up her skirts and stalks off. Richard follows fast. He catches her wrist.

"Alison – "

"Let me go."

"Not like this."

Suddenly they are standing close, breaths coming foggy and fast in the stark winter sunshine.

"Alison." His voice holds a plea. Her anger disappears. She rests her head on his chest, giving in for now. He strokes her hair carefully. Cue theme music, softly underpinning the emotion of the moment. Eventually Alison looks up. She is close to tears.

"Richard. What are we going to do?"

"Pass us the four-hole punch, would you, Cathy?"

Cathy came crashing back to earth, blinking in confusion. Her heart was beating fast.

"Cathy?" Patsy was looking at her peculiarly.

"Sorry, Patsy." Cathy reached across for the puncher. The tips of her fingers felt scorched after handling the script.

"Is it any good?" Patsy asked, nodding at the script. Her idea of good was the sensationalist true-life stories in the gaudy magazines she read in her lunch-break, such as 'I Was a Lesbian Escort' and 'Quadruples! Again!'.

"It's pretty okay," Cathy mumbled, hoping that the four-hole punch would confuse Patsy to the extent that Cathy would be left in blessed peace to pull herself together. She was in shock and had been since Jean handed her the script an hour ago and asked her to re-type it.

But Patsy was in the mood for a chat. She was leaving in two weeks' time for her new job and was inclined to slack off more than usual. "It used to be a play," she said knowledgeably.

"Yes. I know."

"It was in the Abbey Theatre. Five years ago."

"Yes. I know." *I was bloody in it*, she wanted to shout at Patsy. Instead she turned back to the script, hoping that Patsy would take the hint. No such luck.

"I love period dramas, don't you?" she said with a sigh. "There was one of Jane Austen's on the telly last week, it was great. I hope she writes another."

"Jane Austen is dead, Patsy," Cathy pointed out heavily.

"Oh, is she? That's a shame," Patsy said cheerfully. "Still, leaves more room for new talent. Like Carl Tallon."

At the mention of his name, Cathy jumped nervously.

"He's gorgeous, isn't he?" Patsy went on. She looked at Cathy. "Oh, sorry, you haven't met him yet, have you?"

It was a huge effort, but Cathy managed a negative nod. Patsy leaned in conspiratorially. "He's a bit of a ride." She clamped a hand over her mouth and giggled at her own audacity.

"Great," Cathy said desperately, wondering what it would take to shut Patsy up.

"He has lovely eyes," Patsy confided dreamily. "You could kind of drown in them, if you can imagine that."

Not only could Cathy imagine it, she had been there and done that one. Numerous times in fact. She knew all about Carl Tallon's eyes.

"Great," she bleated again. "Look, Patsy, I really should get back to work. Jean wants the script typed up as soon as possible."

Patsy immediately became efficient. "Don't forget to make back-up copies on floppy disks," she sternly instructed Cathy. She was still top-dog in the office and liked to remind Cathy of it from time to time.

Cathy looked back at the script. Her brain was a jumble of conflicting emotions and she felt sick again as she saw Carl Tallon's name printed on the front page.

Of all the agencies in town, you had to walk into mine.

This wasn't strictly true. It seemed that Jean had taken Carl Tallon on before she'd hired Cathy. If Cathy had known, she would not have ventured within a million miles of The Jean Ormsby Agency. But she had not known. And now here he was, in her face again. After all this time.

She had managed not to think about him in years – *really* think about him. It was amazing really, the brain's capacity for shutting out things that are too unpleasant or painful to deal with. London had helped, of course. There was no danger that she would run into him down the local pub or find herself sitting opposite him on the 46A bus. She didn't have to listen to casual gossip about him, or get second-hand news from friends. Who in London knew anything about Carl Tallon?

Dublin was different. It was too small – so small that they had both somehow ended up in the same place on the same day. Fate had the sickest sense of humour sometimes.

She had to stifle the impulse now to jump to her feet, grab her coat and sprint out of the office, never to return. She eyed the door speculatively. Three strides of her long legs would take her there and she wouldn't have to think about him again.

No. That would be running away again. And you've done quite enough of that, she told herself severely. If anyone was to run this time, it would not be her. Besides, if she was brutally honest with herself, she was dying to stay and read the script.

It drew her like a magnet now and she smoothed the top cover with her hand. *Outsiders*.

When Jean handed it over this morning, Cathy had

Clare Dowling

already hardened her heart against it before she'd read a single word. So she had once starred in the play version – so what? She had starred in other plays, hadn't she? And okay, so *Outsiders* had been a good play, but big swing – there were plenty more good plays out there. Just because Carl Tallon had twisted someone's arm to get it made into a film was no reason to go to *pieces*.

Anyway, Cathy had assured herself, it would probably be awful. Didn't they often say that plays never translated into good films? Yes, she decided stoically, it would be the worst kind of crap. Pretentious, probably. Up its own bottom. Carl Tallon would fall flat on his face with this script and she wouldn't be human if she didn't enjoy that.

She couldn't have been more wrong. From the very first line, it made her heart sing. Like the original play, it was sexy, romantic, moving, tragic. The dialogue was fantastic, the descriptions luscious. The setting in the heart of rural Kilkenny was so realistic that, at times, if Cathy breathed deeply enough, she swore she could get the faint whiff of fresh hay and cow-dung. No matter how she tried to fight it, she felt that old magic creep over her again.

"Oh feckit, it's brilliant," she muttered.

Reading it hurled her right back into the past; she was on the Abbey stage again, she was Alison, the servant girl who fell in love with the rich and powerful Richard Butler, a love that was doomed. She found herself muttering lines from the play in tandem with the script, and whispering encouragement to the lovers with every page turn. She

107

groaned aloud when yet another obstacle was put in their paths; when they stole illicit moments together, she was on the very edge of her swivel-chair with excitement. And when they finally consummated their relationship in a frenzy of desire she found, to her mortification, that she was aroused. And that was only the first fifty pages.

He had done it, she reluctantly conceded. No matter how much she hated Carl Tallon, she would give him that much. He had pulled it off spectacularly.

She felt peculiar now, she felt like crying. Ridiculous. She was just being sentimental for her time in the Abbey. And for Alison, the best female part she'd ever played.

She wondered who would be playing her in the film version. Some big film star, probably. She hoped that she would be good, whoever she was. Alison was too precious, too complex to throw away in a lightweight performance.

Listen to me, she thought. She had no claims on Alison. None.

"Cathy?" Patsy had a hand clasped over the phone receiver. Her face was full of recrimination. "It's those soap commercial people. They want to know if you can audition tomorrow afternoon."

"Sure, great." Cathy watched guiltily as Patsy wrapped up the call and replaced the receiver a little harder than necessary.

"Three o'clock," she muttered in Cathy's direction.

"Patsy," Cathy began. They'd had this conversation before. "I promise I'll leave as soon as I get a part, okay?"

"I shouldn't be doing this," Patsy replied.

She had a point. It was wrong to be involving Patsy in

the pretence that Cathy was actually on Jean Ormsby's books instead of a part-time secretary employed to type for four pounds an hour.

But Cathy didn't see that she had any choice. It had been too late to correct the confusion when Jean had assumed that Cathy had come for the typing job. Besides, Jean had made it very clear that night that she was not taking any actors on. Cathy couldn't come clean. Besides, the money would come in handy to supplement her miserable dole.

It had only occurred to her later that she could turn the situation around to her advantage. Guiltily, she'd convinced herself that she wouldn't really be doing anything *wrong* – she would simply be telling a white lie in order to gain entry to auditions. And the minute she landed a part she would hand in her notice and nobody would really be any the wiser.

Unfortunately, it had been necessary to elicit Patsy's help. Patsy answered all calls and, obviously, would not be passing on any enquiries about Cathy Conroy to Jean. Patsy had also been persuaded to send out Cathy's CV and photo to potential employers while she was sending those of the agency's legitimate clients.

So far, Cathy had landed two auditions, one for a student film and now this commercial. She hoped that something big would come along soon. She disliked subterfuge and dishonesty and hated putting poor Patsy on the spot. It was also debatable how well Patsy would carry it off in the long term – the Brain of Britain she wasn't.

Cathy was also afraid of Jean Ormsby's reaction,

should she find out. Cathy was slightly in awe of her new boss, and not a little intimidated. Jean was gorgeous for starters, straight from Cosmo in her sharp suits and her precision-cut, shiny hair. She was so neat and well-made that Cathy felt like a hulking monster beside her. Many of the agency's male clients frequently turned up for appointments reeking of Obsession and producing spare tickets for the theatre that they had just happened to come by. All of this filled Cathy with envy and a faint resentment towards a God who obviously had His favourites.

Jean had confidence too. Buckets of it. Not an in-your-face arrogance, more a presence that made you look up when she walked into the room. When she spoke, you listened and when she asked you to do something, you did it as well and as fast as you could, simply to win her approval. At least Cathy did, suffering from a mild case of hero-worship.

Jean Ormsby would not take at all kindly to an impostor working under her very nose.

Guilt made Cathy turn back hurriedly to her computer screen. If she was taking four pounds an hour from the woman, the very least she could do was earn it. She was typing so diligently that she did not look up when the agency door opened.

"Oh, hi!" Patsy said breathlessly. Probably one of the agency's better-looking clients, Cathy thought, typing on. Patsy was a trier, she'd give her that much. There was a brief silence.

Then, "I've an appointment with Jean."

The voice pierced Cathy like a hot knife through ice cream. Her head snapped up. She found herself looking straight into Carl Tallon's eyes.

He was staring back. As shocked as she.

"I'll just go and see if she's ready for you," Patsy said enthusiastically, heading for Jean's office.

In the awful silence she left in her wake, Cathy Conroy and Carl Tallon continued to stare at each other. The atmosphere was so laden with tension that the rubber plant in the corner of the room seemed to wilt.

Some part of Cathy's numb brain registered the fact that Carl had not changed at all. Long floppy black hair still fell into his eyes, eyes that were as dark as she remembered. His face was still perfect, except for that crooked nose that looked as if he'd done a round or two in a boxing ring. And he wore a disgraceful denim jacket, frayed around the cuffs and collar. Cathy had given him that denim jacket five years ago on the opening night of the play. It had been new then.

But his eyes had changed. They were harder, colder. And they were looking at her now as though she were something particularly nasty he'd discovered on the sole of his shoe.

Finally, he spoke. Which was just as well, as Cathy was quite incapable of kicking this one off. "I thought you were in London." He made it sound like Timbuktu. And he looked her up and down while he said it in a manner that Cathy could only describe as disparaging.

Her body immediately snapped into defensive mode. She would not sit here like some mouse, apologising for coming home to her own city. Apologising for *existing*, if his manner was anything to go by.

She slowly stood, ostensibly to reach for the pack of floppy disks on Patsy's desk. At her full height of five-feet eleven-inches, she was on an eye-level with him. She offered him a flippant little smile. "Yes, well, I'm back, as you can see."

He did not appreciate this. Black eyes flashed. "Things didn't work out for you then?"

Cathy felt a burst of anger. He sounded hopeful, the bastard. "No, I just got tired of London, that's all."

Another ice-cold silence descended. Cathy prayed for Patsy's return, but there was no sign of her. Unable to bear his wordless scrutiny any longer, she flicked a hand at his filmscript. "I see you've changed direction."

"I see you have too." She saw him looking around the office. "Or are you still acting?"

"Yes." *Shit*. The minute the word was out she wanted to grab it back. Supposing he told Jean that he knew her, that she was an actress? Jean would toss her out on her ear. "I mean no."

He smiled now, a sardonic sneer. "A little confused, Cathy?"

What a pig. How had she ever loved him? "Look, Carl." It went against every grain in her body to ask him a favour, but she had no choice. "Jean doesn't know I'm an actress, okay? And I'd appreciate it if you kept it to yourself. I need this job."

She waited for him to tell her to get lost, that he

owned her nothing. And that he would take great pleasure in telling Jean.

"Why would I tell her? I don't care what you do any more, Cathy."

The words were so measured and cold that Cathy was shocked.

"She'll see you now, Carl." Patsy was back.

Without another glance at Cathy, Carl nodded at Patsy and disappeared into Jean's office. Cathy sank back down onto her swivel-chair, her heart thumping unpleasantly fast.

"I know," Patsy giggled, taking one look at her face. "I had to sit down too the first time I saw him. Isn't he just *gorgeous*?"

"Gorgeous," Cathy said grimly, turning back to her computer and punching keys too hard. The sooner the script was typed and finished, the sooner he and his bloody film were out of her life. She couldn't wait.

Chapter Eight

The media were billing it as potentially the most exciting by-election in years. Already Bill Mackey's face was plastered across the features pages of Friday's newspaper. The air-brushed photo was a masterpiece in composition; he managed to look as serious as befitted an election candidate, yet showed traces of the famous roguish grin that had kept housewives up and down the country in a continuous state of rampant adulation for the past thirty years.

In the ponderous accompanying interview, penned by a journalist distinctly lacking in objectivity, he fondly reminisced about his childhood in Kilkenny: a glowing, happy time revolving around kindly neighbours, walking to school across the fields and lashings of Marietta biscuits. Much was made of his hurling achievements, and he modestly confessed that he still liked to bat a *sliotar* around with his sons on a Sunday afternoon. He talked about his wife of twenty-five years, or his "rock" as he frequently referred to her, crediting her as the inspiration for the many women-related topics he had aired on his radio show over the years. The irony that wife-battering, alcoholism and extra-marital affairs had been the staples of his show was lost on the adoring hack.

The rose-tinted personality profile abruptly gave way to a stinging attack on the rising unemployment numbers in Kilkenny. The contentious issues of the computer multinationals pull-outs and factory closures followed fast. He mentioned the continuing plight of the farmers in one breath and, in the next, pledged to fight for more money for small businesses. By the end of the interview, he had managed to include every dog and divil in Kilkenny. He was doing it by numbers and he was good.

He also got in several attacks on the Government in general and Peter Fisher in particular. He was clever too. He praised rather than ridiculed Fisher's objective of bringing a major movie to Kilkenny. Then, in a back-handed assault, he pointed out that this project embodied all that was wrong with the new Government; in their transparent attempt to win votes, they had lost touch with the ordinary people who desperately needed jobs rather than high-brow notions of "art" and "culture".

He finished up by sombrely paying tribute to Tony Croft and admitting that he had the greatest of respect for the Croft family, including his rival Roger whom he saw as having a great political career – when he had gained the necessary experience and age at some distant point in the future, of course.

Roger Croft got a head and shoulders photo only and ten column inches in which he sounded bland and naïve.

Jean Ormsby folded the newspaper thoughtfully. It was early days yet. Besides, the spin doctors had barely gone to work. Croft was only twenty-seven and had little or no experience of the media. He would learn. He would have to, and fast.

Anyhow, at the end of the day, it would be the provincial papers that counted. The national ones would lose interest now until nearer the election date. There was over four months to go. A lot could happen in that time.

She checked her watch. It was ten minutes to six. All around her, Friday-evening traffic choked the streets as people escaped the city for the bank-holiday weekend. Hopefully, Peter Fisher's secretary would want to do the same.

At exactly five minutes to the hour, Jean got out of rusty Uno, locked it and made the journey on foot around the corner to the Department of Arts on Mespil Road. She smoothed down her grey tailored business-suit at the top of the steps and in her haughtiest, busiest voice, informed the security guard at the reception desk that she had a six o'clock appointment with the Minister.

As she expected, he was anxious to knock off and get to the pub and gave her only a cursory glance before punching out a number on the phone. Her heart slowed a little. Obviously Peter Fisher was in the building. It had been a gamble. When she'd phoned his constituency office in Kilkenny, they'd said he was in Dublin – but who knew where?

The security guard replaced the phone. "I'm sorry. Imelda – the Minister's secretary – seems to be gone for the evening."

This was exactly what Jean had hoped. But her mouth twisted in minor annoyance and she made sure that the man saw the expensive pigskin satchel bursting with papers that she impatiently changed from one hand to the other.

"But go on up," he said quickly. "I'll tell Mark to come meet you."

Jean was already tapping her way across the polished floor. "Thank you, but I know the way."

At the top of the stairs, she had to pause. She had no idea where Fisher's office was but she didn't want any Mark fellow asking her her business. As far as anybody in this building was concerned, she didn't have any.

She took a chance and climbed another flight of stairs. Offices were locked all around her and voices grew quieter as she ascended. On the second landing, there didn't appear to be anybody about at all.

Her shoes sounded ridiculously loud on the hardwood floor as she pushed open swing doors into an imposing reception room. The whiff of power almost knocked her over. For a moment, her courage deserted her and she almost ran out the door and back to the safety of her car.

But the weight of the satchel under her arm reminded her of why she was here. Swallowing, she made her way towards the reception desk, which guarded a huge oak door that must surely lead to the inner sanctum. The door was slightly ajar.

She hesitated, hands steadying herself on the reception desk.

Imelda, she saw, liked Diet Pepsi and Snickers bars, and had a *Far Side* calendar perched by her computer. A jokey birthday card poking gentle fun at advancing age was pinned to a cork message-board. *From Peter.*

Another, more ominous, message was also pinned to the board, in plain view. *All visitors must report to reception downstairs and display a security badge.*

Jean's wonderful idea of ambushing Peter Fisher with her marvellous script was rapidly turning to ashes in her mouth. Nervously, she wondered whether it was an indictable offence to gain entry to a Government building under false pretences and had unsettling visions of herself ringing up her mother from Store Street Garda Station asking her to post bail.

Worse, Fisher might not take this at all in the manner in which it was intended. Instead of admiring her initiative and cunning, he might bawl her out of it for wasting his time and tell her that in future she was to go through the proper channels. He might even refuse to read the script outright, outraged by her audacity.

He can only tell you to get lost. And God knows, you've heard that before.

And if he had even an ounce of human decency, he would appreciate the sheer neck it took to waltz in here like this.

Armed with these reassurances, she put her best foot forward.

A woman's voice burst out from the partially-open door: "You're a right bastard, do you know that?"

Jean froze. It seemed that someone had got there before her.

"Oh, come on. We just don't seem to want the same things any more." Fisher's voice now. Jean had heard it a million times on TV, had spent countless hours listening to it on her beat-up radio stuck in traffic on the M50.

"Well, we all know what *you* want." Fisher's female companion sounded bitter. "You want your fun and nothing else!"

"Now hang on here a minute. I distinctly remember you throwing the word 'fun' about in the beginning."

Jean could hear weariness in his voice. Wildly, she looked about, wondering whether she should abort the entire mission and quietly retreat. Or should she just sit down on one of those black leather chairs over there and pretend that she had heard nothing of this sordid little exchange between the Minister for Arts and what was obviously a soon-to-be-ex lover?

"Sending me a bunch of fucking flowers!" The woman's sneering voice was louder now.

"My mistake. If I recall correctly, you returned them the same day."

"I should have sent them to your wife!"

Jean backed away. It was time to get out before this turned into a fist-fight. Because this woman, whoever she was, was not about to be brushed off lightly.

"But you didn't, Helen. You just made a few hang-up phone calls to her instead."

Jean heard the disgust in his voice. She felt no pity for him. What goes around comes around, Minister, she thought, retreating rapidly past Imelda's desk.

"Oh fuck off, Peter!" The woman's voice reached her again.

The door to Fisher's office was hurled open and an Amazonian redhead, face furious, stalked past Jean.

"Who are you? His latest?" she snapped, storming out.

Jean turned to find Peter Fisher behind her. He was in his shirtsleeves, rolled up to the elbow. His face was inscrutable as he watched her. Jean stared back, her tongue suddenly glued to the roof of her mouth.

"I'm sorry about that," he said quietly. "Are you looking for Imelda? I'm afraid she's gone for the weekend."

"No," Jean said, suddenly finding that her terror had gone. He was only a man after all, and one who cheated on his wife to boot. She could handle him. "I was actually looking for you."

She could see him mentally going through his diary although his expression did not change.

"I haven't got an appointment," she added calmly.

He hesitated. "I'm afraid I don't have much time," he began. Here we go, she thought. He was going to brush her off nicely. "But, please, come in."

He indicated his office and stood aside. Jean hid her surprise and walked past him, catching a faint scent of Givenchy. She was careful not to brush against him.

"Coffee?" he asked.

120

Jean was again taken aback by the courtesy he was extending to an unwanted intruder. "Yes. . . yes, thank you."

"Have a seat. I'll be back in a minute."

Jean found herself alone, grateful for a few minutes to collect her thoughts and prepare herself for the pitch. She cautiously sat on the couch just inside the door and looked around.

Fisher's office looked like a particularly violent hurricane had swept through it, sucking up everything in its wake before depositing it at random over every available surface. His desk top was a chaotic mess of papers, fixit stickers and books. Files were stacked five-high on the floor by the wall. The wastepaper basket was overflowing and a programme manual was propped against a can of coke by the blinking computer.

He was obviously an extremely busy man who did not put much stock on appearances. Two trays, aggressively marked "In" and "Out" in large red letters, were ostentatiously parked in the middle of the desk – a fruitless attempt on Imelda's part to impose some kind of order on her boss, Jean guessed. Fisher's discarded tie was now strewn carelessly in the "Out" tray.

No diplomas or certificates were mounted on the walls but Jean was amused to see a framed photo of what was obviously the family dog with a small girl sitting on its fat broad back. There were no photos of his wife.

Jean quickly averted her eyes from the room to the floor. She felt like she was prying into Fisher's personal life.

"I hope you don't take sugar." He was back, holding out a mug of coffee to her.

"No."

"Good. I couldn't find any."

He smiled suddenly and Jean was completely disarmed. She felt colour creeping up her cheeks and fought it back down. She gulped her coffee as Fisher sank down into the chair behind his desk and turned to his computer.

"I'll just turn this off." He hesitated, looking up at her. "I don't suppose you know anything about spreadsheets, do you?"

Jean blinked. "Um . . . yes, actually, I do."

Automating the agency was one of her new goals.

"This manual isn't very clear . . . how would I go about customising a spreadsheet?"

He cocked his head to one side and watched her, waiting.

"Well, you'd have to go up to the Tools Bar," Jean managed, completely thrown off course by the way this interview was progressing. "You should find a list of options under 'customise' and. . ."

"Slow down," Fisher said, working the mouse. "What do all these categories mean?"

Jean attempted to see the computer screen from her faraway position on the couch.

Fisher motioned her forward. "If you wouldn't mind . . . Imelda gave me a run-down but I'm afraid I'm a bit slow."

Again, that broad, self-deprecating smile. Jean

reluctantly crossed the room and edged around his desk. Fisher scooted sideways, fully expecting her to share the computer with him. Poker-faced, she did so, and found herself more or less hanging over his shoulder like some groupie.

Wildly, she wondered whether he was making a pass at her. He didn't seem to be any slouch in that department, if the unfortunate Helen was anything to go by. If he did, not only would she put him firmly in his place, but she would not keep it to herself either. She had visions of what the sleazier papers might print. *Minister made Pass at me over Spreadsheet!*

"What do you think?"

He was looking up at her – and with a purely professional interest too, she noted, wondering why she felt so disappointed. Feeling foolish, she reminded herself that she was hardly in the league of the six-foot flame-haired Helen.

"I think you need to create a template," she said, painfully aware of the forced intimacy of the situation.

Fisher nodded vigorously. He obviously knew exactly what a template was. "Excellent. I thought that might be the solution, but I wasn't sure."

Two seconds later, he had executed a couple of commands and the job was done.

"Thanks," he said cheerfully, switching off the computer.

Jean nodded and retreated, glad to be away from his rather disarming physical presence. This time, she chose to sit in the chair directly opposite him rather than attempting to win him over from the back of the room.

"Forgive my manners," he said. "I haven't even asked your name."

"Oh. Jean Ormsby. I'm an agent."

"And what can I do for you?" he asked, watching her carefully.

Jean had the rather uncomfortable feeling of being under a microscope. It was like he could see straight though her. She decided that it would be folly to beat around the bush.

"You need a filmscript," she said. "And I have one."

Fisher did not say anything. Jean forced herself to ride out the silence. Either he wanted to read it or he didn't. She would not be forced into doing a cold-sell on it.

"Have you submitted it to the Film Board?" he eventually asked.

"I'm not interested in general funding. This script is specific to your project."

Fisher leaned back in his chair. He never took his eyes off her. "Then you'll know that Jack Thornton is the director on this one. He is picking the script."

"But he's in LA. I thought it would be more expedient to get it to yourself," Jean said blandly. "If you thought it was any good, then you could pass it on to him."

Fisher's eyebrows rose just a fraction in amusement. In effect, she was saying that she was not relying on Thornton's ability to spot a good script if he saw one. But he could not fail to ignore something that Fisher had given the thumbs-up.

"What's it about?" he asked.

"I'd rather not influence you before you've read it," Jean said nicely. It was imperative that she pique his interest. "I'll just say that it's a film about the Butler family. As you know, their seat of power was in Kilkenny."

He was enjoying her now, she could see it. "Yes. What a coincidence."

"Indeed," Jean agreed. "So you could call it a period extravaganza. The kind that Americans love. In fact, it's not unlike that English film that won nine Oscars last year."

He was smiling openly now. "That certainly would be a bonus, wouldn't it? And who wrote it?"

"Carl Tallon."

She watched as he immediately made the connection. "It was originally a play, wasn't it? I thought Jay Devaney was directing."

"*Was*," Jean corrected.

Boy, what a scene that had been. Jean wasn't particularly proud of herself for having poached Carl Tallon's script from Devaney and didn't really blame Devaney for his choice of language when he'd rung her up to complain. He'd threatened to sue. He didn't have a leg to stand on, of course. Nothing had been signed. But it had been a colourful conversation nonetheless. According to Devaney, Jean would not be eating lunch, dinner, breakfast or any other meal in this town ever again.

"You're a literary agent then?" Peter Fisher asked.

"Not exactly," Jean admitted. "I'm an actors' agent."

Fisher tapped a biro off the desk. "You would have an interest in the casting then?"

"Certainly I would be putting forward some of my people," Jean said reasonably. "Like any other agent."

Best not to tell him that she had no intention whatsoever of handing over her precious script unless there was an understanding between her and Thornton that several of her clients would get at least some speaking parts. After all, she wasn't in this for the greater good of mankind.

Neither did she mention Bill Mackey's crowd-wowing interview in today's paper. She did not need to. The paper was wadded into a ball in Fisher's wastepaper basket.

Fisher shot her another penetrating stare and suddenly threw down the biro. His mouth twisted. "Look, we haven't announced it yet, but I think you should know. We have a script."

Jean felt sick. "What?"

He looked uncomfortable now. "Jack Thornton is writing it himself."

She was gutted. It was a huge effort to hide it from him. "You should have said earlier," she said coldly.

"I wanted to hear what you had to say first."

"You wanted to watch me grovel first, you mean," she said in a flash of anger. She felt like a fool.

He looked indignant. "That's not true. It's not even a hundred percent certain yet – Thornton hasn't finished the script. I shouldn't even have told you."

But Jean knew that it was already cut and dried. Jack Thornton was coming to Ireland to film his baby and that was that. She gathered her things and stood.

126

"I won't waste any more of your time. Or mine. Goodbye."

He caught up with her as she passed Imelda's desk. "Wait."

"What."

"Let me read it."

She felt tired now. "Please. You don't have to humour me."

"I'm not," he insisted. "It sounds good."

"You already have a script."

"It might be suitable for something else. Let me read it anyway."

She handed it over wordlessly. Thirty seconds later, she was standing on the street, looking up at the light shining from his office window. Maybe he would read it. Most likely he wouldn't. It didn't matter now.

The hard truth was that she had gambled and she had lost. Worse still, she had gambled with Carl Tallon's talent and now she had to face him and tell him that the Government would not be making his film, for all her inflated optimism. He would be furious. She wouldn't blame him.

She looked back up at Fisher's window. She felt used somehow. He could have told her straight up. Why bother with all the rigmarole?

He's a politician, she reminded herself. Politicians probably did this kind of thing all the time, hedging their bets in case something better came along. Well, to hell with him. Her script was probably lying in his "Out" tray right now while he prepared to leave for some glittering reception full of important, beautiful people. She thought of her own evening ahead in her little cottage in Castleknock, picking at a Marks & Spencer's cottage pie and watching TV alone. It seemed a lonely and pathetic existence.

She shook herself slightly, annoyed at her self-pity. A figure appeared in the window above. Fisher, looking down. His eyes met hers for a long moment. Jean started slightly. Then she turned on her heel and walked rapidly away.

Chapter Nine

It was her own daughter who broke the news to her.

They were having afternoon tea in a hotel on Stephen's Green. It was Fiona's school mid-term break and Tess had taken her out for the day as a treat. They had already gone on a rampage up and down Grafton Street with Peter's credit cards.

"Mum?"

Tess eyed her tea suspiciously. The colour wasn't good. "Yes, love?"

"Mum, there was something. . ." Fiona trailed off hesitantly.

Tess sniffed the tea now. "What, Fiona?"

"Well, it's just . . . Oh for God's sake, Ma, there's nothing wrong with the tea!"

Tess eyed her over the rim of the cup. "The tea is off, Fiona. And please don't call me 'Ma'. You'd swear you were born in Tallaght."

"Don't make a scene," Fiona begged.

But Tess was already summoning the waiter. "Your tea is stale," she informed him politely but firmly.

The waiter clearly believed himself to be a cut above the hotel's clientele. "I think you'll find that Earl Grey is supposed to have a distinctive flavour."

"And I think you'll find that it's musty," Tess said clearly. "Change it, please."

The waiter tried to stare her down. He lost badly and at the end of the brief stand-off, was sent scurrying off with his tail between his legs.

Fiona had kept her eyes trained on the table throughout. She was mortified.

"You know what they're saying about us in the kitchen right now, don't you?"

"I should imagine they're calling me a cantankerous old bag," Tess said cheerfully.

"And probably spitting in the bloody tea," Fiona added with relish. "Or peeing in it."

"You have to stand up for yourself in this world, Fiona. People will walk all over you – "

"– if you let them, I *know*." Fiona threw herself back in her chair and flicked her eyes heavenwards in abject despair.

Tess hid a smile. God, how she loved her. Sometimes it took her by surprise, the sudden rush of emotion when she looked at this strong, tall, volatile girl who was her daughter. It was almost a physical pain. Nobody had told her she would ever feel like this about another human being. Certainly, it seemed incredible that she and Peter, two fairly flawed people at the best of times, could produce someone as perfect as Fiona.

"What are you looking at me like that for?" Fiona asked warily.

"Like what?"

"Like you've just swallowed a lemon."

"Charming. I was thinking how nice you'll look in that outfit we bought."

"Oh. Yeh,"Fiona said unenthusiastically. She grabbed a strand of her long hair and wrapped it around her finger. Her eyes, so like Peter's, were cloudy and shuttered. Tess suddenly remembered how the conversation had started. "What was it you wanted to tell me?"

Fiona looked at her briefly and furtively. "Nothing," she mumbled.

Tess's hand went to her throat. "Oh God."

"What?"

"Oh *God*, Fiona. You're not. . .?"

Fiona was horrified. "Ma! No, I haven't gone and got myself pregnant! What do you take me for?"

Tess felt weak with relief. She was careful not to show it. "Sorry."

"Jesus!" Fiona huffed. "We do have sex education in school, you know." She shot Tess another accusing look. "And before you ask, no I haven't done it with anybody yet and when I do, you'll be the last one to know."

Tess couldn't help herself – she laughed aloud, but the point was taken. Like Peter, there was a line with Fiona that you didn't cross. Tess crossed it anyway. She had to know.

"So you don't have a boyfriend then?"

"Ma!"

"I'm just asking!"

It was only a matter of time. Fiona was tall and slim and beautiful, a girl with intelligence and confidence. She would be a prize for any man. The thought sometimes filled Tess with dread. Please God she'd pick someone who would treat her well.

"It's just that I worry about you," Tess said apologetically. "No, no, don't pull a face. Every mother worries. I don't want you making the same mistakes I did."

"You haven't made any mistakes. You're perfect, Ma."

"You're making fun of me."

"I am not. You've the life of Reilly."

Tess supposed that maybe that was how it looked. What other woman could get out of bed on a Wednesday morning and decide to take off for a day's shopping, with no worries about work or money or having to be home to cook a husband's dinner? And tonight she would get dressed up for an important and glamorous black-tie dinner in Dublin Castle along with Sheila Burke and Edel Kennedy and the other Minister's wives and it wouldn't matter a damn what time she got to bed because who had to get up in the morning?

She had no right to feel restless, to feel that something was missing.

"What would you have changed?" Fiona was curious now.

Tess smiled. "Nothing, I suppose. And anyway, we were talking about *your* mistakes."

"I haven't made any yet," Fiona said with a grin.

It wasn't Fiona's mistakes that worried Tess. There was an awfully big world out there and not all of it good. Tess was determined that if anybody did anything to hurt her daughter, then they would have to reckon with her.

Not for much longer, Tess noted sadly. Fiona was fifteen, practically an adult. Soon she wouldn't need or want Tess's protection. And what would Tess have left then?

Peter, of course. And he had never needed or wanted her protection.

"Regina was saying something the other day," Fiona said suddenly.

Her eyes were too bright. Tess was immediately wary. "Oh?"

"About Dad." She looked at Tess, unsure.

"Fiona. You can tell me anything, you know that?"

Fiona bit her lip, then blurted, "Regina said that he was seeing Helen Boyd."

Tess froze. Fiona was winding the strand of hair around her finger so hard that it looked like it would break.

"I didn't know whether to tell you, Mum, I didn't know what to do. But if it was me, I would like to know." She slumped back in her chair as if all the wind had been knocked out of her. She watched Tess, her face riddled with worry. "I shouldn't have told you. You're upset, aren't you?"

"What? No, no, love, I'm not upset."

Tess was raging. Boiling with fury. How dare that stupid, *stupid* Burke girl shock Fiona like this, how dare she go telling tales her even stupider father had imparted to Sheila Burke once he had a couple of Jack Daniels in him? Did they have no feeling, no sense of what news of a father's affair could do to a fifteen-year-old?

One look at Fiona's miserable face calmed her down. It wasn't the Burkes' fault, of course. It was Peter's. Always Peter's.

"How long have you been keeping this to yourself?" she quietly asked.

"A couple of weeks."

The poor child. She would murder Peter.

"Regina's Mum said that you knew."

Thank you, Sheila, Tess thought.

"Did you, Mum?"

Of course she knew that Peter had been carrying on with Helen Boyd for months now, the whole of bloody Dublin knew.

"You were perfectly right to tell me," Tess said, not answering the question.

Fiona fiddled again with her hair. There was more. "But Regina said yesterday that they had broken up." She was wondering how much to reveal. Tess looked at her encouragingly. "Harry Burke said that there was some kind of scene in Dad's office. That he'd sent her some kiss-off flowers or something."

Tess nodded clinically, as though this were all mildly interesting news. But in the back of her throat, a burning sourness made itself felt. The rotten bastard. For their

134

wedding anniversary last week there had been no flowers. Just a casual invitation to accompany him that night to the opening of Michael Goldin's new film at the Savoy, freebie tickets that he had received as a matter of course. And a big box of Belgian chocolates, when he knew damned well that she could never afford to touch anything sweet. She had pleaded a migraine and sent him packing to the film on his own. Whether he remained on his own was entirely debatable. She told herself that she didn't care whether he slept with Michael Goldin himself that night.

"Is it true, Mum? Did he have an affair with her?"

Tess looked at her daughter's white face. Fiona didn't know about any of the others, that much was obvious from her question. Tess was glad. And there had been others, plenty of them. But nobody like Helen Boyd.

She had been a danger. What had promised to be another of Peter's whirlwind affairs had dragged on for the better part of six months. Sheila Burke had kept Tess informed of the increasing frequency with which Peter spent evenings at Helen's place in Donnybrook. There had been two dinners in remote, dimly-lit restaurants, supposedly secret but Sheila had her contacts. Helen Boyd had been seen more than once coming out of his office late at night.

It was the most blatant Peter had ever been and Tess had felt a growing sense of dread as the weeks crawled by. She had not been afraid that he would leave her; that would be political suicide and it would never, ever happen while he was in office. The Irish public's adoration of

Peter Fisher would not extend to forgiveness should he abandon his family for a redhead in her twenties.

What Tess feared was that Peter would genuinely fall in love with the trollop and sustain his affair over a matter of years instead of months, leaving Tess to join that despised little group of wives who were spouses in name only. Everyone knew who these women were and felt nothing but pity for them, knowing that they kept their positions for political expediency solely. Tess would rather die than become one of them.

But it was over now, the affair. And the news had come from her own daughter's mouth.

No wonder Fiona had been so offhand and belligerent with Peter in recent weeks. She must have been desperately confused, wondering whether to tell Tess or not. Tess really would kill Peter for this one.

But first she had to deal with Fiona. And Fiona was still waiting for her to answer her question. Waiting for Tess to confirm whether or not her father was a cheating, lying bastard.

The temptation was fierce and strong. It would be so easy to blacken him forever in her eyes, to say that yes, he had betrayed Tess with Helen Boyd. That he had been doing it for years now and was unlikely to stop. After all, it was only the truth. Why should she defend him? Why should she lie on his behalf?

Because of Fiona, of course. He was her father, she needed him still. She was too young to learn that he was a mere mortal like everyone else. The shock would be too great.

136

She had him on a pedestal, of course. Her gruffness and insolence only underlined that fact. And how could she not? He was the great Peter Fisher after all, a glamorous, famous figure who was larger than life, a spokesman for all that was honest and right in politics. How many teenage girls had a father-figure like that in their lives?

It would be cruel to expose him now as the shabby, cheating man that he was, to dash all of Fiona's inflated illusions. She would find out for herself in the fullness of time. As indeed Tess had.

In the meantime, she had to be protected. Her parent's sham of a marriage could not, *must* not, be revealed to her yet.

"I'm sorry you had to hear about this business, Fiona. It's very hurtful, I know."

"Never mind about me! What about *you*, Mum? Are you not desperately upset?"

"Of course I'm upset," Tess agreed calmly. "I'm upset that people are going around saying this kind of thing."

"But is it true?"

The child was in agony. Tess knew that she had to make this sound good. She looked her straight in the eye. "Was it true when people said last year that Carol Taylor wasn't paying the mortgage on her house out of her own pocket?"

It had been a silly little tittle-tattle rumour that had done the rounds of Dublin.

Fiona was impatient at the evasion. "Of course not – "

"No, of course not. And was it true when we heard

137

that Harry Burke had been caught drink-driving and had been let off?"

Harry Burke had indeed been stopped in a car under the influence, except that he was comatose on the back seat while his perfectly sober chauffeur was driving.

"Well, no . . ."

"No!"

Fiona was looking less sure of herself now.

Tess hammered the point home. "And was it true when they said that I needed psychiatric help for a mental breakdown?"

Tess had been amused when she'd heard that one, a week after she'd been to a specialist for an ingrown toenail.

"No! Of course not!" Fiona was outraged.

Tess gave her a measured glance. "So you see the kind of world we live in, Fiona? The world of politics?"

"So it's not true then? Dad and Helen Boyd never had a thing going?"

"If we believed everything we heard, Fiona, we would drive ourselves mad." Fiona was still now, watching Tess. "I gave up listening to the gossips years ago," Tess added forcefully. "I suggest that you do the same."

She saw the colour slowly creeping back into Fiona's cheeks. She had succeeded.

"I told Regina that she was lying, you know," Fiona said. "I told her that it couldn't be true. She said to come and ask you."

"And now you've asked me," Tess said with finality.

Fiona smiled with relief and her whole face lit up.

"I'm sorry, Mum. I shouldn't have said anything at all. But I thought you should know what they were saying, that's all."

"Thank you," Tess said quietly.

"And you're not upset?"

"No, no."

Had Tess been a woman given to tears, she might have cried now, here in the sympathetic company of her daughter who meant everything to her. She would have given vent to her feelings of anger and hurt at the casualness with which her husband betrayed her time and again. She would have wept at her continuing degradation in front of family, friends and political acquaintances, all of whom witnessed the parade of her private life. She might even have shed a tear or two of regret for a marriage that had once been content and happy if not bursting with passion. And for those long, empty nights in bed alone in her beautiful house in Dalkey wondering where Peter was and with whom.

But Tess Fisher had cried all her tears the day she discovered Peter's first affair. The time to confront him, to demand that he stop or she would leave, had come and gone. She had weighed up her feelings against her goals and there was no competition. No matter what he did, she knew that she would never leave him because what would she have left then? Nothing. Of even greater importance was Fiona, a mere toddler then. Could Tess condemn her to a childhood where her father was a presence only on alternate weekends?

Lastly, Tess had still loved Peter. She had still wanted

to be with him, could not imagine life without him. And if that meant turning a blind-eye, then so be it.

Once the decision had been made all those years ago, tears were both futile and hollow. She had not let herself cry over Peter since.

She sat up straighter, irked by her self-indulgence. Things had gone far enough. She never wanted to have to lie on Peter's behalf to their daughter again. Neither did she want sit to here feeling like an old, cast-aside fool, always the last one to know. And Fiona must not be exposed to this kind of thing again.

Something would have to be done.

Chapter Ten

Jack Thornton was late.

Peter Fisher hung up his mobile and swallowed his annoyance. If it had been anybody else he would have walked out of the Shelbourne bar ten minutes ago. But of course Thornton figured he could make him wait until doomsday. Peter's guess was that he was busy with Shelley, the brunette he had picked up last night. Or was it Shirley? Whatever.

He didn't know where the man got the energy. Peter himself felt like the walking dead. They'd been out for dinner and drinks in the Clarence Hotel last night, before Thornton had got the idea of visiting the hotel nightclub. Peter had felt wholly ridiculous skulking in the shadows in his suit, watching eighteen-year-olds stamp about to music that had neither rhyme nor rhythm to it. He'd left after an hour, anxious to escape before some staff photographer from one of the dailys got lucky. As he was going, Thornton was on his way to another club with Shelley/Shirley. The man was a powerhouse.

Well, the fun and games had to stop. And right now.

In his briefcase, Peter had the finished script that Thornton had sent him five days ago. After all Thornton's guff about admiring films with integrity and a strong story, it was obvious to Peter that he was incapable of producing the same himself. His script was awful – a testosterone-laden buddy-buddy detective yarn with a couple of vacant blondes and a lot of heavy artillery thrown in. Sexism was rife, although it was debatable which sex came off worse. And, purely as an afterthought, Thornton had gone and set it in rural Kilkenny, populating it with every Irish stereotype in existence, all of whom went around saying "begorrah" and "bejasus" whilst brandishing AK47 machine guns. It was a mess. Worse, it was the kind of stuff that was guaranteed to raise the hackles of the voters in Kilkenny. Thornton had sentimentally dedicated the script to his long-dead great-grandmother.

Peter was caught between a rock and an extremely hard place this morning. The facts were that the Government did not want Thornton's appalling script. But they still wanted the money he could raise from the studios. No matter what way he sugar-coated it, he did not think it was a pill Thornton would easily swallow.

And time was running out fast. This film had to be on the road in less than a month. Which was why Peter had sent by return post the script that was his own choice. Thornton had not even confirmed that he'd received it. Peter was almost afraid to ask.

"Peter! Am I late?"

Half the bar did a double-take as Thornton strode in, voice booming. The other half tried their resolute best to snootily ignore the fact that a movie legend was in their midst.

"Yes." Peter did not smile.

"Sorry about that," Thornton said easily, sinking into a chair and tucking in his shirt which was hanging out. Peter tried to banish the vision of him and Shelley/Shirley rolling about on the Shelbourne's white linen sheets.

A waiter was on top of Thornton before he had finished crossing his legs. "Double scotch," Thornton barked. "And good stuff, not that shit you sent up with room service last night. Peter?"

"Just a coffee."

Thornton unearthed a fat cigar and bit the end off it. He lit up and fixed Peter with a laddish smile. "Pity you dashed off so early last night. You sure got some hot broads here in Ireland, don't you?"

Peter was not about to get into a discussion on the temperature of his countrywomen.

"I haven't got much time," he said pointedly.

"Sure, sure, sorry. Anyway – I had an early breakfast meeting with that producer guy, Declan Mahoney, this morning." He pronounced the name like "baloney". His loud American accent got on Peter's nerves.

"Good," Peter said. He knew all about the meeting. Declan had phoned him afterwards. The upshot was that everything was ready to roll into pre-production. They were just waiting on final decisions about the script, the director, the stars and the money, Declan had added sarcastically.

"He seems pretty together," Thornton said magnanimously. Peter would not be imparting this gem to Declan, the most successful and experienced film producer in Ireland. He'd turned down two major British TV series to come on board this film. It had been an act of faith on his part and Peter owed him more than one.

"Jack," he said. It was time for the bullshit to end. "About your script . . ."

Thornton was alert. "You liked it?"

"It's certainly different," Peter said carefully.

"I've worked for two years on that script," Thornton said fervently, and Peter felt his heart sink. "That's why I didn't go straight to the studios on my own. It's too personal for me to allow them to hijack it, Peter." He grinned then. "But I know you guys will let me do it my way."

This was going from bad to worse.

"It needs a little more tweaking," Peter said, striving for tact. "I don't think it's quite ready."

"I guess I could do more work on it," Thornton said slowly.

Peter couldn't lie any more. He had lost him anyway. Might as well give it to him straight. "I think it's lousy actually, Jack. Sorry, but there you go."

"Well, fuck you," Thornton said, hurt.

"I'm not doing either of us any favours by lying to you. We both want to make a good film here. Which is why I'm wondering whether you've read the script I sent you last week."

Thornton was still scalded. "I read it all right. But the deal was that I got to direct my own script."

"You can't. We're going with this new script, Jack. We'd very much like you to direct."

"And if I don't?"

They were interrupted by the waiter. As he deposited the scotch and coffee, he informed Thornton in the most reverential tone that there was a phone call for him and would he like to take it in the booth down the hall? As Thornton stomped off, Peter changed his mind and ordered a scotch after all. He might need it when Thornton came back.

That was less than two minutes later. Thornton's face was black. "That was my agent."

Peter wasn't surprised. When he'd phoned on the mobile ten minutes ago, he'd been put through straight away.

"You told him that you were going to offer that script to Robert Mills."

Robert Mills was possibly the biggest director in Hollywood right now.

"Correct," Peter said.

Thornton leaned closer, his craggy face ugly with aggression. "What the fuck is this shit?"

"As I said, we'd like you to direct it." Peter was entirely reasonable. "But we'll understand if you don't. In which case we'll go with someone else. But we've offered you a twenty-four-hour option on it."

Thornton did not appreciate this act of generosity. He was livid. "What about the studios?"

"Oh, we think Robert Mills is quite capable of attracting studio money, don't you? Come to think of it, he *owns* his own studio."

He almost enjoyed the look on Thornton's face as the suspicion dawned that these Irish hicks did not think he was as shit-hot as he did. Peter fully expected him to storm upstairs and possibly even home to LA, doubtless after tossing his scotch in Peter's face.

But again Thornton displayed that capacity to elicit a grudging admiration from Peter. A slow smile crept over his face. "You should be in LA, you bastard." It was as near to a compliment as he would give.

"Sorry about your script, Jack. I mean it."

"I guess it wasn't so hot," Thornton admitted. "To tell you the truth, I couldn't bear to go and rewrite it again."

Peter hastily got off the subject of Thornton's masterpiece. "So? Do you want to direct this script or not?"

"Do you want Jason Blake or not?" Thornton enquired loftily.

He was the sly fox now, lifting one foot to rest on the table and expertly rolling his cigar between his teeth, like the canny cowboy he had played in one of his famous Westerns. He had just lassoed Peter and they both knew it.

Peter's weariness suddenly lifted. Maybe this movie was going to get off the ground after all – and in a big, big way.

146

"You've got Jason Blake hooked?" The question was rhetorical but he needed to know that this wasn't some joke of Thornton's.

"Listen, I knew when I got your script last week that it was the one for us. I just didn't want to admit it. But I put out some feelers just in case. And, like every other actor in Hollywood, Jason Blake is dying to do a period piece. He'll be fantastic as Richard."

Peter could not give a good goddamn if Jason Blake turned in a turkey of a performance in the film. The pertinent fact was that he was one of the top five names in world cinema right now, having starred in the two biggest-grossing movies of all time. Put Ewan McGregor, Brad Pitt and George Clooney into a blender and Jason Blake would come out the other end. He was not merely a physical bombshell, he could also act up a storm when it suited him – as his two Academy Award nominations had proved. The combination of Thornton and Blake would be the sweetest bunch of carrots ever dangled under the studios' noses.

Along with the script, of course, the best thing that Peter had read in years. In the ten days since Jean Ormsby had dropped unannounced into his office, Peter had carried the script around in his briefcase as though it were his bible. He had read it close on ten times and it got better each time. He'd had to stifle the impulse to go rushing into Jean Ormsby's office and buy the thing straight away before someone else got there first. But Thornton had kept him waiting. Now he was itching to wrap up this meeting and get hold of Jean Ormsby.

"We're in business then?" he asked.

"Yep," Thornton said with satisfaction. "The only question now is the female lead. She's got to be Irish, the genuine article. I don't want any Meryl Streeps putting on brilliant accents."

Peter agreed. "Let's get together with Declan and Phyllis and draw up a short-list."

Phyllis Harding was already on board as casting director.

Thornton wasn't happy with this. "You don't see any new talent with short-lists. Just the same old faces."

"We don't have time to do open auditions," Peter pointed out. He cut off any further protests by standing. "Our top priority is to get this film in on time, Jack, okay?"

Bill Mackey had been all over the papers again today. And rumour had it that a poll due to be published tomorrow would reveal that he had a twenty-percent-lead on any of the other four candidates. The squeeze was on.

Thornton uncrossed his legs, the spurs on his cowboy boots jangling loudly. "I guess I'd better go meet this agent and sign this script up."

Peter surprised himself by saying, "I've dealt with her so far, Jack. Let me hammer out a preliminary deal with her and then we'll set up a meeting." It would be much easier just to let Thornton go with Declan Mahoney, it wasn't even Peter's department. But he felt a curious relief when Thornton shrugged in acquiescence.

"And you'll sign a director's contract this afternoon," Peter added, getting to his feet.

"You don't take my word for it?"

"No."

Alan, his driver, was waiting for him outside the hotel in the car.

"Dame Street," Peter said, climbing in.

Traffic was terrible. As the car crawled around Stephen's Green, the script sat idly in Peter's lap as he thought about Jean Ormsby.

She would throw some stipulations at him about casting, of course. She wanted her piece of the cake and he was prepared for that. She would probably try to nail him on the question of money. He was ready for that one too. He was sticking to the fee guidelines of the British Writers' Guild but he was open to negotiation.

He was not in any way prepared for the peculiar and entirely inappropriate feeling of excitement and apprehension at the prospect of seeing her again. She had come into his mind continuously and at odd times since she'd gate-crashed his office last Friday week and he had spent a ridiculous amount of time trying to figure out exactly what it was about her that so intrigued him.

She had courage, of course, and plenty of street-smarts. You could see that she'd dragged herself up by the bootlaces all right and hadn't arrived yet – the car keys she'd unearthed from her bag as she was leaving did not fit a Merc. But her ambition hadn't jaded or hardened her, not like many of the successful people Peter met on a day-to-day basis.

She was beautiful, granted, that genuine kind that wasn't all make-up and clothes. But Ireland was full of beautiful women and Peter had met quite a number of them. And she was obviously intelligent and had a sense of humour.

What bothered Peter was that he found that he cared about her opinion. In his experience, this was a reaction that was both immediate and inexplicable. He would say that he had felt the same upon meeting Carol Taylor, for example, for the first time. It was a type of charisma that certain people possessed without trying. It was nothing to do with anything he later learned about their value systems or personalities. Over the years, he had cared about the opinions of people others would regard as renegades.

People of that kind, while he admired and respected them, also made him extremely uncomfortable. After himself, they were his hardest judges – not actively, they simply caused him to step back and look at himself. He had not always liked what he'd seen.

Which was why he'd found himself running around making coffee for Jean Ormsby that night, and asking for her help with his computer problem – trying stupidly to convince her that he was an okay guy after all, rather than the disgusting brute she had witnessed upon her arrival, when Helen had been dispatched along with the rest.

It was because of Jean Ormsby that he'd made a phone call to Helen to apologise, only to be told to fuck off again. This depressed him even more, but what had he been expecting? A pat on the back for trying to make everything okay, when from her point of view it patently wasn't?

He'd stayed late in the office to read the script, and several times had to stop himself from punching out Jean Ormsby's home phone number which was printed on the front page. Besides, a woman like her would not be sitting at home on a Friday night waiting for somebody to call. She would be out with her boyfriend, or more probably in with her boyfriend with the phone off the hook. Peter found that he was insanely jealous of this boyfriend he had never met.

"We're here." Aidan looked around, half-amused at his boss's introspection. "Are you getting out or what?"

"Thanks, Aidan. Take the rest of the day off." For reasons not yet clear to himself, Peter didn't want Aidan hanging around waiting for him to finish up with Jean Ormsby.

"But what about your man? I'm collecting him from Heuston in half an hour."

Aidan did not like Roger Croft and referred to him only as "your man". Peter had forgotten that Roger was due in Dublin today to meet with John Graham and the election strategists.

"Take him to lunch with John. Tell him I'll meet him at my office at three. He can make his own way there."

Aidan drove off. Peter had to caution himself to slow down as he took the stairs to Jean Ormsby's office two at a time.

The tall, willowy girl who was diligently typing did not recognise him even when he gave her his name. From the screensaver flashing on her computer behind her, saying *Cathy's Computer*, he ascertained her name.

"Do you have an appointment?" she asked efficiently.

"Well, no – "

"Are you an actor?" She looked at him doubtfully.

Peter swallowed a smile. Although he supposed that he did his fair share of acting for the TV cameras and the Pat Tynans of this world.

"No. I'm actually the Minister for Arts."

This did not have the impact to which Peter was accustomed. "Listen," she sternly, "Are you trying it on?"

"What?"

"There was an actor in here last week who told me that he was Gay Byrne's son.

Just so he could get in to see Jean."

"Gay Byrne doesn't have a son."

"I know!" Cathy said indignantly. "The cheek of him! Jean was really mad at me."

"I'm not trying it on," Peter assured her, trying to keep a straight face.

"Have you any ID?" she asked.

Peter could not remember ever being asked for identification in all his years in public life. "I'm afraid I don't," he said, fighting to hold back laughter. She looked at him even more suspiciously, like a terrier who would bite his ankles if he pushed her too far. Peter had visions of himself, esteemed Minister and public representative, being turfed out upon Dame Street by Jean Ormsby's zealous secretary and found it even more comical. He must be working too hard. Or else, as he suspected, the prospect of seeing Jean Ormsby again was making him as giddy as a teenager on the proverbial first date.

"I'm sorry," he said, recovering. "If you'd just get Jean to have a look at me, she'll verify who I am."

She was unconvinced. "Well, she's with someone but I'll tell her."

She picked up the phone and mumbled into it in that incomprehensible shorthand that secretaries the world over seemed to use. "She'll be out in two ticks."

"Thank you," Peter said meekly and opened the script, pretending to read.

Out of the corner of his eye, he drank in this space that was Jean Ormsby's, intrigued. It was a shabby little office, with a threadbare carpet and a rubber plant that looked as though it had been chosen for its ability to survive in adverse conditions rather than for any aesthetic considerations. A battered blow-heater was effective only in that it stirred about the stale air. Thrust under the coatstand in the corner was a pair of old running shoes that he guessed Jean Ormsby changed into to drive home.

Tess did that too. At the thought of her, Peter jumped guiltily. She was taking Fiona out today, a mid-term-break treat. Peter was due to meet them later for dinner. He was making an effort with Fiona, trying to break down this peculiar hostility she was displaying towards him recently. Hormones, Tess had said magnanimously, as always smoothing over troubled waters. She was good at that. She held the family together, she always had.

Pity it didn't extend to their marriage. Peter had made

an effort there too, only to find it thrown back in his face. For their wedding anniversary last week he had organised special tickets for the new Michael Goldin film première and, as a surprise, had arranged for them to join some of the stars of the film later on for dinner. Tess would have loved it, he knew. But she'd lamely pleaded a headache and turned away. He had been mystified. And hurt. Sometimes he didn't understand Tess at all.

"Excuse me?" Cathy was watching him shyly over her computer screen. "I couldn't help noticing what you're reading . . . it's *Outsiders*, isn't it?"

He saw the way she looked at the script, hungry-eyed. "You've read it?"

She nodded.

"And what did you think of it?"

She seemed a little surprised that he wanted her opinion. "I think it's brilliant," she admitted.

"Good. So do I." He smiled at her and she smiled back, as though they shared some kind of secret. She really was quite striking, he noticed for the first time – all jawbones and intense eyes. Memorable.

"Are you involved in it?" she asked, then reddened immediately. "Sorry, it's none of my business . . ."

"No, no," Peter said quickly. "I suppose you could say that I have an interest in it."

Those big eyes of hers were on the script again. He suddenly had the feeling that she had an interest in it too – a huge interest. He was about to ask what, when she shook herself slightly and smiled politely, putting an end to the conversation.

"I hope it goes well for you."

So do I, Peter thought fervently. He found himself still watching her as she went back to work. There was definitely something about her, something that made you want to look at her.

His head snapped up as a door opened and now here was Jean Ormsby, all clean shiny hair and another of those tailored suits, a dark blue this time that made her look classy as hell. Peter found himself on his feet with no recollection of getting there, a wide smile on his face and his hand thrust out.

"Minister," she said.

Her hand was warm and dry and Peter felt the shock of the first physical contact. He hoped it didn't show in his eyes.

"I'm sorry to keep you waiting," Jean said with a sharp glance at Cathy. Cathy looked terrified. Peter saw her look quickly at him, wondering whether he was going to shop her.

"Oh, not at all," he said smoothly. He liked the girl, had found her refreshing, and didn't want to get her into trouble. "Cathy and I were having a great chat."

Cathy shot him a grateful smile and went back to her computer.

Peter turned to Jean, savouring the moment. "I've some good news for you," he said, anxious to make her day, to see her smile in delight. To look at him with pleasure, dammit.

"I know," she said. And she stepped back to reveal Declan Mahoney.

Peter felt incredibly piqued. "Declan," he said, nodding at his producer.

"Thornton rang me. I came straight over for a meeting," Declan said, looking thrilled with himself.

That damned interfering Thornton – after Peter had *told* him he would deal with this.

"Great," Peter said blandly. "Have you started?"

"Just finished. I think we're both happy with what we've worked out?" Declan looked to Jean for affirmation.

"I'm very pleased," she said with all the togetherness of someone who pulled off million-dollar deals every day of the week.

"Great," Peter repeated parrot-like. "I guess I'm not needed then."

"Yeh – go back and run the country," Declan said, good-humoured. "Jean and I are off for a celebratory lunch."

Peter generally worshipped the ground Declan walked upon but right now he'd have liked to kick him in the nuts. For the first time, he noticed how bloody good-looking the man was, all stubble and faded jeans. He was at least ten years younger than Peter too. Already he could sense the easy familiarity between Jean and him.

"Won't you join us?" Jean asked quietly. "If you've got the time, that is."

Peter felt like an old fool who never learned. "No, I'm afraid I don't," he said in clipped tones. "Let me see everything before it's signed."

With a nod at them both, he left.

Chapter Eleven

He wasn't a day over nineteen. Fresh. Pure as the driven snow if his Aran jumper and baggy jeans were anything to go by. And a country boy to boot, if Roger wasn't mistaken. He would bet that the rucksack he had carelessly jammed into the corner of the train seat and now lounged against contained a cake of soda bread his Mammy had baked for him that morning, along with six free-range eggs to see him through the college week. She was clueless that her boy was learning a lot more in Dublin than Applied Mathematics.

Roger loved the young ones. If you caught them just when they were discovering that those secret desires they'd harboured for years were shared by others, accepted and encouraged by them, you were in for a treat. Freed from the stifling confines of rural communities and family homes, they displayed boundless energy and no fear, and a sweet enthusiasm that could excite even the most jaded palate.

The boy looked over at Roger again and away quickly.

What marvellous eyes he had. A lovely clear green, and it was cute the way he could sustain that been-there-and-done-that-twice look for only a few seconds at a time. No, he hadn't been on the scene long at all. Roger would enjoy this one.

He checked his watch. They wouldn't be arriving in Heuston Station for another twenty minutes yet. Plenty of time.

He carefully folded his jacket on the seat beside him and stepped into the aisle. Without walking too slowly, he made his way up the carriage. As he passed the boy's seat he paused, as though the movement of the train had momentarily caught him off balance. He gave the boy a single look and walked on.

The toilet was wet and cramped. Roger was careful not to touch anything as he waited. His heart was pounding with excitement and his mouth dry.

He knew he should not be here but, as always, the danger and risk of the casual encounter was too much to resist. It was the only kind of relationship he had ever known and would ever know. Ever since his father had discovered him in an embrace at the age of seventeen with an older man who looked like Burt Reynolds, his had been a twilight existence of chance meetings in parks, toilets and certain backstreets in Dublin.

His father had called him into the kitchen that night, his kindly, paternal face open and concerned. Roger gritted his teeth in resignation. Knowing his father, he would want to talk the whole thing through, before making embarrassing offers of support and help, as though Roger had some kind of unspeakable disease.

"You disgust me," his father said pleasantly instead. "And if I ever catch you with another shirt-lifter, I swear to God I'll kill you with my bare hands, you fucking little pervert."

Roger sat frozen. He had never in his life heard his father utter a threat; never heard him swear. But even more shocking was the naked hatred on his face. He was like a stranger.

"Daddy . . ." The childish form of address slipped out in Roger's fright. Surely his father wasn't serious? Tony Croft, Government Deputy, the man they called the "champion of the underdog"?

Fragmented childhood memories came rushing at Roger, words and phrases his father had used when someone had annoyed him – "a queer, of course", "fag-hag, your woman", "I wouldn't bend over around that fella". Some of them almost laughably quaint, most of them unutterable in this politically correct age, and all of them revealing the fact that kind, loveable Tony Croft was a raging bigot.

"Daddy," Roger said again.

His father recoiled from Roger's outstretched hand as though he were poison. "Get out of my sight."

He never again looked at Roger directly if he could help it. It took Roger two years to decide that, really, he didn't give a shit. He had discovered the joys of the one-night stand and there was no stopping him. Some of his brief lovers had told similar tales of being ostracised by parents, friends and family and there had been some horror stories. Roger had murmured sympathy and moved swiftly on to the next. He would not give in to his father by becoming a victim. He simply did his thing and enjoyed every minute of it.

He'd been discreet, of course. It wouldn't do to further enrage good old Dad, and besides, who wanted every neighbour for miles around whispering behind his back, crowd of old women that they were? Roger preferred his private life to remain private. For all intents and purposes, he was the lad about town, downing pints with his mates and picking up the odd woman or two. He'd even slept with a couple, a distasteful and entirely frustrating experience he did not intend to repeat. Their company repelled him almost as much – all that giggling and tittering, and analysing even the simplest thing to death. For the last couple of years, he hadn't bothered with even the pretence of dating, although his other life was still entirely secret, known only to himself, his dead father and those young men who came and went in the night.

All that could change now, of course. Voters liked to see their candidates settled down, married or at least "doing a strong line", preferably with a member of the opposite sex. Roger was young enough to get away with the marriage bit maybe, but they would wonder about his single status. The media worried him more, with their nasty little habit of digging into candidates' private lives.

The possibility of discovery at such a crucial time in Roger's career gave an added *frisson* to today's little rendezvous. He could not give this up. Not yet.

Where was the boy? What was keeping him? Roger waited another minute and then opened the toilet door. He smiled. The boy was standing outside, in a lather of sweat. He had obviously never done this before, had no idea of the rules.

"Do you fancy a coffee?" he blurted.

So cute. "I fancy *you*," Roger said, pulling the boy into the cubicle and securely shutting the door.

"What's your name?" the boy stammered.

"Peter Fisher," Roger said, stalling further boring conversation by reaching for the zipper on the boy's pants.

Fisher's driver Aidan was waiting for Roger at the train station, shuffling from foot to foot and smoking a cigarette, which he would never have dared to do had he been waiting for Fisher. Still, he looked good in his uniform and he half-stood to attention as Roger stepped off the train.

Aidan reluctantly picked up Roger's bag when he made no move to do so himself. Other passengers were watching now, sure that Roger must be someone important – maybe a diplomat, or an American businessman at the very least. Roger pretended to ignore them.

"Where did you leave the car?" he asked just loud enough for passing commuters to hear.

"In the carpark, Einstein," Aidan said politely.

Roger coloured slightly, but quickly told himself that the indubitable Aidan was merely a small man in a small job.

He made Aidan wait while he put on his cashmere coat, a pre-election present to himself. Nothing could spoil his mood today. Apart from the fact that he was about to meet the big guns, the election and PR chaps, the boy had not been disappointing. After some persuasion, he had got down on his knees, his cherry mouth working Roger into a delicate frenzy, sustaining it until Roger thought his cock would burst.

Then, the impatient knock at the door as a disgruntled passenger waited to relieve himself. The interruption had shocked and thrilled Roger and the boy both, adding an extra dimension to the intimacy. Finally, Roger could bear it no more and pulled the boy's head close, erupting in an orgasm so intense that he thought he would faint.

Yes, he had been worth the risk.

"The Minister said to give you this, you're to read it in the car," Aidan said, handing over an immaculate manila folder containing information about press strategies and meetings that afternoon. "And you've lunch with John Graham and his people in twenty minutes."

"Fine," Roger said, admirably containing his excitement.

He could get used to this – the glamour, the ceremony. Being treated like he was a somebody for the first time since his glory days in the Student Union.

Aidan hoisted the bag onto his shoulder and turned away. Roger was about to follow when the boy sidled shyly up to him.

"Do you want to meet up later?"

Roger went cold. The boy was all eagerness and

162

innocence, stupid little sod. Could he not tell the difference between a quick shag and a life-long commitment?

"No, I can't," Roger said out of the side of his mouth, pushing past him.

The boy looked hurt now, and trailed along after Roger. Roger walked faster. Oh Christ, he wasn't going to make a scene, was he? Better to attack it head-on. Abruptly, he swung around and stuck his face close to the boy's.

"Do you want something?" he asked harshly.

Aidan looked back now and slowed, his dull eyes suddenly becoming sharp. Roger could sense a major catastrophe about to happen.

The boy's eyes were filled with hurt. "After what happened . . . don't you want to see me again?"

Roger felt a flash of savage hatred for this teenager with his ridiculous Aran jumper and battered rucksack. How dare he accost him in public in such a manner? Embarrass him like this with nonsensical demands for a continuing relationship? Roger had made a bad mistake choosing him.

"No. Now please leave me alone." Roger's voice was full of venom but there was a smile on his face, as though he had just given the boy directions. With his peripheral vision, he saw Aidan walk back towards them.

The boy was wounded. But he still persisted. He tentatively put out a hand. Roger flinched before he saw that the boy held a scrap of paper.

"It's my phone number," he said.

Aidan was nearing now. Roger had to get rid of the boy and fast. He caught the boy's wrist so hard that he could feel the slender bones through the Aran jumper.

"Listen, you little shit," he hissed. "I don't want your phone number, I don't want to see you ever again, do you hear me? Now fuck off."

The boy was stunned. He might even burst into tears. He stood forlornly on the platform as Roger released him and strode away, features schooled into blandness again.

"Is there a problem?" Aidan enquired.

"Some pathetic homeless person looking for money," Roger said shortly. "They shouldn't allow them in here."

Aidan looked at him oddly. "You mightn't want to say that kind of thing in public before the election."

In the car, Roger hit the button to raise the smoked-glass partition, blocking out the sight of the odious Aidan. He made a mental note to see what could be done about removing him from his position.

As he opened the manila folder, he was surprised to find that his hands were shaking. The boy had nearly ruined everything. What if the dimwit Aidan had grasped the situation and had a word in Fisher's ear? What if the boy had a journalist friend?

It took only one rumour to ruin a political career; Roger had learned that if nothing else under his father's roof.

It was his own stupid fault for giving into temptation in such seedy and open circumstances. Especially now.

It was a time to be careful. Very careful. Possibly he might need to curtail his activities entirely until the election was over. Although the film might offer some opportunity – he would not be so tied to the campaign trail and could slip away more easily unnoticed.

Fisher would be on his back of course, as always. He kept tabs on Roger as though he were some kind of prize pig they were rearing for slaughter. Well, Fisher was no one to preach. If he could take time out to screw, then so could Roger. It was simply a matter of logistics, and keeping the voters, the party and the media ignorant. It could be done.

Roger Croft. Twenty-seven. Five-foot-eleven and clean-cut. Attractive without being too handsome. Nice clear brown eyes. He looked good.

John Graham lit another cigarette and studied again the studio photo he'd ordered of Roger Croft. There was a certain softness around the chin that bothered him. An indication of a weak character perhaps? Or maybe it was simply the roundness of youth. Time would tell.

Underneath the photo was a thick file, official background information on the lad – education, family, career-to-date. All standard biographical stuff to feed to the press.

In Graham's briefcase was a thinner file, unofficial information for his eyes only. A purely precautionary measure, of course. Apart from some unfounded nonsense about college union funds, nothing in the slightest bit worrying had turned up. But the full report had yet to come in.

Graham never liked to rush these things. He was by nature obsessively thorough and never left anything to chance. But there was no time to finish his homework on Croft.

The by-election was already well underway. Graham thus found himself in the unenviable position of promoting a candidate whom he did not know as well as himself. It bothered him. That and the weak chin.

He turned once again to the photo. Roger Croft smiled back at him, confident and calm, and Graham felt better. The background check would continue, but what could the lad possibly have hidden that might pose a problem?

He was being too paranoid. He was letting Ulick get to him. Bill Mackey had opened a new centre for disadvantaged children in Kilkenny yesterday afternoon, and Ulick had seen to it that the public and the media had turned out in force. It had all been disgustingly sentimental and over the top and Graham was green with envy. Ulick was smart all right. Graham would just have to be smarter.

He turned his attention to the film now. Croft's profile was largely dependent on that of the film. And apart from the initial rush of interest in Thornton as director, media interest had flagged a little. It was time to fire it up again.

Slowly, Graham's little grey cells galvanised. He smiled. On his mobile, he punched out Jack Thornton's number.

Chapter Twelve

There was an American made-for-TV film on the telly. A plastic-looking brunette with a frightening number of teeth on view sobbed on the broad shoulder of a man whose hair looked like it had been painted on.

"Oh Brad! I wish I were dead!"

"Come now," Cathy sternly told the brunette. "Things aren't that bad, are they?"

The brunette burst into fresh tears. Things were obviously terrible.

"I know the feeling, honey," Cathy murmured in sympathy, sticking a thermometer into her mouth. She waited a minute, then extracted it and had a look.

It said ninety-eight. She had no fever. And a quick look in the mirror told her that her eyes were bright, her tongue nicely pink and her cheeks roundly ruddy.

Damn anyway. There was no sign at all of the flu which she was going to pretend was striking her down. She looked as healthy as a horse.

She could plead a migraine, she supposed. People

were often laid low by mysterious migraines, weren't they? But on second thoughts, no. It was too convenient. Carl Tallon would see through it straight away.

An accident, perhaps? Could she ring Jean and claim that she had fallen down the stairs? Nobody was to know that there were no stairs in her smelly little flat on the North Circular Road.

She liked this one and thought about it some more. She could say that she had sprained her back and couldn't walk. No, too dramatic. Better to say that she had an accident in the kitchen – involving hot oil, or something gruesome like that. Not too gruesome, though. She might be expected to produce scars as evidence or something. Or worse, Jean might insist on rushing over and taking Cathy to Outpatients.

Oh feck, Cathy thought. Surely there was some perfectly reasonable excuse that could be made to get out of tonight? Because there was no way she was going. No way at all.

The brunette was still whinging on the telly. Cathy grabbed the remote control and channel-hopped – anything to take her mind off the fact that she was standing here in her gladrags, and should have left ten minutes ago for a night on the town with Jean and Patsy, who had been persuaded to turn down her new job and stay on at the agency. They would be joined by Carl Tallon for a big celebration dinner to mark the signing of his film deal today.

Jean had thought that it would be a nice thing to do. A treat for them all.

Jean had some rotten ideas sometimes.

The TV offered no respite. The end of the news was on. Once again, they were talking about *Outsiders*, and the fact that Kilkenny Castle was rumoured to have granted permission for a limited amount of filming to take place inside its walls.

Cathy's finger hovered over the "off" button on the remote control. Did she really want to hear another thing about the bloody film? They were probably going to announce that they'd just cast Wynona Ryder or Gwynth Paltrow as Alison. Cathy didn't think she could stomach it.

Curiosity, of course, got the better of her. She turned the volume up. Now a shot of a very excited cub-reporter standing outside Kilkenny Castle, breathing into a microphone. "The latest news on the Jack Thornton period film, due to begin shooting in three weeks' time in Co Kilkenny, is the announcement that there will be a nationwide search for the Irish female lead, to star opposite Hollywood actor Jason Blake. Movie buffs are calling it Jack Thornton's search for Scarlett O'Hara."

Cathy nearly choked. Her eyes bulged as Jack Thornton burst onto the screen, looking oh-so-LA in his baseball cap and three-day stubble. "Yeah, I'm looking at everybody, and I mean *everybody*. I want to get this girl just right. We're asking anybody interested to submit a three-minute video."

The piece finished up with a brief cutaway of a young guy Cathy learned was Roger Croft, the Government's candidate in the Kilkenny by-election. He was relaxed and smiling, entering into the spirit of the piece. "Naturally, we're hoping down here that it'll be a Kilkenny girl."

The news moved on to a more sedate piece about the sharp dip in sheep prices.

Cathy remained glued to the spot. A Scarlett O'Hara search for Alison? Were they for real?

Immediately, she thought of Carl. Oh, how he was going to *hate* this one – if he even knew. She could hear him now: "It's a fucking gimmick! Hollywood bullshit! I will not have my script compromised in this way!" Well, tough, she thought nastily.

Because if there was one thing in this world that was important to Carl Tallon, it was his work. She would go so far as to say that his work was the *only* important thing in his world. She had first-hand knowledge of that.

His artistic fervour was what first drew her to him. He sat at the back of the studio on the first day of rehearsals for *Outsiders*, drinking black coffee and watching proceedings with brooding eyes. He spoke to nobody, he did not laugh at any of the funny lines in his play. Neither did he go to the pub with them all afterwards to celebrate the first day of a fantastic play. He went straight home instead, only to arrive in the following morning with ten pages of rewrites, having managed the incredible feat of improving on perfection.

He brooded, refused drinks, and rewrote for a week. Nothing seemed to please him. Because of that, of course, everybody tried harder. Cathy especially. Carl Tallon seemed to watch her more than anyone; she would turn around to find those eyes on her constantly, following her every move. Sometimes she thought that he hated her as Alison. As the days crept by, she found his silent presence at the back of the room more and more intimidating. And extremely attractive. Not only did Carl Tallon look good enough to eat, it was quite obvious that he was some kind of a tortured genius.

On Friday evening, the end of the first week of rehearsals, he approached her for the first time. In his hand, he held a page of rewrites for the character of Alison. Cathy was gutted. What was she doing wrong?

He stood silently as she read them, tight-throated. They were fantastic.

"It's just a suggestion," he said shortly. He took her terrified state for disapproval. Cathy watched in amazement as he reddened, his eyes falling to the ground. "But if you don't think they're appropriate . . ." he'd muttered. "I mean, you're so good as Alison . . . I've been watching you all week – look, maybe we could talk about it in the pub?"

A genius *and* vulnerable! At that point, Cathy was lost.

That night was the first of many spent huddled together in the pub discussing the script. His brusqueness was only a front for perfectionism, she thought fondly. There was no aspect of the play that he did not want her opinion on. And she gave it readily, only too happy to nurture his talent.

Fooling herself, of course, that it was her he was really interested in. Oh, he'd been happy enough to amuse himself with her for two short months, but all he had cared about at the end of the day was his precious play.

Because when it was over, they were over too. She had rung him from London. Begged him to come and see her, that she desperately needed him. He, about to sign a contract for his next masterpiece, had refused. End of story. End of them.

She was expected tonight to sit opposite him for at least three hours in a restaurant, pretending to be delighted that his film was all signed up.

She kicked off her shoes and sank down on the couch. At least she could spare herself half-an-hour of misery by being late. They wouldn't miss her anyway. They would all be too busy talking about Jack Thornton's search for Alison.

I'm Alison.

The thought burned in her brain before she could stop it. But she had been the first to play the character, to take her from the printed page and breathe life into her. She knew the way Alison spoke, how she moved, the way she pinned her hair up in the mornings. She identified with the character down to her toenails, because she had helped create her. Hadn't Carl Tallon even gone off and re-written aspects of Alison on Cathy's suggestion? How could anybody else play her better?

Abruptly, Cathy pulled herself up short. If she

wasn't careful she would start to sound like those awful actresses who thought that because they once played a role, they owned it. Or worse, she would start to sound as arrogant as Carl Tallon.

Alison was gone. Let Jack Thornton look at his videos. He wouldn't be getting one from Cathy Conroy, that was for sure.

There would be other films, she stoically told herself. But it rang hollow.

On the telly, the brunette was bonking Brad. Neither of them looked as though they were particularly enjoying it, although there was an awful lot of sighing and screaming going on.

Cathy felt very tired all of a sudden. It had been a long week, and now she had to muster the energy to put on a front for tonight. To show Carl Tallon that she didn't care.

Which she didn't, she assured herself, as the brunette on the telly laid her head on Brad's shoulder went to sleep.

She was woken at midnight by a knock on the door. She stumbled to her feet in confusion, swiping at the trickle of saliva that had escaped down her chin. "Hold on!"

The knock came again, impatient now. She hurled the door open, bleary-eyed. *"You."*

Carl Tallon's face was carefully bland. "Sorry to disturb you. But when you didn't bother showing up tonight, Jean was worried." *He* wasn't, she noted. "She asked me to drop by on my way home to check that you were alive." Even his silences managed to be sarcastic. "Which you obviously are."

"I, um, yes, sorry about that."

Another dead silence as he eyed her distastefully. Cathy's hackles rose.

"I fell asleep, I'm afraid," she said curtly. "I'm sure you all had a very nice evening without me."

"Lovely, thank you," he agreed.

She would not let him see how rattled she was. "Good," she said, dragging a pleasant smile to her lips. "I'm sorry I missed it."

She waited for him to go. But it appeared that he was determined to be as pleasant as she.

"Yes. So, ah, how are things going?"

Cathy was a little bemused. Carl Tallon was not one for engaging in small talk.

"Fine."

"Any acting jobs coming up?"

She wondered was he trying to get the knife in. But his expression was one of polite interest, as though they were strangers passing the time of day on the street.

"No. Not yet. And you?" She could play the game too. "Any more high-profile writing gigs on the horizon?"

"I'm too busy with the film. But I've started on something new. A play."

"A *play*. You're a busy beaver." This time, her sarcasm was unmistakable.

He glowered, but still made no move to go. Behind her, Cathy pulled the door of the flat closed. She did not want him to see her little home. He would probably sneer. And what was he hanging around for anyway? Why didn't he just go?

"You saw the piece on the TV?" he asked after a pause.

"What?"

"The Scarlett O'Hara stuff."

He was going to bang on about the fecking film again. The guy was unbelievable.

"Yes. I saw it alright," Cathy said with as much civility as she could muster.

His face darkened. "It's a gimmick, of course. Hollywood bullshit. I won't have it, I . . . "

"Won't let your script be compromised in that way?" Cathy helpfully supplied.

His eyebrows sprang together in suspicion. "Are you laughing at me?"

"I wouldn't dream of it," Cathy told him heavily. "Please, carry on."

He did. He was obviously dying to get it off his chest. "Sending in videos. What a heap of nonsense! Well, don't you agree with me?"

He was looking at her with that old intensity. Cathy felt something stirring in her and swiftly clamped it down. "I don't have any opinion on it one way or the other."

She couldn't believe that Carl Tallon had the brass neck to stand here and try to have a conversation with her about his damned film. About Alison, for God's sake!

The incongruity was obviously lost on him. "They won't find Alison like that. Not in a million years. *You* know it too, Cathy."

Again, that piercing look. Cathy felt her fingernails bite into the palms of her hands. What did he want from her? Reassurance that everything would work out for him and his script? Was he *that* stupid? Her days of stroking his ego were long gone.

"It's nothing to do with me," she said coldly. "Now, goodnight."

"Cathy – wait."

She swung back, unsure. "What?"

Carl Tallon suddenly seemed to have difficulty looking her in the eye. "You played Alison first . . ."

"Yes?" A tiny flicker of hope licked at her insides. Could he be suggesting . . . ? No. Impossible. He hated her. He would never put her forward for the role of Alison. Or would he?

"And you were so good," Carl mumbled. "Nobody could do it like you. So, I was wondering . . ."

"Yes?" Cathy said again, her eyes starting to shine. This was it. He was going to put their mutual dislike to one side for the sake of the film. Black eyes met hers now and she found that she was hot.

"I was wondering whether you'd lend me your copy of the video of the original play," Carl Tallon said casually. "Just so they know what to look for when they start the casting process."

Cathy felt like she had just been kicked in the stomach. "You want my copy of the video?"

"Yes, I seem to have mislaid mine," Carl agreed pleasantly. "I want them to be able to tell a good performance from a bad one."

"I see," Cathy said, smiling nicely, giving no indication of her shock, her gut-wrenching disappointment. Her *fury.* "I'll see if I can find it."

She was back on the landing a minute later, handing over the video. She'd have liked to throw it at him.

"Cathy . . ." he said again, fingering the video.

She could not look at him for another second. "*Goodnight*, Carl."

The belligerence was back in his eyes. "You know, you could just have said you had the flu tonight, or something. I know the evening would have been a trial for you, but you could have come up with some excuse."

Her patience finally snapped. "I told you, I fell asleep!" she almost shrieked.

"Really." He favoured her with a long, measured look. "But then again, you have a habit of not showing up, don't you?"

Cathy wasn't quite sure she had heard correctly. By the time she had opened her mouth to retaliate, he had turned on his heel and was loping away.

Chapter Thirteen

It was *the* launch party of the year.

It was held in the grounds of Kilkenny Castle, a massive publicity coup, where many of the later scenes in the film were supposedly being shot. All the stops had been pulled out to capture the ambience of the film and to ensure that it was an evening to remember.

Thus guests were met from their cars by a fleet of braying donkeys and escorted into the castle in traps festooned with flowers. Twenty stable-boys greeted the arrivals with goblets of ale and mulled wine before they stepped into the floodlit banqueting hall where two cows, Maisie and Daisy, wandered about excitedly despite John Graham's best efforts to keep them in check.

"Whose fucking idea was the cows?" he swore, forgetting that it had been his. He had worked in close tandem with the film production people on this one and went off now to round up the Celtic band, an extraordinary-looking bunch of long-haired middle-aged men who looked and smelled like they hadn't washed in a month but who made the sweetest music Graham had ever heard.

At one side of the hall was a lavish medieval banquet: tables were laid out with honey-cured hams, whole turkeys, sides of beef, nutty brown bread, mounds of mashed potatoes, stew, salads, pickles, chutneys, relishes, Guinness cake, warm apples-pies and clotted cream. Irish whisky was being dispensed as fast as the crew of authentic-looking milkmaids could work.

A huge open turf fire had been built at the far end of the hall, tended to by a shepherd who was on twenty pounds an hour and all the Guinness he could drink. Waiters, dressed as farm boys, wove in and out of the crowd with trays laden with smoked salmon and black-pudding treats, while a lone harpist on a podium at the top of the barn played a haunting tune to warm up the crowd.

The finishing touch was an obese pink sow – whose name right now escaped

Graham – glaring balefully from her pen near the fire and standing protectively over her eight piglets who were loving every minute of the attention.

It was all gloriously tacky, incredibly vulgar and completely, utterly kitsch. It was also a runaway success, Graham observed with no little satisfaction. He threw an expert eye over the laughing, chattering crowd and absentmindedly patted Maisie who had wandered up.

They had all turned out for this one. There was Carol Taylor and her posse of Ministers, all down from

Dublin. Not that this was any surprise to Graham; he had made it known in his inimitable fashion that their presence would be required. All the big industry names were here, of course – famous Irish film directors and producers littered the sawdust. Actors too, although Graham had tried to put a limit on these to make room for the usual compliment of leggy models and beautiful women who were famous primarily for getting their pictures in the gossip columns of the Sunday papers.

And Eileen Burnstein and Neil Pasternak of Cinerama, of course, the guests of honour from the big Hollywood studio that Jack Thornton was squeezing for fifty million in funding. Not that that was public knowledge yet – negotiations were supposedly on-going but it was no secret that a positive announcement would be made on Monday morning.

The media were here in their droves. It was most unusual to have any kind of launch party for a film; the wrap party when it was over was the main event. But after many hours of argument with the film people, Graham had won the day for the Government. He could not risk the film coming in behind schedule, and losing all that publicity. Besides, Ulick had wiped his eye last Saturday with a prime-time radio interview with Bill Mackey. This ensured that Mackey's mug was plastered all over the Sunday papers, edging him a couple of points ahead in the race.

But Graham's Scarlett O'Hara search was paying off in spades. Not that anybody remembered that it had been his idea in the first place. That crude Jack Thornton had hijacked it as his own. Still, that wasn't important right now. The fact was that half the hacks here tonight would never have made the journey down to Kilkenny but for the fact that they thought the winner would be announced at the party.

No such luck. They hadn't found her yet. Graham's great plan of having her arrive on a white stallion specially borrowed from a studfarm in Kildare was down the tubes. Oh well. It was the only fly in the ointment in an otherwise perfect evening.

A loud, frightened bellow interrupted his self-congratulations and sent him running towards the banquet table. Daisy had broken through the protective cordon and had eaten half a vat of mustard before she realised that her mouth was on fire. Graham arrived just in time to see her lift her tail and let fly in a glorious stream of brown and green.

"Is Jason Blake *really* going to turn up later on?"

"He really is." Peter smiled indulgently at Fiona. She looked lovely tonight, demure and sweet in a white dress that reached her ankles. And there were no wisecracks from her either. Whatever was eating her recently seemed to have resolved itself.

Peter was relieved. For a while he had been worried that she was growing wild. There had been reports of drinking and truancy from school. But looking at her now, sipping orange juice and looking around enthusiastically, he decided that he had been wrong. She was still his little girl.

"Can I visit the set some day? When you start filming?" she asked now.

"Sure." He eyed the crowd, glad that so many had turned out.

"You know how boring the summer always is." She pulled a face.

A thought struck him. "How do you fancy a summer job?"

Her eyes shone. "On the film?"

"Nothing fancy, mind. Making tea and things like that."

"I don't care, I'd love it!"

Peter was gratified. "I'll have a word with Jack Thornton."

Peter could see him now across the room. And there was Eileen Burnstein. He really must go and talk to her. Out of the corner of his eye, he saw Jean Ormsby walk in with Carl Tallon. He felt his pulse jump.

"Dad?"

"Sorry – what were you saying, love?"

Fiona's mouth twisted. "It doesn't matter."

"It does."

"Oh, go off and mingle, Dad. We both know you're dying to."

He must have looked guilty. "Sorry, it's just that some of these people are important. . ."

The minute the words were out he realised what he had said.

Fiona's face closed. "Don't let me keep you then."

"How are the rewrites coming along?"

"Don't fucking talk to me."

"I don't have any choice," Jean said tartly, sipping her wine. "I think you're the only person I know here."

At least she had succeeded in wresting a smile from him. Jean had known several writers in her time, but Carl Tallon gave new meaning to the word "brooding". In the weeks that she had been working on the script with him, she had learned that he was not given to small-talk, smiles, or, indeed, any of the other pleasantries that were the currency of everyday life. She found that she liked him more because of this.

"I'll have the final rewrite next week, okay?" Carl informed her tersely.

"You were supposed to have it *this* week."

"I know, I know. But I'm working on another project, okay?"

Jean's self-interest rose to the fore. "Oh? A filmscript?"

"A new play."

"I see." Not as sexy as a filmscript, true, but Carl Tallon had proved that he was a bankable name. "Maybe you'd let me read it when you're done."

He looked at her and laughed. "You agents. You're never off the job, are you?"

Jean smiled back demurely. "You need us as much as we need you."

"True. Anyway, we'll see. I haven't finished it yet." He looked around disparagingly at the party. "It's a bloody circus, isn't it? Who *are* all these people?"

Jean shrugged. "Somebody seems to know *you*."

"What?"

She nodded to her left. "That guy over there has been watching you for the past ten minutes."

Carl Tallon gave a cursory glance over and sniffed. "Never saw him before in my life." He moodily slugged his drink. "Jack Thornton should be working on the film, not throwing parties to impress people."

"He *is* the director, Carl," Jean said magnanimously. "He's trying to drum up interest in the film."

"He's a goon," Carl said baldly.

Carl Tallon, Jean had also learned, was not the kind who prostrated himself before Hollywood legends.

"Pulling a fucking stunt like that!" Carl went on heatedly

Jean sighed. It was obvious that he was still raging over the Scarlett O'Hara search for Alison.

"He's looking for the right actress."

"He won't find her that way."

"Well, have *you* any suggestions?" she asked a little impatiently.

"It's not my job to cast the film," he returned, face black.

She decided to move onto safer territory. "So! Who played Alison in the original play?"

He fixed her with a ferocious look. "What?"

"I just asked who – "

"I know what you asked. And I can't remember."

"You can't remember?"

"That's right," he barked. "It's a complete blank."

Well! Jean thought huffily. What had rattled *his* cage?

Fed up of writers and their ridiculous sensitivity, she

184

turned to look around at the party – and found herself gazing right into Peter Fisher's eyes. He half-smiled in acknowledgement. She smiled back.

"I'm going home," Carl Tallon announced.

"But we've only just arrived."

"You stay if you want. I've better things to do."

"Cows," Sheila Burke sniffed.

"This *is* the countryside," Tess returned mildly.

"You look marvellous." A hint of envy.

"Thank you, Sheila."

Tess was manicured, plucked, styled, waxed, and painted to within an inch of her life.

Sheila jabbed a fat elbow into Tess's ribs lewdly. "If I didn't know better, I'd think you were trying to catch someone's eye."

Tess was not about to tell her that the only eye she was out to catch tonight was Peter's.

She had felt slightly foolish dressing up for her own husband after sixteen years of marriage. But the Helen business had shaken her more than she'd first cared to admit. She had grown too complacent, too busy with her own life. Not that this excused his behaviour in any way. But things had been let slide far enough.

And perhaps she was partly doing it for herself. To assure herself that she still had what it took to hold her husband.

The launch party had seemed a perfect opportunity to do a little re-launching of her own. It was in Kilkenny, where she and Peter had met, courted and married. She had come down yesterday and aired the family home. She had put fresh flowers in vases and a bottle of champagne in the fridge. They would open it later on, after Fiona had gone to bed. Tess didn't have any great expectations of what might happen, but perhaps they might start talking again – really talking, instead of the indifferent civility that had become the norm.

Maybe Helen had shaken him too. Certainly he was around more. He and Fiona were getting on better. There had been several unplanned family outings – nice, happy times that they had all enjoyed.

And there had been no other woman since. Tess knew this. The film was keeping him too busy in any event. But the coast was clear and she intended to keep it clear for as long as she could. It was worth a try.

"I didn't know Fiona was going to be here," Sheila said pointedly. "I'd have brought Regina otherwise."

This was exactly what Tess had been avoiding. "Fiona decided to come at the last minute," she lied.

The friendship between Fiona and Regina had cooled. Tess had seen to that. There would be no more news of Peter's affairs reaching Fiona's ears from the Burke quarter.

Peter was purposefully coming towards them now, resplendent in black-tie. He held two glasses of wine and he smiled directly at Tess – that old smile, sexy and slow. Tess felt a warm buzz inside, surprised at how pleased she felt. He had noticed her efforts. Excited, she left down her drink.

"If you'll excuse me, Sheila."

She hurried through the crowd towards Peter, confidence adding an unfamiliar bloom to her cheeks.

Before she reached him, he moved off to the left. He handed the glass of wine to a young, dark-haired woman in a red dress. He was captivated.

Without missing a step, Tess turned smoothly away and joined Eileen Burnstein and Neil Pasternak from Cinerama.

Jack Thornton's all-American smile could have lit up the entire banqueting hall by itself and saved John Graham the effort and expense of installing the floodlights he had hired from a football club in Dublin. Inside, Thornton was seething.

"Tell me again, Phyllis, honey. Exactly how many do you have on the shortlist now?"

Casting Director Phyllis Harding fixed him with her peculiar pale-blue eyes.

"Three," she said. "Honey."

Before Thornton could retaliate, Gabrielle sashayed up and laid a hand on his arm. He brightened. He had met her in Dublin the night he had dumped Shelley. Gabrielle was sweet and fun, nothing like Shelley who had turned out to be an out-of-work actress with an eye on the main chance.

She was also stacked. Thornton knew that half the men in the room were watching her and trying to control stiffening cocks. Let them, he thought smugly.

"You *promised* that you wouldn't talk shop tonight," Gabrielle purred. "Let's go pat the cows. They're so cute!"

Thornton smiled her indulgently. Sweet and fun she might be, but not too hot in the brains department. Still, she wasn't a gold-digger. Thornton had had a bad run of those lately.

He turned back to Phyllis. "Three shortlisted, you say. My, my." Sarcasm dripped from his tongue.

"So?" Phyllis said defiantly.

"So we start shooting in nine days' time. Nine frigging days! And we have no female lead!"

"It was your idea," Phyllis retorted loudly. "You try watching two thousand fucking videos!"

Thornton tried to still his nerves. It was all going dreadfully wrong – after such an auspicious start too.

John Graham had started the ball rolling immediately after suggesting the idea of a star search to Thornton, who had loved it. The competition was announced first on television and then in double-page colour spreads in almost all the publications. Thornton's personal favourite was a wonderfully inane piece in one of the tabloids: a stills photo of Marilyn Monroe was splashed under the caption *Could this be you*? A piece of purple prose informed readers that Hollywood was knocking on the door of every Irish girl, if only they would send a three-minute video of themselves to Casting Director Phyllis Harding, who would be delighted to view them. The new-born starlet would start a glorious career opposite Hollywood heart-throb Jason Blake.

Tacky, yes. Effective, most definitely. It had started an avalanche of publicity and the papers and TV had given it almost blanket coverage for days. In the weeks since the hunt was announced, over two thousand videos had arrived at the casting office.

But the bald facts were that while the videos had turned up hundreds of girls with great potential, not one of them was suitable for the role of Alison. It was reaching crisis point.

Thornton was more concerned about Cinerama. The launch party tonight was largely to impress Eileen Burnstein and Neil Pasternak, over there chatting with Tess Fisher. Not that they needed much convincing; they loved the script and they loved Thornton. It was pretty much in the bag that they were throwing fifty million dollars behind the project. But it would have been the icing on the cake had Thornton been able to produce the new female star tonight. After all his talk too.

"I told you," Phyllis couldn't resist saying. "You should have used an established actress."

How he loathed her. "We can't back down now," he said coldly. The entire country was waiting for the "discovery". It would have to be someone who had sent in a video. "I want a shortlist of ten girls by Monday, Phyllis."

"Monday? It's Saturday now, for God's sake, I can't – "

"You can. And you will. That's the final deadline."

Thornton slung an arm around Gabrielle and ostentatiously paraded her to the bar.

"Watch that cow – she's eating your handbag."

"Oh! Thanks."

Jean shushed away one of the demented-looking cows and turned back to Peter Fisher. She felt oddly shy.

"Everything signed, sealed and delivered script-wise?" Fisher enquired. The crowd surged forward to let the cow past and Fisher suddenly seemed to be on top of her.

"Yes, we exchanged contracts last Friday week," Jean managed.

Up close, she could see the five o'clock shadow bursting forth from his skin. She watched the tiny dimple in his chin, fascinated. His eyebrows were really quite luxuriant and the hair at his temples was showing the first signs of grey.

"Good." He nodded vigorously. "And how are the re-writes coming along?"

"With difficulty," Jean admitted. "Carl is very protective of his script. A perfectionist."

"Writers, eh? Worst in the world."

They smiled politely at each other. Jean shifted uncomfortably in the silence that fell. Surely now his duty was done; he had given her two minutes of his precious time and now he would run back to his own – the rich and famous who stood around in dresses and suits that probably cost more than The Jean Ormsby Agency's entire yearly turnover.

But he didn't move. He just kept half-smiling at her, looking as awkward as she felt. She took a long pull from her drink.

"I meant to ask you," he said eventually. "About the

role of Alison – have you anybody hopeful on your books at all?"

He knew full well that she hadn't. She'd already put forward her entire client list for every role going in the film. As it was, it looked like five would be cast in fairly substantial supporting roles. Fisher and Thornton were keeping to their part of the agreement – they got the script, and they also got some of Jean's clients whether they liked it or not.

"I heard that you were still looking," she said.

This was an understatement. All the agents in town were tearing their hair out trying to be the one who found the new star. To Jean's knowledge, there was not a single actress left in the country who had not submitted a video.

"I'm sure someone will turn up," Peter Fisher said, admirably playing down the crisis.

Another silence descended upon them. Jean looked at her glass, her shoes, the cows and back at Fisher. He looked at her at the same time. Jean's mouth suddenly went dry.

"Would you like another drink?" he asked.

Say no politely and walk away, Jean told herself. Somehow it seemed desperately important that she get away now, right this minute.

"Yes, please."

John Graham watched Carl Tallon's departure with a mixture of anger and relief.

Tallon had had a puss on him that would sour milk and had barely concealed his disdain for the party going on around him. Graham would have liked to put him straight on the fact that his little film would still be gathering dust under his lumpy mattress were it not for the efforts of Graham and others.

At least Roger Croft was making more of an effort. He had a natural charm and intelligence that shone once Graham had managed to rid him of the worst of his pomposity during two days of a crash-course in presentation and media skills. His crisp good looks were a definite bonus and Graham was glad to see that he had dispensed with that awful cashmere coat which made him look like a pimp.

Graham was pleased with his little find all right. Even more so now that the background check was almost done. Nothing had come up. It appeared that Roger Croft was squeaky clean.

The background check was curiously silent on Roger Croft's romantic life, except for a couple of girls who claimed to have dated him. But he did not appear to have a steady girlfriend and this worried Graham.

Graham watched now as Geraldine Day sidled up to Roger, all hungry eyes and thrusting chest. The woman was rampant and Graham was well aware of her shenanigans with younger men. Between them, she and Peter Fisher had given Graham many a sleepless night.

Roger was smiling back at Geraldine Day. Graham hoped to God that Roger Croft wasn't one for the women. The last thing he needed was a posse of ex-girlfriends crawling out the woodwork to tell tales to the media. Or, heaven forbid, to produce a love-child or two.

He would order another background check. In the meantime, he resolved to have a firm but vague chat with Roger about the relationship between the media and his private life.

Gabrielle had gone missing.

"You mean you've mislaid her?" Tess Fisher enquired politely.

Thornton was wary. Was she laughing at him? No. It was just his imagination, surely. But Tess Fisher disconcerted him. She gave him the impression that she could see right through him.

"So, how are you enjoying the countryside, Jack?" she asked, but he could see that she was giving him only half her attention and he was piqued. Her eyes seemed to be fixed on some distant point of the banqueting hall.

Thornton noticed for the first time how good she looked – a little old for his taste, of course, but she was pure class.

"I'm sure as hell enjoying the scenery," he replied with a lewd wink. Immediately he wanted to bite his tongue out as her smile slipped. It was so utterly the *wrong* thing to say to Tess Fisher.

"I've got a big mouth," he blurted.

"Yes, Jack. You have."

She turned on her heel and walked away. Thornton looked after her in admiration.

What in God's name was the old fart on about?

"The media, you see, are obliged to print whatever

they consider to be in the public interest," Graham was murmuring.

"Yes, yes," Roger said impatiently. What was his point? The man had a dreadful habit of waffling on, and was suffused with a sense of his own importance. But at least he had rescued him from that odious Geraldine Day. The woman had practically propositioned him.

What a pity Carl Tallon had dashed off. Roger had watched him surreptitiously from across the room. How he would have loved to have brought a smile to that sulky little mouth. Still, it was obvious that he didn't sing to Roger's tune. Those sorts never did, worse luck.

Peter Fisher had certainly found amusement, in the shape of that little morsel in the red dress who had been chatting to Carl earlier. It was possible that she was simply a business acquaintance. But there was something about Fisher's face that made Roger suspect that it went deeper. Either way, it was worth keeping an eye on.

"So we must be careful," Graham droned on. "Because we don't always see eye to eye on the issue of what exactly *is* in the public interest, and what is merely salacious."

"I understand perfectly," Roger said, anxious to get back to the party. He had never seen so many glamorous, important people in one room before; he was hobnobbing with the best of them and loving every minute of it.

"Well done on that TV piece on Thursday, by the way," Graham said.

"Yes, it was rather good, wasn't it?" Roger said arrogantly.

What a coup it had been – a two-minute interview at the end of the nine o'clock news. Graham had tipped the station off that Croft would be meeting Jason Blake off a plane in Dublin Airport. Blake was over for a weekend of costume-fittings and script meetings and, of course, the launch party. The piece was divine: the two of them on the tarmac, all windswept hair and chiselled good looks, smiling and buddy-buddy. A couple of words with Blake before he was whisked off by minders and then a lengthier piece with a clearly-enthusiastic Croft, "Like anybody else, I'm excited about the project coming to Kilkenny. It's a film that everybody in the city and county will be involved in, in some way."

Roger felt wonderful afterwards. He had been fantastic, he thought. And the bit about everyone's involvement had been inspired – almost as inclusive as Mary Robinson's "diaspora". Graham's office had received twenty-three fan letters for Croft, including two marriage proposals.

Rumour had it that opposition leader Frank Tavey was so sickened that he had refused to even RSVP to the invitation to tonight's launch party.

Croft's time in the sun was coming, he could feel it. And he was ready. As he looked around at Carol Taylor, Peter Fisher and Harry Burke, he wondered what any of them would do without him.

"So you'll mind what you say to them?"

Graham was still fussing like an old woman.

"Yes, yes, I won't discuss my private life," Roger assured him, before turning his back and rejoining the party.

Tess Fisher thought that the effort would kill her. But she kept nodding and smiling at people, as though it didn't matter at all that her husband was practically salivating over that Jean Ormsby woman. In front of all these people, how could he?

She had been an idealistic idiot. Had she really thought that a night in Kilkenny, and a little careful dressing on her part, could rekindle their marriage? That some magic would miraculously occur, that he would look at her in a new light? Fat chance.

But he didn't have to rub her nose in it with a woman ten years younger than her.

Her eyes searched the room for Fiona. Had she noticed too? But Fiona was deep in conversation with Roger Croft, oblivious.

"Tess?"

She looked up quickly with yet another manufactured smile. Jack Thornton was hovering nervously. "I'm sorry about that remark."

"That's perfectly all right, Jack."

Over his shoulder, she watched her husband laugh.

Thornton looked straight into her eyes. "It's just that you look pretty damned stunning tonight. That's all I meant to say."

Tess was amazed when two tears sprung to her eyes.

Never had she needed reassurance so badly. But she had not expected it to come from Jack Thornton.

"Tess?" He looked alarmed.

"Nothing, Jack." She smiled then, and it was genuine.

"That buffet looks good," Thornton said. He cleared his throat loudly. "You hungry?"

Tess hesitated. "Starving."

Thornton beamed. "You wait here. I'll be right back."

Peter knew damned well that if he didn't move away from Jean Ormsby soon, tongues would start to wag. He was shamefully ignoring the other guests but he simply didn't care.

She looked so good tonight in that red dress. And she had that ability to give you a hundred-and-ten-percent of her concentration; it was a curiously giddy feeling, as if you were the only man in the room.

He was glad that she had come on her own. The boyfriend who loomed so large in his imagination was nowhere to be seen. That didn't mean that he didn't exist, mind. But she hadn't mentioned him.

She hadn't said much at all, for that matter. Peter felt sure that he must be boring her rigid with his inane conversation. Normally, he had any number of glib topics to drag out at these social gatherings. Tonight, they all deserted him. He was content just to look at her.

He saw Tess across the room and was suddenly suffused with that familiar guilt. Here he was hanging over a woman young enough to be. . . well, young anyway, while his wife was over there on her own.

"I really should go and mingle," he said to Jean regretfully.

"Of course. So should I."

The atmosphere cooled immediately. Fool, he told himself, as she left quickly with a brisk nod. Immediately, she was surrounded by men, or so it seemed to him at any rate.

He joined Tess. "Enjoying the party?"

"Yes, thank you."

Her smile did not conceal the anger and disappointment in her eyes. She had noticed, of course. He felt sick.

"Just doing the duty rounds." The lie stuck in his throat. "We don't have to stay much longer – we'll drive back to Dublin and maybe have a late drink somewhere?"

He would make it up to her. He had behaved like a pig and he knew it.

Tess was as cool as ice. "I thought we might stay in Kilkenny. I've opened up the house."

He was confused. She hadn't mentioned this. "But I've that radio interview first thing in the morning. In RTE. Didn't I tell you?"

"No, Peter. You did not."

He felt even worse now. "I'm sorry. Come back with me."

Tess shook her head. "Someone has to stay and lock up the house again. And anyway, there's Fiona."

Half to alleviate his own guilt, he put an arm affectionately around her waist. "I really am sorry. But come on, let's get some of that food, enjoy ourselves.

And don't go on about your diet again – you're perfect and you know it."

To his relief, she smiled too – then he saw Jack Thornton bullying his way through the crowd towards them, holding aloft two plates of food.

"You're too late, Peter," she said, stepping out of his embrace and joining Thornton.

"Bloody hot in here, isn't it?" she said, downing her orange juice in one go. It was heavily laden with alcohol, Roger knew. He could smell it from here.

He hid a smile. She was trying so hard to be grown up. *Look at me, I'm drinking and swearing and chatting up men.* And she was only a child.

Still, who could blame her for rebelling when she had the misfortune to be the offspring of Peter Fisher? It must be sheer hell having *him* for a Daddy, Roger thought.

She looked like Fisher too. All long limbs and dark looks. Roger supposed that she could be described as extremely attractive. But when he looked at her, all he saw was Peter Fisher.

"I have to go talk to some people," he said dismissively. It was bad enough having to share the same air as Fisher tonight; he didn't have to entertain his tipsy teenage daughter too.

She recoiled. "Sure. Sorry," she mumbled, all bravado gone. "I only wanted to wish you good luck with the election."

She *fancied* him. It was written all over her. Roger was tickled pink – Peter Fisher's daughter hot for him.

What a kick. If he had been heterosexual, he would have given her a one-night stand, broken her heart and sent her crying back to Fisher. Oh well. Still, he couldn't resist winding her up a little all the same.

"That's very sweet of you." He was rewarded by the sight of her cheeks reddening.

"If there's anything I can do to help . . ." she said eagerly. "I'll be around a lot this summer."

"Is that so?" Roger said, bored again.

"Yeh. I'm working on the film. Dad's getting me a job with Jack Thornton."

Nothing like a little nepotism, Roger thought cynically. But she might be useful all the same.

"Good for you. By the way, who's that woman in the red dress?"

"Phyllis?" Gabrielle simpered.

"What?" Phyllis said rudely, eyeing up the shepherd tending the fire and wondering whether he was in the market for a little nooky.

"I want to try out for the part of Alison."

Phyllis Harding looked at the fluffy blonde and almost laughed. Almost.

"I didn't know you were an actress," she said as kindly as she could manage.

"Well, I'm not really," Gabrielle assured her. "I'm actually a model. But I'd love to get into acting."

"Fancy that," Phyllis said.

"So? What do you think?"

"I think you should go ask Jack, honey."

Gabrielle's pout turned mean. "I think he might take it the wrong way. He might think I was using him or something."

"Which you're not, of course," Phyllis clarified.

"Of course not! But I'd like to test for you, Phyllis."

Christ. This was all Phyllis needed. Thornton's bit of skirt after the part of Alison.

"Send in a video."

The journalist from one of the tabloids had her notebook out.

"It's a marvellous opportunity for Kilkenny, both economically and culturally," Roger said earnestly. "We're very proud to host this film."

The journalist looked around restlessly. Roger knew that he was losing her. Her notebook was probably stuffed with soundbites about the film, and from more important people than Roger. Unless Roger came up with something fresh, he would not be featured in the paper tomorrow, he knew.

"Cinerama are funding it, of course," he blurted.

Now he had her interest. "I thought nothing was official?"

It wasn't. But everyone knew anyway. It wouldn't hurt to feed her a little information.

"No, but I'm aware of the negotiations," he said importantly.

The journalist opened her notebook again. "How much?"

Roger hesitated. But faint heart never won fair

maiden, and it certainly never won any column inches. "Fifty million. Give or take a million."

Jean left at midnight. The crowd were milling around Jason Blake, who had just arrived on a stallion of all things, and her departure would not be noticed.

Not that her presence had been noticed much either, mind. Everyone was too busy checking out the players and working the room. She was glad to get away.

She adjusted the car seat in the Uno and caught sight of herself in the rear-view mirror. Lord. Her eyes were glittering like she was drunk, and her skin was vaguely flushed. It was the heat in the barn, she told herself quickly. It was nothing at all to do with Peter Fisher.

All right, she conceded; so he was an attractive man, and an extremely powerful one and he had paid her a lot of attention tonight. It was enough to turn any woman's head and she had momentarily given in to it.

She had been brought swiftly to her senses by the sight of his wife. Now she felt ashamed of her simpering behaviour. The man was married, for God's sake – a father, not to mention a political figure continually in the public eye. And a man who was a proven adulterer.

Jean slammed the gear-stick into neutral and stuck her key into the ignition. She had been very foolish tonight – stupid, even – to allow a bit of flattery to go to her head, and in front of a roomful of people, too. She simply had been too long without a boyfriend now, she reasoned fiercely. She had let herself down.

Well, no more. She would go back to Dublin and let them all get on with their film.

She had no reason to be in contact with Peter Fisher again and she told herself that she was glad.

The Uno wouldn't start.

"No . . ."

She tried again. The ancient engine lurched in pain and settled into a deathly silence.

She was stranded in the middle of Kilkenny with no means of escape.

She was working out exactly how much a taxi to Dublin would cost when there was a rap on the window. Of all the hundreds of people here tonight, it *would* have to be Peter Fisher.

Chapter Fourteen

Jean sat in the passenger seat of the Ministerial car with her back ramrod-straight, her knees clamped stiffly together and her hands bunched into fists. This was going to be the longest two hours of her life.

"I hope I'm not putting you out," she said.

Peter Fisher shot her a sideways glance as he negotiated his way out of the town. "I was going to Dublin tonight anyway. I have to be in RTE in the morning. They're doing a piece on the film."

Jean still tingled with mortification and cursed her Uno. It was going onto the scrap heap the minute she got it back to Dublin.

"Well, thanks for the lift." She sounded very ungracious.

"No problem." He seemed quite content to sit in silence for the next twenty minutes. Jean stared out the window at the rain as though it fascinated her.

"You wouldn't reach into the glove compartment, would you?" Fisher asked eventually, startling her.

"Um, sure." She fumbled with the clasp. What did

he want, some important Ministerial portfolio that he intended to scan while driving? A mobile phone to make an urgent call? The keys to the Dáil chambers?

"You should find a bag of peppermints," Fisher advised her. *Peppermints*? "I've indigestion," he added apologetically. "All that rich food, I'm afraid."

Jean found herself unwrapping a peppermint for him. It seemed a terribly intimate thing to do. She held it out, wondering whether he was going to take one hand off the steering wheel and come get it, or whether he expected her to reach over and pop it into his mouth.

He held his hand out for it. I'm going mad, she thought.

"Have one yourself," he said generously.

She did. This is truly surreal, she thought, as she and Fisher sped through the night noisily sucking peppermints.

"Do you find me amusing?" he enquired politely.

"Sorry?"

"It's just that you're smiling."

"No, no." Now she couldn't *stop* smiling.

He tried to look indignant. "I happen to suffer quite a lot from indigestion. It's all these functions, all that food."

"It's a hard life you have all the same," Jean said tartly, surprising herself. He laughed. Please God, she implored, don't let me start to *like* him as well as fancy him.

"*You* can talk," he said, bantering back. "I'm sure you're out to lunch every single day with some big client or other. And probably a film première every night."

Jean knew that he had seen her decrepit little office, was aware of how badly she needed the commission on this film, and that he was just being kind.

205

"It hasn't been easy," she said suddenly. She had meant to laugh lightly and make some harmless joke in response.

"Nothing worth having ever is," he said.

"This film . . . it's a break, you know?"

"I know." He glanced over at her. "How did you get into it, anyway? Casting?" He sounded genuinely interested.

"It all started with the Millie Mathew School," she confessed rather sheepishly.

"And who, pray tell, is Millie Mathew?"

"Oh, sorry – she ran a speech and drama school. I joined when I was five."

He laughed again.

"My mother's idea," Jean hastily added. "She was dying to get her daughter on the stage. Every Saturday morning from nine until twelve, down I'd go and sing and tap-dance with the rest of them. I hated every minute of it."

"Not much of a singer?"

"Not much of a tap-dancer either. And then the Christmas concert was coming up. I was cast as one of Santa's Elves. I had a solo number – I had to get up in front of the whole school, and all the parents, and sing 'Silent Night'."

"While tap-dancing?"

"I was supposed to mime wrapping Christmas gifts, actually," she corrected indignantly. Then she laughed, embarrassed. "This is all silly stuff, you don't want to hear it – "

"I do."

She saw that he was enjoying this. "There's no great drama," she said reluctantly. "I just forgot my lines. Imagine, to 'Silent Night'."

"No!" Was he teasing her? "In front of all the parents?"

"I didn't even get that far. It was the night of the dress-rehearsal."

"And Millie had a fit?"

The humiliation was as fresh now as if it had all happened yesterday instead of twenty-odd years ago. "Yes. She realised that I was incapable of doing it. There was consternation – because who would mime gift-wrapping at such short notice?"

"Whilst singing 'Silent Night'," he clarified. She shot him a look and thought she saw him grinning.

"Well, yes. And, of course, Anita would have been perfect. She had a lovely voice, you see, and she was marvellous at mime. So I went up to Millie and suggested her. And Anita did a brilliant job on the opening night. That was my first piece of successful casting," she finished rather proudly.

"Well done," he said.

It was the first time she had ever told anybody that ridiculous little story and was shocked at herself now. Silly and all as it was, she felt she had revealed some desperately intimate part of herself. Anxious to make up for lost ground, she turned to him.

"And what about you?" she said. "How did you get into politics?"

"Me? Oh, it all started at the Party Political Conference of 1960. I was five and I was required to entertain the esteemed councillors with a singing-and-mime routine . . ."

He *was* laughing at her.

"Sorry," he said. "I wish my beginnings had been as auspicious as yours. Mind you, I forgot my lines too the night of my first election. I was so sure I wouldn't win that I didn't prepare a victory speech. I was probably too nervous to have delivered it anyway."

It was odd to think of Peter Fisher on tenterhooks. Odd to think of him as anything other than the go-get-'em politician she saw on the TV at least once a week.

"But you did win," she said.

"I wonder how it would have turned out if I hadn't," he mused. "I miss working for myself, like you do."

"What did you do before you were elected?" Jean felt she should know this, but didn't.

"Architecture."

Of course. He had been a partner in a big Leinster firm, Jean couldn't remember the name of it.

"I still do some consultancy work when I can." He looked at her, as if to ensure that he wasn't boring her. "I design innovative stuff. It's not to everyone's taste. But change is good, don't you think?"

"I wouldn't mind a bit of stability every now and then," Jean said wryly, thinking of her ever-fluctuating bank balance. Unfortunately, it always seemed to fluctuate downwards.

"Sure. But it's better than getting stuck in a rut." He sounded a bit depressed. She had a feeling that he was talking about something other than architecture.

"No danger of that in the world of politics, surely?" she said, a little uneasy.

"Rat race," he said succinctly. "I'll put in another couple of years and then I'll see."

"Oh?" She was surprised. How could anyone in his position want to give it up?

"Mind you," he added with a laugh, "if Tess has anything to do with it, I'll be there until it's time to collect the pension."

The mention of his wife's name was like a dash of cold water. For an hour now, she had forgotten the woman's existence, had sat here swapping trite childhood memories with Peter Fisher as though they were on some kind of getting-to-know-you date. At least they hadn't got as far as enquiring how many brothers and sisters each had, and whether their parents were still alive. And they wouldn't either, she resolved.

"Terrible night," she said coolly, turning to look out the window again.

She sensed him looking at her for a long moment, and squirmed as she wondered whether he had deliberately dropped his wife's name into the conversation. Perhaps he had thought she was getting a little too cosy with him and had wanted to warn her off. But he had said it so casually.

And why not? she asked herself fiercely. Tess was the man's wife, for God's sake – it was usual for people to talk casually about their other halves.

"Terrible night," Fisher agreed eventually, frostily.

There were no more peppermints unwrapped, no

more chat about past or present lives. As the miles went by, Jean felt more and more awful, and entirely ridiculous to boot. He had given her a lift to Dublin out of the goodness of his heart, and probably expected a little light conversation to pass the journey; a little civil chat, for Pete's sake. And she had turned around and acted paranoid at the innocent mention of his wife. Oh *God*. He must know now how attracted she was to him – why else would she have reacted in such a fashion? He was probably thinking that she was yet another woman who fancied him and was insanely jealous of his wife.

By the time they got to the outskirts of Dublin, Jean almost had lockjaw, her muscles were so tight.

"You can drop me here," she said quietly. "Thank you very much."

"Don't be ridiculous. Where do you live?"

"I can get a taxi."

"It's two o'clock in the morning and I am not dropping you in Clondalkin. Now do you want to tell me where you live?" He sounded very irritated.

"Castleknock," she muttered, wishing with every bone of her body that this awful journey was over. And now here she was, dragging him miles out of his way. She stole a glance at him; he looked tired and fed up, and she felt even worse.

The car screeched over to the left as he swung it onto the M50. Soon she found herself giving halting directions to her cottage.

"It's the next left," she said, sounding as miserable as she felt.

He pulled the car into her tiny driveway and kept the engine running. With one hand on the door-handle for a mercifully quick escape, she turned briefly to him.

"Thanks. I appreciate the lift," she said formally.

"You're welcome," he said, adding pointedly, "even if it was a bit of a trial to you."

Jean's stomach lurched. "I'm sorry," she said, not knowing quite what she was apologising for.

"I'm sorry too," he said. "In case you thought . . ."

"I didn't think anything," Jean said quickly.

"Oh, me neither," he hastily returned.

"I was just enjoying. . ."

"So was I."

"Indeed."

"Absolutely."

Neither of them had a clue what the other was talking about. Somehow it didn't seem to matter. The hostility lifted like a straggly cloud and Jean felt light again. He wasn't angry with her any more.

"I'd better go," she said.

"I suppose you'd better."

"Good luck in the morning."

"With what?"

"The RTE thing."

"Oh, yes. You too."

"With what?"

"Um, I don't know. Things?"

They were doing it again – filling the air with mindless words which fogged up the windscreen and enclosed them in a tiny, steamy space.

211

All they needed now was the radio playing *Who's Gonna Drive You Home*, Jean thought fuzzily as Fisher leaned over and kissed her, as if it were the most natural thing in the world for him to do. And it did feel right. He had given her ample opportunity to escape and she had not done so; instead, she threw herself wholeheartedly into it because it was beyond her to resist.

She would think of some wonderful analogy for the experience later – kissing him was like licking ice-cream, or some such delightful rubbish. Right now, she didn't bother with any brain exertion at all. She simply enjoyed every tingle and ripple and the gorgeous taste and feel and smell of him.

"I'm terribly sorry," he said against her mouth. "After all I said."

"But you didn't say anything," she reminded him.

"You didn't either."

She fully expected him to kiss her again. He didn't. He took her face in his warm, broad hands and just looked at her, stroking her cheeks softly with his thumbs. The gesture was so intimate that for a moment she felt shaken. He was looking at her like . . . well, like she *meant* something to him, and she couldn't handle it. The kisses, yeh, fine. But this was something else.

She did not know what to do or say. He didn't seem to either, and she was glad. She tried to banish the tiny voice in the back of her head that said that Peter Fisher must have done this kind of thing a million times before with the various Helens of this world; that he had all the right words. She dreaded hearing some pat line now about how beautiful she was, and was she not inviting him in for coffee?

The wind was taken from her sails when he abruptly pulled away from her. "I'd better go."

She looked at him, confused – and followed his gaze to her living-room window.

A light shone from it.

Peter sat stiffly beside her. Obviously, he thought that she had company. He would not meet her eyes.

"There's someone in there," she said. At his look, she clarified, "I mean, a stranger. I didn't leave any light on."

The tension went from his face. "Are you sure?"

"Of course I'm sure."

It must be a break-in. Thank God she hadn't actually been in there when they came.

"Now, relax." Peter sounded very in control and she was grateful. Her own nerves were in tatters. "Let's just see what's going on."

They got out of the car quietly and crept to the front door.

"What will we do, knock?" Jean said, finding her own suggestion ridiculous. It was her home, for heaven's sake.

Fisher took the keys from her cold fingers and opened the door silently. "Wait here, I'll go in."

Jean was over her initial fright; anger had replaced it. How dare somebody come barging into her house like that! And while she was thankful for Peter's presence, she didn't need him behaving like Indiana Jones while she trailed helplessly behind him.

She pushed past him and into her hallway, her face white with indignation.

"Jean, wait – "

He was fast on her heels as she hurled open the living-room door. A man lounged on the sofa with his back to her, watching late-night TV, the remains of a curry on the coffee table. Robbers these days really look after themselves, Jean thought savagely, and alighted on him.

"What the *hell* are you doing in my house?"

The man looked around, startled. A huge smile spread across his face.

"Hiya, love."

It was Ian. Jean noted in a detached way that he looked clean and sober, was shaved and had on smart clothes. He looked absolutely terrific. And he was the last person on earth she wanted to see right now.

"I thought you weren't going to come home at all," he said, jumping up and kissing her familiarly on the cheek. "I had a meal made and all."

It was as if he had every right to be there; as if he still lived there. He must have kept a spare set of keys.

"Ian . . ." Jean began, nonplussed. She looked at Peter. He seemed relaxed and calm. His eyes told a different story.

Ian finally copped that Jean was not alone. His Colgate smile slipped as he took in Peter. He looked slowly back at Jean with a hurt air. Jean realised that he was behaving like a duped husband and she wanted to hit him.

Peter, of course, didn't miss a thing. "Glad that you

214

know the intruder," he said to Jean, jangling his car keys loudly. "I'll say goodnight."

"Who was he?" Ian demanded as Peter left the room.

"Shut up! Just shut up, Ian!" Jean hissed and ran after Peter.

She caught him at the door.

"Peter."

"Yes?"

"He's . . . I'm sorry."

"For what?" He wore an infuriatingly pleasant smile.

Jean shrugged. She had nothing else to say. "Thanks for the lift."

"No problem."

He gave her a look then, as though she had sickened and disappointed him.

Jean felt a flash of annoyance. *She* wasn't the one who was married – Ian wasn't even her boyfriend. And she and Fisher weren't even . . . well, they weren't *anything* to each other! So what was with the jealous-boyfriend routine?

She did not wait for him to get safely to his car before closing the door. And then she went back in to Ian.

Chapter Fifteen

Phyllis Harding was in a foul mood. Her ulcer was kicking up again and she had heartburn like you wouldn't believe.

"Stop," she grunted.

Either Kieran didn't hear her or he didn't care.

"For Chrissake, I said stop! She's hopeless!"

The video playing on the widescreen TV in front of Phyllis ground mercifully to a halt. Her assistant looked at her submissively as he ejected the video and put in the next. Phyllis tried not to look at the pile on the floor waiting to be viewed.

"Well! Who's this one?"

"Marie Devlin," Kieran whispered.

"Experience?"

"Um, none."

"Christ. Well, go on, play it!"

Marie Devlin got exactly five seconds of fame.

"Stop!"

The video went into the reject-bin and Kieran

fumbled for the next. Phyllis knew that she could not watch one more talentless fool cavorting around on a home-video without a very strong coffee.

"Gimme five minutes," she bellowed. "Oh, and get me two aspirin, would you, sweetie?"

She lumbered from the room and down the corridor to the toilet, her bladder bursting with the dregs of at least a gallon of caffeine consumed already today.

As she sat on the loo, she automatically checked her pulse, carefully timing it against her watch. On top of the ulcer and the heartburn, she had high blood pressure and threatened diabetes, the result of twenty years of too much nicotine, too many vodkas and tonics, and too little sleep.

"You cannot burn the candle at both ends," her Blackrock consultant had told her sternly only last week. "You are slowly killing yourself."

She paid the little shit two thousand pounds a year and all he could give her was bad news? And a guilt-trip about the couple of drinks a night she allowed herself, and the odd cigarette or two? Then he had refused to prescribe the little while pills that she needed to relax. To function, dammit!

It was all Jack Thornton's fault, of course. At the very thought of him, Phyllis's pulse skipped angrily and speeded up. Then it stopped entirely. Mother of God, was she having a heart attack?

She sat paralysed on the loo and then, thankfully, her pulse kicked in again. She was still alive. Although whether that was something to be thankful for was a matter for debate.

She hitched up her knickers and stumbled from the cubicle. Her face was a mess staring back at her from the mirror. A quick repair job was executed with shaking hands. She needed another bloody face-lift too; this one was falling out very unevenly – the right eyebrow was at least a quarter of an inch lower than the left, making her look as though she were scowling ferociously all the time.

Anyhow. She digressed. The real problem, of course, was Jack Thornton.

"And Scarlett O'Fucking Hara," she said murderously, smearing lipstick on haphazardly.

Where he had got the idea was beyond her. It was typical LA bullshit and fantasy, the entire thing. She hadn't got to where she was today, which was the number one Casting Director in these islands, without recognising a bullshit idea when she saw one. She'd told him that, of course, in the plainest terms she knew. "It's a fucking bullshit idea," in fact were her very words. But he'd just laughed; treated her like she was some idiot who wouldn't know a good actress from a crater in the ground.

Well, she'd cast some of the very best movies in Britain, and in the States too. She'd worked with adults, kids, foreigners, dwarfs, every animal species known to mankind – she'd even done a film about aliens and two with cartoon characters. She'd cast horror, drama, comedy, westerns and a porn movie once when the times had been lean. She'd auditioned the male lead personally on that one, an old war story that always brought a smile to her face.

But not today. No sirree. Heads were going to roll

today. And hers would be the first on the chopping-block.

"By Monday," he'd said. A shortlist of ten. Just like that! Did the idiot realise how *long* it all took? The sheer manpower? And she couldn't delegate. This was one she would have to do all by herself – as well as casting the rest of the film. When she'd mentioned this to him, he'd winked.

"I have every confidence in you, Philly."

How dare he call her Philly. She had added an extra five grand to her fee just for the insult. And she'd add more too, before this fiasco was over. By God, he would pay through the nose for putting her through this.

She'd complained to Peter Fisher. But Thornton had done a job on him too.

"Why not? Think *The Commitments*, Phyllis. Think *Gone With The Wind*."

"Think the money," Phyllis had butted in. It was time to get her fees straight right away.

"We'll take care of that," Fisher had said smoothly. "Besides, we'll make it back at the box office. This kind of publicity is worth millions."

"And you lot sure could do with the publicity," she'd said sarcastically. She read the papers like everyone else. She knew who Bill Mackey was, for heaven's sake. Fisher couldn't pull the wool over *her* eyes.

"You're very insightful, Phyllis," Fisher had said. It was only after she'd hung up that she'd realised that he had been making fun of her.

Her hand shook with the injustice of it all, her

blusher now two red gashes down her fat cheeks. Oh, they'd get their moment in the sun for this stunt, the lot of them. But it would be a different story when they got the poor unknown cow who had probably never acted in her life before onto the set on that very first day.

Phyllis had seen it all before: the stage fright, the sudden discovery that the girl couldn't act at all, the fury of the frustrated cast and crew and, most unforgivable of all, the disastrous rushes which would only highlight the costly mistake that had been made at the casting stage. But it was too late then. Phyllis as a rule never said "I told you so", but she always made a point of saying it loudly and rudely when those first rushes came in.

Phyllis fumbled in her handbag and unearthed her vial of white pills. Little did her consultant in Blackrock know that he was not the only one. Phyllis had been seeing two others behind his back for the past year. He had no idea. Phyllis tossed two pills to the back of her throat and swallowed them dry. Men were such fools.

As she waited for the pills to do their thing, she tried to quell her feelings of doom. She had her shortlist of ten all right, but could she honestly say that even one of them was a serious contender?

It wasn't for the lack of trying. Since the launch party on Saturday night, Phyllis had been closeted away in her office with her video-player and Kieran. They had mowed through hundreds of tapes. Not a single one had gone unviewed.

Oh, how they had nearly made Phyllis *cry*. With each clip of a sniggering, pubescent girl, her heart grew heavier, her ulcer got worse and her heartburn rose. Over a bottle of vodka with Kieran at midnight last night, watching a clip of a redhead murdering *Romeo & Juliet* and being prompted by her doting father, she actually *had* cried. She'd laid her head on Kieran's shoulder and had bawled. He had cried too. Then she'd torn off his trousers and had her way with him. Afterward, they'd shared four lines of coke which Phyllis carefully laid out on the video of the redhead.

She smoothed down her too-short skirt over her too-fat thighs and hobbled back to her office. It took longer each time for the damned pills to work.

Kieran was waiting for her eagerly.

"What are you gawking at?" she snarled as she fell into her chair. "Next!"

Kieran was unperturbed. He'd been with her for five years now and only stayed for the abuse, weirdo that he was. Phyllis couldn't get him to do anything at all on a Monday morning without a good tongue-lashing and maybe a crack or two of her fist.

The video-screen flickered to life.

Kieran briefly consulted the video-box. "This one is Cathy Conroy."

"Never heard of her," Phyllis sniffed. That was nothing new.

"It's a full-length video," Kieran said, examining it.

"Are these people stupid?" Phyllis groaned. "*Three* minutes. That's all we want!"

"And it says here she's got an agent," Kieran added. "Jean Ormsby."

Phyllis sat up a little straighter. So, another of Jean Ormsby's little protégés. Jean Ormsby was already a big thorn in Phyllis's side. Not only did she represent the script, but she had some kind of deal going with Fisher and Thornton whereby her people automatically got parts in the movie. The movie that *she*, Phyllis Harding, was casting. It was outrageous. Normally, Phyllis wouldn't have stood for it. But Fisher and Thornton had been firm. Well, it was time for a little revenge on Jean Ormsby.

"Next," she said to Kieran.

"But I haven't started the video yet – "

"I don't think she'll be suitable," Phyllis said with relish. "Throw it in the reject-bin."

She felt better now. That would show Jean Ormsby who was boss. And to look at her at that launch party on Saturday, you'd think butter wouldn't melt in her mouth. All the time, she had Thornton and Fisher wrapped around her little finger. She was probably sleeping with both of them. How else did a nobody like her have such clout?

And so the video of Cathy Conroy was thrown, unviewed, into the large cardboard box that contained the rejects.

By the time Jack Thornton, Peter Fisher and Declan Mahoney arrived, the chemicals were working and Phyllis was in control. On top of things. *There*. Let Thornton just try and mess with her head today.

"Gentlemen," she said crisply, shaking hands all around. "I've got ten videos for you to view, as promised. I'm sure we'll find the star of the film amongst them."

"We're lucky we *have* a film at all," Thornton muttered darkly, shooting a black look at Peter Fisher.

Phyllis was lost. "Is there some problem?"

Peter Fisher brushed her off. "No problem at all, Phyllis."

"Except that certain people can't keep their fat mouths shut," Thornton growled. "Especially when talking to the press."

Phyllis felt her paranoia grow. "I haven't said anything to anybody! About anything!"

"Let's get on with watching the videos," Declan Mahoney said with a sigh.

Phyllis waved a hand towards the back of the room. "Hit the lights, Kieran. And get coffee for everyone."

"Mineral water," Thornton corrected rudely.

Phyllis's blood pressure began a slow and steady rise again. Goddamn that man. As the room went dark, she scrabbled in her handbag for her precious vial of pills.

When Kieran put the lights on again, there was a deathly silence in the room. Phyllis looked at her shoes in apparent unconcern.

"I thought number four was quite good," she said forcefully.

"She couldn't act," Thornton said stonily.

"She looked right for the part," Phyllis shot back.

"Jesus Christ Almighty! She has to carry the whole frigging film and you chose her because she *looked good*?"

Peter Fisher held his hands up in an attempt to halt certain bloodshed. "Let's go through them in sequence, okay?"

"Fine," Phyllis snapped. "Number one."

"Crap." That was Thornton.

"Not bad." Fisher.

"Not good," Declan Mahoney said flatly.

"Number two!" Phyllis shouted, furious.

"Crap." Thornton again.

"Not bad." Fisher.

"Not good." Mahoney.

And so on and so forth, right down to number ten.

"You think they're all crap," Phyllis said accusingly to Thornton.

"They are not all crap. But not one of them is right for Alison."

Nobody disagreed with him. Phyllis was on the verge of tears. "These are the best! I've watched them all, believe me! And if you think you can do better, then good luck to you!"

"I sure as hell couldn't do any worse than you!" Thornton paced the room now, eyes wild. "We're shooting in seven fucking days!"

"You don't like any of them because you want your girlfriend to get the part." Phyllis immediately wished she hadn't spoken as Thornton's face went black. Fisher and Mahoney looked appalled.

"I beg your pardon?" Thornton hissed.

Phyllis had no choice but to go on. "She asked me on Saturday if she could test."

Thornton leaned in very close to Phyllis. She felt mildly afraid. "Gabrielle is not testing for the part. Now stop trying to deflect attention from your own pathetic performance."

Phyllis was speechless. Words eluded her even when Thornton roughly pushed past her and began rummaging through the piles of videos.

"We're going to start watching these all over again."

"What?" Phyllis was outraged.

Fisher once again stepped in, that sneaky, diplomatic son of a bitch. "Perhaps it's a good idea."

"But those are the rejects! They're hopeless!"

Thornton ignored her, dumping an armful of videos onto the conference table. Everything was going out of control on Phyllis. She had to get it back, and fast.

"Fine," she said graciously, allowing a patronising smile to cross her face. "If that's what all you good gentlemen want. I think you'll find it's a waste of time, however."

She had the satisfaction of watching Fisher and Mahoney exchange doubtful glances as they sat through footage of Marie Devlin, Gemma Murphy and Orla O'Riordan. After a while, nobody bothered to read the names on the video-boxes any more, and a numb look crept over their faces. Phyllis was now smiling widely. Ha! Maybe now they had some appreciation of her skills as a casting director, maybe now –

"Your services are not needed any more."

"My services were never yours to begin with, sir."

Phyllis froze. Those were lines from the script. From

Outsiders. She could recite the damned thing backwards in her sleep.

She abruptly transferred her gaze from her fingernails to the television screen. The hairs rose on the back of her fat neck. Bloody hell, who was *she*?

The video was of poor quality, shot in what looked to Phyllis to be a darkened theatre. The girl on the stage was scarcely in her twenties, dressed in servant's garb. She was lean and lanky, with a peculiarly gamine face and spiky brown hair. Slowly and jerkily, the camera zoomed in on the stage, and as the girl turned towards it, her liquid brown eyes literally grabbed you and sucked you in. She said nothing at all; her very stillness was transfixing.

She held the screen, *devoured* the screen, for perhaps an entire minute without uttering a syllable. Then, as the actor playing Richard came into grainy view, she picked up her skirts and walked rapidly away. He caught her arm.

"Alison – "

"Let me go."

"Not like this."

"Alison."

Then a most remarkable thing happened; she turned to Richard and her entire face, body, her *being*, radiated the most intense emotion of desire, so strong that it seemed to waft off the video-screen and wash over the darkened room like a scorching breeze.

"Richard. What we are going to do?"

Thornton froze the frame; the girl was captured in that luminous pose.

"Good God," he whispered.

"That's the play," Phyllis said, stunned. "A video of the original play."

Declan Mahoney was unable to look away from the screen. "Who is she, Phyllis, for God's sake?"

Fisher stared hard at the girl. "I've seen her somewhere before . . ."

Phyllis scrabbled about on the table for the video-box, her throat tight. She had never seen the girl before in her life. *How could she have missed this video?*

"She's. . ." Oh hell. The video-box was nowhere to be found.

Fisher spoke again. "She's Jean Ormsby's secretary."

"What?" Phyllis was now green. Surely this wasn't the video she had ordered Kieran to throw into the reject-bin?

"Her name – it's Cathy," Fisher went on. "It was on her computer."

"Cathy Conroy," Phyllis supplied dully, having found the video-box.

"It doesn't matter what her real name is," Thornton said, before announcing simply, "She's Alison."

Phyllis made a desperate attempt to cover her back. "She's not sexy enough, she's too tall, too angular . . . Jesus, she looks like a boy!"

"So? I found her attractive," Peter Fisher said.

Any woman with a heartbeat was attractive to *him*, Phyllis viciously thought. But it seemed that Declan Mahoney felt the same.

"She's different. Unusual."

Jack Thornton put an end to the matter. "She's the most interesting-looking woman to step in front of a camera in years. Any idiot can see that. Except you, Phyllis, it seems. Why wasn't she shortlisted?"

"I. . . I must have missed that video," Phyllis choked. She looked at Thornton timidly. "Will I get her to screen-test?"

"Fuck screen-testing," Thornton said curtly. "You just find her and find her fast."

Phyllis burned with humiliation as she left the room. Thornton would no doubt tell this pretty tale to half of LA; how Phyllis Harding was unable to recognise talent even when it came up and bit her size-eighteen ass. Her little act of vengeance against Jean Ormsby would cost her dearly in terms of future work; she saw her pink retirement villa on the Costa del Sol slowly go down the tubes.

She barely made it to the loo before she threw up – a putrid mixture of coffee, pills and malevolence. Cathy Conroy, whoever she was, would pay dearly for this one, Phyllis would see to that.

Chapter Sixteen

Carol Taylor barely had time to take off her coat on Tuesday morning after a brief break in the West when Peter Fisher burst into her office.

"Well? Have you spoken to him?"

"I haven't had a chance, Peter."

"We're going to have to do something to stop him."

"Why don't we all have some coffee?"

Peter belatedly realised that she was not alone. Geraldine Day was curled up like a spiteful cat in a chair by the wall. She was flanked by Harry Burke and John Graham. Peter nodded curtly at them.

"We'll talk about it later," he told Carol.

Geraldine Day snorted. "For God's sake, Peter. Surely you can discuss Government business in front of your own cabinet." She paused meaningfully. "Unless, of course, it's personal."

Peter had no doubt that she knew of his midnight run up the country with Jean Ormsby last Saturday night.

"Who could hope to have a personal life around here, Geraldine," he said viciously.

She was taken aback by his tone and wisely shut up.

"So?" Harry Burke boomed. "What's up, Peter?"

"You know bloody well what's up, Harry," Peter snapped. "You *do* try and keep up with the newspapers, I hope?"

"Of course I do," he blustered, looking to his left and right for help, hoping to God that Peter wouldn't put him on the spot.

"Well, then you know what Roger Croft did," Peter added sarcastically.

"Let's calm down here," Carol interjected.

Carol wasn't half as het up about this as Peter had expected. Perhaps three days in Connemara had softened her brain. Too much Guinness and oysters, he thought sourly. As for himself, he had been simmering since he opened the newspapers on Sunday morning.

"He's a liability," he said forcefully.

Carol Taylor looked a little impatient. "Aren't you exaggerating, Peter?"

"Exaggerating? Roger Croft nearly blew the whole deal! A fifty-million-dollar movie and he almost ruined it single-handed!"

"Well, he didn't, did he?" Carol replied. "Cinerama came on board in the end."

Peter leaned both hands on her desk and eyeballed her. "Only after Thornton and I got down on our hands and knees and grovelled! And this was after I'd grovelled to Thornton, to keep *him* from walking!"

230

Geraldine Day piped up again. "Croft is young and inexperienced, that's all."

Peter turned on her. "He knew that no announcement of Cinerama's backing was due to be made until Monday morning. We had a press conference organised, for Jesus' sake! And he goes and shoots his mouth off at the launch party – the next thing we know, Cinerama are reading of their involvement over Sunday brunch!"

Peter knew he sounded dangerously angry and he did not care.

"I've already had a word with him," John Graham said quickly. This looked bad for him. His boy had fucked up big-time.

Peter ignored him. "It goes farther than the film, Carol."

"What, has he done something else?"

"No," Peter said flatly. "But it's only a matter of time. And he could really burn us."

Carol still was not taking this seriously, he could see that.

"It was only a newspaper article, Peter," Harry said, trying to be the voice of reason.

Peter could already smell the bourbon off him. It was not yet eleven o'clock.

"He's allowed one mistake," Geraldine chimed in.

Peter crossed his arms over his chest and looked around at them all slowly. "You don't know him. Not like I do. I've been around him for the past two months. And it's not just youth and inexperience." They watched him silently. "He's egotistical and arrogant. He is not a team-player in any sense of the word. He will do anything to get himself elected and, frankly, that worries me."

Carol Taylor was at last concerned. "Apart from the leak to the papers, has he stepped seriously out of line?"

"Well, no."

"Done or said anything to damage the party?" Geraldine shot.

Peter wanted to kill her. "No," he ground out. He had only his own gut-feeling that Croft was a time bomb. Just as his gut-feeling told him that it was Croft who was going through his private files in his constituency office in Kilkenny. "Again, I will say that it's only a matter of time."

"Based on what, exactly?" John Graham asked curtly.

"Well, Peter?" Carol wanted to know too. But she wasn't being sceptical. She was simply weighing up the facts.

"Based on his track record, for example. We have a candidate who stole funds while he was in college."

"There is no proof whatsoever of that," Graham said decisively.

"I know that you've no *proof*, John."

Graham didn't like this. But Peter knew that, like himself, Carol suspected the story was true.

"Do we really want a deputy we cannot trust?" he asked quietly.

Carol was very still. "What do you suggest we do?"

She wouldn't like this, none of them would. "Get rid of him."

Geraldine Day's pop-eyes rolled. "Are you mad?"

"Not that I'm aware of."

"Come on, Peter," Harry Burke rumbled. "We're nearly halfway into the campaign."

"We can find someone else," Peter said adamantly. "I'll hand-pick him myself, I'll push him all the way, we can still do it. . ." He trailed off as he caught quick glances flying back and forth across the room. None of them were in the slightest bit interested, he realised. Croft could dance a jig naked for the political correspondents in Leinster House and they would not be all that concerned.

"What's going on?" he asked.

Geraldine Day smiled smugly. "Carol's had a chat with Andy Walshe over the weekend."

Carol Taylor's head whipped around. "Thank you, Geraldine. When I want a mouthpiece, I'll ask."

Geraldine sat back in her chair, chastened.

Carol looked at Peter. "I came back by Galway yesterday. To see how the land might lie with Andy Walshe."

Peter was stung. He hadn't known about any such scheduled meeting with Walshe, Independent TD for Galway.

"It was very casual, Peter. But I think we can count on his support."

"And what did you have to offer to sweeten him up? Half of next year's budget-surplus for the good people of Galway?" Peter smiled without any humour.

"Hardly. But there has to be some give and take," Carol returned sharply.

Peter would bet that Andy Walshe had asked for a lot in return for voting with the Government should Roger Croft fail to get elected. He had never liked the man. Backbone was not one of his strongest attributes.

"So we've covered our asses and we can all let Roger Croft run wild and free," he said loudly.

John Graham looked testy. "Despite what you think, he's doing very well, Peter."

"And how would you know?"

Graham fixed Peter with his flat grey eyes. "We've had our own poll done. Roger Croft has almost twenty-five percent of number-one votes in Kilkenny."

Peter was floored. He knew Croft was not doing badly on the ground, but this was a surprise. "I see."

"He's exceeding all expectations," Harry Burke said proudly, as though Croft were his discovery.

"So, you're worrying about nothing," Geraldine finished archly.

Peter buttoned his jacket. There was nothing left to discuss.

"You'll speak to him about the press leak," he threw at Carol. He was so annoyed with her that he could not look at her. She had not told him about the poll either.

"I'll tear strips off him," Carol promised, but Peter knew it was only a sap.

"Maybe you'd also speak to Thornton. He's very upset. Entirely understandable, I would say."

He had ruffled her feathers now. "Indeed," she said coldly, "given that Croft stole his thunder. And maybe yours, Peter?"

He never drank at lunch-time but it took a scotch in Fitzers restaurant on Dawson Street to calm him down. Carol – all of them – obviously thought he was blowing the whole thing out of proportion. They were so full of their victory with Andy Walshe that they couldn't smell what was under their noses. Ordering a second scotch, Peter conceded reluctantly that perhaps he *had* overreacted a little, but he still stood by his instinct that Roger Croft was bad news. There was something about him that set Peter's senses on red alert; some innate coldness, a lack of empathy with other people. He was the kind of man you would not turn your back on if you had any sense.

Peter was stuck with him now, Carol had made that much clear. All he could hope to do was monitor him as closely as possible. As soon as the election was over, he could wash his hands of him.

He felt tired and disillusioned, as he had increasingly of late. He was fed up of being manoeuvred into position every time he turned around; sick of the politicking and the diplomacy he was forced to resort to in order to keep Thornton, Carol, Cinerama, Geraldine Bloody Day and everybody else happy.

He sipped the scotch slowly. It was turning into a long week. The days were crawling by in agonising indecision over whether or not to contact Jean Ormsby. He could think of a million reasons not to: he was married, she practically was by the looks of that live-in boyfriend of hers, it was only a kiss at the end of the day, there had been a full moon of all things, et cetera, et cetera.

There was only one reason for: he wanted to so badly that he couldn't sleep at night.

But he had resisted the impulse. As the days passed, he knew he would continue to do so. He had started enough affairs in the past knowing full well that they were interludes. But Jean Orsmby was different. If he contacted her, he knew that he would be in over his head. If he wasn't already.

Anyway, for all he knew, the need was all on his side. She certainly had made no attempt to seek him out. And why should she, when she had that blond Adonis stashed at home?

He looked out the window, feeling every day of his age. He could see Tess approaching, immaculately turned out as ever. She was bang on time, knowing that he had to be back in Leinster House for a meeting at two. He knew that she would have his reading glasses, which he had forgotten this morning, in her bag for him, and that it was she who had made sure they got a window table for lunch, in the no-smoking section that Peter preferred. Little things. Wifely things.

The scotch suddenly tasted foul. What had she ever done to deserve being cheated on? Except remain steadfast and loyal throughout? Her reward was to watch her husband flirting publicly with another woman at a party before driving off into the night with her.

Any other woman would have had a fit. But Tess, strangely, had not said a word. It made Peter slightly nervous. Was it possible that she hadn't noticed? Either way, she deserved a hell of a lot more respect than he had been showing her of late.

With renewed determination, Peter banished Jean Orsmby from his head and rose to his feet as Tess entered, pulling out her chair with a flourish and a smile.

He was riddled with guilt. It was written all over him, from the stoop of his shoulders and his over-solicitousness to the way he admired her appearance.

"You look fantastic, Tess."

"Thank you, Peter."

She wondered whether men genuinely didn't realise how transparent they were, or whether they simply did not care. His praise was akin to other men buying their spouses expensive and unexpected gifts; both usually stemmed from their own unbearable sense of guilt. As if being nicer to their poor, cuckolded wives would somehow make their actions okay.

Tess was an old hand at recognising the signs. It was the same every time he embarked upon, or was contemplating embarking upon, a new affair.

She did not know whether he'd slept with Jean Ormsby on Saturday night. The woman had been seen getting into his car, that was all. But along with his brazen attention to her all night at the party, it was proof enough. Tess had gone home alone and thrown her new dress into the bin.

Peter was looking at her anxiously. "Are you okay?"

Tess wanted to slap his good-looking face, tell him to

pack his bags and that he would be hearing from her solicitor – a not entirely unreasonable response given the circumstances. Instead she smiled.

"Fine."

He looked at her for a long moment, as if waiting for something more. Tess half-smiled; where, he was wondering, were the subtle recriminations for making a fool of her in public on Saturday night? Where were the veiled barbs, the looks of disgust and hurt that usually marked her discovery of a new affair?

Instead, he was confronted with a remarkably benign woman, a smiling Stepford Wife who had not uttered a single cross word since the launch party. He was wondering whether he'd got away with it, or whether she was making him wait for his punishment.

His nerves must be in shreds. It she hadn't been so hurt, she would have found his predicament amusing. She wondered why she hadn't copped before now that, with Peter, she didn't need to exert herself to punish him. A man like him, whose sense of morality was as strong as his sexual appetite, would do it all by himself. She simply had to smile and make him hate himself even more for betraying such a damned nice woman.

Tess suddenly felt jaded, as if she and Peter were dancing the same macabre dance over and over again. And she did not have the courage to stop the music.

She watched him now as he squinted myopically at the wine list; a slightly-greying man with a lean, weathered face, shorter in real life than he seemed on TV. Still shockingly good-looking, of course, but the familiarity of sixteen years of marriage had naturally reduced her appreciation of that. It seemed impossible to her now that she had ever experienced passion with this man; that they had ever drunk each other in the way new lovers do. Had she ever really lost her appetite in anticipation of a date with him, or breathlessly analysed his every word with her friend Kathy afterwards?

"Peter?" she said abruptly.

He looked up, wary.

"Do you remember when we got engaged? And you insisted on coming around to ask my father's permission?"

"Yes," he said slowly, looking at her as though she had lost her marbles.

"And you were so nervous that you asked for his hand in marriage instead?" She was eager now, smiling. "And he thought you were making fun of him."

They had laughed themselves almost sick in Peter's Ford Cortina afterwards, huddled together for warmth.

"Do you not remember, Peter?"

It suddenly seemed desperately important to her to establish that there had once been something meaningful between them, even if it had only been humour. Surely there had been more to them once than this pantomime?

"Well, yes, of course I do," he said a little impatiently. "Why?"

Tess's smile slipped. "No why. It was funny, that's all."

"It was." He reluctantly smiled too, but she knew he was only doing it to please her and that was no good at all. "But why are you thinking about it now?"

"Oh, just forget it," she said sharply. She felt silly now. Mawkish. What was the point in dredging up a past that obviously meant more to her than to him?

He was watching her with that horrible schoolboy-caught-smoking look, as though her reminiscences were some attempt to lay a guilt trip on him over Saturday night.

She felt intensely irritated with him, and herself.

"What's she going to do about Croft?" she asked, abruptly changing the subject.

She saw the familiar tightness around Peter's mouth at the mention of Croft and the newspaper article.

"Slap his wrist. That's it."

Personally, Tess had found it all rather amusing, if indeed anything could amuse her last Sunday morning. Croft had wiped the eyes of the big boys all right, and that was no mean feat. He had managed to put several very important people off their croissants and café latte and, at the same time, endear himself to the press. He was an insufferable little prig, of course, but he was already displaying the essential qualities of underhandedness, ingenuity and absolute selfishness that were necessary to get on in politics, as far as Tess could see.

"She's got Andy Walshe on board," Peter blurted.

Tess was thoughtful. "She would be negligent if she hadn't tried, Peter."

"They think they're home and dry, Tess. The lot of them. They're not worried about Croft or about anyone."

"Carol won't get complacent," Tess assured him.

"She already has. And she's not going to listen to anything I have to say."

Tess could see that he was worried. He watched her intently, wanting her opinion.

"You'd better be careful," she said slowly. "You can't trust the Independents. They'll jump whichever way the most money lies."

"My thoughts exactly. But if Croft bombs, Walshe is our only hope."

Tess tapped a finger on the back of his hand. "You're just going to have to come down hard on Croft, Peter. I'd rather put my bets on him than on Walshe."

Peter looked at her gratefully, glad for one voice of reason. "I'll speak to John Graham this afternoon. We'll put a muzzle on Croft if necessary. Thanks, Tess."

He was being over-solicitous again. She smiled back, over-nice again, before deciding that the cat-and-mouse game had gone far enough. It was time to snag the mouse.

"There's something I've been meaning to say to you, Peter."

The hunted look was back in his eyes. Here comes the fallout for Saturday night, he was thinking. Well, he was right, in a fashion. It just wouldn't be what he expected.

"Now that you'll be moving more or less permanently back to Kilkenny . . ."

He was puzzled. "I'll be travelling to Dublin all the time."

"Yes, yes. But you'll be based in Kilkenny."

"I suppose."

"And Fiona, of course, will be down there working on the film."

"Only for a couple of weeks, Tess. I'll look after her, if that's what you're worried about."

She could see that he had no idea where this was leading. She made him wait for it, before announcing brightly, "I'm not worried at all. Because I've decided to move down with you."

His face was a picture. She almost enjoyed it.

"But Dublin, Tess, all your friends. . ."

Tess's nose wrinkled delicately. "I know, they just don't compensate when your husband is a hundred miles away."

The implications were just sinking in for him. Tess kindly helped him along. "So we'll be spending much more time together from now on, isn't that great?"

Unless he intended sleeping with Jean Ormsby in the Kilkenny marital bed with Tess two feet away, he wouldn't be sleeping with her at all.

"Great," he echoed.

Tess had that feeling again that they were simply playing a game. She might have won this time, but it was a hollow triumph. She forced a brilliant smile to her face. "Let's splash out and have a bottle of champagne to celebrate, shall we?"

Chapter Seventeen

Jean felt hot. She turned over in bed and tried to push the duvet down but found that she couldn't move.

"Peter?"

Of course it was Peter, planting tiny kisses down the side of her neck. Jean threw her head back onto the pillow, helpless to resist. The weight of him on top of her felt so solid and right. She lifted her arms and threw them around his shoulders, drawing his mouth down to hers.

"I've missed you," she whispered.

He didn't say anything, he just eased the bed covers slowly down. Jean impatiently kicked them the rest of the way off and they landed on the floor. Now nothing separated them except the thin silk of her nightdress.

He kissed her deeply before pushing aside the flimsy straps. She closed her eyes tightly as he stroked her softly, lovingly. Her arms tightened around him, as though trying to draw him inside her own skin.

"I love you," she said suddenly, the words spilling out at the same time as the realisation.

He merely smiled and burrowed further down the front of her nightdress, rough now. Through her excitement, Jean felt the first stirrings of unease. He wasn't looking at her face, just at her breasts, her belly. His didn't kiss her again, too busy grappling between her legs. She tried to banish the disquiet, to recapture the passion of the moment, but it eluded her.

She put her hands on either side of his face and lifted his head to look at him. His eyes weren't soft with love, but glazed with desire. Confusion must have shown in her own eyes. He smiled down – a lewd, debauched grin. His teeth seemed sharp and predatory, like those of a wolf. She felt herself go cold, and twisted sharply beneath him, trying to get him off her. She didn't want him any more, not like this. It was all wrong. But he was heavy and strong and she felt weak as a kitten.

"Stop," she mumbled, turning her face away into the pillow.

She woke from the dream with a start, wild-eyed and sweating. It took a second for the realisation to hit that there really were two arms wrapped around her. Fingers softly and insistently caressed her through her nightdress.

"What the hell do you think you're doing?" she choked, her voice heavy and thick with sleep.

Ian was lying half on top of her, sprawled across the bed. *Her* bed. In *her* room. Uninvited.

"Giving you a wake-up call," he murmured, eyes half-shut with desire.

Jean tried to sit up. "How dare you!" Her voice, intended as a roar, came out as a squeak.

He laughed and tickled her ribs.

"Ian – stop – " Her voice was a mere whisper now, as she fought for breath under the onslaught of tickling.

Naturally, he took this as a further invitation. He rolled closer and managed to plant a kiss on her cheek.

"Come on, admit it – you're missed me, haven't you, Jean?"

She was too astonished for a moment to struggle. "What?"

"There was a phone call for you, I came in to wake you. And from the look on your face, that was one hell of dream you were having."

He smiled knowingly. It came flooding back to Jean with a start. Peter Fisher. And the torrid dream. Him making love to her, of all things. Oh God: Her cheeks felt as though they were on fire.

"I want you off me and out of my bedroom, Ian," she commanded.

He didn't believe her. "Let's drop the pretence. We both know we want to get back together."

He tried to kiss her again. A stinging slap across his cheek soon put a stop to that.

He was horrified. Hurt.

"Off, Ian. Now."

He got off her without another word and retreated to the window. She was out of bed fast, grabbing a bathrobe and belting it tightly around her. She didn't have time for this crap this morning, but it had to be done.

"There are a couple of things we need to get straight, Ian."

He watched balefully from the window, all tousled hair and long legs. They had done a good job on him at the clinic this time. His skin had lost that grey pallor and his eyes no longer looked as though they lived in the back of his head. He had put on a little weight too, which suited him, and he had obviously availed himself of the clinic's gym. She had never seen him look better. She had also never fancied him less.

"I said that you could stay for a couple of days, Ian. That was all." She tried to sound friendly but firm.

"Oh come on, Jean. I used to live here, remember?"

Pity they hadn't been able to do anything about that whine at the clinic. Self-pity had become his trademark in recent years.

"Not any more," she pointed out.

"I can't get an apartment. I've no money." He looked at her, a puppy dog about to be heartlessly tossed out by its malevolent and unfeeling owner.

You are not responsible for this man, Jean fiercely told herself. Seven years is enough time to give him, to give anybody.

But she still felt a choking guilt as she said, "You could stay at your mother's until you get yourself sorted."

He gave a mirthless laugh. "My mother's? She locks away the aspirin every time I cross the threshold."

Wise woman, Jean thought. She took a deep breath. "You can't stay here, Ian."

He stepped forward. "I did it for you, Jean – signed myself into the clinic for you. To show you how serious

I was about staying clean. Can you not give me a chance here?"

"I've given you too many chances." Her voice sounded tired and dead to her own ears. This conversation was one they'd had a million times before. He knew it too and stepped up the attack.

"I know what you're thinking. But this time is different. I swear," he said fervently, taking her hands in his.

"I hope it is, Ian," she said with feeling. "For your sake. It's too late for us."

"Don't say that. I'll make it up to you. If you'd just let me." As always, his emotions were written all over his face. "I love you, Jean."

Jean twisted her hands from his. Her palms felt cold and clammy. "But I don't love you any more, Ian. I'm sorry. And I'm afraid you can't stay here any longer." She had to look away from his bewilderment, his disappointment. "I'm going to have a shower."

His voice, venomous and low, stopped her at the door. "It's him, isn't it?"

She was glad she had her back to him. "Who?"

"You know bloody well who."

"Ian – "

"Fisher. Mr Big-Shot Politician. How long have you been seeing him?"

She refused to rise to the bait. "You don't know what you're talking about."

"Oh? I know that he was here at two o'clock in the morning last Saturday."

"I already told you. We thought you were a burglar."

"Yeh, right."

She had never heard him sound so bitter and was shocked.

"You were going to screw your ass off with him, weren't you?"

She swung around, white-faced. "Shut up, Ian."

His lip curled. "Sorry to have spoiled the party. I suppose this place must be handy for your little rendezvous. I mean, it's not as though you can be seen in public together, is it?"

Jean clamped down on her anger. "Are you finished?"

"I note your lack of denials, Jean."

"My private life is none of your business." She was shaking. "Now get your stuff, please, and get out."

She did not look at him as he crossed the room. He stopped briefly by the door. "I just hope you know what you're getting into," he said quietly. "I mean, he does this kind of thing all the time, he's famous for it. It won't last, it never does with him. You're worth more than that, Jean."

She stayed in her room until she heard the front door close behind him. Then she went to the kitchen and made breakfast, slamming the fridge door hard enough to take it off its hinges.

She was drained and raging at the same time. He was a leech, she stormed to herself – manipulating himself back into her life and ready to take advantage at the first opportunity. And she had let him. Practically *invited* him to trample all over her again. Would she never learn?

248

She could not quite believe how ugly things had got. Ian could be pathetic, clinging and egotistical at his worst, but she had never known him to be vicious. It was like discovering that an old and amiable, if misguided, friend liked to torture animals in his spare time.

The smell of the toast made her want to throw up. She threw it into the bin and gulped strong black coffee instead. But no amount of caffeine could mask the sour taste his remarks about Peter Fisher had left in her mouth. He hadn't even known about the kiss in the car that night, yet he had managed to make it all sound so cheap and tawdry and small. What was worse was that he was right.

She had gone around for days now hugging her little secret to herself, waiting for the phone to ring, sure that no matter how they had left things on Saturday night, Peter Fisher would ring. He would make some effort to contact her, because surely what they had shared had been special?

He had not tried to contact her. And he wouldn't now, she knew. It was ridiculous to have even harboured the hope. After all, he was a married man and nothing could ever change that fact.

Her stomach lurched unpleasantly again as she remembered herself grappling with him in the steamy car, his wedding ring gleaming under the interior light. It hadn't been special at all. It had been a sordid little encounter and she a romantic fool for thinking otherwise.

She should be grateful, really, that Ian had inadvertently intervened. Otherwise things might have gone farther. Much farther. That didn't bear thinking about.

Well, she had had her moment of madness and there would be no more. She was not the type of woman who cavorted with older, married men, drunk on their power and position. As Ian had said, she was worth more than that; worth more than Peter Fisher. Why, then, did she feel so depressed now?

She took out some of her frustration by loudly slamming the fridge door again.

"Hello? Hello there?"

She almost jumped out of her skin at the tinny voice, which came from somewhere near her elbow.

"Hello?" the voice said again.

The telephone receiver lay off its hook by the fridge. She snatched it up suspiciously. "Hello, yes?"

"Is that Jean Orsmby?"

"It is." She was mystified.

"Some man told me ages ago that he was going off to get you," the male voice on the telephone said.

Ian. He'd mentioned that there was a phone call. Jean had forgotten all about it. Obviously so had Ian.

"You must be holding ages," she said into the phone, astonished.

"Oh, no bother at all," the man assured her hastily. "This is Kieran – Phyllis Harding's assistant?"

"Um, yes?" This was a turn-up for the books. Phyllis Harding had never once phoned Jean.

"We *do* apologise for calling you so early, and at home. But do you think you could spare a minute to speak to Phyllis?" The man was grovelling.

Jean was wary. What was going on? "Yes, of course."

"Oh *good*. We think you'll be very pleased."

"Peter-Piper-Picked-a-Peck-of-Pickled-Pipper." Wrong. "Pickled-*Pepper*."

Those P's were tricky. Cathy tried again.

"Peter-Piper-Pecked-a-Pick-of-Pickled-Pepper." Feck. "*Picked-a-Peck*."

Cathy diligently started over again, booting up her computer at the same time. She had taken to practising her voice exercises in the morning before Patsy or Jean came in. It had become part of her little routine. She had learned the exercises in acting school but had shamefully neglected them during her years in London.

Being back in Dublin had made her take to doing them again. It reminded her that she was an actress. Her spectacular lack of success in landing any acting roles sometimes made her forget.

"Peter-Piper-Picked-a-Puck. . ." Puck? Fuck.

"Peter-Piper-Picked-a-Peck-of-Pickled-Pepper," Carl Tallon reeled off smoothly.

Cathy whirled around. He was closing the agency door behind him and throwing himself into his favourite chair by Patsy's rubber plant.

"You used to practise that every morning before rehearsals for the play," he added quietly, seeing her face.

He had remembered. She used to stand in front of the mirror in his flat, naked after a night of hot and passionate sex, and do her voice exercises. He would stand beside her, naked also, shaving and poking gentle fun at her. Sometimes she didn't get to the end of Peter Piper. Sometimes they had ended up back in bed.

She blushed madly now, wondering if he was thinking the same thing. It was impossible to tell anything from those black eyes of his.

"I presume you've spoken to Jean?" He was watching her intently.

Cathy didn't know what business it was of his. "Yes, as a matter of fact."

"And?" He was eager, she saw, although he was trying to hide it.

She was confused. "And she's going to be late."

"And?"

"And what?" she asked haughtily.

He sat back slowly into his chair. "Suit yourself, Cathy," he said coldly.

Cathy was at sea. "I have no idea what you're talking about."

"I'm sure," he bit out, before taking out a battered copy of the script and proceeding to ignore her completely.

Cathy did her best to ignore him too, turning to open the post noisily. But her fingers seemed thick and clumsy. Out of the corner of her eye, she saw him lazily cross his legs, fingers drumming casually off one knee. Under his breath, he whistled a jaunty little tune.

He obviously didn't give two hoots, she told herself.

So why was she getting herself into a knot? At least Patsy would be in any minute – she could entertain Tallon.

The whistling was getting on her nerves. She suspected he was doing it just to irritate her. When he tossed several pages filled with his handwritten scrawl onto her desk, she was even more annoyed.

"What are these?" she demanded.

"Rewrites." He fixed her with a breezy look. "For Alison."

Cathy clutched the pages with white-knuckled fingers. "I see." She wondered whether he got some kick out of deliberately hurting her. He had never seemed like a sadist, but then again, you never knew these days.

"Around here, we say 'please' and 'thank you' when we want something done," she said sharply.

"Huh?"

"I presume you want me to type these up for you. A little manners wouldn't go astray."

The confusion cleared from his face. "Oh. Of course I don't want them typed up. I want to know what you think of them."

"You mean you're looking for my *opinion*?" Was he certifiably insane?

"Yes." He spoke as though it were the most reasonable request in the world.

Cathy was again gobsmacked by his insensitivity. After all that had happened between them, did he really expect her to act as his little muse again, a sounding-board for his work and his monumental ego? To give him advice on Alison so that he and some other actress could benefit?

Obviously he did.

A quick glance at the top page told Cathy that the new stuff for Alison was going to be dynamite. The ache in her chest grew.

"You've got some neck," she blurted, abruptly pushing the pages away.

She was unprepared for the look of hurt on his face.

"What? But you have to read them."

What as he on about? "I don't *have* to do anything for you any more."

He roughly raked back that black hair of his. Immediately, it flopped back into his eyes. "Jesus Christ, Cathy! We have to learn to work together! Establish *some* kind of professional relationship!"

Cathy wasn't quite sure where this was coming from. Did he expect her, as Jean's secretary, to make him a coffee or something? He'd be in for a long wait.

"I fail to see why."

"Oh, you *fail* to see why, do you? Well, I'll tell you why! Because I can't concentrate on the film with all this hostility going on!"

Somewhere deep in Cathy, a gasket blew. "Oh, well, pardon *me*! I had no idea that my hostility was disrupting your precious work! I will cease and desist immediately!"

Her outburst stunned him into silence. She should have shut up then. She didn't.

"But you always come first, don't you, Carl? You and your bloody work. You'd step over a dying dog on the street to get to your typewriter! Just like you stepped all over me!"

She clamped her mouth shut. But it was too late. He was wild-eyed. And leaning forward for the attack.

"You were the one who went to London for a long weekend and never came back."

Cathy recoiled at his venom. "I rang you, Carl, asked you to come over. You wouldn't!"

"You were only going to be gone for three days! And I was supposed to drop everything and get on a plane? For no reason? Or, at least, no reason that you would give!"

"I asked you," Cathy said quietly. "Wasn't that reason enough?"

Their eyes were locked in battle.

"Not when I was in the middle of negotiations for a new play." His voice was quiet now too. "If I had gone, I would have lost the commission. And you wouldn't tell me why, Cathy. If it had been important, then of course I would have gone."

Cathy felt peculiarly calm now. She had been *so* right to stay in London, she told herself. He was so cold, so detached. Looking for reasons and explanations, cross-examining her at every turn.

"Well, you didn't," she said with finality.

He seemed about to say more, to ask questions to which Cathy would not be giving him answers. Not now and not ever.

She was never so glad to hear the sound of footsteps on the stairs outside. Patsy was here. At last.

It wasn't Patsy. It was Jean. And one look at her face was enough to turn Cathy's heart to stone. The game was up. Her goose was well and truly cooked – no, burnt, incinerated. Somehow or other, Jean Ormsby knew that Cathy had been taking her name in vain.

Like all good torturers, she made Cathy wait. She took off her coat, bid Carl Tallon good morning and picked up her phone messages. Cathy was left to speculate wildly on how she had found out. It didn't matter. She had, that much was obvious. This morning was turning from fiasco to farce.

Finally, she looked at Cathy. Her face was one Cathy had seen many times in her nightmares.

"You, Cathy, have some explaining to do."

"I'm sorry," Cathy blurted. "Really sorry." She was. She should never have taken advantage like that, it was unforgivable.

Carl Tallon looked on quizzically and suspiciously. Jean turned to him.

"I take it you've told her?"

He was bemused. "Well, no. Phyllis said that you would. . . you mean she doesn't know?"

Cathy barely heard them. She was too busy gathering her things. The floor never opened up and swallowed you when you wanted it to, she thought, her whole head on fire with mortification.

"And just what do you think you're doing?" Jean snapped.

"Leaving. You don't want me here now," Cathy mumbled. "Look, I came here that evening to see if you

256

would take me on your books. . . you thought I was here for the typing job. I didn't think there was any harm . . ."

Jean snorted. Carl Tallon watched from his chair. He *would* have to witness her humiliation.

"I'm sorry," Cathy said again limply, stuffing her pencils and pens into her handbag, incapable of looking either Jean or Carl in the eye.

Jean unearthed the keys to her office and jangled them grimly. "We'll discuss this later."

Cathy felt the first stirrings of hope. "You mean I get to keep my job?"

"No."

"Oh."

"But as Patsy isn't in yet, I'll need you to type up your contract."

"What contract?" Cathy said dumbly. Surely she meant letter of termination?

Jean smiled and it held a hint of menace. "The agent's contract between you and me, Cathy. You landed an acting job this morning. And seeing as I have made myself look a complete idiot on your behalf, you will repay me by giving me ten percent of your earnings and letting me push you around. Agreed?"

"Agreed," Cathy stammered, euphoria starting to kick in. She had an acting job. And an agent. If it hadn't been for Carl Tallon sitting there looking at her sourly, she would be the happiest woman on earth.

"What's the part?" she belatedly thought to ask, as Jean ushered Carl into her office.

Jean looked at Carl. "Will you tell her or shall I?"

He shrugged indifferently. "You tell her."

"It's Alison, Cathy," Jean said finally. "You landed the part of Alison in Carl's film."

Cathy had to hold onto the side of the desk to stop herself falling. "What?"

"They saw the video. They want you."

"But . . . I never submitted a video."

"Oh. Well, it doesn't matter. Somebody did. It was a video of the original play."

Cathy's eyes flew to Carl. He stared back, unblinking.

Jean smiled at last. "You never said you were in the play, Cathy."

"I guess it must have slipped my mind," Cathy said, her gaze still pinned on Carl.

Jean looked from one to the other. "And neither of you said that you knew each other, imagine! So, you'll be working together again, isn't that great?"

Her smile faltered somewhat as Cathy Conroy turned away and Carl Tallon stomped off into her office.

Chapter Eighteen

The fifty-three sheep in Packie O'Connor's field in Graiguenamanagh in Co Kilkenny raised their heads in mild interest as the convoy of lighting trucks, catering vans, accommodation trailers, jeeps, cars and motorbikes slowly trundled into the field next door at dawn. The peace of the June morning was shattered as all kinds of strange-looking people alighted and began running around the place, yelling into walkie-talkies and mobile phones.

The sheep trotted along the dividing-fence alongside two particularly scruffy individuals who unravelled miles of cable along the grass, finally attaching two cameras to the end of the cable.

"Shag off," one of them roared at the sheep, frightened. The sheep left them to it and went down to see what all the commotion was at the bottom of the field. Three limousines were slowly pulling in off the road. A handsome chap emerged from the first and was immediately set upon by a gang of people with cameras. Flashbulbs exploded.

"This way, Jason!" one of the snappers shouted.

259

Obviously he was pretty important. The sheep waited avidly to see what star would emerge from the second limousine. A tall, gangly girl stumbled from the back seat and jumped in fright as she was set upon by the photographers, who were even more excited than before.

"Cathy!"

"Smile, honey!"

"Cathy! A question!"

"Yes?" she mumbled.

"How does it feel to be playing opposite Jason Blake?" someone shot.

"Um. . . pretty good."

"First day of the shoot, Cathy – are you nervous?" someone else asked.

"Um . . . pretty nervous."

Oh come on, the sheep thought. She wasn't a patch on Uma Thurman.

She was ushered away by a stern-looking woman with a clipboard as the doors to the third limousine flew open. A big brawny man stepped out, followed by a girl with a lot of hair and cleavage. The photographers and reporters went wild.

"Jack!"

"What scenes are you shooting first, Jack?"

He smiled lazily. "The outdoor ones, you genius."

"Is it definite that you're shooting in Kilkenny Castle, Jack?"

"Confidential information, fellas. If I tell you, I'll have to kill you."

The reporters and photographers guffawed heartily.

The woman with the clipboard descended again. Jack waved at the cameras. "Gotta go, guys."

But the blonde lingered while the photographers snapped voraciously, mostly focusing on her chest.

"Deirdre," Jack snapped, jerked his thumb impatiently. The blonde pouted and tripped delicately across the grass after him on six-inch platforms.

"That's all, boys," the woman told the reporters and photographers. "We'll have a full press briefing later."

Several cars and tractors stopped now on the road and people got out to gawk at the spectacle in their midst. Only locals, the sheep saw, and moved up the fence in search of more excitement.

It was all to be found at the catering truck. Three girls in white aprons dispensed coffee, bacon butties and chocolate croissants to a ravenous cast and crew, supervised by a fat woman with a name-badge that said "Dympna". The atmosphere was tense with the excitement of a first day.

"I want muesli. And a decaff." The strident demand rang out across the field and half the crew stopped eating. The sheep tensed in excitement.

The speaker was a smooth-faced fellow wearing an immaculate suit. He looked totally out of place.

"We have cornflakes or branflakes. That's the choice," Dympna said stonily.

Half the crew sniggered. The man's face glowed pink. He had obviously never been on a film set before and did not know the first and most important rule of survival: Never Piss The Catering People Off.

"I'll have some toast then. Wholewheat," he said.

Dympna leaned forward meanly. "I don't see any ID."

Everybody else was equipped with plastic identity cards pinned to their T-shirts.

"I'm Roger Croft," the man said imperiously.

The cast, the crew, the catering girls and the sheep all held their breaths. Dympna slowly and deliberately snatched back the cup of coffee he had helped himself to.

"No ID, no breakfast," she said nastily.

The drama was interrupted by a loudspeaker blaring across the field.

"Principals to make-up and costume! Stand-ins, positions please! Technical rehearsal, scene 27!"

All of a sudden, the catering van was abandoned as people legged it in all directions.

Silence fell as work started in earnest. There would be nothing else to see now until the stars came out and shooting began.

The sheep drifted away disconsolately, bitterly regretting the fact that they had not been cast in *Babe*.

It took ten minutes of wrangling and a phone call to Fisher's constituency office before the beefy guy with the crew cut in the production trailer was persuaded that Roger was neither a marauding tabloid journalist nor a psychopathic intruder.

"This is ridiculous," Roger said.

"Listen, matey," the beefy guy said. "I've got a list here of all authorised visitors. And you're not on it."

After his humiliation at the hands of that bitch Dympna, Roger was not anxious to antagonise this fellow.

"There's obviously some mistake," he said nicely. "Can you please tell me where I might find Jack Thornton?"

After several exchanges on his walkie-talkie, the beefy guy reluctantly pointed him in the direction of Thornton's trailer.

"Do you have an appointment?" Thornton's personal assistant Miranda asked condescendingly, standing like a guard dog outside the door.

"Well, no. I'm Roger Croft."

"Can I see your ID?"

"I don't have any ID!" Roger forced himself to calm down. "Look, if I could just have a word with Jack."

The assistant knocked and poked her head inside Thornton's trailer.

"He's busy," she told Croft baldly.

It began to sink in with Roger that perhaps he had messed with the wrong man in Thornton.

"Please." The word stuck in his throat. "It'll only take a minute."

The assistant hesitated. "If you wait, you might catch him on his way out. They're shooting in twenty minutes."

She set off across the field towards the farmhouse where two exterior scenes between Alison and Richard were to be shot that morning.

Roger was left to cool his heels outside the closed door of the trailer and fume.

Standing there like some kind of groupie begging for two minutes of Thornton's precious time was just the

latest in a series of humiliations at the hands of Peter
Fisher. Roger was an election candidate for God's sake,
the most important person to the survival of the
Government at this very moment in time. He should be
out there with the stars getting himself photographed,
not standing around in a mucky field waiting for
Thornton's wrath.

He had only barely recovered from the meeting with
Carol Taylor yesterday. He'd played it all innocent and
light, had expressed shock and regret at putting
everybody in a difficult position. He had turned the
wattage up full-blast on his smile. And she had made
mincemeat of him.

"Put a foot wrong again, Roger, and you'll be
answerable to me. Understand?"

He found that he was afraid of her and hated himself
for it. On the train on the way home, he vented his
spleen into a lukewarm cup of coffee. Bloody
superwomen. They had more testosterone than your
average man and probably had a pair of balls hanging
between their legs. Dykes, of course, most of them, out
to score points off men. Their problem was that they
had been allowed to crawl out of the kitchen in the first
place. Oh, how he would love to see Carol Taylor
booted out of office and to the backbenches, from where
it was only a small step back into the obscurity of a
housewife's existence, on her hands and knees
scrubbing floors. Not that this scenario exactly fitted in
with Roger's electoral ambitions, of course. But the little
fantasy helped to pass the journey.

Then off the train and a bollicking from Peter Fisher. And a list of rules and regulations as long as Roger's arm governing future press strategy, public appearances, media relations. Fisher was coming down like a ton of bricks. Roger would no longer be allowed to go to the john without Fisher's written authorisation. Both Fisher and Graham would be breathing down his neck and at every turn.

"This election will be run my way from now on," Fisher had said harshly. "Or not at all."

Roger was not slow to catch his drift. Besides, his sources in Dublin had already fed him the news that Fisher had tried to get him off the election ticket. Had tried to get him *canned*. Only Carol Taylor had saved his skin – this time.

Roger decided now that he had underestimated Fisher. The man was extremely dangerous to the health of Roger's future. Fisher would be on the lookout now for every mistake of Roger's and would pounce. And Roger had no comeback at all as it stood.

Something had to be done. Roger needed some percentage, something to keep Fisher in line should things get ugly again.

Across the field, he saw Fiona Fisher. She was ferrying tea and coffee to the crew, dressed in the obligatory uniform of jeans and a baseball cap. As if aware that she was being observed, she looked up suddenly and caught Roger's eye. She blushed.

Sweet, Roger thought.

There was still no sign of Thornton. Roger's mouth

twisted in distaste as he heard a girlish laugh come from
the trailer. Thornton was probably banging the make-
up girl in there, walking cliché that he was.

Roger looked around for Miranda in the hope of
soliciting her intervention. But there was no sign of her
in the throngs of people milling about the farmhouse.
There was Jason Blake now, in full costume, looking like
some kind of dashing, romantic hero.

There was a palpable air of excitement as he arrived
in front of the cameras. Roger saw the Irish girl who was
playing Alison – he couldn't remember her name –
being shepherded from her trailer by an aide.

His blood pressure jumped sky-high as Carl Tallon
appeared from nowhere, strode across the grass and
lingered at the very back of the group, dark eyes flashing.
Roger drank him in, from his too-long black hair to the
ever-present denim jacket and the long, lean legs
encased in jeans. His gaze moved back up to linger on
Tallon's mouth. He felt his trousers grow tight.

Beside him, Thornton's trailer began to rock in an
unmistakable rhythm. The man was definitely screwing.

Roger wasn't going to hang around for the grand
finale. He turned up the collar of his coat and set off in
the direction of Tallon.

Deirdre was inexhaustible.

Her toned brown thighs moved in perfect rhythm up
and down as though she were a prize show-jumper
taking a series of never-ending jumps, effortlessly and
gracefully. Her knees were firmly clenched around

Thornton's hips, expertly holding him inside her as she rose ever higher and plunged ever deeper.

"Christ," Thornton said between clenched teeth, as her buttocks slapped down on his thighs again, her two pink nipples bouncing energetically inches from his nose. He watched, almost hypnotised. He'd met Deirdre shortly after he'd dumped Gabrielle. Deirdre was not a model or an actress, but a nurse. He was sure about that. And she was beautiful.

"All right, honey?" she asked in a sexy growl.

"Keep going, baby, keep going," Thornton said. She had been astride him for twenty minutes now. Sweat coated her round face and he knew she must be feeling the strain. But she stoically lifted her rump and slammed down on him again. Thornton gritted his teeth and looked to heaven. *Please God, make it happen this time.*

It was the film, he told himself, as Deirdre pumped some more without success. The strain of finding a female star with mere days to the shoot had taken its toll. And with shooting due to start in ten minutes, his mind was naturally on other things.

Like the script, for example. Wonderful and all as it was, there was something missing between Richard and Alison. The passion just wasn't expressed in the stuff Tallon had written for the love-making scene, the most crucial scene in the entire movie to Thornton's mind. The explosive nature of the protagonists' love wasn't coming across; the lust, the sheer, uncontrollable animal attraction.

Thornton had an idea that would turn this scene on its

head and blow it out of the water. Declan Mahoney agreed with him on it. The problem was, would Carl Tallon? And, more crucially, Jason Blake and Cathy Conroy?

Thornton decided that he would not tell any of them just yet. Better to get a couple of weeks' shoot in the can and then he would drop the bombshell.

A knock sounded on the trailer door.

"Go away," Thornton grunted.

It was probably Roger Croft, even though he'd told Miranda to get rid of him. Thornton was still trying to live it down – his very first movie as director, and that little shit nearly blew it all. Fisher, Graham and Carol Taylor had all been on to him, of course. Sorry, Jack, terribly sorry. Well, tough. The Government had interfered enough in this film as far as Thornton was concerned. It was his gig from now on and it was high time that they and Roger Croft realised it.

Deirdre bounced down hard on him again, hurting him, her way of expressing her annoyance that his attention had wandered.

"You're beautiful," he told her by way of appeasement, rubbing her fluffy triangle of pubic hair, which he suspected was dyed. "Keep going, honey," he urged again.

She looked at him doubtfully. "Maybe you want to get on top?"

"Let's do it doggy," he suggested. That had always revved his engine.

In one fluid movement, Deirdre lifted herself off him and in an abrupt about-turn, presented him with her perfect, rounded bottom, her sex peeking through her parted legs.

Thornton swallowed. His cock instantly grew harder. This time, it would happen for him. *This time.*

With renewed determination, he positioned himself behind her and drove into her so hard that she moaned aloud, the force almost sending her down onto her elbows. This excited Thornton even more.

"That feels so goooood," she panted, and even though he didn't really believe her, he went at it harder. Sweat broke out on his forehead. He kept his eyes on the sight of her gorgeous, glorious, raised bottom and waited for the rush –

His penis went limp.

Goddamn.

It was always the same. He slowly slid out of her, as soft as a sherry trifle.

"Sorry," he muttered, turning away to hide his terrible shame.

Deirdre was unfazed. After a weekend with him, she was used to it by now. "Will we try something else?"

"No." Thornton couldn't bear it. "I need to go to work, okay?"

But Deirdre, with her nursing background, decided to tackle the problem head-on. "There are things you can take, you know. Drugs."

Thornton dived into his jocks, face stinging. "I know what things I can take, okay?"

"It's completely curable, you know," Deirdre went on briskly.

"What is?"

"Impotence."

"I am *not* impotent."

"Well, no, I just meant – "

"I'm just frigging tired, okay? And stressed! Christ, just because I can't get it up once in a while doesn't mean I'm impotent!"

He was raging now. He hated himself and her. He hated every last one of the parade of young, bouncy girlfriends, not one of whom he'd managed to satisfy.

They got dressed in silence.

"I was only trying to help," Deirdre said eventually.

Thornton's anger went as quickly as it had come. He shouldn't have taken it out on Deirdre. She was a nice girl. And she was obviously concerned about him.

"Let me take you out to lunch later," he said, determined to make it up to her.

"Okay," she agreed slowly. "I suppose I could stick around, maybe watch you working."

She wasn't going to hold any grudges, she really was a nice girl.

"Great, honey."

"And if you needed any background people – you know, extras and stuff – you could always use me, couldn't you?"

Thornton felt that familiar leaden feeling creeping over him. "I don't need extras this morning."

"But you might tomorrow," Deirdre pointed out meaningfully. "My mother always said that I should give up nursing and go into acting."

"Maybe we should take a raincheck on lunch," Thornton said brusquely.

The penny dropped quickly with Deirdre. "I'm all right to screw, but not to put in your film, is that it?"

Pretty much, Thornton thought. He hastily zipped up his pants. "I didn't think we were seeing each other for the benefit of our careers," he said sarcastically.

"You think I'm with you only for kicks?" she almost shouted. "Get real, Jack. Jesus, you can't even get it up!"

With a toss of her hair, she stormed from the trailer.

Jack looked after her, stunned and incredibly hurt. Although he wasn't sure why; he should have seen it coming. *You think a girl like Deirdre would be with you, legend or not, unless there was something in it for her? You're old enough to be her grandfather.*

He leaned heavily over the wash-hand basin in the corner of the trailer, sick. In the tiny mirror over the basin, his lined, middle-aged face stared back at him; the face that had launched a thousand movies, movies where he had kicked ass and blown up buildings, wielded machineguns and rode off into the sunset on white horses, testosterone spilling from his every pore. And he was a limp-dick in the sack.

How his fans would love *that* one.

It had been this way for five years now, since his last block-buster had failed to do the business at the box office for the first time in his career. His star was in the descent and he knew it. The succession of girlfriends had started then, each younger and more beautiful than

271

the last. All had held the promise that they would cure Thornton's affliction. None of them had, especially when they opened their pretty mouths and asked him for a leg-up in the business. How was a man expected to perform when he knew that none of them wanted him for himself?

Starlets, he thought grimly. They were users and abusers. And he had let himself get sucked into their game in a pathetic effort to prove to himself that he was still a man.

No more, he swore. The next time he got involved, it would be with a real woman; a woman he could talk to, share things with. The rest would sort itself out then.

He found himself wondering when he would see Tess Fisher again.

Carl Tallon was unaware of the fact that he had not drawn breath in over a minute. He had only blinked twice. His cigarette was burning a hole in his fingers and he never felt a thing, so totally focused was he on the drama unfolding in front of him.

"I have no choice, Alison. It's for the family."

"Marry her for the sake of your family then. But don't stand there and tell me that you love me."

"But I do!"

Alison swung around and, in one fluid movement, whacked Richard across the face. It was a good one. He almost fell sideways.

Carl Tallon felt his own cheek tingle in response.

Before Richard could respond, Alison gave him a single

look and went into the farmhouse. Slam. The door shut in Richard's face. Richard standing alone now, torn, already thinking of ways to make amends.

"Cut!" Thornton roared.

Carl Tallon jerked, remembering where he was. His heart was beating fast. Wow. This was surreal, watching the story he had created, nurtured, *lived* with for five long years being played out in front of him for the second time. It was incredible.

And unnerving. Half of him wanted to snatch his script back protectively. He felt ridiculously naked and exposed, as he had with the play five years ago. It was as if he were revealing some secret and precious part of himself to all these buffoons standing around in their baseballs caps.

The other half of him was thrilled and amazed at watching the characters of Alison and Richard come alive again – speak, walk, breathe, laugh, love, feel – like two ghosts from the past. It was almost eerie, as if a part of his life was being replayed. Nonsense, of course. There was no point in coming over all sentimental.

Jason Blake was stunning. He had dropped the star-crap the minute he'd set foot on the grass and become so wholly Richard that Carl knew he would have difficulty in ever thinking of him as anybody else. He would buy the guy a pint of Guinness later on, he decided generously.

And as for Cathy . . .

He had not been able to take his eyes off her. He had thought that her original performance in the play could not be bettered. He had been wrong. She had matured as an actress, bringing an emotional depth to the role that he had not seen her do before. It was as if she had changed somehow, as if something had happened in London. It was in her eyes.

Not that he cared what had happened to her, if anything. The point was that she was turning in a fantastic performance and that was all that mattered at the end of the day, wasn't it? And so what if he'd had to resort to a little subterfuge to ensure that she landed the role? She wouldn't have gone forward for it if he'd suggested she submit a video to Phyllis Harding; she'd made it quite clear that she wanted nothing to do with him or the film. He'd had to resort to "borrowing" her copy of the video of the original play and submitting it himself.

She hadn't even thanked him when she'd won the part. He had shown her that he was big enough to put personal considerations aside and she had not had the grace to pick up the phone to him.

Well, to hell with her. Annoyed with himself for indulging in such petty emotions as rancour, he watched now as she walked by on her way back to her trailer, all big eyes and flushed cheeks.

"Nice one," Thornton told her with a wink.

"Brilliant, Cathy!" the line producer twittered.

"Hey, *star*!" one of the crew joshed her.

Carl Tallon snorted. He saw her look at him and slow down, as if to say something to him. It was the first time she had acknowledged his presence all morning. If she was waiting for him to tell her how fan-fucking-tastic she was, she'd be in for a long wait. He turned deliberately away. She walked on fast.

"Good, isn't she?"

Carl had forgotten all about Roger Croft who had walked right up and introduced himself half an hour ago. He had then proceeded to annoy the hell out of Carl by talking most of the way through the shooting of the scene.

Croft too was looking after Cathy Conroy. He probably fancied her. He was welcome to her.

"She's a *star* now," Carl replied, surprised at how sourly it came out.

"Hey – nobody would be here today if it wasn't for you and your script," Roger Croft said earnestly.

Carl Tallon knew blatant flattery when he heard it. But he was slightly mollified all the same. Today he felt small and insignificant in the face of the mighty machine Jack Thornton had organised around this film, and more unsettled than he'd expected by Cathy Conroy's presence.

"Want to go grab a coffee?" Roger Croft asked.

Carl most certainly did not. He was itching to get back to his typewriter. There were some more rewrites to be done on the filmscript. And then there was the new play, which was occupying more of his headspace than anything he'd ever written before.

He was about to brush off Croft, but three large security guards got there before him. One of them laid a large hand on Croft's shoulder.

"What's going on?" Croft was furious.

"You're off the set."

"*What?*"

"Jack Thornton's orders. Don't set foot on it again."

Chapter Nineteen

Tess took her tea out onto the patio. It was eight thirty and she was still in her dressing-gown and slippers, an unforgivable breach of her rigid morning routine. But who of any importance was going to see her down here buried in rural Kilkenny, surrounded by haystacks, dung and endless green fields?

It had been nearly a month since her self-imposed exodus from Dublin. Once her mind was made up, she had moved with ruthless efficiency, transporting furniture, clothes, herself, Fiona and Peter back down to the old family home two miles outside Kilkenny City. A cleaner had been hired to come to the house twice a week and Tess had organised a whole new schedule of weekly appointments with the local hairdresser, manicurist, beautician and exercise consultant.

These were the sort of details Tess thrived on, and she was proud of the fact that she had made the transition as smooth and painless as possible. The minutiae of the move had also occupied her mind admirably for days on end, and she had almost convinced herself that this was some kind of jolly little adventure that she was quite enjoying.

"Are you sure about this, Mum?" Fiona had asked doubtfully.

"Quite sure," Tess had said cheerfully. "It'll be nice to get away for the summer."

"But I'll be out on the set all day, and Dad's never around anyway."

"So? I can amuse myself."

"Mum, I hope you're not doing this for me. I'm old enough to look after myself. Dad thinks so too."

Typically, it hadn't occurred to either Fiona or Peter that Tess might be doing it for herself. Sometimes she felt that she existed simply to orbit around the pair of them.

"I'll try not to interfere," she had said, but the irony was lost on Fiona.

On her second Monday morning in Kilkenny, Tess woke early to the alien sound of birds tweeting incessantly outside her bedroom window. Apart from that, the stillness was terrifying. She lay in bed, desperately racking her brain for the pressing schedule that she was sure must lie ahead. Slowly, it dawned on her that she was in a house that ran itself, with no lunch meeting to dash off to, no phone calls to return, no dinner date to prepare for that night. In short, she had no life. And she had done it to herself.

I'm going to go mad, she thought clinically. That was the first day that she didn't bother getting dressed for breakfast.

The temptation was to pick up the phone to Sheila Burke or one of the other wives and dash back to Dublin for an impromptu lunch gathering. But that would be admitting defeat before she had even got her toes wet. Her pride wouldn't let her. She gritted her teeth and put her Filofax to the back of the writing bureau. It was only until the by-election was over, she kept reminding herself. Then she could go back to where she belonged.

That week passed slowly. Fiona and Peter were both gone at dawn, leaving Tess's days to take on an almost surreal quality. For perhaps the first time in her adult life, she had nothing but time on her hands. The prospect was daunting, but she was determined not to be beaten. She went for walks. She explored the city which she hadn't really been back to in years. She read books, something she usually never had time for. Pat Kenny and Marian Finucane kept her company on the radio.

To her surprise, the weekend eventually came around and she had not gone mad. By the end of the month, the worst of the homesickness had passed. She had settled into a kind of peaceful routine of walks and late lunches and worrying about nobody but herself.

Sheila Burke had rudely interrupted her little reverie last night with a phone call just after dinner.

"Poor Tess. Is it *terrible* down there?"

Tess found the pseudo-sympathy irritating. "It isn't that bad."

"I know, but still. All those country hicks. And no decent shops at all. I simply don't know *what* I would do without Brown Thomas."

Tess could imagine her smug, bovine face at the other end of the line. "You'd survive, Sheila, like I have."

Indeed, Tess had been pleasantly surprised at how much Kilkenny had blossomed in terms of shopping outlets and exclusive boutiques. The place definitely had more cachet than she remembered.

"So you're adjusting all right then?" Sheila pressed, anxious for a tale of doom and gloom.

"It's not exactly Outer Mongolia," Tess said tightly. "And, of course, I'm right on the doorstep of the film."

That took the wind out of Sheila's sails momentarily.

"I hear it's going very well," she said magnanimously.

"Fantastically," Tess agreed. "Jack was telling me that they're ahead of schedule."

She enjoyed the brief silence across the phone line.

"Jack Thornton?"

"Yes, of course. We had dinner with him."

Tess didn't know why she said "we". She alone had dinner with Jack Thornton, at his invitation. It was the third time he had asked her out, and the first time she had accepted. Peter, as usual, had been off at some meeting or other. Fiona had said she was needed on the set until late. Tess had found the prospect of a night on her own unappealing. And from what she remembered of Jack's company at the launch party, he was entertaining and fun. The evening had turned out to be very pleasant, with Jack on top form. It was all perfectly innocent and above board. But for some reason, she had not told Peter about it.

"I suppose you're seeing lots of Jason Blake and all those Hollywood types as well?" Sheila asked, sounded envious now.

"No, not really," Tess said, again surprising herself. A month ago, she would have immediately pounced on this opportunity to elevate herself socially, to regale Sheila with tales of intimate cocktail parties and insider-gossip from the film set, knowing full well that they would spread like wildfire around her former social circle in Dublin.

She found that she couldn't be bothered, not this time. All this country air was definitely affecting her brain.

"And how's Peter keeping?" Sheila enquired over-casually. She too had witnessed his behaviour with Jean Ormsby at the launch party. She couldn't keep her nose out of it, of course.

"Desperately busy," Tess replied crisply. "He's out canvassing with Roger Croft most of the time. And he's spending a lot of time on the film set."

"We haven't seen much of him in Dublin at all," Sheila said meaningfully. Her spies were obviously on the look-out for any secret rendezvous between Peter and Jean Ormsby.

"I know," Tess said sweetly. "We're both quite enjoying the break. And it's nice spending a bit more time together."

Let Sheila make of that what she wished.

"I think you're very brave," Sheila declared.

Brave in what way she didn't say, but there was an underlying note of pity in her voice.

"I really have to go," Tess said, annoyed. She didn't.

"Me too," Sheila said hastily. She was leaving for

Spain in the morning with Harry Burke on their annual holiday now that the Dáil had recessed for the summer. She had already bored Tess with details of their flights and hotel. "I can't seem to get Harry's suitcase shut. I don't know *what* he has stashed in there."

Probably a dozen bottles of Jack Daniels to get him through three weeks with Sheila, Tess thought grimly as she rang off.

She sipped her tea now and looked out across the back garden. She had forgotten what it was like to be in the countryside in summertime. The June sun was just breaking through the slight mist and the farmers had not taken to the fields yet. It was all very refreshing. Even the birds' endless twittering didn't get on her nerves so much.

"Tess? Have you seen my mobile phone?"

It was Peter, shouting from the kitchen, running late this morning. Normally, Tess would have sprung to her feet and led the search. Today, she decided that he was big enough to look after himself.

"Try the hall table."

She heard him rummaging about. He was off for another day's slog with Roger Croft. There would be no luxury holiday in Spain for *them* this summer, Tess knew, Dáil recess or no Dáil recess. There wouldn't even be a long weekend in Kerry, not with the by-election and the film running simultaneously. She would be here for the entire summer by the looks of things.

Peter ducked out onto the patio. "I brought you another cup of tea."

She smiled. "Thanks."

He had also brought some toast. She hadn't known that he was aware that they actually possessed a toaster.

"I'll be out all day," he said. "And I may have to go to Dublin tonight. Carol Taylor just rang. Cabinet business."

He was letting her know that it was a bona fide journey, that she could surreptitiously check with Carol Taylor's office if she so wished.

"Okay," she said.

"If not, maybe we'll go out for dinner?"

"Maybe."

He hesitated. "You'll be all right on your own today?"

"I'll be fine."

He planted a kiss on her cheek. "Bye."

She watched as he got into his car and drove off with a wave.

She had to hand it to him. He really was trying very hard. The move to Kilkenny had changed him too. It was there in the small gestures, such as the morning cup of tea, and the bigger ones, such as his daily recital of where exactly he would be and with whom.

Tess didn't know whether his model-husband bit stemmed from the usual guilt, or whether he was actually trying to bring them closer together. She found that she did not really care. She was simply grateful for his efforts, and responded to them. She liked the easy companionship as they watched TV in the evenings together, or ate out in the local pub. It was all very pleasant and nice and easy-going, and something they had not shared often before.

But it was not the stuff of passion. It would light no fire under the embers of their marriage. It was as if by some silent mutual agreement, they were behaving like old friends who were going to make the best of the summer together. And that suited Tess just fine.

She wondered whether he yearned after Jean Orsmby. Also by some unspoken agreement, the agent's name had not been mentioned by either of them. Tess knew that she had been down to the film set several times. Thornton had told her.

Peter wasn't seeing her – that would be impossible in the present circumstances. But as Tess lay beside him at night in the dark, listening to his breathing and knowing that he was awake, she wondered if he was thinking of her.

She supposed that he probably missed sex at any rate. She had not slept with him since the night of the launch party. And he had not asked. It wasn't malice on Tess's part nor, she suspected, fear on his. It just seemed inappropriate somehow; embarrassing even.

She peered down the drive as a black jeep swung in, scattering dust in all directions as it sped towards the front door.

"Morning, Tess!"

Jack Thornton jumped energetically from the driver's seat. His cowboy boots crunched loudly on the gravel as he made for the lawn and the patio. The perennial cigar was clamped between his teeth. All he needed was a ten-gallon hat to look like some ageing cowboy come to sort out the baddies before sundown.

Tess was momentarily flustered. Here she was in her dressing-gown and slippers, her face devoid of the tiniest scrap of make-up, her eyes still puffy from sleep. She wasn't equipped to receive visitors, certainly not those of Hollywood-legend ilk. Either she could make some lame excuse and rush upstairs to repair the damage, or she could simply continue with her breakfast. She stayed put.

"There's tea in the pot," she told Thornton.

"A woman after my own heart."

"It's too early for insults, Jack."

He laughed out loud.

She knew that she had played it exactly right. He found her refreshing, she knew, because she did not pander to him, she did not seek him out. But still, his attention to her was inexplicable.

"What can I do for you this morning?" she enquired.

"Nothing. Just passing," he drawled.

Sure. The Fisher house was in the other direction from the film set.

"On a go-slow this morning?" she teased, looking at her watch. "Although I suppose you didn't finish up until late last night."

Thornton frowned. "We finished at six."

"Oh." Fiona hadn't come home until nearly midnight. A night-shoot, she'd said. Tess shrugged. She must have picked her up wrong.

Jack was eyeing her breakfast. "Don't I get some toast?"

"Sure. The kitchen's behind you."

"You're a hard woman, Tess."

"No. I'm just too old to go running after men any more," Tess said succinctly. "Even big important stars like you, Jack."

He was nonplussed, unable to believe that someone was taking the mickey out of him. Eventually he laughed again, louder this time.

"Seeing as you've refused all my invitations to come down to the set, I decided to come get you myself," he said cheerfully.

He had rung almost every day since their dinner date. Tess had been mildly perplexed. Surely her company hadn't been *that* sparkling?

"No thanks," she said. She did not want to be anywhere in the vicinity of Jean Ormsby if she could help it.

Jack looked a little put out at her bald refusal. "But why?"

"Oh come on, Jack. You don't need me there to show off to."

Now he really did look annoyed. "That isn't why I'm inviting you."

Tess carefully wiped her buttery fingers on a napkin. "Why *are* you inviting me?"

"Forget it," he said gruffly, surprising Tess by getting to his feet with such force that the patio chair fell backwards. When he looked at her, she saw that he was genuinely hurt.

"Tell me one thing, Tess. Did you enjoy dinner with me last week?"

Tess was bewildered. "Yes, of course, it was lovely."

"I didn't offend you in any way?" he asked.

"What? No, of course not."

"No more than I usually offend you, that is," Jack added sardonically. "With my crass American ways and my brashness."

Tess really was perplexed now. "Jack, where is all this coming from?"

He was stomping around the patio, his cowboy boots hitting the concrete with force.

"I just don't know what it takes to impress you, Tess," he blurted.

Tess sat very still. Part of her wanted to laugh – she found it hilariously funny that Jack Thornton, legend, icon, et cetera, had been trying to impress her and she hadn't even noticed. Another part of her was confounded. From the look on his face, it was obvious that the man had a crush on her. On Tess Fisher, sitting here with no make-up on and in her dressing-gown. It was incredible.

"I . . . like you, Jack," she said, wondering whether the words sounded as lame as they felt.

"Thanks a bunch," he shot. Obviously they did.

He did some more stomping about. Again, she had a crazy impulse to laugh. She bit down hard on her lip.

"Jack, I'm married," she began eventually.

"Yeh. To a serial cheat," he returned baldly. "Blissful, I'd say."

Tess was shocked. Perhaps it was a mistake to treat him like a clown. How had he known of Peter's affairs? Obviously he had made it his business to find out.

"My marriage is my own concern."

He hauled up the fallen patio chair, planted it beside hers, and sat.

"Stop fooling yourself, Tess."

"Look, what do you want, Jack?"

"You," he said simply.

"Well, you can't have me," she said, feeling foolish. This was turning into a scene from some bad B-movie.

"You're an attractive woman, Tess. Young still. What are you doing burying yourself down here for the sake of a husband with hot pants?"

"I like it down here," she said coldly, realising with a small start that it was true.

Jack looked disbelieving and Tess felt stab of anger. "And who the hell do you think you are, marching in here with your demands and your opinions that nobody asked for?" Her lips curled dismissively. "Go back to Gabrielle. Or is Deirdre?"

"She's gone," Thornton said meaningfully. "I sent her back to Dublin."

"I hope you didn't do it for me," Tess blurted.

"Now who the hell do *you* think you are," Thornton said sarcastically. Tess coloured. She was learning fast that Jack Thornton was not a man to be trifled with.

"I'm sorry, Tess – I shouldn't have said that. I'm just disappointed, that's all."

"Maybe so am I, Jack," she said, more to appease him than anything else. "Perhaps if the circumstances were different . . ."

"Yes," he agreed. "But we can still go out to dinner again? As friends?"

"Certainly," Tess assured him, half-aware of the fact that he was edging closer around the breakfast table. Surely he wasn't trying it on?

"And maybe you'll come down to the set with me today?" he murmured, his knee brushing against hers under the table.

He *was* trying it on, the old codger. Curiosity kept Tess silent. She was wondering how far he'd push it.

"You'll have to give me ten minutes to get ready," she said.

"You look just perfect to me," Jack said. "Speaking as a friend, of course."

"Of course," Tess managed, as his large face loomed closer. My God. He was going to kiss her. And she was going to let him.

Sanity prevailed at the last possible moment. She jerked away and found herself on her feet.

Jack was looking at her knowingly, she saw. He knew he had rattled her all right.

"Get yourself some tea, Jack. I'll be right down."

She walked quickly into the house, astounded by herself. What had got into her? She had almost kissed Jack Thornton on her own patio. In her dressing-gown. Over a cup of tea and toast.

It was those daft birds, she thought grimly. Twittering and tweeting away. It was enough to addle anybody's brain.

She felt Jack Thornton's eyes on her back all the way up the stairs.

Chapter Twenty

The first rushes of the film were ferried back from England under the strictest of security and viewed only by Jack Thornton, Declan Mahoney and Cinerama. Then they were placed in a fire-proof vault under lock and key.

How John Graham managed to get a copy he would never say. This was the Government's movie and he had simply made it his business.

The stuff looked okay to him, as far as he could tell. Period pieces had never been his thing; he preferred gory nature documentaries any day. But he would be able to tell the Government that Thornton was bringing in the goods all right.

What a pity. Thornton had thrown them all with his little stunt of banishing Roger Croft from the film. Declaring it a closed set. Graham was still trying to smooth that one over. What good was a beautiful film to them at the end of the day if it didn't get their candidate elected?

The fax beside Graham churned into action, spewing out an advance copy of the latest poll on the by-election, due to be published in the newspapers tomorrow.

Graham skimmed it. Roger Croft had twenty-five percent of number-one votes all right. But Bill Mackey had forty.

He turned to look out the window. The light was on in Ulick Pearse's office at the far side of the block. Ulick appeared at the window now and saluted.

Graham laughed. "You bastard."

Ulick drew his hand sharply across his throat – *You're dead*, he was saying.

Graham laughed again, then reached over and flipped down the blind, shutting out Ulick's grinning gob.

Graham tapped the fax against sharp white teeth. Roger Croft's little leak to the media about Cinerama's funding hadn't done him much good – except to rile the Ministers, of course.

The lad was either very smart or very stupid. Either way, he had taken things into his own hands and Graham didn't like that. It was time to put a stop to Roger Croft's gallop and run this election Graham's way. Which was as it should be.

"Breathe in," Marie commanded.

"I *am*," Cathy gasped.

"Breathe in some more!"

Cathy sucked in air, her lips puckered like those of a long-distance runner. She felt the bones of the corset tighten inexorably around her ribcage and waist, squashing her lungs like sponges and forcing her belly back into the region of her kidneys. Her breasts were suddenly under her chin, while the cheeks of her bum were brutally hoisted up towards the small of her back where they quivered like two frightened ferrets.

"I feel dizzy," she protested.

Marie was unsympathetic. "That'll pass."

"But they didn't wear corsets in the sixteenth century!"

"So? You're wearing one today and that's that."

"But why? I've never had to wear one before!"

Marie said nothing. It was Jack Thornton who had ordered plenty of cleavage. And when it came to creating cleavage where none had previously existed, Marie, head of costume on the film, was an expert. Forget Wonderbras. Forget lumps of loo roll stuffed into A-cups. Nothing created a more authentic-looking cleavage than a good, old-fashioned corset.

It was also increasingly obvious to Marie that Cathy Conroy was ignorant as to why exactly she needed cleavage this afternoon.

"Breathe in!"

"Bloody hell, I am!"

Marie hid her sympathy behind another show of dourness. "Quit your bitching. Most girls would kill to be in your shoes right now!"

Cathy bit her tongue. Marie wouldn't understand if Cathy told her that she had almost turned the film down.

Jean hadn't understood either. "Cathy, are you mad? Stark, *raving*?"

Cathy had felt very ungrateful. "I just don't know if it's right for me."

"I've seen the video. You'll be fantastic. You've played the part before, for God's sake!"

"All the same. . ."

"What's going on?" Jean had asked, eyes suddenly canny.

"Nothing!"

She certainly couldn't tell Jean that the prospect of spending two months in Carl Tallon's company on a claustrophobic film set was the last thing she wanted.

And the last thing he wanted too, she was sure.

Why, then, had he submitted the video? The video he'd borrowed from her under false pretences? It was all too confusing. And too dangerous. Their heated exchange in Jean's office that day had proved that they were incapable of letting the past rest. Who knew what kind of secrets might come tumbling out in the heat of the moment when they were confronted with each other day after day on a film set?

Cathy had felt a sense of dread at this. She would never tell him. *Never.* And so she couldn't accept the part.

But Jean was too smart for Cathy. She had left a copy of the final draft of *Outsiders* on Cathy's desk and told her to sleep on her decision.

Cathy, of course, had sat up half the night reading it, as Jean knew she would. And the old hunger made itself felt. By morning, Cathy knew she wanted to play Alison again.

All she had to do was avoid Carl Tallon as much as possible, she told herself. That should be easy enough on a set of eighty people, shouldn't it? And certainly *he* wouldn't be seeking her out. It would all be okay. She could have her cake and eat it.

Armed with these reassurances, she had signed the contract the next day.

There had been no time for regrets. With less than a week to the start of shooting, Cathy's life changed overnight, and so dramatically that her existence behind a desk in Jean Ormsby's little office seemed like a distant dream now.

Here she was on a fifty-million-dollar film set, waited on hand and foot by a whole team of people. It was almost embarrassing. Her every wish was their command – a telephone so that she could ring Jean Ormsby? No problem. A special pass so that her Mum could visit her one day on the set? Absolutely, and here's twenty more for all the family. And was she sure that the mini-bar in her trailer was adequately stocked with champagne and Belgian chocolates?

She still didn't believe it. This kind of thing simply didn't happen to the Cathy Conroys of this world. It happened to girls with names like Tamara Ball, gorgeous creatures with hour-glass figures and mops of white-blonde hair – the kind of girls who were born to sprawl across a white leather couch for a double-page spread in *Hello!* magazine and whose seventeen-year-old big bouncy breasts had never seen a corset in their lives.

It all seemed too incredible to Cathy. This was the big time, the kind of stuff that every actress dreamed of. And she would be lying if she said that part of her wasn't enjoying it.

It was frightening too. She would never forget that heart-stopping moment when she'd stepped – or rather, been pushed – in front of the cameras for the very first time. And there was Jason Blake, Hollywood star, smiling at her casually, so near that if she reached out she could actually touch him.

"Hi, Cathy," he had drawled easily. "Glad to be working with you."

"Duh," was all that came from her mouth.

To his credit, he had pursued the conversation.

"It'll all be fine," he had said reassuringly.

Cathy had nodded and grinned desperately. Her entire body had felt as though it were deep-frozen as the camera swung towards her, in position. The lines in the scene they were about to shoot were jumbling around in her brain like alphabet soup. She'd never known such fear. Had it not been for the forty or so people standing watching her, she would gladly have given in to her urge to faint, or vomit, or both. Then those terrifying words, blared from a loud-speaker –

"Rolling!"

"Action!"

Somehow or other, her body had unlocked. Her feet had moved of their own accord across the grass to her marker, her mouth had opened and she had said the first line.

294

And suddenly, it was okay. She forgot about the people watching, about Jason Blake. She was Alison again. She was lost.

Then someone was shouting "Cut!"

She had no recollection whatsoever afterwards of doing the scene. But it must have been okay. Jack Thornton ordered it printed after only two takes.

"Well done," Jason Blake had whispered.

"Duh," Cathy had said again.

Then she was being ferried back to her trailer in preparation for the next scene, passing a sea of smiling faces, not one of which she knew.

Except for Carl Tallon's. There he was, lurking at the back of the crowd. She reminded herself of her promise to stay far away from him, but his scowl and scruffy denim jacket were so familiar and welcome that she had an insane urge to run over and fling her arms around him. To ask him whether he thought she did Alison proud. His approval, she realised abruptly, was more important to her than anybody else's. It always had been.

And he had turned his back on her. Blatantly. She had faltered only slightly before marching past, her throat tight with hurt.

Afterwards, she was furious with herself. Her days of begging for a moment of his attention were over, she told herself brutally. And she should be glad he was avoiding her too. It would make life easier all around.

He had not been on the set since. Re-writing, somebody had said. Working on his new play, somebody else had said. Cathy told herself she didn't care. In fact, it was positive *relief* not to feel his glowering eyes burning a hole in her back while she was trying to work.

And what hard work it was – from dawn till dusk most days. She would fall exhausted into the narrow bed in her little trailer on the set, too tired even to make the short journey to her hotel in the city. But after months and years of being out of work, getting her teeth into the part of Alison again was bliss. In fact, the only cloud on the horizon was the reappearance of Carl Tallon on the set this morning.

"There." Marie had finally succeeded in bullying Cathy into the corset and was now advancing with a magnificent green satin dress.

"That's not Alison's costume for today." Cathy was puzzled. The fabulous green dress was for later, when Alison masqueraded as a noblewoman and attended Richard's wedding to another woman.

"Change of plan," Marie mumbled.

"What change of plan?"

"*I* don't know, do I? Now, arms up!"

Cathy meekly obeyed. Marie threw the gown over Cathy's head. For an age, she fussed and fretted, tugged and rearranged. Then she swung Cathy around to face the floor-length mirror.

Cathy was speechless. Surely that couldn't be her? She had *breasts* for a start, two white globes of things spilling out over the bodice. And every one of her five-feet eleven-inches was just right in the dress; she looked willowy and regal, someone to be reckoned with. And why had she never realised before that green was definitely her colour?

"You're a genius," she said, hardly noticing that the corset had also raised her voice an octave. "But I think you've got it wrong, Marie. We're doing an outdoor scene after lunch."

Marie sighed heavily. "Go and speak to Jack Thornton."

"Why?" Cathy was suspicious now.

Men were such bastards, Marie thought with relish – Jack Thornton a bigger one than most. She reached into her vast sewing kit and unearthed several pages. *She* for one wouldn't go along with this charade of keeping the leading actress in the dark until the last possible moment.

"Here. Read this."

Cathy took the pages and skimmed them. Her eyes jumped up to meet Marie's.

"The *love-making* scene?"

Marie looked at the ground.

"We're shooting that this afternoon?"

"It would appear so."

Cathy felt sweat pop out all over her body. Nobody had told her. Nobody had given her a chance to *prepare*, for God's sake.

In the script, Richard and Alison finally consummated their relationship on the night of his nuptials, a protracted and frenzied love-making scene that Cathy had managed to put to the back of her mind until now. It had been ages since she had even snogged a man; how was she supposed to convincingly have sex with Jason Blake? She'd bet he was no slouch in that department either – his gorgeous model-cum-actress girlfriend had flown in from LA last week and Jason had been spending a lot of time in his trailer since.

"Why didn't they tell me?" she demanded. "I haven't even brushed my teeth!"

"Maybe Jack didn't want to worry you." Marie tried to be conciliatory.

"Big of him," Cathy said sourly. Well, if it had to be done, then that was that.

Marie was again mysteriously mute. What was *wrong* with her this afternoon?

"Marie!"

"Read page two," Marie mumbled.

Cathy did.

"I don't believe this."

She read it again. She still didn't believe it.

"No way," she said slowly. "No way in hell!"

Marie felt bad now. "Look, why don't you go and talk to your agent – "

"I will bloody not! I know exactly who I'll talk to!"

With Marie flapping helplessly in her wake, Cathy stormed out of the trailer.

He was propping up the bar at the catering van, reading a newspaper and drinking coffee.

"You!" Panting, Cathy jabbed a finger in the direction of his chest.

"Me?"

Oh, how infuriating he was.

"Yes, you!" she almost shouted. The catering girls looked over, surprised at this show of drama from their normally placid star. "What the hell is this all about?"

"What?"

"This!" She shoved the sheet of crumpled paper at Carl Tallon.

He sipped coffee, his eyes cynically travelling down the length of her green dress and back up again, coming to rest on her newly-installed cleavage. Cathy felt as though he had touched her. Her cheeks flamed.

"Well?" she demanded tightly.

"I believe it's called a re-write."

Cathy wanted to shake him. "And why wasn't I told?"

"You're being told now," he said calmly.

"I'm sure Jack Thornton will have something to say about it!"

He didn't bat an eyelid. "It was his idea."

Cathy was shocked, yet she should have known that Carl Tallon couldn't go changing the script without Thornton's say-so.

When she spoke again, her voice was pure ice. "It's a stupid idea. The love-making scene was fine as it was. There's no need to change it to a nude scene."

"Jack feels that the story needs it at this point. I happen to think he's right."

"Jason Blake won't agree to it."

"He already has."

Cathy felt herself sink deeper. It seemed as though it was all decided and nobody had bothered to ask her.

"I won't do it," she said finally.

Carl Tallon shrugged as though it were a matter of supreme indifference to him. "I guess you'll have to take that up with Jack."

Cathy stared at him in silence, bewildered and hurt. Whatever else had gone on between them, she had thought that they'd always respected each other's work.

"Why didn't you consult me, Carl?" she asked quietly. "Doesn't my opinion count for anything any more?"

He looked away. "I'm the writer. Not you."

"Oh, and that gives you the right to do what you want?"

"What?"

"You played God in my life once before, Carl. You're not doing it again."

He looked mystified. She didn't care.

"And you can forget about your nude scene. Pigs will fly before I'll do it."

Chapter Twenty-one

"Faster," Phyllis Harding commanded.

She was sprawled on her back on the middle of her desk, happily naked from the waist down. Kieran, her assistant, was doing his best to keep apace, his trousers bunched around his spindly ankles.

"Giddy-up, you little runt," she said savagely. This excited Kieran to such an extent that he pumped faster. A box of paperclips went spilling to the floor. He knew that she would make him get down on his hands and knees later and pick them up one by one while she watched, and he moaned in ecstasy.

"Don't you dare come," Phyllis warned, her legs almost up around her ears.

She was always at her most voracious first thing in the morning. She preferred a good fuck to a cup of strong coffee – it set her up for the day.

"Jean Ormsby's waiting outside," Kieran reminded her breathlessly.

Phyllis smiled in pleasure. She liked him to talk

business while he screwed her. And it got her going even more to know that she was keeping that little madam waiting while she took her pleasure.

"Woof," she said, panting.

Kieran reluctantly withdrew. This was the signal that she wanted to do it doggy-style.

With some considerable effort, he heaved her bulk over on the desk. The huge white mass of her ass stared up at him and he swallowed in trepidation.

"Go!" Phyllis directed. "And mind my skirt for Chrissake."

He dutifully rolled up her skirt another couple of inches before easing into her. Phyllis clutched the rim of the desk and rolled her eyes gratefully. Thank God for at least one man who would do exactly what she told him to.

She'd had Jack Thornton and Declan Mahoney on the phone to her this morning. Sort it out, Phyllis, they had ordered.

As if any of this mess was her doing. As if it was part of her job description to sort anything out for the *bungling* men. Her fury built to such an extent that when Kieran inadvertently scratched her rump now with a fingernail, she reached back and lashed him across the side of the head with her fist.

"O-o-ohhhh." His red mouth drooped open as he looked at her in shock and hurt. Two fat tears gathered in the corners of his eyes.

"Sorry, baby – Mummy's sorry, okay?" Phyllis was immediately repentant. She reached back with the offending hand to cup his balls and squeeze them in comfort. "Mummy didn't mean it."

Kieran lapped it up. The tears melted away and he stared at her with renewed adoration and lust. Phyllis's excitement built again. He would really go to work now.

"Mummy's been a bad girl. You'll have to punish her," she said slyly.

It was like a red rag to a bull.

"Jesus, Mary and Holy Saint Joseph." Phyllis had to hold on to both sides of the desk as Kieran gripped two handfuls of her fleshy bum and used them to keep his balance as he bored into her like a man demented, driving her up the desk six inches. Reports, pens and more paperclips went crashing to the floor.

"Atta boy," she yelled in encouragement, holding on to the polished wood for dear life. Kieran began the assault in earnest, forcing her down onto the desktop. Her nose came to rest on a copy of Cathy Conroy's contract, open at Clause 23.

She quivered with anticipation as she thought of what she would do to Cathy Conroy and her uppity little agent in a few minutes' time. Vengeance would be hers. The prospect, combined with the lashing Kieran was giving her from behind, proved too much. The tightness inside her stretched exquisitely and then burst in a glorious, heart-stopping orgasm. Saliva dripped from her slack mouth onto Clause 23 as she let rip with a scream. Kieran jerked, thrilled at the spectacle of Phyllis in the throes, pushed into her one last time and let rip himself.

"Mummy Mummy Mummy," he squealed.

"You little pervert," Phyllis murmured affectionately and collapsed onto the desk, pleasantly replete.

"I had a lovely time last night."

She really was fresh and sweet and innocent beneath that tough exterior. And she had popped open an extra button on her blouse just for him, Roger knew.

"Good. So did I," he murmured.

A blush stained her cheeks. Roger was amused. It was amazing that she had reached the age of fifteen and never been touched. *Really* touched. Most of these young ones were at it hammer-and-tongs from the age of twelve. But something about the way Fiona Fisher dipped her eyes made him think that she was virgin soil all right.

"Didn't drop you home too late, did I?" he enquired politely.

He'd taken her out for dinner and drinks. No expense spared. Then a fast drive around the city in his sleek black Lexus. The silly girl had loved every minute of it.

"I can go home any time I like," she said with a defensive toss of her head.

Yeah, right, Roger thought. He would bet that Tess and Peter Fisher had had their heads glued to the net curtains all night long.

Not that they would have seen much. Roger had dropped Fiona at the end of their driveway, as he had on all their previous dates in the past three weeks. He knew that Peter Fisher would put a swift and brutal end to any romance his darling daughter might be conducting with Roger. And Roger was not ready to dispense with Fiona yet. She was his only life-line to the film since that egomaniac Thornton had banned him from the set.

He shouldn't even be here now. They were sitting inconspicuously at the back of the catering tent. Fiona had got her hands on a temporary pass and a free cup of coffee.

"I don't see why we have to keep it a secret. Us," she said now, big wounded eyes fixing on him.

"Because I'm an election candidate, Fiona," he explained patiently for the hundredth time. "And you're a little on the young side for the voters."

"I'm fifteen, old enough," she said with a pout.

Didn't the daft girl realise that he could be arrested?

"It's better for me if I look like I'm single. They like that."

"The *women* like that, you mean," she said jealously.

"You don't have anything to worry about, sweetheart," Roger said with a winning smile.

"Do I not?" That annoying puppy-dog expression was back on her face. She was so anxious to please that Roger felt contempt.

But anything would annoy him this morning. It wasn't the most pleasant start to the day to wake to the sight of Bill Mackey's smug face on the front page of *The Kilkenny People* newspaper, along with results of the latest poll. Mackey was a whole fifteen points ahead in the race, and climbing. The man was so bloody confident that he had gone off to Greece on a week's holidays.

And who could blame him? He had nothing to worry about at all, Roger thought moodily.

"It's early days yet," John Graham had smoothly said when Roger phoned him at eight this morning.

Early days? Didn't the fool realise that they had barely seven weeks to go to polling day?

"Eight weeks," Graham corrected in that maddeningly calm voice.

What, Roger demanded, were they going to do?

"We'll step up your public appearances," Graham eventually decided. "There's a community centre being opened in Ballycummin tomorrow. I didn't think we could fit it in, but perhaps we should now."

A community centre. In Ballycummin. Roger almost choked. Was that *it*?

"No, no," Graham assured him. "I think we should also set aside more time for door-stepping."

"*Door*-stepping?"

"The most important thing is to meet as many people as you can before polling day," Graham said mildly.

"Listen, John – maybe you chaps could come up with something a bit more radical. I'm doing everything I can down here."

"Yes, we've noticed your efforts." Graham's voice was as dry as old wood. "Especially with the press."

Roger was raging at this reference to the leak over the Cinerama funding. At least it had got his picture in the paper. Graham and the rest of the fat-cat spin doctors were content to sit on their asses while Roger went out there and got himself noticed. And then they had the temerity to turn around and lecture him?

Roger wondered how on earth the likes of Graham had ever got to where they were today. *No* imagination. *No* drive. *No fucking idea* how to use the most important election tool they had – the media.

Forget door-stepping, accosting dotty old dears with blue rinses who did not want to talk to Roger, nor Roger to them. John Graham's tactics would not win a raffle, never mind the most important election in the country in years. It would be up to Roger to find a new angle that would put him ahead in what he knew at the end of the day was a media race. But it was obvious now that he was on his own.

John Graham sensed something of this on the other end of the phone. "We know what we're doing, Roger. We *did* win the last general election, you know. You do your job on the ground and leave the rest to us, okay?"

"Have you sorted things out with Thornton at least?" Roger asked, voice shaking.

This movie was supposed to be *his* – the pet project that would woo the voters and earn him some publicity. And he wasn't even allowed on the fucking set.

"I'm working on it," Graham murmured. "But media interest in the film has died down anyway. We've got all the mileage we're going to get out of that."

Get with it, Granddad, Roger thought, slamming down the phone.

Roger sipped the coffee Fiona has stolen for him, lost

in contemplation. There were two things going against him right now. Firstly, Graham was right – after the initial frenzy over the film, nobody really gave a toss any more. Secondly, Bill Mackey had the women's vote in his back pocket. After years of being their best buddy over the national airwaves, he was home and dry. Trying to wean away their support would be like sucking blood from a stone. It was a conundrum, and Roger didn't have the answer. Yet.

He could do some work on Fiona though.

"Any idea what your father has planned for me in the way of a campaign budget for posters and the rest?" he asked casually.

"He doesn't talk about work to me."

"But you could ask – discreetly, of course."

"Why can't you ask him yourself?"

Because Fisher would tell him to get lost. "I have, and he said he'd left the figures at home." A delicate pause. "You could have a look for me, couldn't you? On the sly?"

Fisher kept nothing like that in the office. Roger had already found that out.

"But that would be sneaky," she said a little coldly.

Roger saw that he had been too hasty. Sometimes you had to be careful with Fiona. Just when he thought she was the world's biggest pushover, she turned around and defended her ground with a strength that was surprising.

Anyway, it didn't matter, not really. Posters were not going to win this election for him, however much money Fisher threw at them.

He laid a hand on her thigh, conciliatory. "I'm sorry, honey. I'm just a bit nervous about the campaign."

She softened. "You'll win, I know you will."

Putty in my hands, he thought, hastily releasing her thigh. "Hadn't you better get back to work?"

"No rush."

Roger suddenly noticed that the set was very quiet – and the catering tent very full.

"What's going on?"

"Nothing." She was lying.

"Aren't they shooting this afternoon?"

"No. . . look, we were told to say nothing to anybody."

Roger felt his sixth sense kick into action. Something was going down. "That doesn't mean me, surely?"

She was unhappy. "I can't, Roger. Declan Mahoney and Jack Thornton's orders."

"I won't say a word to a soul," he promised, putting his hand back on her thigh.

"Well. . . there's some hold-up about the love-making scene. They tried to change it to a nude scene. There's all kinds of trouble."

"Really?" Roger was fascinated.

He heard how Cathy Conroy had dug her heels in and said no, and that there had been harsh words from Thornton and Declan Mahoney. The row had escalated and production had ceased as of yesterday afternoon.

"There's war," Fiona confided. "We were told to say nothing because Jack Thornton doesn't want Cinerama finding out that filming has stopped. They'd have a fit."

"I'd imagine so would your father," Roger added innocently.

Fiona bit her lip. "They don't want him finding out either."

Despite himself, Roger felt sorry for her. She was caught between two stools.

"Don't worry," he assured her. "He certainly won't hear anything from me."

He didn't notice her grateful smile. He had other things on his mind. This little crisis had distinct possibilities.

"*I* wouldn't do it," Fiona announced. "Take my clothes off in front of all those people . . . can you imagine?"

Roger could and delicately suppressed a shudder of distaste.

"Don't tempt me," he said with a lascivious smile.

He watched as she melted like an ice cream in the sun, and then jumped a little as he found the length of her leg pressed against his under the red-check table top.

"Maybe we can meet up tonight." She paused meaningfully. "And if you liked, I could say that I had an all-night shoot."

Illicit sex. My, my, Roger thought. She really was a chip off the old block.

He smiled roguishly. "Ah, wouldn't I love that!"

Her eyes lit up. Roger enjoyed this, even though he knew that things could not go on much longer the way they were. She was pushing hard for a full physical relationship. So far, he had got away with a few chaste kisses and a quick grope of her breasts. It was painfully obvious from the way she responded to even the slightest touch that she was ripe for it. And her insistence was growing with each date.

"Well?" she said now, leaning over to kiss his neck.

Roger endured it, detached. While on one level she repelled him, on another, it was enormously stimulating to watch Peter Fisher's daughter beg. As she grew more desperate, her self-respect went out the window, as it was doing now, with her hand sliding up the inside of his trouser leg. Even more of a kick was turning her down, watching her disappointment and frustration. Roger found it a huge aphrodisiac.

"But I've got a radio interview early in the morning. I need to be up fresh and early," he said, thoroughly enjoying the profound disappointment on her face.

"We never seem to have any time together," she said in a small, pointed voice. "Sometimes I wonder whether you find me attractive at all, Roger."

Careful, he warned himself. "Don't be silly. You're gorgeous, you know that."

She was still doubtful.

"But I totally respect you," he added meaningfully. "And I want things to happen properly between us. I want us to get to know each other fully first before we take things onto another level."

The words were pure phoney, but he could see that they were exactly the right ones for the moment.

"Me too," she said shyly. "I suppose we can wait a little longer."

"Not too much longer," Roger said with false lust.

"Can't we meet for a drink tonight anyway?" She was begging now.

Oh, the power, he thought.

"Sure," he said.

He wondered how much longer he could hold her off.

Phyllis Harding had gone to get them coffee. Alone in her office, Jean tried to marshal her thoughts. She had no doubt that Jack Thornton had briefed Harding fully on his phone conversation with her last night.

"Cathy Conroy's too fucking sensitive," he had bawled.

Jean had told him that unless he tempered his language, she would terminate their conversation forthwith. Things had scarcely improved from there.

"You were sly, Mr Thornton. You should have told her upfront."

"I didn't tell her upfront because I knew this would be the reaction."

"And you went behind my back too. I am also the agent for the script, in case you've forgotten."

"Your input into the script is long over."

"You're getting my input whether you like it or not. I represent an actress you are attempting to coerce into doing something her contract does not require her to do."

"I have *not* tried to coerce her." He sounded enraged. "I don't coerce actors. I was one myself for a long time. Still am."

"All communication regarding this scene is to go through my office from now on," Jean stated baldly. "I

312

don't want my client bothered again. She's trying to make a film down there."

"Jesus Christ. Isn't that what we're *all* trying to do down here?"

Declan Mahoney had tried to pour oil on troubled waters. It was his suggestion that Jean take the matter up with Phyllis Harding this morning. It was bound to work, he'd thought. Two women together and all that – after a bit of a gossip and a bonding giggle, surely they could iron out this little problem between them without dragging Cinerama or the Government into it?

Big mistake. Jean Ormsby and Phyllis Harding disliked each other on sight, having already disliked each other from a distance.

Jean briskly opened her copy of Cathy's contract and tried to swallow her nerves as Phyllis stomped in and dumped two cups of coffee on the desk. She sat and watched Jean silently out of red-rimmed eyes.

Jean refused to be intimidated. "In my copy of Cathy Conroy's contract, Clause 23 clearly states that nudity is not a requirement."

Phyllis Harding still said nothing.

"I have taken legal advice," Jean went on tersely. "And you cannot force Cathy Conroy to do a nude scene if she doesn't want to."

Phyllis Harding carefully rearranged a box of paperclips on the desk, her pasty face malevolent. Jean waited for the threats, the harsh words, the loophole in the contract that Phyllis would use to send her scurrying out the door with her tail between her legs.

She was astonished when Phyllis smiled cosily and leaned forward, planting her two fat elbows on the desk.

"If it's a question of money, I'm sure we can up her fees to reflect this new development. Would a couple of thousand help?"

Jean was even more surprised. The offer of money was more or less admitting that she and Cathy were in the right.

"Money is not the issue, I'm afraid, Miss Harding."

And even if it was, they'd have to come up with a hell of a lot more than two thousand. If Linda didn't get out of bed for less than ten thousand, then Cathy Conroy would not take off her kacks for less than thirty if Jean had anything to do with it. Maybe even fifty if she could raise a big enough stink.

Phyllis looked even more conciliatory now. "Is there anything we can do to make her happy about this, Jean?"

The woman was even resorting to first names.

"I don't think so," Jean said cautiously. She had expected a dog-fight. Not this "name your price" game, as though Phyllis were already licked.

Phyllis looked at her sagely. "I hope you realise what a boost this could be to her career?"

"I beg your pardon?"

"Come on, *everyone* takes their clothes off these days," Phyllis confided. "Jesus Christ, they complain if they *don't get* to take their clothes off! Look what it did for Demi Moore – who was she before she appeared in the raw on the front of *Vanity Fair*? As for Playboy – it's an *honour* to be asked to strip off for them, you know.

314

And the men too – how many times now have we seen Michael Douglas's butt?" She grinned owlishly at Jean. "If I were Cathy, I'd be grateful for the chance."

Jean stared back levelly. "What does Cinerama think about all this?"

Phyllis smiled sweetly. "They're behind Jack Thornton a hundred percent. As is the Government."

Jean was dismayed. She was not only up against Harding and Thornton, but Cinerama as well. And Peter Fisher.

She felt anger take over. She would not be bullied by them. By *him*.

"I'm afraid my client does not want to do it and there really is no way that you can force her."

Phyllis's chummy smile mutated into a snarl, frighteningly fast. "Is there not?"

She had been altogether too civil so far, Jean realised. She should have known that the woman had something up her sleeve after she had kept Jean waiting in reception for the best part of an hour. That was not the action of someone who did not have a trump card.

"Cathy Conroy is not indispensable to this movie," Phyllis said softly, her neck arched like that of a cobra.

Surely she couldn't be serious? "I doubt that you're going to re-cast at this late stage," Jean said, managing to sound calm.

"I would remind you that there is less than one tenth of the film in the can, Ms Ormsby." Phyllis was showing her true colours at last. Her mean little eyes shot sparks of odium in Jean's direction. "I've done everything I can to keep you happy today and you're just not going to meet me halfway, are you?"

This was a blatant lie. Phyllis Harding had offered nothing but a paltry sum of money.

"So," Phyllis spat softly, "If you refuse to drop Clause 23, I have no option but to draw your attention to Clause 47. Which clearly states that your client can be fired at any point during the project. 'Artistic differences'."

It was the one clause in the contract Jean had not liked. It was also a standard film clause, Declan Mahoney had argued at the time, and it was staying.

The two women stared at each other, the air coloured with confrontation. Jean knew that Cathy's career was in her hands and she had to make a snap decision. She hoped to God it would be the right one.

She stood and picked up her briefcase. "Goodbye so."

Phyllis's lazy voice followed her to the door. "Twenty-four hours, Miss Ormsby. If your client still refuses to do the scene and holds up production any longer, I'm going to recast."

Jean saw now that Phyllis Harding was loving this; that she had been waiting the entire meeting for Jean to walk out. And that nothing would please her more than to boot Jean and her client off the film. The problem of finding a replacement actress would be a small worry in the face of her satisfaction.

Jean left without a backward glance, knowing what she had to do.

Chapter Twenty-two

The fifty-three sheep in Packie O'Connor's field in Graiguenamanagh knew that something big was going down in the field next door. Things hadn't been right since yesterday, of course, when all production on the movie had completely ceased.

Today's developments had started just before lunch outside the farmhouse, where the sheep knew that there was some big meeting going on. A big crowd of people had gathered, and there had been lots of raised voices and tension. The focus of all the drama seemed to be a woman in a sharp red suit, who had marched out of the farmhouse with that tall girl, Cathy Conroy, in tow. Both had disappeared into one of the trailers with a slam of the door. Then Jack Thornton and Jason Blake had appeared, unearthed mobile phones, shouted some more into them, and stomped off into their own trailers.

The rest of the cast and crew stood around picking their noses until it was obvious that nobody was going to tell them what to do. En masse, they drifted to the catering tent, faces red with excitement and trepidation.

Shortly afterwards, the cars had started to arrive – big, black, important-looking cars; Mercedes, BMWs and a Saab. A well-dressed couple had jumped from that one and disappeared into Thornton's trailer, the man muttering into yet another mobile phone.

Declan Mahoney, Carl Tallon, the line producer – all had traipsed in and out of Thornton's trailer, looking volatile and belligerent. That Miranda girl, Thornton's assistant, ran back and forth across the field, ferrying coffee, scripts, contracts and two spare mobile phones in case anyone ran out.

And there was no sign at all of Cathy Conroy and the mysterious lady in red. What, the sheep wondered, was going on?

They edged closer to the catering tent. If anyone knew, it would be the catering girls.

"Jean Ormsby's pulled her off the set," Marie, head of costume, announced.

"No!"

The catering girls huddled closer together, agog. Marie nodded wisely.

"In the middle of a meeting Jack Thornton had set up with Cathy Conroy *and* Jason Blake to talk about the nude scene."

"No!"

To walk off on Jack Thornton and Jason Blake? The girls exchanged boggle-eyed looks. Was Jean Ormsby completely barking? Either that or she was incredibly, suicidally, brave.

Dympna, the fat boss of catering, elbowed her way closer to the epicentre of the gossip.

"Agents," she sniffed disparagingly. She for one thought the whole thing a storm in a teacup. "Should have their heads boiled, every last one of them."

"Oh now, I don't know about that, Dympna," Marie returned with spirit. "Why should the men get away with trying to turn us all into sex symbols?"

"*She's* no sex symbol," a trainee catering girl chimed in disparagingly. She was a failed actress herself and harboured a strong grudge against Cathy Conroy.

The rest of the catering girls joined in the debate now.

"I think she's very attractive. In a Twiggy sort of way."

"Twiggy! I think she looks like a fella."

"Thornton will never stand for it, Twiggy or not."

"Jason Blake's already been on to his agent in LA."

"I wouldn't blame him."

"Oh come on! It's not as though we're going to see his dangly bits in any nude scene!"

"Shame."

Several sniggers accompanied this.

"But *her* boobs and fanny will be everywhere, you can count on that! Jack Thornton's no feminist."

"She's just looking for attention." Dympna was sticking to her guns. After twenty years in film catering, she had developed a healthy disrespect for actors and their demands. Anyway, the very fact that they chose to spend their lives pretending to be someone else was proof enough that they all had screws loose in the first place.

"Apparently, she had no choice but to walk off," Marie confided in a whisper. "The casting agent in Dublin said she would be fired if she didn't do the scene!"

"*No!*"

This was a juicy bit of news indeed. Several sceptics immediately changed their allegiance from Thornton to Cathy.

"That's blackmail."

"It's a bloody disgrace."

"It's because she's not known. Do you think *Kate Winslet* has to put up with this crap?"

"Will they re-cast?" the failed-actress trainee enquired breathlessly, having visions of herself being "discovered" as she handed over a chip butty.

"Probably," Dympna said imperiously. "We're only a couple of weeks into the shoot." She knew about these things.

Marie sniffed haughtily. "It's not up to you or me, is it, Dympna? And maybe not Jack Thornton either."

"What do you mean?" Dympna barked.

The catering girls held their breaths, knowing that there was more to come. Marie savoured the moment.

"*Apparently*, Cinerama have got wind of it."

"*No!!!*"

"*Apparently* they're hopping mad."

"They don't want a nude scene?" the trainee enquired.

Marie sniffed at her naïveté. "They couldn't care less

if Cathy Conroy was buck-naked in *every* scene! The fact
is that production has stopped and they're losing
thousands of pounds by the hour! And as for recasting
. . . if Jack Thornton thinks that they'll pay for a reshoot
with a new actress, he's insane."

"So what's he going to do?" someone asked, looking
to Marie for the answer. Dympna started to get annoyed.
The costume department was, as usual, stealing all the
attention. It was the same with the Oscars. When,
Dympna wondered dourly, were they going to get around
to handing out a Best Catering On Location Award?

"Nothing," she bellowed authoritatively. "It's up to
Peter Fisher."

"He *knows*?" The girls were in a frenzy of excitement
now.

"Oh yes. And he's here."

Dympna saw that she had buttered Marie's parsnips
with this snippet of gossip and she was delighted.

"Holed up in Thornton's trailer with that wife of
his," she elaborated.

They had all seen Tess Fisher on her visits to the set at
Thornton's invitation. There had been endless
speculation as to whether she and Thornton were
carrying on. The consensus in the end was no. Since he'd
got rid of that pneumatic nurse, he'd followed Tess
Fisher around like an over-eager puppy but she, the
girls decided, wasn't interested. And why should she
be? With a dish like Peter Fisher for a husband? None
of them would kick *him* out of bed for eating crisps.

And then there was her daughter Fiona, of course.

She was an okay kid, even if she had only got a job on the set because of Dad.

"Fisher's furious," Dympna imparted casually, as though she were Fisher's closest confidante.

"It's not his film," Marie said loftily.

"Oh yeah?" Dympna shot. "Why was his little lapdog Croft hanging around here like a dose of the runs until Thornton had the sense to get rid of him?"

Everyone pulled a face. Roger Croft had not been sadly missed.

"He'll sort this nude scene out fairly pronto," Marie stated. "The Government doesn't need the embarrassment. And they certainly don't want it getting out to the press."

"Indeed," Dympna agreed heartily. Nothing worse than reporters holding up the lunch queue with their stupid questions. And it was Chicken Korma today, the crew's favourite; little pets.

"Carl Tallon's as much to blame as anyone," someone else offered. But she got little support. The catering girls thought he was a dreamboat, with his long black hair, soulful eyes and tatty denim jacket. And he always said "please" and "thank you" – he treated them with a little respect. The girls always made sure he got extra big portions at the catering hatch.

"He didn't have any choice. Thornton insisted," another girl offered, exonerating Carl from any blame. "Anyway, I heard he feels pretty bad about the whole mess."

This sparked another wave of debate.

"But he hates Cathy Conroy. Anyone can see that."

"I think it's just an act."

"What, you think he *fancies* her?"

"They used to go out together."

"What?"

"During the play five years ago. A friend of mine was stage manager. She said they were stuck to each other like glue."

"What happened?"

"Some big bust-up. Nobody knows why."

They pondered on this mystery.

"Well, something will have to be done," Marie finally declared.

"Or else we could all be out of a job," Dympna added ominously.

The two women eyed each other fearfully and edged a little closer together, comrades again. There was nothing like the threat of unemployment to bring a little harmony.

"What do we do now?" the trainee enquired.

"Nothing. We sit and wait."

"I *never* told Phyllis Harding that she had the authority to fire Cathy Conroy. I said *negotiate.* She took matters into her own hands." Declan Mahoney was red-faced with indignation. "I don't know how she's going to get us out of this one – "

"You can forget about that." Thornton's voice was leaden. "I already fired her."

"Oh, so it's up to *me* to go and pat down ruffled feathers?" Declan demanded.

"I think you've done enough," Thornton snapped.

"The nude scene was your idea, Jack."

"As you've pointed out four times already."

"Oh shut up, the pair of you!" Peter Fisher snapped. Thornton and Mahoney shot him belligerent looks and lapsed into a tense silence. Peter rubbed his eyes tiredly. This was all he needed today, after Bill Mackey's triumph in the newspaper polls. It was a beautiful summer's day outside – he should be living life. Instead, he was stuck in a tiny trailer with a pair of raging egos who were creating even more problems. For two pins, he would walk out the door.

He looked across at Tess. She obviously didn't feel the same. Her face was keen and interested, her eyes bright for information. He supposed that this little crisis must be a welcome diversion for her after the boring summer she was having so far. To give her her due, she hadn't complained at all about her staid new living conditions, but Peter knew that she must be missing the bright lights. Why else did she spend so much time on the film set these days?

He looked at Thornton, then Mahoney. "You two have created this mess. Now what are we going to do?"

"Can we recast?" Thornton ventured hopefully. "It's not too late."

"Yes, it bloody is," Peter growled. "Cinerama will have a fit for starters. And to dump Cathy Conroy because she won't do the scene would make us look even shoddier than we look already."

This whole nude-scene business was a headache

Peter did not need right now. The movie was supposed to work to the Government's advantage. Instead, Thornton was managing to turn them into a crowd of pornographers.

"I think we should wait it out," Declan Mahoney declared. "Jean Ormsby is just calling our bluff."

Peter made a small involuntary movement at the mention of her name and hoped that nobody else had noticed.

It was strange really. It had been nearly a month since that fateful Saturday night and instead of receding, the longing for her had only grown more fierce. He thought about her constantly, wondering at odds times of the day what she was doing. Sometimes he drew little similarities between his life and hers; for instance, he thought about her as he ate his breakfast, knowing that she must be breakfasting at that time too. Or in his car on the way home, he would imagine her negotiating her way though rush-hour traffic on her way back to her little cottage in Castleknock.

It was all very domestic and mundane, and sometimes he would redden at his own fantasies. He had never seen her in rush-hour traffic, for God's sake. And what was he doing, fixating on her eating a bowl of breakfast cereal?

She mightn't even eat breakfast, for all he knew. In fact, he knew nothing much at all about Jean Ormsby. She was a virtual stranger. He knew how she looked, the way she tasted and felt during that brief kiss, he'd had an hour or so of conversation with her in his entire life. And that was all he was basing his great romantic feelings upon. If anybody else had confessed this to him, he would have laughed in amusement and told them that they simply had a crush.

Maybe he had too. Perhaps an unsatisfactory marriage and an increasingly unsatisfactory career had led him to project all kinds of romantic feelings onto a perfectly ordinary woman. In that case, he was a sad old fool who had obviously learned none of the lessons life had tried to teach him along the way.

He was annoyed with himself for indulging in yet another Jean Ormsby Retrospective.

He took it out on Thornton. "Why don't you make life easier for us all by just dropping the bloody scene?"

Thornton didn't appreciate this. "I'm the director. I have to stick by what I think the movie should be."

"*What* movie? Jesus Christ, you haven't shot a single scene since yesterday afternoon! If you think Cinerama are going to stand still while you waste their time and money, you've got another thing coming!"

Thornton was furious now. "Oh come on, Peter, you don't give a fuck about Cinerama! All you care about is your precious by-election!"

"I care about the original filmscript that I read, Jack. And there was no nude scene in that!"

"What's the point in recriminations?" Tess said pointedly to Peter. "Surely we should be looking for a solution?"

Peter was surprised. What was she coming down on Thornton's side for?

"Indeed," he said sarcastically. "Before the papers get hold of it."

This was the most pressing concern. Nobody – not Thornton, Cinerama, and certainly not Carol Taylor and the party – wanted it to hit the airwaves that their lead actress had walked off the set, citing exploitation. None of them would come out of it smelling sweet. But with each passing minute, the danger increased that someone, somewhere, would spill the beans.

"Will you consider dropping the scene?" Peter again asked Thornton, voice tight.

But Thornton's pride was choking him now. "No! Now you just keep on pushing, Peter, and see where it gets you."

The threat was clear. Thornton would walk if he didn't get his way. Peter was raging at his petulance.

Declan Mahoney hurriedly stepped in. "Could we water it down? Would they go for topless only?"

Thornton looked gloomy. "They're on a fucking crusade now. I know Ormsby's type. You wouldn't know what she'd be holding out for."

"An apology, perhaps?" The words were loud and sharp and they came from Tess.

The three men turned to look at her, surprised.

"You messed up, Jack, by not being upfront," Tess went on. "Phyllis Harding messed up by issuing threats. If I were Jean Ormsby, I'd have done exactly the same thing."

She looked at Peter directly as she said the agent's name. She wasn't afraid. She wasn't afraid of Jack Thornton either.

"This isn't about anyone taking their clothes off. It's

about respect. If you started by apologising for the spectacularly shoddy way you've treated Cathy Conroy, you might get somewhere."

Thornton didn't like this. But he swallowed it. He looked at Tess and turned his hands palm-upwards, conceding that she was right. She nodded almost imperceptibly. It was the kind of body language that only people very familiar with each other shared, Peter realised with a start.

Could she be . . . ? No. Impossible. Sure, she was spending a lot of time on the set lately, but wasn't that because of Fiona? And she had been out a lot in the evenings recently, but Peter had no reason to believe it was with Thornton.

He shook his head slightly, wondering whether he was losing it entirely. Tess would never throw over her status and position for an affair, no matter how famous Thornton was. Of that one fact, Peter could be a hundred percent sure.

Tess stood decisively, her point made. "If you'll excuse me – I'm meeting Fiona for lunch." She looked briefly at Peter. "I'll see you later."

She stepped from the trailer, leaving a faint trail of Dune behind her. Declan Mahoney and Jack Thornton looked after her with something akin to awe.

"Let's finish this up," Peter said sharply.

"Jean Ormsby won't accept any apology from me," Declan Mahoney declared. "As far as she's concerned, I set Phyllis Harding on her."

"She'll think I'm apologising just to get my own way,"

Thornton said. He had no desire to deal with Jean Ormsby again. She had looked at him this morning in a manner that would strip paint. The hardened Hollywood babes that Thornton dealt with on a regular basis weren't a patch on her.

"Wonderful! I guess that leaves me," Peter said, hoping that his sarcasm masked his nerves.

"You need this movie more than any of us," Thornton replied with a nasty little smile. "Now go and get Cathy Conroy back on set."

Cathy was bundling clothes into a rucksack.

"What are you doing?" Jean demanded.

"I thought I'd better make a start," Cathy explained.

"What?"

"You said on the set this morning that I was to pack my things."

"Jesus! That was for the benefit of Thornton. You hardly thought I was serious?"

"I don't know, do I! If we walked off the set, why are we sitting in my trailer? We're still *on* the bloody set!"

Cathy looked wounded and not a little bewildered by the sudden turn of events this morning.

Jean felt bad. It had all seemed a great idea at the time. The drama was wonderful and the timing perfect. Let's show Thornton, Phyllis Harding and everyone else that we can get out the big stick too! Let's get tough with the tough guys, let's barricade ourselves into our trailer until they come crawling on their hands and knees *begging* Cathy to come back! Yeah! High fives all around!

The euphoria had lasted an hour. It dwindled slowly as time ticked by and nobody came knocking on the trailer door. Jean's mobile taunted them with its silence. Now, three hours into the siege, things were looking distinctly Not Good.

"Sorry, Cathy," Jean eventually said. "I'm a little uptight."

This was something of an understatement. Under the trailer table, her knees were doing a nervous little dance of their own and her stomach was somewhere in the region of her sling-backs.

What was Thornton *doing* a hundred yards across the field? Was he simply calling her bluff just as she had called his? Or was he at this very moment setting up a casting session for a new actress to take over the role of Alison?

No. They wouldn't, would they? Without even *trying* to sort it out?

The desperate reassurances were starting to ring a little hollow. Maybe she had just made a huge mistake. After all, Jack Thornton had the might of Hollywood behind him. Did she really think he was going to roll over for a small-time Dublin agent? Hell, he was probably making paper airplanes out of Cathy's contract right now and cackling that Jean Ormsby was finished in this town.

Her knees started to bounce off the table top.

She looked at Cathy's miserable face and it was like a dash of cold water. Here she was worrying about herself when it was Cathy who was the injured party.

She should have thought this thing through properly before she jumped in her car outside Phyllis Harding's office and broke the speed limit to Kilkenny. She had acted in the heat of the moment, fuelled by her own sense of outrage and a desire to show them all that they couldn't walk all over her. She had been *selfish*.

"Where are you going?" Cathy asked, as Jean stood up.

"To talk to Jack Thornton."

"What?"

"I have to try and see if we can work something out before this goes any farther." Maybe she could salvage this yet and get Cathy back on the set today. If necessary, she would eat as much humble-pie as he demanded.

"No."

"Sorry?"

"I said no." Cathy's mouth was set and Jean saw fierce determination in her eyes.

"But Cathy, you could lose the role."

"I haven't done anything wrong. I'm not giving in."

"That's very noble of you. But principles won't pay the rent."

"I don't care. Now I respect your opinion, Jean. But I have the last say. And as my agent, I don't give you permission to talk to Thornton on my behalf."

Jean shrugged and sat back down. She hadn't realised Cathy had so much backbone. She'd had her pegged as another actress on the make who would do anything to get a part – including pretending that she was on Jean's books.

"So what's your bottom line, Cathy? Will you do the scene or not?"

"Of course not!" She looked at Jean suspiciously. "What, are you saying now that I *should*?"

Jean sighed. The whole thing was a minefield. On the one hand, there was the crowd who would holler "exploitation" at the very sight of bare female skin. On the other hand, there was the mob who would go on about women reclaiming their bodies and banishing taboos.

To Jean, there was only one way to look at it.

"Have you read the script?" she asked.

"Of course I have," Cathy said impatiently.

"*Really* read it, Cathy? You're not letting anything influence your judgement?"

"Such as?"

Jean shrugged. "It'd be understandable if your back was up over the way this has been sprung on you. Anybody would dig their heels in."

"I am not letting Jack Thornton's behaviour colour my view, if that's what you mean!"

She sounded so vehement that Jean believed her. But there was *something* bugging her.

"You think I should do it, don't you?" Cathy said incredulously.

Jean looked her in the eye. "No. For two reasons: firstly, they pulled a fast one, and secondly, I suspect Jack Thornton's motives for having a nude scene in the first place. But I don't have a problem with the actual scene. No, hear me out, Cathy, please. I worked on that script for weeks during the rewrite stage. And whatever about Thornton and the rest of them, the scene as it is written is good and strong and is in no way exploitative of you, Jason Blake or anybody else."

Cathy was silent for a moment. "Maybe," she muttered.

"Carl Tallon is too good to let that happen," Jean finished.

Some peculiar emotion ran across Cathy's face before she could hide it. Jean watched her carefully. They were getting to the crux of the matter now.

"You used to go out with him, didn't you?"

Cathy jumped.

"Look, Bernice Gannon told me. She worked on the Abbey production of *Outsiders*."

"So what if I did?" Cathy was baldly hostile now.

"If there's some kind of problem there – "

"There's no problem."

"Okay, but maybe I should get him in here, you could talk through the scene –"

"No."

Jean was taken aback by the ferocity with which this came out.

"Cathy, it makes sense. I represent both of you."

"I've already tried to talk to him. And I'm not going to again. Okay?"

Jean was not going to get far down that road.

"Okay, fine. But you should know that I've already spoken to him, Cathy. He didn't change his script for cheap thrills. He's got more integrity than that."

Cathy did not reply. Jean eyeballed her.

"And you've got too much talent and intelligence to allow your emotions to spill over into your work."

It was an age before Cathy replied. "If we were to do the scene – and it's a big if – I would want to view the rushes."

Jean's admiration for Cathy grew. "Right. But let's not jump the gun here, Cathy. There will be no nude scene until that shower over there in Thornton's trailer start behaving like professionals."

They both started slightly at a knock on the trailer door. Jean felt relief wash over her. Thornton, at last.

"Well, well," she said. "Let me do the talking, okay?"

When she opened the door to Peter Fisher, words completely eluded her. She had no idea he was here today.

"Can we talk?" He was direct and courteous.

"Not here," Jean said evenly. "Perhaps we could drive into town for a coffee."

She had already decided that any compromise would be reached far away from the set, which was firmly marked as Thornton's turf. It would be on neutral ground.

"Okay."

As Jean gathered her bag and phone, Fisher nodded to Cathy. "I hear the rushes are great. Well done."

It wasn't bluster or false flattery. Cathy nodded back quickly, embarrassed and pleased.

"Stay here," Jean told her quietly. "Don't say anything to anybody. I'll phone you, okay?"

Chapter Twenty-three

Peter Fisher drove directly to a big hotel on the outskirts of Kilkenny without consulting Jean. Reception was bright and open-plan, with plenty of people milling around, several of whom recognised him and nodded. Jean immediately understood that he had chosen this venue so that there could be absolutely no suggestion of impropriety, no question that this was anything other than a business meeting. She didn't know whether she was annoyed or relieved.

"Are you hungry?" he enquired politely.

Jean looked at her watch and noted with a start that it was almost seven o'clock. The afternoon had disappeared.

"Yes."

They got the best table in the restaurant. The manager had also recognised Peter Fisher. The hotel had a planning application in for an extension.

There was very little said until they were seated and had ordered from a nervous young waitress. Jean refused wine. She could be as officious and businesslike as him. The waitress went and they were alone.

Peter rearranged his cutlery carefully. "It would be better if we were to keep the press out of this."

At the question in his eyes, Jean felt a flash of annoyance.

"I certainly haven't informed them." Did he think that her actions today were some kind of media game?

"I just don't think it would help matters."

"Like I said, they won't be hearing anything from me," Jean sharply clarified.

He nodded. "Thank you."

Another silence fell.

"Would you like to – " he began.

"I was thinking – " she said simultaneously.

Both cut off sharply, looking at each other in embarrassment. Peter waved a hand, giving her the floor.

"I was going to say that, upon reading the script again, Cathy and I are open to compromise. We want the scene shot exactly as it's written – no frills or cheap stunts from Thornton. No full-frontal shots and nothing explicit below the waist. We also want a closed set. And we get artistic veto. If we don't like what we see in the rushes, then the scene is cut." She had laid her cards squarely on the table. "And you?"

He reached into his coat pocket and produced two sheets of paper. "I was going to ask whether you'd like to read these now or later?"

Jean looked at the pages warily. Was it some kind of

notice of a lawsuit from the movie's fleet of slick LA lawyers? For a moment, she thought she was going to be sick.

"These are two written apologies," Peter Fisher said. "One is from Jack Thornton. The other is from Cinerama. They faxed it over this afternoon."

Jean couldn't have been more surprised. She managed to hide it.

"But they still want the nude scene?"

"This is between you and me," Peter Fisher said.

"Yes. Of course."

"Jack Thornton does. If you feel really strongly about it, I'll force him to drop the scene. But if you're prepared to compromise, then maybe everybody will be happy at the end of the day. We will certainly agree to everything you've just asked for. I will personally see to that."

It was a feat of enormous self-control to hide her delight and offer Peter nothing more than a poker-faced nod.

"Thank you." She looked at the two apologies and was gratified as she imagined Jack Thornton and Cinerama bending over the pages, gritting their teeth. They might think twice about pulling something like this in future. "I'll pass these on to Cathy. I'm sure she'll be pleased."

"And she'll be back on the set in the morning?"

"First thing," Jean assured him.

A great weight lifted from her and she felt almost dizzy with relief.

"Agreed, then," Peter Fisher said.

"Agreed."

The triumph quickly passed as it dawned on her that a whole meal stretched before them with absolutely nothing left to discuss. After all, she thought, what had they in common except the film and a kiss in his car that night? They had already covered the first topic and the second was hardly suitable for a little light dinner conversation.

Tell me, did you enjoy our little kiss? Oh good, so did I. We really must get together and do it again sometime. I'll check my diary and have my secretary get on to yours. Oh, and maybe the next time you might follow it up with a phone call, you bastard.

She shifted in her chair and wished heartily that she had not ordered a starter. He seemed to be thinking the same thing, judging from the way he was looking around for the waitress. The silence stretched.

She would *not* give into the impulse to fill the embarrassing void with nonsensical chatter about the weather. Neither would she go to the loo to pass a little time between courses. Why should she be the one to make the effort? And why pretend that she was enjoying this dinner when, patently, it was a disaster? Deliberately she laid her napkin on the table.

"I'm not hungry after all," she said quietly. "Maybe it's not too late to cancel our order?"

If he wouldn't put an end to this sham, then she would.

"If that's what you'd prefer," he said eventually.

Oh come on, she thought. Both of them knew damned well that he was dying to run out of the place too.

Her impatience with him made her say abruptly, "And what *you'd* prefer. I just have the neck to say it."

She was prepared for hostility, for annoyance. Instead he smiled.

"I don't think there's been any question about your 'neck' today. I'd never seen Jack Thornton rattled before, you know. Not a pretty sight."

She didn't want to be flattered. And she didn't want to get into Jack Thornton and the whole nude scene again, not when everything had been settled.

"He had it coming," she said shortly.

Peter Fisher was looking at her curiously, head to one side. "Why are you so prickly?"

Prickly? What did he think accounted for the tension between them tonight, a bad case of PMT on her part? Didn't he understand anything, *feel* anything? There she was, putting herself on rack for the past month about Peter Fisher, analysing every last second of that night together in his car, turning it over in her brain at least ten times a day, while he thought that everything was hunky-dory between them except for a mild case of inexplicable "prickliness" on her part?

Obviously, the incident in his car had not bothered him in the slightest. All the more proof that he did that kind of thing all the time. He probably groped young women over the gear-stick twice a week.

Well, to hell with him. If she was going to turn herself into a nervous wreck over some man, he would at least be worth it. And she had thought that he would actually *phone* her? Delusion wasn't in it.

"Will you cancel our order or will I?" she asked crisply.

He was cool now. "I will."

The hapless waitress thought his curt beckon was an indication that they wanted to speed things up, and went scurrying into the kitchen. Jean felt her fingernails bore holes in the palms of her hands.

"And contrary to what you seem to think, I would have enjoyed having dinner with you," he added in a hard voice. "I didn't think we were on such bad terms."

Now not only had she possible PMT, but some bizarre grudge against him.

"We aren't on bad terms," she said abruptly. "We aren't on *any* terms."

He recoiled slightly; he looked hurt. She wasn't prepared for this.

"Well, we aren't, are we?" she added desperately.

"Not when you put it like that, no," he said, sounding angry now.

Jean was confused. And angry now too. Why was he acting like the injured party here? *She* had done nothing wrong.

There was still no sign of the waitress. "It's too late to cancel our order. Let's just pay the bill and go, will we?" she said, fumbling for her purse.

"I'll get it." He reached for his wallet.

Pride made her back stiffen. She might be a penniless agent, but she would not be humbled before him – him with his black Saab and huge expenses allowance.

"I said I would get it," she said sharply.

"And I invited you for dinner," he returned stubbornly.

"Look, I owe you, okay? You gave me a lift to Dublin that night."

She wanted to bite back the words the minute they were out. The last thing she'd intended to do here today was bring up the night in his car.

She stared at the tablecloth, sweat popping out on her upper lip. Across the table, Peter Fisher was still. Probably mortified, she thought, and looking for the quickest exit.

"I haven't stopped thinking about you since," he said.

Jean felt as though she were teetering on the edge of a cliff. Step back and *fast*, the sane part of her yelled. Stand up and walk out now. She stayed sitting.

"I know. I've been the same," she said, looking him straight in the eye.

The waitress arrived breathlessly with their Caesar salads, asked whether they would like some dressing, was completely ignored, and eventually left.

Peter pushed the salad aside. His eyes burned into hers. She had no impulse or desire to look away.

"Sometimes I tell myself that I hardly know you and that I shouldn't feel this way. But I do."

"Me too," she said, knowing that she was apeing him but not caring. He was saying all the things she felt.

"And no matter how much I tell myself that this shouldn't happen, I can't help myself."

"No," she agreed.

He didn't seem to mind her momentary lack of verbal dexterity. Her face was all the encouragement he needed.

"It all points to one thing really," he said.

"Yes, yes," she said, nodding furiously.

"I suppose I must be in love with you," he finished quietly.

The words were like a small shock. She was very still now.

"Me too. With you, I mean."

Neither of them breathed for a moment. The air was thick.

"Is it off or something?" The blasted waitress was back, having been dispatched by the manager posthaste. "Your salad?"

"Yes," Peter said.

"He means no," Jean said.

The waitress looked from one to the other nervously, then over her shoulder at the manager. She could feel a P45 coming on.

"I can get you something else if you'd prefer."

"I'm not hungry," Peter managed. "Jean?"

"I couldn't eat a thing."

"Just the bill, please," he told the waitress.

They found themselves in the hotel foyer, looking at each other. Jean shifted from foot to foot, unsure. What to do now? After such declarations on both their parts, surely he wasn't going to drive her back to the set?

"Do you want to go somewhere?" he asked instead. "To talk?"

Jean felt relieved. There was so much to be said yet, it was all just beginning. But where could they go? They couldn't continue any conversation in the middle of a

342

hotel foyer. And they could hardly go back to his house. He seemed as uncertain as she.

"Why don't I book into a room?" she found herself saying. "I'm staying down here for the night anyway . . ."

She trailed off. A hotel room was very private. And it also had a bed. Neither of them could fail to be aware of this. But there was nothing else for it. They couldn't wander from hotel to hotel all night.

"All right. But. . . Jean. I would have to go up separately."

There would be subterfuge involved on his part, he wanted her to know that. And if she found it all too seedy and wanted to back out, then that would be okay. She thought about it, but only briefly.

"In that case, I'll go up first," she said.

Alone in the elevator to the second floor, she waited for reason to prevail, for her own well-honed sense of self-protection to hit her with a dose of reality.

It didn't. She knew what she was doing, she'd had plenty of opportunity to say no. She wanted Peter, she had for months now, and she could not deny it. Neither would she fool herself by blaming it on impulse. She was going into this one with her eyes wide open.

The room she'd booked in her name was as bare and anonymous as every other hotel room. She found she was nervous, terrified. While she waited for him, she wandered about the room, turning on and off the TV, checking out the bathroom. She finger-combed her hair and applied fresh lipstick. Ridiculous, she thought, and quickly scrubbed it off again. All the time, she avoided looking at the double bed with its seductive peach sheets, which seemed to get larger and more imposing by the second.

Finally, she perched on the edge of the sofa, her back deliberately to the bed. She checked her watch. Peter was taking a long time. Too long.

The first slivers of doubt began to eat away at her. Wildly, she wondered whether he had really said all those things in the restaurant. Was he regretting it all now and sprinting for his car? Or had he somehow or other gone to the wrong room?

Just as she was seriously contemplating leaving, the door opened and there he was.

"Sorry. I was cornered downstairs by someone I know. I got away as fast as I could."

"That's okay."

He advanced a few steps and then stopped. She stayed sitting on the sofa. Things were awkward now. She wasn't sure what would happen, what he expected. Did he think she would hurl off her clothes and get down to it straight away with him on that big bed with the peach sheets that seemed cheap and brash now? She wouldn't blame him if he did – she was the one who had suggested booking into a room.

When he sat down on the sofa beside her, she tensed involuntarily. He reached over, but instead of grappling at her clothes, he carefully took her hands in his. The gesture was comforting and even loving, and she found it incredibly erotic because of that.

"I'm married, Jean. You know that," he said eventually.

Instead of being taken aback, she felt a fierce rush of gladness. He was not going to wait for her to bring it up. He wasn't going to brush it under the carpet.

"Yes."

"What about you?" he asked.

She knew he meant Ian.

"He's an ex-boyfriend. That's all."

Peter nodded slowly. "What do you want to do?"

Jean was momentarily confused. Did he mean right now, this minute?

"I'm not free, Jean. Before we . . . before this goes any further, you have to realise that. I can't offer you anything, no matter how much I want to. Is that going to be enough for you?"

Jean had already asked and answered these questions for herself. She had made her decision at the dinner table tonight. Maybe she had made it weeks ago, when she had hoped against hope that he would phone. But she was grateful that he had asked her himself.

"Yes," she said simply.

He was so close that she could feel the heat from his body. The pressure of his hands on hers was curiously numbing and she felt giddy.

He kissed her then. It wasn't tender or soft, it wasn't a tentative getting-to-know-you kiss. Roughly, greedily, they clasped each other close and devoured one another.

His hands were on her face now. She felt his fingertips smoothing her cheeks, moving around to the nape of her neck as his held her closer. It was like he was trying to eat her whole; like he could never get enough of her.

The feeling was mutual. Her hands were buried deep under his suit coat. She was not interested in delicate exploration. She did not want to slowly discover him inch by inch and marvel in wonder. A month of pent-up frustration had put paid to that.

The kiss deepened until she was unsure where her lips ended and his began. They were making those wet, sloppy noises that she had always found embarrassing when she watched couples kissing on the TV. This was different, it was fantastic.

Finally, he drew away. "These terribly serious business suits of yours . . . I've always wondered what you had on beneath them."

She laughed, glad for the brief respite from the intensity of it all. Then the double bed with its peach sheets groaned as he gently pushed her down on it

It was only then that the enormity of what she was about to do dawned on Jean. Things were getting to the point of no return. Was this what she really wanted?

"What's wrong?" he asked.

She quickly shook her head. "Nothing."

He looked at her for a long moment. Then he lifted his hand and gently stroked her hair, then her face; long, slow, sweeping strokes. The touch was devoid of lust. It was pure affection and tenderness and it made all her doubts vanish, doubts that she saw now were not about her own feelings but his, for all his words earlier. This wasn't just another roll in the hay for him. She meant something to him, she knew that now, he had not been lying.

He was looking down at her anxiously.

"Jean. We don't have to. . ."

"Yes. We do."

And she drew his head down for another kiss. Closing her eyes, she gave herself up to it.

Chapter Twenty-four

Gobnait Purcell was sore at the world and had been since birth. Not only had her parents lumbered her with a ridiculous name, but she had been the middle-born child in a gang of seven. The older ones were able to shout louder than her and the younger ones were cuter. Her father was too busy to listen to her tales from school and her mother had heard it all before. When her siblings came down one by one with measles, mumps and chicken pox requiring hours of care and attention, she remained gloriously healthy and ignored. All through her childhood, nobody ever listened to a word Gobnait Purcell had to say.

It was the same story in college. Twice a week, she religiously sprayed Go-Blonde onto her light brown hair but was never beautiful enough to command attention through looks alone. She wasn't bright enough to run with the ultra-intelligent crowd who hobnobbed with the tutors after class. She didn't excel at sport or debating. No matter how hard she tried, there was nothing about her that made people sit up and take note.

Her anger grew. By the time she got a work-placement position in the accounts department of a freebie local newspaper in her final college year, she was a cauldron of boiling rage underneath that pleasant, smiling, imminently-forgettable exterior.

One day a run-of-the-mill article on hairdressers failed to be handed in on time for the next edition of the newspaper. On her lunch-break, Gobnait idly dashed off a vitriolic attack on the types of establishments that charged exorbitant rates to turn brown women into blondes, and on the types of men who fancied blonde women in the first place. It was witty and vicious and vengeful, and the sub-editor found it and loved it.

Gobnait Purcell had finally found a voice.

In the next six months, she penned and got published an exposé on college lecturers who slept with students and one on a possible dope scam in inter-faculty sports. She progressed to freelance contributions to an evening newspaper where her writing got more vicious and more popular. Finally, she landed a full-time permanent position on the biggest national daily, where she quickly rose through the ranks to become the top investigative journalist. Those who met her at functions and press do's thought her personable and nice. Those who unwittingly antagonised her vomited up their breakfast a week, or a month, or even a year later, as they found themselves named and shamed in one of her exposés, depending on her mood.

It was sheer bad luck tonight that Gobnait had a hot date with Gary from Features. They were going for a late dinner and drinks, and the anonymous story tip had just come in. Frank had already gone for the night and Pauline was too busy finishing up an editorial.

"Strictly filler-piece," the sub-editor said with a yawn. "Don't bust a gut."

Gobnait made three quick phone calls. Some rumpus about a nude scene on the Jack Thornton set. Big swing.

Jack Thornton's assistant Miranda snootily gave a "no comment". Gobnait then obtained Cathy Conroy's mobile number but the uppity little cow had had the nerve to hang up on Gobnait. John Graham was still working in Leinster House when Gobnait reached him. He promised to phone back in ten minutes. Gobnait waited thirty. By now, her sub-editor was screaming for the piece and Gary from Features was mumbling about a raincheck.

That's it, Gobnait thought furiously, and started to re-work the article. By the time she was finished, what had started out as a mildly sensationalist and gossipy filler-piece had mutated into a five-hundred-word scathing attack with a decidedly political edge. Without rereading it, she sent it down the line and left for her date.

The sub-editor hurriedly added the headline *Government Funds Porn.*

This tickled the night-editor so much that, at the last minute, he pulled the piece on airport taxes from page one and inserted Gobnait's piece instead.

Down in the basement, the huge presses started to roll.

Cathy wished that she still smoked. At least it'd be something to do. Anyway, wasn't that what all great movie queens traditionally did when things didn't go their way – sit tragically in their trailers and chain-smoke and drink vodka neat? Marilyn Monroe, Jayne Mansfield, Jean Harlow – dashing, romantic stars of the silver screen, thwarted by men and by life, burning brilliantly and briefly in the hearts and minds of millions of people and then passing gloriously into the realms of the unforgettable, icons forever. Wonderful, Cathy sighed, drifting to the minibar in the corner of the trailer with a suitably tragic air.

Neat vodka tasted pretty foul but she stoically tossed it back. The second miniature bottle went down a little easier.

Abandoned, she thought morosely, by everyone. Jean, Jack Thornton, even that nice Peter Fisher. Left to moulder away here alone for the past six – no, seven! – hours with not even a phone call to let her know what was going on.

Her movie career could be over right this minute for all she knew. From the look on Jack Thornton's face earlier, she wouldn't be a bit surprised. She'd probably never work with him again. She'd probably never work again full stop.

Feeling very sorry indeed for herself, she opened the top of the third miniature bottle of vodka with her teeth.

She knew that her self-pity stemmed from the fact that Jean Ormsby had been absolutely right, feck her. It was Carl Tallon who was under her skin, not any potentially dodgy nude scene. Cathy had allowed her professionalism to be compromised for the sake of a few silly emotions. She had been weak.

As if he was worth it. As if he was worth a single *thought*, never mind the amount of anger she had invested in all this nonsense.

"About time," she grumbled as a knock sounded on the trailer door. Aggrieved, she flung it open, expecting Jean.

Carl Tallon stood on the grass outside.

In her surprise, Cathy hiccuped.

"Well? What do you want?" she said ungraciously.

He held up a large brown paper-bag. "Jack Thornton sent me around with this."

Cathy eyed the bulging bag as though it contained semtex. "What is it, more rewrites?" she snapped sarcastically. "Maybe now you want Alison to give Richard a blowjob while she's at it?"

He looked at her silently. He made her feel crass. Crude.

"What is it?" she asked, more muted now.

"Chinese food."

"What?" Did Jack Thornton seriously think she could be bought off with sweet 'n sour chicken?

"He wants us to talk."

"Does he now," Cathy said coldly.

Carl Tallon glared. "Look, I don't want this any more than you do. But we have an obligation to tell him that we at least tried – seeing as our agent and Peter Fisher seem to have disappeared off the face of the earth."

Cathy hesitated. She would look churlish and small if she refused to talk to Carl – and she would feel even more unprofessional if she let her emotions stand in the way of a compromise.

"Five minutes then," she snapped.

"Five too many for me," he snapped back, stepping in.

She watched as he rummaged for plates and forks, and tried to summon up outrage at the familiarity with which he treated her trailer. She sat and swigged more vodka and pretended to ignore him as he efficiently dished out food from cartons.

"None for me, thanks," she said in a small poignant voice, fixing him with a particularly tragic look. Marilyn couldn't have done it better.

"You smell like a brewery," he said brutally. "How many of those have you had?"

"Only three." This tragic thing wasn't washing at all with him. "I'm not drunk."

"Bully for you," he said, slapping down a plate of steaming food in front of her. He plonked himself at the small table opposite her with another plate for himself.

"Eat," he said.

"Please don't order me about."

He shrugged indifferently, lifted his fork and dug in. Chicken chow mein, fried rice, beef in black-bean sauce, noodles – all went down the hatch.

Cathy tried not to watch. It was hard to be soulful when she was salivating furiously. The vodka was making her feel even hungrier. And it had been an awfully long time since breakfast.

To his credit, he didn't sneer when she picked up her fork and nibbled at a prawn. It was so good that she had another. The noodles were good too.

She snuck a glance across the table at him. He glanced up at the same time and caught her eye.

She started to bluster. "Listen, about the nude scene – "

"I know, and I'm sorry, okay?" he cut in abruptly.

"What?"

"About springing it on you like that. But Jack Thornton only told me about it this week. He said that he would discuss it with you."

Cathy eyed him warily. "Did he send you here to butter me up?"

"No!" He shook his head furiously. His hair flopped onto his forehead and Cathy barely managed to restrain herself in time from reaching over and flipping it back, like she used to do a hundred times a day.

It was the vodka, she told herself hastily, that was making her entertain wild fantasies about Carl Tallon's fringe. But, funnily, she had never felt more sober.

"I'm apologising off my own bat, okay?" he muttered. "You were right. I should have consulted you."

He looked embarrassed and took great interest in his prawns. A little glow like a pilot light ignited in Cathy's chest and warmed her. Stop it, she told herself. But the warm glow persisted.

"And I just wanted to see if you were okay," he added in a rush.

The pilot light in Cathy's chest was fanned into a

flame. She felt a flush creep up her neck and hoped to God he didn't notice.

He was looking at her now as though he meant it. Cathy desperately tried to think of something witty and interesting to say.

"Um. Thanks." Oh, brilliant. She tried again. "And I suppose the scene is . . . okay. I mean, it's not half as bad as some nude scenes." Oh, *fantastic*.

She dived into her noodles. But she felt his eyes on her over the trailer table which seemed to have shrunk. This little encounter was not progressing at all the way she'd anticipated. Why weren't they shouting at each other as usual?

"That took some guts today, you know," he said slowly. "To walk off the set like that."

What was with him this evening? Why was he being so *civil*?

"It was Jean's idea."

"You didn't have to go along with it. After all, you were risking your career."

As if she needed reminding. "Yes. Well. Something had to be done."

He nodded again. More black hair flopped down onto his forehead. Cathy's fingers itched to get at it but she managed to hold herself back.

"Anyhow. I'm sure Jean will work it out," she finished limply.

"Yes. I'm sure she will," Carl agreed.

Her fork sounded very loud against the plate in the silence that followed. Well, that was the nude scene dispensed with. What were they supposed to talk about now, she wondered wildly. The weather? The shocking rise in house prices?

"Cathy, about the other day . . ."

She tensed. "What about it?"

"You said that I had played God in your life."

She choked down a lump of beef. "Did I?"

"I was wondering what you meant."

"Nothing."

"You must have meant *something* by it."

The piece of beef was working its way back up her throat. "We were having an argument, Carl. People say things they don't mean when they're having arguments."

"Not you, Cathy. What did I do to you that made you think I was playing God?"

Cathy bitterly regretted that accusation now, thrown out in the heat of the moment. It had been stupid. Even more stupid when the poor eejit hadn't even been aware at the time of what he had made her do.

"Nothing," she said brightly. "That beef is a bit tough, don't you think?"

His shoulders lifted in defeat. "I'll say no more. Except that . . . well, I was wrong." He looked her straight in the eye. "I should have gone to London when you phoned."

Cathy was speechless.

"I'm sorry, okay?"

He tensed, as if expecting her to come back with some nasty put-down.

"Why are you saying this now?" Her voice sounded a bit funny.

"I don't know," he said honestly. "Except that it would be nice if we could finish this film on speaking terms. As friends."

"Yes," Cathy agreed inanely, her heart racing. It would *not* be nice if they could be friends. Friends didn't hide things from each other, friends had pints down the pub and confided their deepest feelings to each other, their regrets and their secrets. And Cathy had no intention of sharing those with Carl.

"Yes, well, thanks for apologising."

She sounded brittle and he was surprised.

"I mean it, Cathy. I let you down. Badly."

He was waiting now for her to say that she too was sorry. Sorry for not coming back from London and for giving him no reason. Sorry about the whole sad mess. And when they were finished crying into their noodles and saying sorry, the explanations would be expected. Because there was no point in saying sorry unless you explained what you were sorry about.

She could imagine the scene if she laid it on the line to him. His conciliatory tone would disappear as fast as whiskey at a wake. He would roar and shout that she'd had no right at all. And she could say sorry until she was blue in the face and he wouldn't listen.

She would mean it too. She *was* sorry. But sorry never changed a thing at the end of the day.

She wondered now if, given the chance, she would do things differently. But she had only been nineteen, young and rash and frightened. And he had been scarcely older, full of idealistic notions about how they would take the world by storm, him as a writer and her as an actress. They had their whole careers ahead of them, he had been fond of saying. With *Outsiders* under their belt, nothing could stop them now. Nothing would stop them.

Well, she had made sure that it wouldn't.

He was watching and waiting now, sure that she would open up the same way that he had. Well, he was out of luck. This wasn't some AA meeting where Cathy was going to get things off her chest, spout a few tears, announce that she felt like a new person and hugs-all-around.

"Carl, it's late. I'm tired."

She wasn't lying. She felt weary all of a sudden. Nothing was ever simple.

He got to his feet quickly. "Of course, sorry."

She saw that she had hurt him. Thrown his offer of friendship back in his face.

"I just don't think we're cut out to be bosom buddies, Carl," she said, trying to make her voice light.

"No. You're probably right," he said slowly. "It was all or nothing with us, wasn't it?"

"Um, yes."

She too bolted to her feet abruptly, wanting to put an end to this conversation. But the trailer wasn't designed for two very tall people to be standing at the same time. And to get to the door, he had to get past her.

She hastily stepped to the left. So did he. She

suddenly found herself jammed up against his scruffy denim jacket.

"Sorry – "

"No, my fault – "

She now stepped to the right. Of course, he would have to do the same. This time, she actually collided with him. Oh, *mortification*.

"Terribly sorry."

"These trailers . . ."

"Oh, I know, poky as hell."

She decided that she wouldn't move at all this time. He obviously decided the same.

And so they stood frozen, inches apart, Cathy's face growing redder with each excruciating moment.

She could smell him, she noted with a shock. Aftershave, the same stuff he used to wear years ago. And soap. And the unmistakable smell of himself, that gorgeous, sexy Carl smell.

The physical attraction they had always shared washed over her like a tidal wave. Bloody hell, she was practically dribbling.

When she finally found the courage to look him in the face, she saw that he wasn't too steady on his feet either. Or maybe it was just the dim light of the trailer that made him seem more intense than usual. And how was it possible for someone's eyes to look so *black*?

"I should go," he said, making absolutely no move to do so.

"You should," she agreed, not budging an inch to let him pass.

As if some magnet had attached itself to their chests, they leaned in towards each other, eyes locked.

They were going to kiss, Cathy knew in that part of her brain which was still functioning. And neither of them was going to stop it . . .

A mobile phone rudely exploded.

Cathy blinked. Carl started.

She pulled away from him abruptly. Reality had come calling with a loud knock.

Carl seemed to feel this too. He was turning away from her, scrabbling at his denim jacket for his mobile.

"It's mine," Cathy said, amazed that her voice still worked. She plucked the phone off the table. "Hello?"

It was some reporter from a national newspaper.

Cathy's brow wrinkled. She felt Carl looking at her. "What do you want?" she asked, mystified.

The reporter asked her whether there was any truth in the rumour that she was refusing to do a nude scene in the Jack Thornton movie.

Cathy was shocked. "How did you find out about the nude scene?"

The reporter simply persisted with her questioning.

Cathy, in her fright, mumbled, "No comment," and hung up.

She turned to Carl, stricken. "That was a reporter – "

"Yes. I gathered." His voice sounded so cold that Cathy was sure that she must be imagining it.

"They know about the nude scene."

"Fancy that."

She was not imagining it. He was furious. Livid.

And unless she was very much mistaken, it was directed at her.

"Carl – you don't think . . . ?"

He did. "Who knows what you and Jean dreamed up together?"

"Carl!"

He was gone out the door.

"Roger?"

"Hmmm?"

"You seem very distracted."

"Sorry, Fiona, honey. I'm just wondering whether a certain person got a phone message I left for them."

"Was it important?"

"You could say that."

Her hand descended on his knee. He headed her off at the pass. "Anything happen on the set today?"

A flounce of her shoulder. "Jean Ormsby pulled Cathy Conroy off the set, did you hear?"

"Really?" Of course he had heard. So had Gobnait Purcell by now.

"Dad and Jack Thornton and Declan Mahoney are trying to sort it out. Everyone is pretty tense."

"It must be terrible for you," Roger said, tongue in cheek.

Fiona snuggled up closer. "Still, I have you, don't I?"

"Yes. And it's way past time that I dropped you home. We don't want you to miss your supper, do we?"

Her face set in suspicious lines. "Are you patronising me?"

He hadn't known the word was in her vocabulary. "Honey! It's just that you told me you had to be home for dinner at eight, that's all."

She relaxed a little. "There's no rush. Dad's not going to be home either. Mum probably won't even bother cooking."

The minutiae of the Fisher domestic routine was of little interest to Roger. Besides, he was too busy eyeing up a student at the bar, a gorgeous young thing in tight jeans.

"I hope he can work things out. Dad," Fiona said now.

"Work what out, honey?"

The student had a pair of buttocks as round and delicious as two fresh cob loaves.

"The nude scene thing. With Jean Ormsby."

Roger's head snapped up. "They had a meeting?"

Fiona snuggled a little closer. "Yeah. They left the set hours ago."

Well, well, Roger thought. He wondered whether the mouse had come out to play.

"Where?"

"What?"

"Just wondering where the meeting was."

"I don't know. Some hotel in town."

He wasn't responding to her cheek-stroking. She moved her hand down to his chest instead, fingering the material of his Hugo Boss shirt suggestively.

"We're good together, Roger, aren't we?" she prompted.

He patted her hand absentmindedly. "Dynamite."

362

Chapter Twenty-five

The local radio stations had a field-day. Their phone lines were jammed solidly all morning as the women of Kilkenny spilled their thoughts into every kitchen across the county.

"I'm disgusted, Barry. *Disgusted*. On our own doorsteps. Filth, that's what it is. *Sleaze*."

"The producers of this film would say that you were over-reacting, Mary." The DJ was deliberately riling her. "What if it were all done in good taste?"

"I don't know what good taste there is in naked. . . *breasts*." Mary could hardly get the word out. "They should pack their bags and go back to Hollywood, the lot of them. I hear they all go around with naked breasts there."

The airwaves burned up with her Catholic outrage. Barry egged her on some more and then cut over to Trish on line two.

Trish was altogether more reasonable. "Surely the issue is not Jack Thornton's film, but nudity in general in film?"

Barry didn't want to hear this. It didn't make for good headlines. He gave Trish less than a minute of airtime and moved on to Edward, another sanctimonious guardian of Irish morals who lived a hundred yards from the film set.

"*I* heard that there wasn't only nudity involved, Barry, but some kind of obscene sex act too."

Exactly what kind of obscene sex act Edward couldn't possibly say in the interests of decency. Women in kitchens across Kilkenny were left to exercise their imaginations. More reached for the phone in outrage.

In her own kitchen, Tess Fisher gritted her teeth. What were these people *on*? It was sickening, all of it. Common sense and perspective had gone out the window in favour of prurience and sensationalism on the part of a few.

The media were partly to blame, of course, and whoever had fed them the story in the first place. They liked nothing better than to whip up cheap emotions in the public and cause a racket where none had previously existed.

But who could blame them when they had little else to go on? Tess knew this from reading that Purcell woman's piece in the paper. It was obvious that she had had no concrete information. The film's PR machine had messed up badly there last night, as had Peter's office. If they had given a clear statement, much of this nonsense could have been averted.

"*I* heard too that – "

What Edward had also heard Tess didn't care. She snapped off the radio, thus missing the DJ's announcement that, later in the programme, he would be speaking to by-election candidate Roger Croft on the issue.

The phone rang shrilly for the ninth time. Tess considered not answering it. But some lingering foolish hope that it might be Peter, with some plausible explanation for the fact that he had not come home last night, made her snatch it up.

"Hello?"

The hope was short-lived. It was a reporter, looking for Peter.

"No, I'm afraid he's not here at the moment to issue a statement," Tess said. It took a huge effort to sound calm and pleasant. "Maybe you'd try his constituency office?"

Let his gofers try and explain Peter's absence. She dispensed with the caller and left the phone off the hook. She would not suffer the indignity of having to lie on his behalf again this morning.

The worst had been last night, when John Graham had rung at midnight from Leinster House. He apologised profusely for the late hour, but needed to speak to Peter urgently and Peter's mobile appeared to be switched off. Tess was forced to admit that her husband was not at home. John was so clearly embarrassed that Tess had found herself making excuses in an attempt to make him feel better – Peter was at a late meeting with Thornton, probably, or on his way home now. *She* had been consoling *him*.

Tess had burned with humiliation. And this was after she had spent the evening worrying about Fiona, who had been due home at eight. She'd arrived in at eleven, looking like she'd been dragged through a hedge backwards.

"Where have you been?"

"Out."

Tess had reddened. Fiona had been uncharacteristically secretive the last few weeks. And the old insolence was back, only this time it was directed at Tess. And it was the last straw this evening.

"While you're under my roof you'll abide by my rules, Fiona."

"Oh come on, Mum!"

"Who is he?"

"What?"

"Fiona, I know that you're seeing someone – "

"I am not!"

"And I am not stupid! You've been lying about working late, and you've been seen in pubs in town."

Fiona was momentarily floored. Like Peter, she too seemed to think that Tess was some kind of blind fool who could not see what was going on under her nose. It cut Tess to the quick.

She took a deep breath. Shouting was not going to help matters. "You're only fifteen, Fiona. I worry about you."

But Fiona was not appeased. "You're not worried. You just want to control me!"

"What?" Tess was shocked.

"Like you try to control everything else in your life!" Fiona's face was red. "But you're not my keeper! No wonder Dad stays away so much – it's like an inquisition every time you walk through the door here!"

She had stormed off to bed, leaving Tess gutted.

Maybe Fiona was right; maybe she was a control freak, the kind of woman who drove her husband away with demands and questions. Was it possible that Peter's affairs over the years were simply a knee-jerk reaction to a woman who tried to tie him down hand and foot?

No, Tess thought sharply. Peter had always had his freedom. Maybe too much.

But she had lain awake most of the night listening to the tick of the grandfather clock in the hall downstairs, sick with doubt over herself and her marriage. Wildly, she hoped that Peter had been in a car accident or something. Or that there really had been some emergency Government business. He would ring any moment, however late the hour. They had been getting on too well recently for him to treat her this way. It could well be a car accident – he drove like a lunatic.

As dawn broke, Tess was cold and calm. There had been no phone call. There never had been all those nights in the past, either. Would she never learn? And to think that she had defended him to John Graham last night, made excuses for him. Why did she have to make it *easier* for him to cheat and lie?

Long ago she had told herself that this was the price she must pay if she wanted to hold on to her husband and her position. Lately, the price seemed too high. And she was too tired.

There was no hint of that tiredness this morning. Careful make-up and dress had taken care of that. When he eventually came home, he would not see a woman who had lain awake all night over him.

Fiona had already gone to work. She had left no note of apology or explanation – nothing. Tess was more worried. Something was happening to her daughter and she didn't know what to do about it.

Brakes screeched on the drive outside. It was Jack Thornton. Tess sighed. She didn't know whether she had the energy for him this morning.

As usual, he strutted into the kitchen as though he owned it.

"Christ!"

He threw the morning papers onto the table.

"Yes," Tess agreed. "Coffee?"

He ignored this and hurled himself into a chair. "When I find the mouth that leaked this . . ."

"You'd be better off occupying yourself with a little damage-limitation. Which, incidentally, you should have done last night."

He was wounded by her lack of sympathy, she could see that. "I didn't know that bitch – Gobnait whatsername – was looking for me. Miranda didn't tell me. I've already torn strips off her."

Tess let him rant on.

"What bugs me is the way they're twisting all this!"

Tess's impatience spilled over. "God, Jack – does it always have to be someone else's fault?"

Huffing loudly, he jumped to his feet. "I can see that I've got you at a bad time – "

"Oh, for heaven's sake, Jack. Sit down and have a cup of coffee with me."

Reluctantly, he did. "And that little shit Roger Croft

has been on the early news, stirring it too," he grumbled. "What has Peter to say about *that*?"

"I don't know," Tess said tiredly.

"I've got the press breathing down my neck. I need to speak to Peter," he went on belligerently. "And your phone seems to be off the hook."

"Yes," Tess agreed, giving no explanation.

"I left two messages with his answering service and he hasn't got back to me," Jack went on bitchily.

You and a hundred others, Tess thought.

"So – he upstairs?" Thornton jerked a thumb towards the ceiling.

"No." She busied herself with the coffee.

"Come on, Tess, I really need to speak to him!"

"And I am not his keeper, Jack!" She found herself saying the words Fiona had thrown at her last night. " I don't know where he is, but he is not *here*!"

She spilled the coffee. Jack wasn't one to miss a trick. He sat in silent comprehension as she grabbed a cloth and mopped up the mess. Only when she had her face under control again did she turn around and set the two cups on the table.

"Some breakfast?" she offered.

"Tess . . . I'm sorry."

"Is that a yes or a no?" she asked sharply. She did *not* want his sympathy.

"No." He paused. "Last I saw of him, he was going to meet Jean Ormsby."

Tess had known full well that it would be her and yet it came as an unpleasant shock. Maybe subconsciously she had still been waiting for that phone call from the hospital.

"The bastard," Jack swore quietly, watching her face.

"Jack, I know you're trying to help, but you're not." Her voice was colourless as she reached for her coffee. "Oh. I forgot to collect the milk."

Jack clamped a large brown hand over hers, stalling her. "Don't pretend around me, Tess. Don't treat me as if I were some stranger, as if I meant nothing to you. It's insulting."

Tess's tiredness caught up with her. "What do you want me to do, Jack? Wail on your shoulder? Hand you a pair of scissors and ask you to help me cut up all his clothes? Would that reassure you that you 'meant something to me'?" Her voice grew angrier. "Right now, I don't care too much about your feelings. This isn't about *you*, you know."

Standing on the porch, clutching two bottles of milk, Tess calmed down a little. It wasn't fair to take it out on Jack. But why did the men in her life always have to take priority over her? Worse, how had she allowed it to happen?

Back in the kitchen, she supposed that Jack's silence meant that he was sulking. He could sulk away. She was past humouring him or any man this morning.

"Tess? I'm sorry. You were absolutely right," he said eventually. "I was just being selfish."

She was mildly surprised. "Yes, well, don't make a song and dance about it, Jack. I'm not."

"But why?" he asked. "I mean, surely you're not going to let him get away with this?"

She didn't know what she was going to do yet.

"Tess, you deserve better. You deserve someone who can offer you a hell of a lot more."

"Like you?" She tried to lighten things up.

"Yes," he said simply, rising from the table to take her in his arms. Tess neatly side-stepped him.

"Jack. No."

"Don't keep pushing me away, Tess."

That was exactly what Tess intended to do, had been doing for weeks now. After that near-kiss on the patio, there had been no more intimacy of any kind. She wasn't really sure why. Jack was intelligent, sexy, rich, powerful beyond most people's wildest dreams. And he was mad about her, that much was obvious. The more she demurred, the deeper he fell. He was hers for the taking.

But she held back. For all that Peter had done to her, she still felt a strong sense of loyalty to him. And to Fiona. There was something deeply unsavoury about getting involved with another man while she remained a wife and a mother. Something tawdry. Perhaps it was because she had been at the receiving end of so many of Peter's affairs over the years. She knew the emotions involved. And they were cheap coinage as far as she was concerned.

And there was something about Jack that was all too familiar. Men like him didn't play second fiddle to anyone. Their energy was all-consuming and anyone around them inevitably ended up taking a back-seat. After sixteen years of marriage to a prominent politician, Tess recognised that those kind of people didn't need equal partners – they needed foils. And she was not about to step into that role again.

Her weeks of near solitude in Kilkenny had changed her, she was slowly realising. Or perhaps it had just made her more aware of what her life was and what it was not.

"I'm not going to wait around forever, Tess."

It held the hint of a threat.

"Good," Tess returned with spirit. "Then I won't have to worry about you wasting your time."

If she had hoped that this would put him off, she was wrong. He simply took it as a further challenge and rose to meet it.

"We belong together. You and me – we'd make a great team, Tess."

"No. When this film is over, you'll go back to Hollywood and we'll send each other postcards and things."

"You could come with me."

"What?"

"To LA."

"I wouldn't fit in at all those launch parties," she said with a crooked smile.

He wasn't amused. "Stop it, Tess."

"No, *you* stop it, Jack. I'm too old for you, too plain. You'd soon get tired and go running after nubile twenty-year-olds again."

He put his hands on her shoulders and looked deep into her eyes. "I'm finished with them. None of them ever meant anything. Not like you."

He was too intense. Tess tried to wriggle out of his grasp, but his hands tightened.

"One night, Tess. Spend one night with me and then make up your mind."

Tess laughed. "Oh *God*, Jack. Sometimes I wonder about you."

The look on his face sobered her. He looked as belligerent as a bull in the ring.

"You think I couldn't satisfy you?"

"What?"

"You think maybe I'm deficient in that department or something?"

"Jack! I didn't mean that at all!" She had no idea where this was coming from. "I just think it would be a complication neither of us need."

"*I* need it, Tess. One night."

He looked too serious for her to make light of it again.

"Jack. I'm married," she said simply.

"He's married and it hasn't stopped him," Thornton said brutally. "How many more times has he got to do the dirt on you before you'll see sense?"

And he was gone, his cowboy boots clunk-clunking across the kitchen floor.

Tess looked after him, more than a little bemused.

It was the first time in her life she had been the recipient of an indecent proposal. If she hadn't been so damned angry and depressed, she would find it quite flattering. Not that she would take him up on it, of course, she hastily added. But it was nice to have been asked, this morning of all mornings.

Her mood dipped again as she thought of Peter. He would probably crawl in any minute. He needed a change of clothes for starters. Well, he wouldn't find her sitting obediently waiting for him. She had plenty of things to keep her busy.

On her way out the door, she put the phone back on the hook. It rang immediately. Without thinking, Tess snatched it up. Gobnait Purcell was on the other end, determined to get a soundbite from Peter on the nude-scene fracas.

Tess's voice was sharp as she advised the reporter that he wasn't at home but perhaps she might try his constituency office.

Gobnait was not palmed off so easily. Did Peter Fisher think that this was exclusively a women's issue?

Tess's patience snapped. What made Peter, betrayer of wives and daughters, an expert on women's issues?

"Perhaps you should ask the women that," she said rashly. "After they've been given the full facts, that is, instead of a mixture of lurid gossip and hyperbole."

Gobnait Purcell was silent. Immediately, Tess regretted her outburst. It was not her job to speak to the press on Peter's behalf, much less to antagonise them.

"As a woman then, Mrs Fisher, do you want to tell me how *you* feel about it?" Gobnait asked archly.

Tess was thrown.

"Unless, that is, you don't have an opinion of your own."

The bitch. Tess grew more annoyed. "I have an opinion all right. And if I give it to you, you'll take it down verbatim and read it back to me over the phone."

Tess Fisher hadn't been on the fringes of politics for over a decade without learning a thing or two about media-misquotes.

"No," Gobnait said laconically. "I'll tape-record it and then I'll fax it to you."

Gobnait Purcell hadn't been in journalism for over a decade without learning plenty about libel suits.

"Agreed," Tess said. They had started to like each other.

At some point during the night Jean must have drifted off. She opened her eyes to find Peter propped up on the pillows looking down at her.

"What time is it?" she asked.

"Almost nine. Time to get up."

He planted a kiss on the tip of her nose and she felt herself relax. He must have pulled the duvet over both of them while she was asleep. Pressed against his warm chest, she felt like she was wrapped in a lovely cocoon that she never wanted to leave.

"Do we have to?" she asked. She didn't want the day to start. She wanted to hide away here in this hotel room with Peter forever, blocking out wives and work and reality in general.

"I'm afraid so. I shouldn't really be here at all."

Guilt gripped Jean. Tess Fisher was probably wondering where in the hell her husband was.

"Of course," she said quickly, struggling to sit up.

"Not so fast," he said. "We can steal another five minutes."

He leaned over and kissed her again. She sighed with bliss. It felt just *too* good.

"You look about seventeen," he teased.

"And you look about . . . forty-four?" she said.

"Ouch."

She smiled. "Sorry. I'm not very good at lying."

"And I wouldn't want you to be." He looked very serious. "I know the circumstances aren't ideal . . . but let's be honest with each other at least?"

"Yes. Of course."

He lightened then, reaching over to pull her on top of him with a growl.

"I might be forty-four, but I still have go in me yet."

"I have no doubt of it," she said, giggling as he tickled her neck with his unshaven chin. Suddenly, she went still.

"*Nine*? It's nine in the morning?"

"Well, yes."

She jack-knifed up in the bed. "Cathy – I told her to stay in her trailer until I rang. God only knows what she's thinking."

"And I told Thornton I'd phone him."

They looked at each other like children caught with their hands in the cookie-jar.

"I suppose one of us had better make contact with the outside world," Peter said, reluctantly reaching for his mobile phone on the night-stand. He handed it to Jean.

"You first."

"Switched off," she noted aloud, teasing. "Had this all planned, did you?"

376

She had not yet started to dial Cathy's number when the mobile erupted.

"And the madness starts," Peter said with a sigh, taking it back.

She watched him dreamily as he answered the phone. He really was gorgeous. And hers, for as long as it lasted. She had no illusions about that. But because she knew it, she would make sure that she enjoyed every last second of it.

"Sorry, John. I was busy last night," he said into the phone, shooting Jean a suggestive glance. His tone changed. "What? You're joking."

Jean saw his shoulder-muscles clench. The caller did not have good news obviously.

"Let's talk again later once we assess the damage," he said curtly, hanging up.

She watched, puzzled, as he swung his legs out of bed and reached for his clothes on the floor.

"Peter? What's happened?"

"Apparently, the press have got wind of the nude scene story. It's on the front page of at least one national this morning."

"What?"

He did not turn to look at her and she felt uneasy.

"They're making a big deal out of it all, Graham said."

Jean sighed. This wasn't good. "But there's nothing to make a big deal out of."

"That's what I thought."

She did not understand the sharpness in his voice.

"Who leaked it?" she asked.

He met her eyes briefly and then looked away. "Nobody knows."

Jean watched him carefully. Surely he didn't think . . .? "Nothing came from us, Peter. Cathy or me."

"I know, I know."

Again, he refused to look at her.

"I was here all night with you. I did not speak to anybody." Her voice was measured and cold.

"Nobody's accusing you of anything, Jean, okay?"

He was not convincing. He was *doubting* her. She could not believe it.

She saw now that he was waiting for her to elaborate; to put his mind at rest. Instead, she flung back the sheets and got out of bed. She would not stoop to cajoling or pleading her case. She had not leaked this and she wouldn't behave as though she had.

"You said we should be honest with each other," she said very quietly. "And I have been. Now, if you can't trust me, then what's the point?"

He looked contrite now. "Jean . . ."

She cut him off by stalking into the bathroom and closing the door. She sat on the edge of the bath, waiting for the sound of the door which would tell her that he had gone.

Roger had rung every hotel in town last night – that is, once he'd managed to expel Fiona Fisher from his car.

God, what a scene. The girl had been rampant. It must have been the four vodkas she'd downed in the pub. She'd been all over him, scrabbling at his shirt, his jacket. At one point she'd actually managed to get her hand down the front of his pants.

She'd found no joy there, Roger thought grimly, just a limp and flaccid organ shrinking further under her touch. Then the confusion in her eyes, the re-playing of the "do you fancy me at all?" scene, the false reassurances on his part, and finally, the reiteration that he had a radio interview in the morning. Which he did now, thanks to Gobnait Purcell.

She'd bought it, but only barely, he knew. Next he would be reduced to pleading a headache. Something would have to be done. She was getting a little suspicious of his evasions now. Perhaps he would have to grit his teeth and actually sleep with her.

The thought raised the fine dark hairs on Roger's forearms.

With a smirk he wondered what of Peter Fisher's had been raised last night. If anything. Time to find out.

He swung the car now into the hotel carpark and cruised up and down. He didn't have to look far. Parked conspicuously near the front doors was Fisher's personal car, a black Saab.

Roger felt disappointed. The hotel had already confirmed last night on the phone that Jean Ormsby was indeed a guest and Roger had left a meaningless message, pretending to be a business associate. Now here was Fisher's car. There was little or no detective work called for on Roger's part. There could be no doubt that they had spent the night together.

Still, better to be sure. Besides, Roger was looking forward to watching Fisher, the sneaky bastard, slide out of the hotel, unaware of the fact that he was being observed. It was too much to resist.

In the foyer, he ordered a coffee and installed himself in an inconspicuous corner, a newspaper strategically held aloft. He didn't bother reading it. He had already savoured Gobnait Purcell's piece on the front cover. It was better than anything he could have hoped for. Oh, but the woman was a bitch. He would enjoy speaking to her later on today. This time he wouldn't need to be anonymous, of course. He would go on the record as an election candidate with a perfectly valid viewpoint. He must make sure to speak to *The Kilkenny People* this morning on the issue, before it went to press. He had a statement ready, one that would stir the hearts and minds of the Kilkenny women. He must leave them in no doubt that he had his finger firmly on the pulse of feminist issues, that he was a man who would look after their interests if only they would elect him. Bill Mackey could never hope to be as authoritative on the subject – especially when he was thousands of miles away in Greece. With relish, Roger imagined the women's vote slowly but inexorably shift on the wind in his direction.

John Graham could learn a few lessons from him on election strategy, Roger thought smugly. Shame he couldn't share this one with him.

"Shit."

He had almost missed him. Fisher was smooth, very smooth. Roger had been watching the elevator near the door, sure that Fisher would try to exit inconspicuously that way. But no, he was coming down the main stairs, confident, crossing the foyer with the air of a man with absolutely nothing to hide. And because of this, nobody gave him a second glance.

Roger hid behind his paper and grudgingly admired the man. He had style. Roger must remember in future to walk away from his various sexual encounters with as much aplomb.

Fisher was gone and Roger thoughtfully sipped his coffee. He wasn't sure yet what to do with this information. The temptation, of course, was to make a quick, anonymous telephone call to Tess Fisher, telling her where her husband had spent the night, and really stir it for Fisher.

But that would be stupid and childish. No, this was far too important to squander on mere revenge. Roger must carefully hoard it for some time in the future. You never knew when it might be needed.

Chapter Twenty-six

The Government sent in the troops the following day.

"Cut the nude scene," John Graham ordered. "Hold a press conference, get Cathy Conroy back on the set and get on with making the film."

Jack Thornton was outraged at being spoken down to in this manner. He was a *legend*, for God's sake. "Oh yeah? Says who? *You* don't have any artistic control over this film."

Graham did not beat around the bush. "No, but Cinerama does."

"Let them tell me so," Thornton blustered. "My contract is with them, not you."

"I know. I've already discussed your contract in detail with them on the phone this morning."

Thornton was more outraged. "Are you threatening me? Listen here, you little gofer – "

"No. You listen to *me*," Graham said quietly. "Cinerama have *fifty million dollars* invested in this film. We've invested heavily too – money, time, effort. And the bottom line is that we want the film we were promised and we want it on time and on budget. And without a nude scene or any more controversy."

Thornton stared back stonily. "Or?"

Peter Fisher spoke for the first time. "Or you're fired. I have Cinerama's authority."

Thornton swung around, his face twisted. "You . . . you went behind my *back*?"

"Yes."

"You bastard."

"Oh come on, Jack! Have you seen the papers recently? You didn't leave us with any choice!"

Thornton looked disgusted. "I thought you were into this movie, Peter, that you were behind it a hundred percent. But you're only after as many votes you can get in this fucking election, aren't you?"

Peter said nothing. He did care about the film, but of course his first loyalty was to the Government. And because of Thornton's notions of artistic genius, the Government had enough egg on its face to make a giant omelette.

"Have we an agreement?" John Graham asked.

Silence. Would Thornton walk or wouldn't he?

"Yeah," he spat, throwing another filthy look at Peter. Peter was mildly perplexed.

This was a business decision – couldn't Thornton see that?

Graham wasn't finished yet. "And let's invite the press onto the set. Throw a party, let them see how well we're all getting on."

Thornton was gob-smacked now. "You want us to hold a frigging *love-in*?"

Peter waved a hand impatiently. "It's simply a PR exercise, Jack."

"A PR exercise? Shame you didn't think of that the night the story broke. Shame you weren't around to issue a statement *then*."

Peter watched him closely. He couldn't *know*. Nobody did. "Same goes for you, Jack. Anyway, it's over now. Let's get back to work." He paused. "I trust you'll speak to Cathy Conroy and Jean Ormsby."

Jean Ormsby Jean Ormsby Jean Ormsby.

For two days now she had filled his head. Her skin, her voice, her laugh. He still did not know whether she was the source of the leak or not.

"You can leave those two to me," Thornton said, throwing another inexplicable black look at Peter. Peter got the distinct impression that Jack would like to deck him.

Thornton had one last parting shot. "You don't fool me, you know, Peter."

Peter froze.

"You barge in here, acting all outraged over the nude scene and the leak. And the only ones who've benefited out of all this are yourselves."

"What?" Peter looked to Graham, astonished.

Thornton smiled cynically. "Don't come the innocent with me. I'm talking about Croft. He did pretty well out of all this, didn't he? Blanket media coverage, with Bill Mackey safely out of the country. Must be really sprinting ahead in the points race."

The implication began to sink in with Peter. "You think I *knew* about this? This has made the Government look as stupid as you lot."

Thornton shrugged in disbelief. "Yeah – except for Croft." He paused by the door. "Don't ever use me and my work again for your own ends."

He stormed from the trailer.

Peter turned to Graham. "Him and his conspiracy theories."

"He has a point," Graham said slowly.

"Croft has been speaking a lot on the issue – I know that," Peter said. "But I thought the interviews were okayed by you."

"And I thought they were okayed by *you*," Graham replied.

They looked at each other.

"Nothing was okayed by me. I haven't seen Croft in two days," Peter said.

Croft. Of course it was Croft. Why hadn't he seen this before? Why had he been so anxious to believe that it was Jean? Was it his own sense of guilt that had made him look for something to sully that perfect night together? She must hate him.

"I'll go through him for a short-cut for this one," Graham swore.

Peter felt a cold rage at Croft replace the sickness in his stomach. "Let me deal with Croft."

He stood. He had plenty of business to take care of. And none of it pleasant.

Jean was back in her office in Dublin when she got the call from Thornton. The nude scene was officially cut and Cathy was back on the set as of now.

"I've just held a press conference. So it's business as usual, okay?"

He'd sounded frostier than she'd ever heard him. But after all that had happened in the last two days, she couldn't really blame him.

She hit the intercom. "Patsy? Can you bring me in that RTE contract for the sitcom?"

It was business as usual in the Jean Ormsby Agency too. Or at least Jean was trying her best to behave in some kind of normal fashion, determinedly ignoring the ache in her head and the cramp in her stomach. She had clients to see and calls to return. The film had finally catapulted her small agency into the realms of the viable, and she was not about to jeopardise that, even if all she really wanted to do was crawl into bed.

Patsy arrived with the contract.

"Any more press calls?" Jean enquired.

"No."

Good. Thornton's press conference appeared to have done the trick. Anyway, the press had worn themselves out at this point, saturated and bloated on the entire issue. Helped along nicely by copious interviews with Roger Croft, of course, Jean thought cynically.

And Peter thought that *she* had leaked this? Maybe he should look in his own back garden before he went throwing accusations around.

"Are you going to the press party on Saturday night?" Patsy enquired now, round face excited.

Obviously, she had been listening in on Jean's phone call with Thornton. On another day, Jean might have fired her for such a breach. Today, she hadn't the energy.

"No."

Patsy's face fell. "Oh. But won't Cathy and Carl need you?"

The way she said Carl's name was a dead giveaway. Poor Patsy. Carl Tallon's eyes were not trained in *her* direction.

"They can manage without me," Jean said shortly.

Peter Fisher would be there. Undoubtedly, he would think that she had shown up purely to curry further favour with the press.

"Maybe you're right not to go. You look absolutely *terrible*."

"Thank you, Patsy."

"I didn't mean – "

"Time of the month, okay?"

"Aaah." Patsy nodded knowledgeably and left.

This was partly the truth. The morning-after pill which Jean's doctor had prescribed had induced a particularly painful and prolonged period. Her entire midriff was creased in cramps and no amount of paracetemol was going to help. She would just have to ride it out.

"You'd want to be more careful next time," her doctor had cautioned with shrewd eyes.

Jean knew she had been foolish. But in the white

heat of passion, who had time to stop and mentally wrestle with dates or, indeed, rubber? She probably hadn't been in any danger anyhow, but she was taking no chances. Still, as another cramp seized her, she wondered what it would be like to carry Peter Fisher's baby. To have a family together.

Ridiculous. Even had they not had that bust-up over the media leak, any kind of rosy future involving kids and pink-painted cottages and family trips to the supermarket on a Saturday morning was out of the question. Theirs would have been a relationship of subterfuge and snatched moments, of lying to his wife and keeping an invisible profile. And as the years passed, she would inevitably have got to the point where her biological clock was howling. She would want what he was not able to give her and they would have gone their separate ways, amicably or otherwise. He would probably start another affair and she would probably be too old to attract anybody save other married men.

None of it was tempting. Any woman with a full set of marbles would run a mile. But such was the life of a mistress, one of endless waiting for those few snatched moments of bliss that were supposed to make it all worthwhile. Only stupid, reckless, foolish women rushed into such relationships.

And women in love, of course. At the end of the day, there was no accounting for the follies women committed in the name of love, Jean thought grimly. It had just been her bad luck to fall for a married man who spent his life in the public gaze.

Love also accounted for her anger with him now. How *easily* he had doubted her word over the press leak, how quickly he had called her integrity and honesty into question. It hurt, and deeply. If she could get her hands on him now, she would swing for him.

And then jump into bed with him, probably. He had shown that he did not trust her and she *still* wanted him.

But that night together had been more than just the best sex she'd ever had. There had been some primal connection with him that she had never experienced with any man before. While on one level she didn't know Peter Fisher very well, on another she felt as though they were soul mates who had known each other forever.

Forget it, she told herself sharply. He had several serious black marks against him. He was hitched, for starters. And he had doubted her in a fundamental way, which she would not easily forgive – not that he had sought forgiveness, for that matter. And, most important, it was dawning on her in the cold light of day that the role of mistress was not one that appealed to her in the slightest. All of which pointed to one thing – no future.

Her queasiness was kept company now by a deep depression that settled over her like a cloud.

"Jean?" Patsy popped her head around the door, looking coy. "You've got a visitor. He wants to know if you can spare ten minutes."

Peter. All reason went out the window as Jean found herself on her feet, light-headed.

"Show him in, Patsy."

Patsy stood aside.

"Hi, love!"

Ian bounded in. Jean's heart went into free-fall.

"Oh. Hi."

Her lack of welcome must have been obvious, because the minute Patsy was out the door Ian launched into a speech.

"Jean, I'm sorry about the way we left things, and I'm not here because I want anything. But I've been reading the newspapers and I figured you were having a tough time with the film. I thought I'd drop by to cheer you up. That's all."

He produced a bouquet of flowers he had been hiding behind his back and extended them with a warm grin. She took them.

"Thanks, Ian."

She was surprised at how glad she was to see him. A friendly face. And he looked so cheerful and energetic, the way he had been before the drugs got him. In the midst of her morbidity, he was like a breath of fresh air.

He looked around the office and let out a low whistle. "This place has come quite a way since I was here last."

The office was the same poky place it had always been, but with the commissions Jean had earned from the film, she had been able to transform it in small ways. It had been painted and there was a new fax machine, filing cabinets, and a sophisticated phone system. The grotty brown lino had finally been replaced with something a little classier. And she had treated herself to a good fake-mahogany desk, wryly promising herself that she would get the real thing when she opened branches in London and New York.

"You've really made this place work, haven't you?" he said in admiration.

"I'm doing okay," she said, pleased that he had noticed. When they'd been together, his interest in her agency had been zero. But then again, his only motivation back then was his next hit.

"I'm not doing too badly myself," he confessed bashfully.

"Oh?"

"I've got a new job and a new apartment."

"That's fantastic, Ian."

"It's a start." He smiled crookedly. "I know I've made all kinds of rash promises in the past about how I would change. This time, I'm taking it slowly and I'm going to do it."

"Good." She actually believed him this time. And perhaps they could start again as friends. She would like that very much.

"Enough introspection," he said, jolly again. "How about joining me for a long, boozy lunch? My treat."

Jean indicated the pile of work on her desk. "I'm snowed under, Ian."

"All right, we'll cut the booze and just have lunch." He paused. "You look like you could do with a break, Jean. Everything all right?"

She was touched by his concern. "It's just been a crazy few days, that's all."

He nodded, not pressing her.

"Maybe I will take you up on lunch after all," she said impulsively. She found that she wanted to spend more time with him. And she was dying to get away from her own thoughts for a couple of hours. She could not bear to analyse Peter Fisher for another second.

"Let's go then."

She smiled brightly and took his arm.

Roger Croft was on the phone in Peter's constituency office when Peter found him.

"A word," Peter said loudly.

With a wave of his hand, Roger indicated that he would be finished in a minute. Peter reached over the desk and abruptly cut off the connection.

"What do you think you're doing?" Roger asked in astonishment. "I was trying to set up a press interview."

"Did you give your name this time?" Peter asked softly.

Roger's face briefly betrayed his surprise – and guilt. But Peter was amazed to see a crafty defiance slowly replace it. A brazenness.

"I have no idea what you mean."

"I think you do. I think you were the one who told the press about the nude scene."

Roger stared straight back. "Prove it."

He was not denying it. His cockiness was unbelievable. Peter's temper snapped. He leaned over the desk, shoving his face into Roger's. His voice was low and loaded with contempt.

"You weasel. You little snitch. I should have known it was you. You haven't the balls to try and win this election on your own merits, have you? Instead you stoop to shoddy little media games where you can manipulate the public. You know what you are, Roger? A conman. You shouldn't be in politics. You should be flogging second-hand cars on the side of the street."

Roger had gone quite pale. Peter saw rage in his eyes.

"And if I had my way, I'd have you booted out of this party and off this campaign so fast that your ass would leave skid-marks."

Roger blinked, and smiled. The rage was under control, Peter saw. He suspected that there was a lot of rage in Roger Croft that nobody had ever seen.

"Go ahead so," Roger said sweetly. "Do it, fire me. Ring Carol Taylor and tell her."

He obligingly held out the telephone receiver.

"Cut the shit, Roger."

Roger laughed and replaced the receiver. "You're all talk, aren't you? You can huff and puff all you like, but at the end of the day, you need me. Carol Taylor needs me. You and her and the rest of that sorry bunch of Ministers are holding onto your jobs by the seats of your pants and I'm the only one who can save you now."

Peter's face felt like it was set in stone. He had no comeback, could say nothing. Because Roger was right.

Roger grinned triumphantly and tossed a bunch of newspaper cuttings across the desk at him.

"See? I'm everywhere. I'm closing on Bill Mackey

fast. So spare me your self-righteous twaddle. You should be glad that I acted on my own initiative. This way you might actually get to keep your Ministerial car."

A fine red mist filled Peter's head. *Don't do it. Don't hit him.*

"Now if you don't mind, I've got work to do," Roger said dismissively.

Peter took a step back. He had to. He did not think that he had ever been angrier in his life.

"I'm not finished yet, Roger."

"Really." Roger looked bored.

"Don't go near Jack Thornton, or his film, or anybody remotely connected with the film, ever again. If you value your health, that is."

"You're scaring me now, Peter."

"And don't say another word to the press about the nude scene. You've played that tune."

"Fine, fine. It's dead in the water anyway," Roger said laconically.

Peter walked away fast towards his own office. Roger was already picking up the phone again. Peter looked over his shoulder.

"You'll have your three years in the sun, Roger. Enjoy it while it lasts."

Roger turned cold eyes on him. "What's that supposed to mean?"

"I'm just telling you now that you will not be re-selected by the party to run in the next general election. You can count on that."

"You can't decide that."

"Ah, but I can. Call it having friends in the right places."

Roger leaned forward. His eyes were slits, curiously bright. Peter got the image of a snake about to bite.

"I'd think very carefully before you do something like that, Peter."

"I beg your pardon?"

"You never know what repercussions there might be for yourself."

Peter whirled around, aggression spilling from every pore. "Get out of my office, Roger. And don't you ever, *ever* threaten me again. Do you hear me?"

Roger picked up his coat. "Oh, I hear you all right."

He fixed Peter with a strangely triumphant look – as if he had some secret goods on Peter.

"Out, Roger!"

Roger paused by the door. "Oh, and Peter? If you're so concerned about press leaks, you should really tell your daughter to watch her mouth."

Peter looked after him, mystified. What he was referring to Fiona for? He didn't even know her.

He shrugged. Roger Croft was all talk. A bag of bluff that would one day be punctured.

He dismissed Roger from his mind. On his desk, a mountain of work awaited him – Government business, constituency matters, campaign strategies that John Graham wanted him to urgently review. He picked up the first of many faxes from a pile. The black print was gobbeldygook to him. All he saw was Jean's face.

Christ, what must she think of him? He groaned aloud as he remembered himself standing in that hotel room, doubting her. Not believing her when she said that she was not responsible. And the bed not yet cold after their wonderful night together.

Self-righteous, cynical fool. He had been in this game too long. He had behaved like the hardened politician, believing that behind every truth there must be a lie. Had he really got to the point where he distrusted everyone, even the woman he loved, sure that she must have an ulterior motive, an agenda? Perhaps it was time he bailed out before his twisted outlook ruined every good thing in his life.

He would have to apologise, of course. He had wronged her badly. He'd do it now.

But even as he reached for the phone, he stopped himself. This wasn't just about the press leak. He had wronged her in other ways too, much worse ways. And it wouldn't be so easy to put them right with an apology.

His own words to her that night came back to haunt him. He had more or less asked her to be his mistress. She had more or less said yes, because he had given her no choice. He had compromised her, asked her to give up everything and offered nothing in return except a relationship based on transience and deceit. Just as he had offered his other lovers in the past.

Peter was sick of himself. Enough was enough. Whether or not Jean still wanted him – and that was debatable at this point – he could not in all conscience live like this any more.

He would have to ask Tess for a divorce.

He had been shying away from this reality for days now. But it was no use. Perhaps Tess knew it too. He had not seen her since the night he'd spent with Jean. She had managed not to be in the house when he was there, and she had moved into the spare bedroom, not getting up in the morning until he was gone.

She knew all right. And she deserved an explanation now. It was the very least she deserved. And Fiona too. This would break her heart. It would break Peter's own to have to admit to her that he had cheated on Tess. Betrayed her mother. But tell her he must. He doubted that she would forgive him easily. She had always been closer to Tess. It would take a lot to win back her trust, if ever.

He must make this as painless as possible for everyone concerned. He would do whatever Tess wanted, give her whatever she needed – the house, the car, generous maintenance, he would not haggle over a single thing. He had no right.

He would also let her break it publicly in her own way. He imagined that she would want to do it quietly. Instead of an announcement, perhaps she might prefer to do things gradually, with him moving out first, and after a year or so they would discreetly murmur about being separated. Then later down the line they would divorce. But he would dance to her tune on it. He owed Tess a hell of a lot and he wouldn't short-change her on this one.

She would hit the roof, of course. It would probably

be an ugly scene. He would undoubtedly deserve everything she would throw at him. But this farce could not go on any longer. And she couldn't be any happier in this marriage than he was. Maybe she would be relieved in a way. She too might start afresh.

Now that the decision was made, a weight lifted from his shoulders. He was glad now that he had not phoned Jean. He had no right. Not until he was a free man. Maybe she would still want him then. Maybe she wouldn't.

He would wait.

Chapter Twenty-seven

"Darling! You look *wonderful*!"

Well, if nobody else was going to say it, Cathy decided that she might as well say it to herself. And she did look good. The Cindy Burke creation she had bought in an exclusive boutique in Kilkenny – the cost of which she resolutely refused to think about – was not her usual style.

This little number did nothing to hide her height or disguise her lack of curves. It was an eye-catching sapphire blue for starters, and clung to her like cellophane. No corset augmented her modest breasts tonight; they sat there, small and proud and braless under the sheer satin of the dress. Kate Moss wasn't in it.

Under the dress, she wore Manolo sandals with three-inch heels. Several times, she almost fell off, but that was a small price to pay for the extra length they gave her already endless legs.

A pair of diamond earrings, a present from herself,

peeked from under the sheer fall of her hair, which she had spent an hour ruthlessly straightening under a hot hairdryer. And for once, her make-up had gone on exactly the way she had intended. No nasty clumps of mascara or dodgy lipliner-jobs *tonight*.

Tonight, Cathy Conroy was dressing out of sheer defiance and she knew it.

"You'll wow them," she bravely informed her reflection in the mirror, doing one last twirl to ensure that the back of the dress wasn't snagged in her knickers or anything equally embarrassing. Jack Thornton had warned everyone that they were to be on their very best behaviour for the press at the love-in party tonight, as it had rapidly become known on the set.

"Ready!" she said loudly. Anything to fill the awful silence.

In recent days, Cathy had taken to talking to herself. It wasn't that she had flipped it, although sometimes she wondered. It was just that nobody else on the film set would talk to her at all. Oh sure, they said "hello" and 'good morning' and all that shit, but apart from that, she was treated to a stony silence from the cast and crew. It had been that way since the day she'd walked back on set after the nude scene had been dropped.

At first she thought she was imagining it. They had lost several days' work, after all; the film was already behind schedule in its first month and everybody was stressed and tense. But in the catering tent, when she'd sat down at the cameramen's table and they had all stood up, she smelled a rat.

"What's going on? What have I done?" she'd demanded of Marie in the costume department.

Marie's eyes were icy. "We don't tell outsiders our business, Cathy."

It dawned on Cathy that it wasn't just Carl Tallon who thought that she was in some way responsible for the whole press frenzy over the nude scene. Everybody else did too, it seemed.

"But I didn't tell them!"

She knew from Marie's face that she didn't believe her.

And why should she? Had Cathy set about swaying public opinion, she couldn't have done a better job. The minute the story broke, the media had taken sides – and that of a put-upon, exploited, young, pretty film star was infinitely more attractive to them than the faceless men in suits. They were the bastards, the pornographers, while Cathy emerged as the shining heroine of the piece, the girl who had fought tooth-and-nail to hang onto her underwear and her dignity. They'd practically turned her into Joan of Arc. Even Roger Croft had spoken out on her behalf. He'd never given her the time of day before now. All of a sudden he was all over the papers and radio talking intimately about her rights as a woman and as an actress. It was all very confusing. And the finger of suspicion pointed firmly at her as the source of the leak. Marie's face was proof of this.

"Look, this might be your first movie, Cathy. But we have a code of honour in this business. If we have differences, we sort them out amongst ourselves."

After that, things were hell. Overnight, she was *persona non grata*. People fell silent as she walked past them and she felt the glare of hostility every time she stepped in front of the cameras. Even Jason Blake, who had been so nice to her up to now, had turned against her.

"The press leak – that was strictly amateur time, Cathy."

She'd cried that night alone in her trailer. Branded as a turncoat and snitch, and she hadn't even done anything! Ostracised by her own people. And she had weeks and weeks of this to endure yet. It was too much.

She should have known, she thought bitterly. Dreams did not come true in the mediocre lives of people like her, or if they did, they were rapidly crushed by a God with a particularly twisted sense of humour. Along with saving souls, he probably had some quota to fill in the Shattered Dreams Department.

She'd run into Carl Tallon yesterday afternoon. He had fixed her with a look so laden with disgust and disappointment that her legs had turned to jelly.

"No nude scene. Happy now?" he'd asked quietly.

It was as if nothing at all had happened between them in her trailer that night. As if he'd never apologised for his behaviour, as if they hadn't almost kissed.

"I did not rat." She would not show him how hurt she was. "You should know me better than that."

She had marched off before he had the chance to say anything more. And to think that she had practically

402

swooned at his feet that night! All he'd had to do was ply her with prawn crackers and a few apologies and she was putty in his hands.

She wondered now why he'd bothered with the sorry routine at all, the "let's be friends" patter. He obviously didn't trust her an inch. For all his supposed regrets over his behaviour in the past, he was quite ready to believe the worst of her all over again at the first opportunity

Well, feck him. It had been a mistake, them trying to patch things up. They would never see eye to eye on anything.

But there was still the physical attraction. She couldn't deny that. And he couldn't either, although she was sure that he would like to. He had wanted to kiss her as much as she had him. And if that damned phone hadn't rung, that's exactly what would have happened.

Cathy looked at herself in the mirror again now, clinical and detached. There must be no more little trysts of any kind, no putting herself in the way of temptation again. It was obvious that she had very poor control indeed over those particular urges and great care must be taken to keep a tight rein on them in future.

Tonight she intended to take herself out a little insurance against Carl Tallon. There was bound to be plenty of men at this party tonight. Surely there would be one or two spare?

And besides, she was the black sheep of the film gang now, and she'd be damned if she was going to hold up the wall all night, shunned by everyone.

She did one last twirl, amazed at how good she looked.

To hell with them all, she thought in a rush of bravado. Cathy Conroy was going to be no shrinking violet tonight.

Ian had persuaded her to attend the party.

"You'll look guilty if you don't," he had argued.

She had told him about the press leak. She had not mentioned Peter Fisher.

Perhaps Ian was right. Anyway, Peter already thought she was guilty, so what did it matter? In the end, Jean decided that for her own self-respect she would not hide away at home. Her place was here, representing her clients, and she had nothing to be ashamed of.

But still she hung at the back of the huge marquee tent erected on the field of the set, courtesy of Cinerama Studio. She was glad that Ian had agreed to come with her for moral support. He was in good form tonight, on top of the world.

"Hey! Is that *Jason Blake* over there?" His voice was loud.

"Stop acting like a groupie," Jean said, mildly embarrassed.

He was undeterred. "Half the Government's here, have you seen?"

She had. Carol Taylor, Geraldine Day, Dan Kilmartin and Harry Burke were present, all decked out in their Sunday-best. And you couldn't swing a cat without hitting at least three prominent County Councillors. She had not seen Peter Fisher yet. She told herself she was glad.

"And there's Jack Thornton," Ian enthused. "My God. Is he wearing *cowboy boots*?"

Thankfully, Thornton didn't hear him, but practically everybody else in the marquee did. Jean again warned him to be quiet. Sometimes he was like this, over-exuberant and too loud. It must be the excitement of being at a celebrity-dotted party.

He had cajoled her into meeting him twice more since their lunch together. They had got on better than they had in years. He had been at pains to assure her that it was only renewed friendship he was after. She had seen no harm in it. But she had forgotten what he could be like when let loose amongst a group of people.

"Let's get another drink," he said.

"You haven't finished the first yet," she said with a laugh.

"Christ, am I not allowed even to get drunk now?" he snapped suddenly.

Jean was wary. "You can do what you like, Ian."

"Sorry, sorry, don't mind me. I'm not let out often enough." He was all over her again, smiling and hugging her. She extricated herself before people really started to stare.

"Another drink so," she said nicely, draining her glass and handing it to him. He set off happily through the crowd, joining two men at the bar whom he seemed to know. Jean did not recognise either man as belonging to the cast or the crew. They were downing free drinks like they were going out of fashion, and laughing with Ian.

Tess Fisher stepped straight into her line of vision. As if sensing Jean's stare, she turned her head slightly and Jean found herself looking straight into cool blue eyes.

She knows.

Somehow or other, Tess Fisher knew about the night Jean had spent with her husband. It was there in the tilt of her head, the twist of her mouth. The contempt in her eyes.

The seconds ticked by. Just as Jean felt she could not bear Tess Fisher's laser perception a moment longer, the crowd shifted slightly and she was gone.

Jean took a few deep breaths, resisting the urge to run out of the place. She longed for Ian to come back – to distract her, to give her a strong drink. She needed it.

So this was what it felt like to be a mistress. An adulterer. A betrayer of other women. The morality of it had bothered her before, of course, but from a distance. Only tonight, seeing Tess Fisher, did the reality of it hit home. And she found it abhorrent.

All the doubts she'd had since that marvellous night with Peter came together with perfect clarity. She did not want him like this. It wasn't her, not Jean Ormsby. And there was no more to be said or thought about the matter.

You'd have thought a film star like her could afford a *whole* dress, Carl Tallon thought, watching as Cathy Conroy's breasts threatened to escape the two minuscule triangles of material half-heartedly holding them in. It was no wonder he hadn't been able to take his eyes off her all night. She was practically giving a free show!

He didn't know why he was here, at this ridiculous party for the benefit of the press, bunch of hyenas that they were. He should be at home, working, as he did every night, sometimes into the hours of dawn. His new play was waiting. With no false modesty, he knew that it was shaping up to be the best thing he had ever written. Why, then, wasn't he hammering away at it instead of standing in an over-crowded marquee gawking at an ex-girlfriend?

He buried himself in his pint as he remembered how near he had come to kissing her the other night. Jesus! It must have been his hormones or something, he reasoned furiously. Because of all the foolish things he had done in his life, to restart something with Cathy Conroy would be the greatest folly of all.

It was Jack Thornton's fault, of course – sending Carl around to Cathy's trailer like an errand boy, armed only with a bag of Chinese food. It had been a stupid idea.

Still, Thornton hadn't been responsible for the way Carl had embarrassed himself once he'd got there. He cringed inwardly at the memory. All that babble about how sorry he was! And then talking shite about them becoming friends? You'd swear he'd been the one swigging vodka, not her.

He stole another look across the room. The press were buzzing around her like flies around a fresh cow-pat. What a surprise. But on closer inspection, he grudgingly noted that she didn't seem all that thrilled. In fact, she looked positively relieved when Jason Blake walked into the marquee with that goddess of a girlfriend of his, and the press stampeded away. Cathy was left standing quite alone, as she had been for most of the evening. She was officially an outcast.

Carl felt guilty. They had given her a pretty hard time on the set in the last few days, himself included. Himself especially. And without so much as a shred of proof that she had been the source of the leak. He felt small and mean and unfair now. But he had wanted to believe it was her. He didn't know why.

You do.

It was the only reason he could think of to stop himself from falling for her all over again.

He almost dropped his pint as the realisation hit him. He was surprised, really, at how he hadn't guessed earlier.

It was all clear to him now. His ham-fisted attempts at apologising the other night were a prelude to getting back with her. He'd thought if they could just sort out that misunderstanding about the past – and it *was* just a misunderstanding, he was sure – then they could start with a clean slate. Be lovers again. Because he did still love her. He had never stopped.

He watched her openly now, standing alone in the middle of the marquee in her glad rags, shunned by most of those present. But she held her chin at a proud angle, as if to convey to everyone that she knew she was an outcast but wouldn't be beaten by it.

Admiration welled up in him. She had guts, he had to hand her that. And talent. And spirit. She had everything he had ever wanted. And he had let her get away.

Maybe this film was fate's attempt to get them back together. Perhaps he was being given a second chance. He wouldn't squander it this time.

His feet moved of their own volition across the marquee towards her now. He would say sorry until she believed him, he vowed. And then they might finally be able to put their differences behind them and start afresh.

"Cathy?"

"What do you want?" she barked, scowling ferociously.

God, but she was lovely, he thought dreamily.

"Nothing."

She looked at him as though he were trying to steal her purse. But her suspicion would go once he explained everything to her, he knew. He decided it was best to cut to the chase. He would tell her straight out that he loved her.

"Cathy . . ."

At that moment, some big hairy brute of a fellow planted himself by Cathy, bearing champagne. Another ignorant reporter, Carl assumed.

"We're trying to have a conversation here," he told the man testily.

"Yeah? Well, we were *having* a conversation before you arrived," the man returned.

Carl noted with a dull shock that Cathy was smiling up at the man brilliantly, taking the champagne. My God. She was *flirting* with him.

"I'll leave you to it then," he said

With a leaden smile at Cathy, he turned his back on them and walked away.

"And the *heat*! Harry, poor lamb, was burnt to a *cinder* by the pool. Luckily, I have wonderful skin, it takes a great tan."

"You look fantastic, Sheila," Tess said insincerely. She deeply suspected that the peculiar orange "tan" Sheila Burke sported tonight came straight out of a bottle. Sheila hadn't seen Tess since her holiday in Spain and was determined to fill her in on all the gory details.

"I missed all the excitement, I hear," Sheila trilled, digging Tess in the ribs. Tess favoured her with a deliberately blank look. "You know, the whole nude scene business," Sheila prompted.

"Yes. All very boring really, Sheila."

Tess's mind was only half on the conversation. She had been knocked off balance by the sight of Jean Ormsby tonight. She'd known she would be here, of course. But it still came as an unpleasant shock.

"Boring?" Sheila's piggy little eyes were sharp. "I heard you were in the thick of it."

"Pardon?"

"Speaking to the press and all that." Sheila was

disapproving. Tess's interview with Gobnait Purcell had caused quite a stir. *A Voice of Reason*, the paper's editorial had proclaimed. Tess Fisher had done more to limit damage on all fronts than the rest of them put together, it seemed, and Sheila wasn't sure she liked it.

But more importantly, it was not the place of a Minister's wife to speak to the press. A certain code had been broken.

"So?" Tess knew she sounded impatient. But she was trying to keep tabs on Peter's whereabouts out of the corner of her eye. So far, he had not gone near Jean Ormsby.

"Did Peter okay the interview?" Sheila shot.

"I don't have to get Peter's permission for anything, Sheila," Tess returned sweetly.

Sheila didn't like the implication one little bit that Tess was her own woman and Sheila was not.

"Besides," Tess added, "He was rather pleased with the piece. I hear Carol Taylor was too."

Put *that* in your pipe and smoke it, you old bag. And the fact that reporter Gobnait Purcell, over by the bar, had gone out of her way to salute Tess earlier.

"Good, good," Sheila said. She smiled wolfishly. "And I suppose one must have *some* excitement stuck down here."

Touché.

"Peter seems to be ignoring us tonight. You two didn't have a little tiff, I hope?" Double touché. Sheila was in a bitchy mood tonight. Tess tried to control her rising colour. So far, Sheila had not clocked Jean Ormsby's presence and she was praying that she wouldn't.

411

"He's working the room, Sheila. You know how it is."

Sheila saw that she had touched a nerve and was pleased. She was prepared to be conciliatory again. "I think it's high time he did a little 'work' on us," she cackled lasciviously, before raising her fat hand into the air. "Peter! Over here!"

"Later," Tess tried to say. She had managed to avoid any direct contact with Peter since That Night and she had no wish to come up against him now, not in public. And certainly not with Sheila Burke witnessing every vibe.

She cursed the woman from a height as another of her bellows reached Peter. He reluctantly extricated himself from Carol Taylor's group and came over.

"Sheila. Tess." His eyes searched Tess's face. She kept it carefully blank.

"Wonderful party!" Sheila said. "Glad we didn't miss it. We're just back from Spain, you know."

"Really," Peter said, his interest zilch. Tess felt him looking at her again.

Sheila was annoyed that her tan hadn't been noticed. "So. How's the campaign coming along, Peter?"

"Glad you asked, Sheila," Peter said smoothly. "And here's the very man who'll fill you in on all the details."

John Graham found himself accosted by Peter as he walked past. "John, Sheila wants to know about the campaign."

Sheila didn't. But she had no choice as Peter practically pushed her on to Graham, who shot him a black look before bearing Sheila off towards the bar.

"That woman," Peter said under his breath to Tess.

"Yes," Tess agreed, almost smiling.

"Where's Fiona?"

He was sticking to neutral territory.

"She's around somewhere . . . Peter, I'm worried about her. She's seeing someone."

"I suppose it's only natural at her age. To start having boyfriends."

She saw that Peter was not worried. Why should he be? He had not been around to witness her behaviour. He'd been too busy with Jean Ormsby.

Tess suddenly wanted to walk away from him. She would not put on a show of civility for the watching eyes tonight. "Look, do you want something, Peter?"

"I called at the house but you had already left," he began haltingly.

"Yes. I came with Jack." There was no challenge in her voice, no attempt to make him jealous. She was just stating a fact.

She waited expectantly, wondering what he would come out with. Excuses? More lies? Or would he try and gloss over it all, pretending that nothing was amiss, as he had so many times in the past?

He didn't. He looked at her with a directness that was unnerving. He had not got rid of Sheila Burke so that he could palm her off with more bullshit, but because he had something important to say. He was too calm. Too in control.

A choking tightness closed around her throat. She felt as if she were on a tightrope, waiting for the words that would send her crashing off.

"We need to talk, Tess."

When they came, they were innocuous on one level. On another, they were the words of doom.

"Yes."

"Not here, obviously."

"No."

"At home, maybe? Tomorrow evening?"

"Fine. I'll be there about six." Surely that wasn't her own voice, so rational and calm? When her world was disintegrating all around her?

"Great. I'll see you then so."

He lightly touched her arm and moved away. Tess stood paralysed for a moment, his words and that compassionate touch coming together with a terrifying clarity.

Sheila Burke was back, damn her to the pit of hell. "That Graham chap. What a *bore*." She looked anything but bored as she leaned into Tess, her hand descending like a claw on her arm as she hissed, "But wait till you hear who I spotted. Jean Ormsby! In the flesh!"

First the first time, she registered Tess's upset. "There's nothing going *on*, is there?" she asked in a voice that said she hoped there was. "Between her and Peter? Oh, *poor* Tess."

Something inside Tess exploded. She shook off Sheila's hand and said quite clearly, "Don't touch me, Sheila, do you me hear me? And keep your false sympathy and your empty friendship to yourself. You make me sick, you and the rest of your cronies."

Sheila Burke's face went green under her fake tan.

414

"You're not yourself, Tess," she blustered.

"No, Sheila. I'm not."

Tess barely noticed her departure, nor Jack Thornton's swift arrival by her side, eyes full of concern. "Tess? Tess, what's wrong? Did she upset you?"

"Not her. Him."

"Who? Peter?"

Tess felt cold all over. "He's going to leave me."

Chapter Twenty-eight

Ian was high.

Jean knew she should have spotted it a mile off. After all these years, she should have recognised the warning signs; the manic energy, the frequent trips to the bathroom, the downing of alcohol as he pretended that he was only drunk.

"Let's go home," she said tightly.

"Why? The party's only getting into its swing," he said, eyes darting all over the place.

"For you, maybe."

"What's that supposed to mean?"

She just gave him a look.

"Jesus, Jean! I'm drunk, that's all. Is that a crime?"

"Who are those two guys you've been hanging out with all night?"

He looked sheepish. "Friends, okay? They gatecrashed. Free drink and all that."

She knew all about Ian's "friends", the strictly fair-weather kind who hung around him for as long as the

416

money and the drugs lasted. Then they moved on to the next.

"You shouldn't have brought them, Ian. They're stoned out of their heads."

She had seen several reporters cast curious looks at them when their laughter and antics had got too loud.

"They're just drunk too," Ian insisted.

Jean didn't bother humouring him. "Why did you show up in my office this week? What do you want, Ian?"

Now he was angry. "I don't want anything! I thought we could still be friends, that's all."

Jean reached for her coat. "Get yourself clean first, Ian. Until then, I don't want to know."

His hand came down hard on her arm. "Where do you get off, being so high and mighty? Okay, so I might have fallen off the wagon tonight, but come on, it's a fucking *party*."

Jean looked around for Cathy so that she could say goodbye to her. There was no doubt that the film people were giving her a terrible time. But Cathy had defiantly refused Jean's attempt at company and was now busy downing copious amounts of alcohol and hanging out of various unsuitable-looking men.

"Ian, let go of me *now*," she said, much as a parent would to a child. "I'm leaving."

"You know what your problem is, Jean?" he said with a sneer. "You never tried it. So don't knock it, eh?"

She said nothing. Best to let him run out of steam.

"You were always too busy working to party, weren't

you. You and that precious agency of yours. Well, I helped you get that off the ground, so don't turn around and begrudge me a good time."

"*What?*" She was mystified now.

"That ten thousand pounds. I bankrolled you when you had nothing, were just setting up."

Jean had to think hard. "Ten thousand pounds?" When it finally dawned on her, she almost laughed in disbelief. "That wasn't your money! That was from a savings account!"

"A *joint* savings account," he clarified. "That we opened when we first started going out together."

Could he really be serious? "And that you never put a penny into," she said, harsh now. She had religiously put by some money every month, knowing one day that she would strike out on her own. Ian, as far as she could remember, had been almost unaware of the account's existence.

"Doesn't matter. My name was still on that account."

She knew now what he wanted. And she couldn't believe it.

"You make me sick," she said heavily.

He couldn't quite meet her eyes. He knew he was in the wrong but he was desperate. He laid a clammy hand on her arm again, pleading. "I need money, Jean."

She bet he did. Coke was expensive these days. Especially when he had to feed his new friends' habits too.

"I thought you had a job."

"I kind of lost it."

Jean snorted. "So you thought you'd sponge off me once again. Forget it, Ian."

Abruptly, he grew nasty. "Legally, half that money is mine. And I want it. Soon."

"You don't frighten me."

"Maybe not, but my solicitor will."

"Jean? Is there a problem here?"

She swung around to find Peter Fisher standing there, looking hard at Ian.

"No. No problem at all," Jean said clearly.

Ian, as always, crumbled in the face of bigger and more sober people than himself. "I'll be in touch," he said to Jean, but his attempt at menace was half-hearted.

He clumsily pushed his way off into the crowd.

"Thanks," Jean said formally to Peter. "But I could have handled him."

"I know you could have."

She found that she was shaking. Who would have thought that Ian, her partner of seven years, could deliver a blow like that? It was incredible.

It was the combination of this shock to her psyche and the fact that Peter Fisher had not come near her all night that made her attack him.

"Do you? How you really know *anything* about me, Peter? You just fill in the blanks yourself as you go along, don't you. One minute I'm a media informer, the next a damsel-in-distress. Well, you're wrong on both counts."

He didn't say anything. She took a few deep breaths, crossing her arms protectively over her chest. She had to fight the thought that this man had seen her naked, had made love to her, knew every inch of her intimately.

"Yes. I *am* wrong," he said. "I'm sorry if I doubted you about the press thing. I know it wasn't you."

"Oh." She had not expected this.

"And I was wrong about other things too, Jean. Lots of things."

His voice could still make her heart melt. It was an effort to maintain some vestige of aloofness.

"I shouldn't even be talking to you now," he went on quietly. "I told myself I would stay away."

"What?"

"Because I'm not free, Jean."

"No," she agreed. It was time to say her piece, to be done with it. "And I won't share you with your wife, Peter."

There. It was out. The hard truth. The irresolvable problem.

"I shouldn't have asked you to."

She looked him straight in the eye. "That's right, you shouldn't."

So this was it. It was over. Finished.

Jean looked at the ground, blinking hard. She wondered what other people did in these situations. Did they say a brief "Cheerio" and walk off? Or shake hands and wryly comment on how good it was while it lasted? She just wanted to burst into tears.

"And I can't ask you to wait for me, either," he said.

Her neck snapped back. "What?"

"Until I'm free."

She looked at him, confused. Was he suggesting she hang around until Tess passed away?

He saw that he had not made himself clear. "I'm going to ask Tess for a divorce, Jean."

Millions of tiny flashbulbs exploded in Jean's head. Was he serious? He was. My *God*. She couldn't believe it.

"Are you doing this for me?"

"I'm not happy, Jean. And I won't be happy unless I'm with you. And that can't happen while I'm married."

Jean could find no words. He watched her carefully.

"I'm not asking you to wait around. I'm telling you that *I'll* wait around." He smiled crookedly. "And if you're still unattached in a few years' time – which I doubt – maybe you might look me up."

The words were like a balm. He wanted her. He *loved* her, she could see that plainly from his face. And she loved him.

"There will be no pressure from me," he added hastily.

He was offering her a relationship on her terms.

"Thank you," she said.

Peter nodded. They stood in silence for a moment.

"You know, we don't have to wait," she said levelly.

"What?"

"I'm willing to place my bets now."

It was his turn to be confused.

"If you ask Tess for a divorce, if your marriage is properly over, then I see no reason to waste years waiting for the paperwork to go through."

"Jean, at least think about it – "

"I have," she said simply. "Unless *you* want to wait?"

"You must be joking."

They found themselves grinning like clowns. They would have buried themselves in each other's arms were it not for the three hundred or so people milling around them.

"Can we meet later?" he asked.

"I'm staying in the same hotel," she said, eyes shining. "Same room, even. I'm a bit of a cliché, I'm afraid."

"I'll take the same elevator," he said, giving her such a scorching look that she expected smoke to rise at any moment. "See you then."

She floated across the marquee and her feet didn't touch the ground until she was out in the open air.

"Fiona, you shouldn't be seen talking to me. Peter might see."

Fiona was on her third vodka. "I don't care." She looked around restlessly. "Let's leave, will we? It's a boring party, full of old farts."

"I need to be here, honey," he said, swallowing his aggravation.

"Don't you want to spend some time with me?" The sexual innuendo in her voice was unmistakable and she dropped her hand until it practically rested on his crotch.

Oh Christ.

"Of course I do."

"Great. I thought we might go back to the house."

"What house?" Surely she wasn't suggesting the Fisher household?

She was. "Mum and Dad will be here all night. We could slip away for an hour, and be back before anyone noticed."

The prospect of despoiling Peter Fisher's daughter under his own roof – in his own bed – was so appealing that Roger almost regretted the fact that he was gay.

"I've got keys," she whispered now.

"We'll see," Roger said noncommittally. He would think of some way of extricating himself – a phone call could be arranged, for example, or an urgent meeting manufactured. But right now, he had more pressing matters on his mind than avoiding Fiona Fisher's advances.

"Did Harry Burke seem funny to you?" he asked.

"Oh. *Harry*." Fiona was disparaging. "He was just drunk."

Roger felt better. He had gone to pay his respects to him only to be more or less ignored. But, of course, the man was a hopeless alcoholic, everybody knew that.

"Roger?" She sidled up to him again.

"Later, Fiona, okay?" Roger said impatiently, looking around. The marquee was stuffed to the rafters with Cabinet Ministers, local Councillors and big party boys. It was an invaluable opportunity to do some networking and Roger did not intend to squander it. It was never too early to lay the foundations for his future political career in the party, now that his victory in the by-election was more or less won.

"I've to go and talk to Dan Kilmartin," he told Fiona. Kilmartin was tedium personified, but he was still the Minister for Justice.

The crowd moved and Roger saw that Kilmartin was talking intimately with Peter Fisher. It seemed to Roger that Kilmartin looked over quickly at him – and disparagingly? No. Roger shook himself. It was only his imagination. He was letting his hatred of Peter Fisher influence his judgement.

"Maybe we'll talk to Geraldine Day instead," he said hastily, as she came towards them.

"No," Fiona said baldly. "I'm bored and I'm going to the bathroom. Then," she paused meaningfully, "we're leaving."

Dream on, Roger thought, as she walked away. He niftily stepped out in front of Geraldine Day.

"Geraldine!"

He always got on well with her whenever they met in Leinster House, knowing exactly how much flattery was necessary to turn her head, silly woman.

"What, Roger?" She seemed in a hurry.

"I just wanted to say that you look wonderful." Her red dress was too loud, too tight, too red.

She smiled at him. "Thank you. I found it in a wonderful little shop in Blackrock that nobody else knows about. I'd tell you where, only then I'd have to kill you."

Roger laughed heartily. *What was she babbling on about?*

"Can I rely on you to canvass for me in the next couple of weeks?" he asked in a winning voice.

"Certainly," she said. "I promised Peter. I had a *marvellous* little chat with him earlier on about you."

Her horsey teeth flashed in another smile. Or a sort of a smile. Roger's own slipped slightly.

"Very informative altogether," she added slowly.

Why was she talking in riddles tonight? Was she drunk too? Roger gave a nervous little chuckle. "All good, I hope?"

She leaned in to whisper confidentially in his ear. "Can't really say, Roger. The place is crawling with hacks and paparazzi. You never know who might be listening, do you?"

With a cheery wave, she was gone.

Roger stood alone, his smile still pinned in place. The bitch *knew*. Fisher had told her. *The bastard.* The bastard.

Gradually, he calmed down. So what if she knew? Peter Fisher had absolutely no proof, Roger had admitted nothing about any press leak. Fisher could tell anybody he liked, but he couldn't touch him, not really. He needed him, Roger reminded himself yet again. They all did.

He threw back his shoulders and looked around arrogantly, confidently. He caught the eye of Noreen and Willie O'Mara, two of the hardened grass-roots supporters here in Kilkenny. Willie O'Mara had already offered to man the phones in the office in the run-up to the election.

"Noreen, Willie, good to see you," Roger called.

Noreen didn't appear to hear him. Willie O'Mara

simply fixed him with a wall-eyed stare. Neither made an effort to come and speak to him. Still, they were talking to Jack Thornton. They could hardly walk away.

Roger turned the other way now, trying to still his growing unease. He found himself directly confronted by Carol Taylor.

One look at her and his heart jumped into his mouth. *She knew too.* Her eyes peered into Roger's very soul and recognised him for what he was.

All at once Roger was a small child again, found out in yet another mean and devious misdemeanour. He saw the disappointment and bewilderment in Carol Taylor's face and he felt weak and small and snivelling.

"I'm sorry," he found himself blurting.

Out of the corner of his eye, he was aware of Dan Kilmartin, Geraldine Day, Harry Burke, Noreen and Willie O'Mara, the local Kilkenny Councillors, all of them, watching. They knew. Peter Fisher had told every one of them.

He felt their contempt and loathing like hot beams on the back of his neck, burning him. For a horrified moment, he thought he might wet himself.

Carol Taylor seemed to loom over him. "We'll talk about it on Monday, Roger, when you come to my office at ten."

Roger looked at the ground. He was trembling with fear, with mortification. Carol Taylor saw this and when she spoke again, her voice was not unkind. "Now go home, Roger, it's getting late. We've a lot of work to do in the next month before the election and you should rest while you can."

She moved off. The watching eyes turned away, backs were presented to him. Roger was alone.

Alone and quite, quite finished. Through the crazy buzzing noises in his head, he knew that as clearly as he had known anything. His career in the party had been terminated tonight by Peter Fisher. Brutally. Irrevocably.

They would help him get elected, of course. They needed him yet. But for all intents and purposes, he was not one of them and never would be now. They would see to that. There would be no meteoric rise through the party ranks, no early appointment as Junior Minister, no chance of a portfolio in years to come. *No fucking chance at all.*

His future with the party now was three years of lunching alone in the restaurant in Leinster House, of skulking on the back seats of the parliamentary chambers. Three years of drinking on his own on a Friday night, and of invitations to functions inexplicably going missing in the internal mail. And when those odious years were up, he would be informed that, regrettably, he had not been selected for re-election in the Kilkenny constituency.

Peter Fisher had warned that it would happen. It already had.

Roger wanted to smash his glass off the side of a table and plunge the broken stem into Peter Fisher's neck, to see him die for what he had done tonight.

"Roger? Are you all right?" Fiona was back and looking at him in alarm.

Slowly, Roger handed her his glass. "Take that for me."

She was mystified. "Did something happen?"

"No."

"Are you sure?" Her persistence made him want to scream.

My life is fucking over, is that enough for you? My career is dead in the water. DEAD. There is nothing left now. And all because of your fucking father.

"It's the heat in here." Amazingly, he sounded half-normal.

She was all concern. "Let's leave, get some fresh air." She squeezed his arm, playful. "And maybe you've had a bit too much to drink?"

She laughed. Did she think this was *funny*?

"Let go of me," he mumbled, as they stepped from the marquee into the blessed cool night air. His head felt like it would explode.

"Oh no," she said. "I'm not letting go of you until I get you back to my room."

She was grinning now, just like Peter Fisher had grinned at him in that marquee. Triumphant. Crowing. She looked so like Peter Fisher that, for a moment, Roger was confused.

He tried to shake her off, to get a breath of air, to *think*. But she was kissing him, her hands crawling all over him, suffocating him. He couldn't bear it.

"Stop."

It came out as a harsh shout as he cruelly grabbed her hands and flung them away. She took a step backwards with the force of it.

"Roger?"

She was like some big dumb animal, waiting for another blow. His own terrible humiliation bubbled over and he had the intense desire to make her suffer, just as he had suffered at the hands of her father.

"Get away from me. Don't touch me ever again," he spat softly. "You make me sick, do you hear me? You're like a dog in heat, mad for it. Go back into the party and find someone with the stomach to lay you. Because I haven't."

The words hit her like a series of missiles and she reeled slightly with each one. Under her make-up, he saw her face go grey. He smiled as he delivered the last blow.

"Ask your Daddy for a few tips. He's screwing Jean Ormsby. Or didn't you know?"

He felt a savage satisfaction as she gathered up the hem of her dress and stumbled off into the darkness across the field. He heard her sobbing, saw her briefly fall as one of her heels snapped. Then he couldn't see her any more.

He stood outside the marquee for an hour in the darkness and the chill air, listening to the laughter and chatter of the party filtering out across the field. Slowly, the white heat of his emotions died down. He found that he could think clearly again and it was a relief.

A small smile crossed his face. All was not yet lost. Far from it. In fact, this could all be turned around to his advantage, and brilliantly. It was a simple plan at the end of the day, but the simple ones were always the best.

He checked his watch. The party would be over soon. He must not miss the two most important people to the success of the plan.

He moved to a darker corner of the field and settled down to wait.

Chapter Twenty-nine

They talked for hours. They sat on the edge of the hotel bed, arms wrapped around each other, drunk on happiness, high. There were so many plans to be made, so much to discuss.

"We'll live in the country."

"We won't," Jean returned with spirit. "What about my agency?"

"We can commute. God, you're beautiful."

"I know. Now back to this business of living in the country."

"We'll work something out."

"Your hair is so *soft*."

"All Ministers use conditioner, it's in our contracts."

They kissed again. It was several minutes before the conversation resumed.

Peter looked more serious. "The divorce will be hard on Fiona. I'll have to spend much more time with her . . . is that all right?"

"Peter!" She was shocked. "You don't have to ask me."

"I love you."

"Me too. Love you, I mean. *Peter*!"

Eventually she fought him off long enough to ask another question. "What about Tess?"

"I'm meeting her tomorrow. I'll tell her then."

"I felt terrible, seeing her tonight."

"I'll do things properly," Peter assured her. "But we're going to have to lie low for a while. The media will probably sniff around once they hear of the separation."

Jean nodded. She didn't mind the secrecy this time. Not now that they were going to be together in the end.

Peter took her face in his hands. "I'm much older than you, Jean."

"Fifteen years isn't that much."

"Seventeen."

"So?"

"So maybe you'll want someone younger eventually."

"No."

"Not even that blond beefcake of a fellow you were with tonight?"

He meant Ian. Ian, her blackmailing, druggie ex. "Certainly not."

The look on her face was enough to satisfy him. It was her turn to get serious.

"And what about you?"

"What about me?"

"Come on, Peter. I've seen you in action, remember? With Helen."

"I know I've had a colourful past, Jean." He was

struggling for words. She didn't help him out. "But all that, it's over. I promise."

"How do I know I can trust you?"

"You don't, I suppose." He paused. "Unless you'd like to marry me."

"What?"

"I'm asking you to marry me. You can keep tabs on me then."

She was unsmiling. "Don't kid about."

"I'm not."

She saw that he wasn't. She thought about it, but only briefly.

"No, thank you very much."

He was hurt.

"You have to win trust, Peter. You don't get it by asking."

Now he was really hurt. "So I'm on probation?"

"Yes, if you like."

"That's a bit harsh."

"What will be "harsh" is if you mess me about. And I'm telling you now, Peter, that I won't stand for it."

It had to be said. He watched her for a long moment, then conceded with a shrug of his shoulders.

"Fair enough. I suppose I was asking for that."

Jean didn't want to ruin the entire reunion with dire threats. "Anyway. Let's talk about something else."

He lightened too. "I'm all talked out."

"Oh?" she said, as he scooted closer across the bed.

"I want to make love to you, Jean."

"Then for God's sake shut up and *do it*."

They still had most of their clothes on when there was a perfunctory knock on the door and it opened. A maid stood there, holding a tray of sandwiches. Her face went bright red as she took in the scene.

"Um, room service?"

Jean and Peter bolted upright guiltily, legs and arms messily entangled. "I think you've got the wrong room," Jean managed.

The maid legged it out the door. Peter looked mortified. Jean collapsed in a fit of giggles.

"I thought you locked the door."

"I thought *you* did. Lock it now, for heaven's sake. And hurry."

It was imperative that Gobnait Purcell play this one close to her chest. It was the kind of scoop every investigative journalist dreamed of, waited their whole careers for. She must be very careful not to blow it.

As the hotel maid approached, she grabbed a tissue and dabbed at her eyes. *Please God, let it not be a hoax.*

"Well?" she asked tearfully.

The maid was a big thick lump of a girl with unintelligent eyes. Gobnait had chosen her precisely for these attributes.

"I'm afraid there was a man in there with her all right," the maid said, wringing her hands.

Gobnait felt sweet relief wash over her. But she pretended more upset. "Could you describe him to me?"

The maid looked at the ground. "Um, I didn't see much. They were, you know . . . at each other."

"Yes, yes, I can imagine," Gobnait intervened hastily, dabbing at her eyes again. "But what did he look like?"

"He had black hair and was fortyish. Oh, and he had on a suit and there was a red tie lying on the bed."

That was Peter Fisher all right. He'd worn a red tie at the party tonight. I'll be damned, Gobnait thought. The tip-off she'd received on her mobile phone less than an hour ago had been genuine after all. Hurrah! This, on top of the titbit that drugs had been rampant at the party tonight. Gobnait had sneaked into the men's toilet and witnessed first-hand three people imbibing, hunched over the hand-basins and snorting like pigs. Wonderful stuff. But it paled into insignificance in the face of this latest discovery.

"Does that sound like your husband?" the maid prompted, obviously ignorant of what her own Dáil representative looked like. Gobnait had counted on this. Had it been a sharper member of staff, the other newspapers would know within the hour that Peter Fisher was holed up in a hotel room with a woman who was not his wife. Gobnait's scoop would have been gone.

"I'm afraid so," Gobnait confirmed sadly. "Thank you very much for your help."

She pressed a twenty-pound note into the girl's hand. The girl hesitated, obviously distressed by Gobnait's plight.

"I'll just sit here for a while until I feel better," Gobnait informed her briskly. "Oh, and you can leave those sandwiches."

Adrenaline always made her peckish. She got on her

mobile pronto. The night-editor was awake for a change.

"I need a photographer down here. Now. And I can't say why so don't ask me," Gobnait barked. "He might have to stay the night. And tell Andy that I've got a front page for Monday morning."

What a terrible pity tomorrow was Sunday. The newspaper did not have a Sunday edition. This little cracker would have to wait until Monday morning.

Still, it might be just as well. Fisher mightn't emerge from the room until morning anyway. Gobnait intended to be right here when he did.

She munched on a cheese salad sandwich and thought about Andy, the editor. He wouldn't want to print, of course.

"Let's leave that kind of thing to the English tabloids," he would piously say. Spineless bastard. The English tabloids might be sleazy, but at least they didn't suffer from the Irish media's sickening deference to powerful political figures.

And neither did Gobnait. It was high time someone blew the whistle on the boys in Merrion Square, who preached one thing and practised another entirely. Why should they dodge accountability in their private lives time and again?

As she settled down for the wait, Gobnait Purcell's conscience was at ease with itself.

And if Andy refused to print, she mused, then she would threaten to go directly to *The Sun* or *The Mirror*, depending on the price.

Andy would print all right.

The film crew weren't so bad after all, Cathy decided. In fact, she couldn't remember why she'd ever fallen out with them in the first place. That fellow James was particularly nice. He'd been plying her with drink for the past hour.

"So. What did you say you did on the shoot again?" she asked, smiling brilliantly and quickly glossing over the letter 's' which she found she was having increasing difficulty with as the night wore on.

"I told you, I don't work on the film. I'm an accountant."

Cathy pretended fascination; in fact, she was feeling rather tired. But she was determined to party on. "Why don't we have another drink?"

He laid a meaty hand on her thigh. "Why don't we skip the drinks and go back to my place?"

Cathy abruptly decided that she didn't like him after all. He had grabby eyes and thick, wet lips. Surely she could do better for herself than him?

"I don't think so," she told him haughtily, picking up her drink and walking off. The room suddenly seemed terribly crowded. She blinked hard and, thankfully, the crowd halved.

"Jason!" she cried, descending on Jason Blake and his girlfriend. He didn't seem all that pleased to see her. Well, fuck him! This was a party and she was going to socialise whether he liked it or not.

"And Shergar." She smiled warmly at the gorgeous girlfriend whom she'd never had the neck to speak to before.

"Charmaine," the girl corrected nicely.

Feck, Cathy thought. She'd thought it was something exotic all right.

"Anyone care to join me in a dance?" she asked. There was some kind of disco area at the top of the marquee.

"No, we're leaving, it's late," Jason said. He looked at her meaningfully. "Maybe you should too, Cathy."

"The night is young yet, Jason. And so am I!" God, but she was witty tonight. With a smile and a wave, she went off gaily in search of a dancing partner.

She found several. She couldn't remember any of their names or indeed anything they said, but they kept her company.

And safely away from Carl Tallon. The guy took her breath away. He'd stood there most of the night staring in disapproval at her dress, his lips puckered like a schoolmarm's. And the cut of *him* – turning up in that denim jacket and jeans. He wouldn't know high fashion if it came up and introduced itself.

Then he'd had the neck to approach her, a most peculiar expression on his face, as though he had a bad case of wind. Cathy had braced herself for more abuse. But thankfully, Greg – or was it Aidan? – had arrived over with a drink. Carl had moved on abruptly. He must have gone home. Cathy told herself she was delighted.

They were playing some kind of smoochy number now. The marquee was almost empty. Cathy felt as though she would drop at any second, but her latest dancing partner was determinedly swinging her around the dancefloor. She'd been with him for the last three songs and he obviously thought that this was a life commitment judging from the way he was feeling her bottom.

Well, that was what she had set out to get tonight, wasn't it? Some man to warm her bed? To chase away the blues? Only, she was going off the idea fast. She was just so tired. And really, this chap wasn't all that attractive.

"I think it's time to call it a night," she asked, her head feeling very light.

He pulled her closer. "Good idea," he said.

Cathy recoiled from his garlic breath. She peered at him out of one eye. She found that when she opened the other, the world reeled unpleasantly.

"So, goodbye then."

He wasn't taking the hint. "I'll walk you home."

"There's no need," she hastily assured him. "I'm going to stay in my trailer tonight, it's just across the field."

"Great," he said, following close behind as she made for the exit. She speeded up, trying to shake him off, but he was like a terrier. She was wondering whether she could hide under one of the tables when she came up against an immovable object.

It was Carl Tallon. At least, it looked very like him anyway.

"The party's over, Cathy." He jerked a thumb at Garlic Breath. "And you. Beat it."

Garlic Breath turned accusingly to Cathy. "You should have said that you had a boyfriend."

"I don't!"

He hesitated, then obviously decided that Cathy wasn't worth the fight. She watched, slack-jawed, as he slunk off. Then she rounded on Carl.

"And just what do you think you're doing?"

"Stopping you making a bigger fool of yourself."

"Step aside, sir!" Cathy said regally, unaware that she had slipped into Alison's lines from the film.

"Stop bloody acting, Cathy."

Her took her arm and she found herself propelled out of the marquee without further ceremony. The fresh, cold air hit her in the face and almost sent her reeling.

"This is outrageous," she blustered as Carl marched her across the grass towards her trailer. Had he never heard of feminism? Men weren't supposed to march women anywhere these days. If he wasn't careful, she would take off her bra, sling it around his neck and burn it. If she had been wearing one, that is.

Angrily, she shook him off and stepped into her trailer with as much dignity as she had left. He stepped in after her, uninvited. The bloody cheek!

"If you're hoping for coffee, you're out of luck," she said coldly.

"I'll bet you were going to offer *him* more than coffee."

"And what business is it of yours what I was going to offer him?"

He didn't reply. She squinted up at him. He looked like he was going to explode at any minute.

"My God," she said slowly. "You're jealous."

"Like hell."

"You are!"

"Jealous of *him*? Although I suppose he was an improvement on some of the toads you've been cosying up to tonight."

His disgust made her defensive.

"I wasn't going to sleep with him!"

"I couldn't care less whether you were going to knock them off one by one."

He was lying. His bottom lip was sticking out, a sure sign. Cathy knew him too well.

She looked at him in wonder now. Was it possible that Carl Tallon still wanted her, despite everything?

All her dire warnings to herself to stay away from him went out the window. In a sudden rush of clarity, she knew that she wanted him too. What was the point in lying to herself any longer? Hadn't she done that for five years now?

"Carl – "

"Oh, go to bed, Cathy," he said abruptly. "Sleep it off."

She did not want him to leave. Not like this. Not without knowing how he really felt.

There was one way to find out.

She took a step closer and put a hand on his chest. She felt him tense. But he didn't pull away.

"Cathy . . ." His voice was all funny and choked. That must mean something, mustn't it?

She grew bolder. She put her other hand around his waist and pressed herself against him lightly. She felt the warmth of him through her thin dress. The sensation was divine. She stole a look at his face. Unless she was very much mistaken, he felt the same. She raised her head for the inevitable kiss.

"Cathy. No."

He pushed her away. Cathy felt as though she had just run into a concrete wall at speed. She turned away, smarting.

"Terribly sorry about that," she babbled. "Gin – I should never touch the stuff!"

"No, it's just . . ."

"Thanks for walking me back."

"Cathy . . ."

"Goodnight now! Safe home!"

Leave, she willed him. Just let him go, now, so that she could die with shame in privacy. He didn't want her at all. She had made a complete idiot of herself.

"Cathy, stop it!"

She would not look at him; *could* not look at him.

"I just don't want you to do something you'll regret in the morning."

"Something *you'll* regret you mean!"

"No. I wouldn't."

She lifted her eyes warily. He was looking at her like . . . well, like he used to. Like he still loved her. Impossible.

"What do you mean?" she whispered.

"What I mean is . . . um, well . . ." He looked miserable. "Oh fuck it, Cathy, I still love you."

No violins erupted into joyous rhapsody. Fireworks didn't explode. Choirs of angels held their song.

Instead, a small bud of sheer happiness blossomed in Cathy Conroy's chest. Carl Tallon still loved her. The angels could go to hell.

The five years of separation and strife melted away as they tumbled into each other's arms. No other words were spoken as the trailer door was locked, the lights extinguished and the narrow bed pulled out from the wall with indecent haste. They didn't bother with blankets. They kept each other warm.

A long time later, Cathy surfaced with a small, ecstatic sigh. She could not believe that she had lived without Carl for all this time. In fact, in the delicious happiness that engulfed her now like a great big lump of cotton wool, it seemed impossible that they had ever let things fall apart in the first place.

Looking at his face now, so soft with love, Cathy decided that she had been quite mad. She should have told him back then, he would have understood. They would have worked it out together; it would have made them stronger, not torn them apart like she had believed. How had she ever doubted him at all? Mad, she told herself again.

She would tell him now. He would hold her close and say he understood. It would be a relief, really. She had carried it by herself for too long.

"Carl, about London."

"Cathy, you don't have to, you know." He smiled at her in a way that almost broke her heart. "That's all in the past now."

But she was eager now to unburden herself. That

way they could really start afresh, she thought fervently, with no secrets and no more lies.

"I got a terrible shock, you see," she said quietly. "That's why I didn't tell you at the time. We had so many plans, so many things we wanted to do, didn't we?"

"Well, yes."

"And . . ." She swallowed. She kept her eyes trained on the ceiling. "And none of those plans included a baby."

Silence. But she knew he would be shocked.

"I found out the week the show finished, Carl. I tried to tell you lots of times . . . but you were so busy with the new play, we hadn't known each other long – "

He sat up suddenly in the narrow bed. Cathy was a little startled.

"You went to London." His voice was strangely flat.

"Well, yes."

"You said nothing to me and you went to *London*?"

There was an ominous change in the air now. But it was all news to him. She had lived with it for years. She must not expect too much too soon.

"Carl – "

He swung himself out of bed and stood over her.

"You went for an abortion, didn't you? Well, didn't you?"

Cathy froze in the bed, clutching the pillow to her chest. She felt almost faint at the look on his face – incredulous, angry. And unforgiving.

"You took matters into your own hands and you

went for an abortion. Am I right?" he almost shouted at her now.

"Yes," Cathy whispered.

He was struggling into his clothes now like his whole life depended on it.

"Carl, please don't go, you don't understand . . ."

He briefly paused by the door, half his clothes on and the rest bundled under his arm.

"I understand enough."

There was such a flatness about it, a finality, that Cathy felt chilled to the bone.

The door flapped shut after him.

She rocked on the bed, her arms wrapped fiercely around her knees and her eyes on the door. He would come back, she told herself, once he had calmed down. It would take a little time for him to think it through. When he realised how hard it must have been on her too, of course he would come back.

She sat up watching the door until dawn.

Chapter Thirty

Government Press Officer John Graham's wife Betty did not like politics. She had no interest whatsoever in her husband's career and was in fact secretly unsure which political party he worked for. All she knew was that he was paid handsomely on time every month, thus enabling her to pay for her real passion in life – garden plants.

On Sunday morning after Mass she made a trip to the garden centre on the Naas Road. She'd heard a rumour that they had just got a batch of willow trees in and she wanted to nab one to replace another that had inexplicably died at the foot of the garden, despite Betty lovingly feeding it cold tea for a week.

Her eyes gleamed as she saw the willows propped against the wooden fence as she drove into the centre. Her fingers itched to be covered in wet, sticky clay. Bliss.

By the time she had parked and got out, the willows were gone. She marched into the centre, highly indignant.

"Excuse me. Do you really need *all* of them?" she asked the purchaser, a middle-aged woman.

"I'm trying to grow a big hedge. Between my garden and my neighbour's," the woman said, apologetic.

Betty immediately felt better. "Willows are no good," she said briskly. "You need Cupressors. They'll spring up in no time, good and thick. You'll have absolute privacy."

The woman was grateful. "That's *exactly* what I want."

Betty companionably helped her choose the best of the Cupressors, having first carefully kept aside a willow tree for herself.

"Bad neighbours?" she asked sympathetically.

"The worst. He was marching around his back garden this morning in his underwear at the crack of dawn, talking at the top of his voice into that mobile phone of his. On a Sunday. And Gerry just over his by-pass."

"Tsk," Betty clucked. "A student?"

"No, a *reporter*." The woman shuddered. "Andy something-or-other, I think he's an editor."

"Oh." Betty's interest was waning fast.

"Apparently Peter Fisher is having an affair. Or else he's on drugs. Gerry said that drugs were definitely mentioned."

Betty shifted restlessly. She wanted to get home and plant her willow.

She spent an hour settling the willow into its new home. She looked at it now through the kitchen window as she and John had lunch.

"Does it look a little crooked to you?" she asked, suddenly worried.

John didn't raise his head from the Sunday papers. "No."

Betty tried to concentrate on her soup, ignoring the tingling in her hands. She must distract herself. "Is Peter Fisher on drugs?"

John rolled his eyes. "Not that I'm aware of."

"Oh good," Betty said. "Then he must be having an affair."

She looked out at the garden again. The willow was definitely crooked. No doubt about it. She got up.

"Who told you that?" John asked sharply.

"Hmm? Some reporter. Or rather, a neighbour of his . . . keep an eye on the potatoes."

Betty hurried into the back garden, pulling on gardening gloves as she went.

They were getting ready to leave the hotel after a very late breakfast in the restaurant downstairs when the call came on Peter's mobile.

"Oh Christ," he said, his face ashen as he told Jean.

Jean couldn't say anything at all. This simply couldn't be happening. Not to her, to them.

"They're going to print, Jean," Peter emphasised, as if willing her to understand.

Jean tried to take it in. Her life was going to be spread across the newspapers tomorrow. It would be so sordid. So cheap. Everything she and Peter had shared last night would be turned into sleaze for the masses.

"Stop them," she said. "You can stop them, can't you?"

"Jean – "

"Jesus, Peter, you're a Government Minister, you must be able to do something!" Her voice was dangerously high.

He took her cold, clammy hands in his. "John Graham has done everything he can to dissuade them. But it's called freedom of the press."

"To hell with freedom of the press! They shouldn't be allowed to do this! To ruin people's lives like this . . ." She stopped, realising how childish it sounded. "I'm sorry. I'm just frightened."

"I know, I know."

"Is there nothing at all we can do?" she asked, praying that he would come up with a solution, that he would save them. But she knew from his face that he could not pull any rabbits out of hats on *this* one.

"Look, Jean, it depends on how they put it – "

"If they're printing the story in the first place, I think we can be pretty sure how they're going to put it!"

Peter stayed calm. "We'll have to issue some kind of statement when they print tomorrow. Try and put our case to the public."

Jean threw her hands in the air. "Case? What case? We have no case, Peter! You're a public figure caught cheating on your wife. And I'm the *Scarlett* woman. No matter how nicely we put it, no matter how sorry we say we are, we can't change the facts!"

A long, chilly silence followed her words. Peter moved away and threw himself on the couch, burying his head in his hands. Jean slumped on the side of the bed, trembling. Everything was falling apart – including them.

After an age, Peter lifted his head. "I'm not sorry."

Jean stared at him blankly. "What?"

"I said I'm not sorry. I'm not sorry that I met you and started a relationship with you."

"Oh, Peter." She was ashamed of her outburst, touched by his words.

"Are you?"

"No. I'm not sorry either. I love you."

It was the truth. She buried herself in his arms, holding him as though she would never let go. No matter how bad the storm would be, they had each other. And the storm would be bad, she had no doubt of that.

Eventually, she had to say it. "You'd better tell Tess."

She didn't want to think about Tess Fisher, didn't want to imagine what the news would do to her. Bad enough that she had to learn that her husband was cheating on her; it would be ten times worse to know that the entire country was privy to it too. Her friends, family, neighbours – all of them would know every detail of her private life. The media would be queuing up to document her humiliation. And then there was their daughter, Fiona . . .

Jean almost choked on the guilt and remorse bubbling up in her now. An entire family was about to be publicly blown apart and she was the cause of it. If she were in Tess Fisher's shoes tomorrow, she would denounce herself as a home-wrecker and a husband-stealer. Jean and Peter could bleat about the unstoppable force of love until they were blue in the face, but there was little doubt where public sympathy would lie. Jean's own sympathies would lie with Tess Fisher.

"I was due to meet her this evening anyhow," Peter said quietly. "John Graham has set up an emergency cabinet meeting for this afternoon. Obviously, my presence is required. I'll drive home afterwards."

He paused, looking uncomfortable. "I'll have to stay with Tess tonight, Jean."

She nodded mutely.

"I'm sorry, I hate not to be with you at a time like this. But in the circumstances . . ."

In the circumstances, his wife came first. Wives always did, they had certain claims on their husbands that no mistress would ever have. But it still hurt.

"But promise me that you won't be alone tonight. That you'll get a friend or someone to stay with you."

"Yes. I'll be okay, Peter."

"If anyone rings you from the papers, don't talk to them, okay?"

"Of course not."

"Maybe you shouldn't go into work tomorrow – "

"I will be going into work as usual in the morning, Peter." She was a little tired at being told what to do. Anyway, she would go mad sitting at home.

"I'm sorry," he said. "I'm just worried about you."

"Don't. I'll be fine." She wouldn't be, but what was the point in putting even more pressure on him?

There didn't seem to be much else to say after that. They gathered their things.

"I'll leave first," Peter said.

Jean swallowed a half-hysterical laugh. It was a little late in the day for that.

He suddenly gathered her close. "I'm sorry about all this. But remember, I love you. And we'll be together no matter what happens."

She must have looked doubtful, because he gave her a little shake.

"We will, Jean. I swear to you. I don't care what I have to give up for you. I'll do it."

And she believed him.

"I'll ring you tonight, okay?"

Jean nodded and embraced him hard. Then he slipped out the door and she was alone.

The small conference room in the discreet hotel in town was ominously silent. For an age, nobody said a word.

"You idiot," Geraldine Day finally declared. "You stupid, *stupid* idiot."

"I know, Geraldine," Peter said heavily. "But what's done is done."

Harry Burke was in the horrors after his excesses at the press party in Kilkenny last night. His hands shook uncontrollably and his mood was terrifyingly belligerent.

"Can't keep it in your pants, can you?" he spat across the table. "You never could, you randy fucker, that's always been your problem."

Peter bit down hard on his tongue. Let him get it off his chest. Let them all have their say, they were going to anyway.

"Bad situation, this," Dan Kilmartin said quietly. "You should have been more discreet, Peter."

Peter squirmed inwardly. He could handle Harry Burke's bluster. It was the quiet disappointment of people like Dan, hard-working and trusted colleagues, that was hardest to bear.

"At a press party! Of all places!" Geraldine was getting into her stride now. "Bloody hell, you might as well have taken out an ad in the newspapers yourself! Saved them the bother!"

Again, Peter didn't reply. However much in the wrong he was, he was not going to justify himself to Geraldine Day.

Harry Burke mistook his silence for a lack of repentance. His jowls quivered in fresh outrage. "I hope you're happy now that you've dragged the rest of us down with you! Sullied the image of this Government and betrayed your poor wife for the sake of some cheap tart who gave you the come-on!"

This was too much. Peter found himself on his feet. "She is not some cheap tart! And you'd better not refer to either her or my wife again in this company, Harry."

Harry Burke recognised that there was a very real chance of being punched in the face. He backed down.

"I think it best if we stick to a political agenda," John Graham said calmly, well over the shock his wife Betty had inadvertently delivered.

"Yes, let's," Geraldine said sarcastically. "Let's not dwell *too* long on the ins and outs of Peter's private life. If you'll pardon the pun."

Bloody cow, Peter thought, praying for some intervention.

It would not be forthcoming from Carol Taylor, who sat at the head of the table in her sharpest suit. Her eyes had not met Peter's once, a reliable indication of the depth of her anger.

So far, she had said very little. She had not joined in any of the abuse, but she had not stopped it either. Peter couldn't blame her. In her book, his affair was not the unforgivable act of folly; his private life was his own business. It was the fact that he had recklessly and selfishly jeopardised something they had all worked so hard for. And she would be the one who would have to pick up the pieces.

Her unspoken recriminations weighed heavy on him now and he had to look away from her. A renewed onslaught from Geraldine Day went over his head as he stared at the polished table-top, head pounding.

Christ, what a mess. What a godawful, destructive fiasco he had created for himself and everyone around him. The grief and hurt he was going to cause to so many people, people that he loved and respected – Jean, Tess, Fiona, Carol. Tess most of all, blithely ignorant on this Sunday afternoon that her life was about to become public property.

His anger at Gobnait Purcell had largely abated now. Earlier, he had entertained notions of going to her house and pleading with her, and if that didn't work, throttling her. But at the end of the day she was doing her job, however odious it might seem. If it hadn't been her, it would have been some other journalist.

And anyway, you had it coming. You've been lucky for years now, but if you play with fire, you'll get burnt eventually. It was only a matter of time.

Peter couldn't shake the thought. In some way, it seemed a punishment for all the casual affairs he'd indulged in in the past; retribution for all the hearts he'd unthinkingly broken – Helen's, others whose names he couldn't even remember. But in some way it seemed rough justice that the very affair that would be exposed was the only one that had ever mattered.

Well, he couldn't turn back the clock. And there was little to be achieved by feeling sorry for himself. He would just have to face the music as best he could and try to limit the damage for all concerned.

"Cinerama," he said loudly. He didn't want to bring it up, but he had to. "They won't like this."

"After all the stuff that's gone down in the last few weeks, I should imagine that they'll have a positive cow," Geraldine Day sniffed. "Another scandal! And at their own bloody press party!"

"I know," Peter said testily.

She went on imperiously, "I suggest we distance ourselves from the film immediately."

Peter was appalled. "Jesus Christ! We brought Cinerama into it the first place! And now we're just going to jump ship?"

Geraldine shrugged. "The film was supposed to get Croft elected. Any further involvement with it can only damage our chances."

"My God," Peter said slowly. "What fine, upstanding people we all are! What a great world we inhabit, the world of politics!"

Dan Kilmartin lifted his head sharply. "Don't try and take the moral ground here, Peter, eh? You look ridiculous."

Peter went hot with humiliation.

"And I agree that we should pull out," Dan went on. "We're a liability to the film now. It stands a better chance without us. Besides, there's months of the shoot to go yet. People will forget."

Nobody disagreed with him. Peter shuddered as he imagined Jack Thornton's face. Still, maybe Cinerama would be glad to be rid of them.

"Never mind the fucking Americans and their film," Harry Burke interrupted viciously. "We've got our own butts to save!"

Peter decided that it had all gone on long enough. He had paid his dues to the Harry Burkes of the cabinet and it was time to bring this farce to an end for everybody's sake.

He got to his feet slowly. All eyes were on him. To his surprise, he found that his hands were steady and his head clear.

"Just a few words." He looked at them all in turn as he spoke quietly. "Firstly, I would like to apologise to you all. Everybody has worked damned hard to make this Government something to be proud of and I never intended to draw either it or any of you into disrepute." He paused for breath. There wasn't a sound. "Unfortunately, I can't undo what has been done. But I must do whatever is necessary to spare the Government and the party further embarrassment."

He took an envelope from his pocket and turned to Carol Taylor. His voice was very formal. "Taoiseach, I would like to tender my resignation as Minister for Arts, effective immediately."

In the stunned silence, he put the envelope containing his typed resignation on the table in front of her. Then he looked briefly at John Graham. "We'll need to issue a press statement this afternoon."

"I'll get on it now," Graham said, slipping quietly out of the room.

Nobody moved as Peter left the table, collecting his coat and briefcase by the door. There was no need to stay now.

"Peter."

Peter turned. Carol Taylor reluctantly picked up the envelope from the table and held it out to him. "Take this back."

"What?"

"I am not accepting your resignation." Her voice was hard but the iciness had melted a little from her eyes. "Now sit down please, and let's get on with the meeting."

Peter sat, a little bemused. He had not expected this.

"I am by no means condoning your behaviour,"

Carol went on. "But I for one will not be coerced by the press. Neither have I any intention of abandoning a hard-working and loyal colleague who has served this Government and this country well. I'm sure the others feel the same."

She looked around the table, in particular at Geraldine Day and Harry Burke. They didn't dare disagree.

"Now I suggest we move on." She briefly consulted some notes. "I think the only possible chance of beating this thing is to confess before they accuse."

Peter waited.

"You'll issue a statement tonight outlining the situation. It gives you a chance to put your slant on it before Gobnait Purcell does her worst."

It was a good idea. A pre-emptive strike. Get in there before they do. At least it would give them a fighting chance of swaying public opinion.

"We'll take it from there," Carol said, briskly standing. There was plenty of work to be done back at Leinster House.

John Graham arrived back in the room. In ten years, it was the first time Peter had ever seen him rattled. He held a fax.

"Well?" Carol Taylor said.

"It's Roger Croft."

Her mouth tightened. "What's he done now?"

Graham's legendary calm completely deserted him. "He's dumped us! The little bastard has dumped us!"

"What?" The disbelieving shriek came from Geraldine Day.

"He's going to run in the by-election as an Independent." Graham held out the fax. "This is his letter of resignation."

Peter's woes receded in the face of this new disaster. Now they were a Government without a majority and not a hope in hell of winning one.

Chapter Thirty-one

Tess Fisher woke with a sense that something was terribly wrong.

When she rolled over in bed and saw Jack Thornton lying naked beside her, she almost vomited onto the pale blue sheets. *No.* This couldn't be happening. This couldn't *have* happened.

She knew that it had. Don't think about it, she ordered herself. Block it out. But when she shut her eyes tightly, the wretched events of the night before played like a film in her head.

Jean Ormsby. Peter's ominous announcement that they must talk. The curious numbness that wouldn't go away. And Jack, so attentive, so protective, insisting on driving her home. Tess, unable to bear her own company, asking him to stay awhile. A bottle of wine had materialised. She had let him take her upstairs . . .

Her fingers grew tight around the sheet and her toes curled with shame. Beside her,

Jack stirred in his sleep. Damn. She forced herself to

breathe deeply and evenly. He grunted and was still again.

He had peeled her dress off, throwing it to the floor. She had taken off her own underwear . . .

How *weak* she had been. To have put herself in the path of temptation when she was in such a fragile state. Where had been her famous self-control?

Jack kissing her naked thighs, her fingers wrapped in his hair, urging him on loudly and insistently . . .

Tess gamely fought down another bout of nausea.

Her fingernails raking down Jack's back, him impatient. Her opening herself to him, waiting . . .

She rode out the memory without flinching. It was getting a little easier now. Or, at least, she was accepting that denial wasn't going to get her anywhere. It was just sex, she told herself fiercely. Just sex.

Jack stopping suddenly. Her confused. Reaching for him. Him trying to turn away. Her joking about his modesty, rolling on top. Only, something funny happened . . .

But what? Tess's eyes flickered open, her mind searching for the memories which she had tried so hard to push away.

Jack, soft and limp. Pushing her abruptly off. Turning his back, silent and cold. Tess confused, but so tired, her head so heavy . . .

They had not had sex. Tess's eyes were wide and clear now. They had not finished what they had started.

Oh thank God. The relief was immediate and sweet.

And short-lived.

Because she would have gone through with it. No

doubt about that. She had wanted Jack and would have had him. All for reasons that had nothing to do with love.

Tess took a cold, angry look at herself now. What had happened last night was a textbook example of the emotional behaviour of a women betrayed. Vengeance, vulnerability, the desire to validate her own sense of self-esteem – the motivations were all there in black and white.

She was no better than Peter. Worse, even. He had never pretended to be anything other than what he was. She, on the other hand, had clung to her self-righteousness for years. It had been her crutch. She had used her moral superiority over him to exonerate herself from any blame for a marriage that was held together only by threads.

It was too late now. He wanted out. She still couldn't believe it.

But she knew Peter too well to mistake the intention in his voice and his eyes last night. Their marriage was over. He no longer wanted Tess, his wife.

It appeared that nobody else wanted her either, including Jack.

She curled into a tight, protective ball as she felt the bed covers rise and fall with Jack's even breath. She had not even had sufficient attraction for a one-night stand. After all his talk of getting her into bed, Jack didn't want her once he got her there.

She could not bear herself a moment longer. She roughly brushed away her tears and took a deep breath.

Peter was coming to see her today, to deliver the blow. She must get ready for him. Even if she all she wanted to do was crawl into a corner and die.

The bedside clock told her that it was almost three o'clock in the afternoon. Tess was astounded. Then she froze. *Fiona.* She must not, could not, see Jack Thornton. Tess listened intently; the house was silent. Maybe she had gone out.

Tess remembered now that she had not heard her come in last night. She assumed that Peter had dropped her home. Please God may she not have heard Tess and Jack making love. The thought of this galvanised Tess. She must get Jack Thornton out of here and fast.

She jumped from the bed and scrambled into her robe. "Jack?"

His breathing was too even. Too deep. She knew that he was pretending.

"Jack!"

He slowly turned over. It was a moment before either of them could meet the other's eyes.

"Morning."

"Afternoon, actually," Tess said in a funny, false voice. "Time for you to go."

"Sure, sure."

He got out of bed and scrambled into his clothes fast. He carefully kept his back to her.

Tess's mortification was rapidly replaced by anger. He could at least have the decency to make some small-talk. He could have the damned courtesy to *pretend.* Was the world really so full of spineless bloody men?

"You'll leave by the back way," she said, her voice like lead. "I'd rather Fiona didn't know you were here." Let him go back to his starlets and his models. They deserved each other.

His shoulders hunched over further at her belligerence. He did not even have the courage to look her in the face as he slunk to the door.

Tess did not think she had ever felt so small, insignificant and unattractive in all her life.

"Don't forget those." She hurled the keys to his jeep at him and turned away.

"Tess . . ."

"Goodbye."

"Tess, I'm sorry."

She looked at him incredulously. Was he actually going to apologise now for the fact that he had found her so unappealing he had been unable to make love to her? He wasn't spineless at all, she thought. He was just incredibly stupid.

"I'm sorry too, Jack. But I never pretended to be a twenty-year-old blonde babe."

"What?"

"What you see is what you get." Her voice was brittle and defensive. She wanted to hurt him.

He seemed bewildered. Well, he was an actor first and foremost she reminded herself.

"Tess, you've got the wrong end of the stick."

She wanted to say something very crude now, but she bit it back.

"It's nothing to do with you, Tess. It's me."

He was really trotting out the clichés this afternoon.

"From where I was last night, Jack, it had everything to do with me."

For the first time, he seemed to comprehend where she was coming from. His ruddy face grew redder.

"Jesus, Tess. You're . . . lovely."

"Oh stoppit, Jack."

"Listen to me! You're beautiful, classy – you're what any man would want."

She laughed bitterly. He seemed even more upset.

"Tess, sit down and listen to me."

"Please go, Jack."

"No. Not until you listen to me."

He made her sit down on the side of the bed. Tess gritted her teeth. Let him get the excuses off his chest. Then he might go and leave her in peace.

"Tess – last night, it was wonderful. I couldn't believe my luck, that after all this time, you were going to let me love you. And I couldn't."

"What do you mean, couldn't?" she snapped impatiently.

He looked miserable. "Um, I'm . . . I've had a few problems . . ."

He shot her a sideways glance, begging her to understand so that he wouldn't have to elaborate further. She did.

"I see," she said.

He didn't look like a great big Hollywood legend now. He looked deflated and confused. He even seemed smaller in stature.

"I thought it would be different with you, Tess. I

465

thought *I* could be different. And I wasn't. I'm sorry. I let you down."

He seemed happier now that the air had been cleared. He even sat up a little straighter.

"It's me, Tess. My fault."

His voice was stronger too.

"It was nothing at all to do with you," he said again with an emphatic nod. "I want you to understand that."

He was waiting for her to say something, do something. He was almost eager, Tess noted with a certain detachment.

The great Jack Thornton had just given her absolution from a crime she had not committed, that of unattractiveness. He was telling her that she was okay after all.

He expected her to be relieved.

"So last night was some kind of experiment for you?" Tess enquired politely.

"What?"

"You thought it would be different with me, you said. Tell me, do you try out many women in the hopes that it would be different?"

He was floored. She did not care.

"Tess, it wasn't like that at all."

"What *was* it like then?" Her voice was still calm.

"Jesus, you think I used you?"

"Didn't you?"

"No!" He was furious now. "If anyone was doing any using last night, it was you!"

Tess was stricken.

Jack's anger died. "I'm sorry, Tess. That was unfair. But maybe you too had your own reasons for going to bed with me last night."

She looked at her hands in silence. Her wedding band gleamed, mocking her.

"I do care about you, Tess," he said awkwardly. "It wasn't just about sex last night, you know?"

She nodded. But it hadn't been about love either. For him or her.

He was anxious to leave now, she knew that. And she would be glad to see him go.

"Peter will be here soon," she said, giving him the excuse.

"Sure, sure. You'll be talking about the separation."

"Who said anything about a separation?" Tess said sharply.

"But you said that you thought Peter wanted to leave you – "

"That doesn't mean that I'm going to let him."

Jack shook his head as if baffled. "I just don't get you, Tess. You still *love* this guy? After all he's done to you?"

Tess was about to say that she didn't love Peter, that wasn't the reason she wanted to hold on to him. But the words died on her lips. How could Jack possibly understand that her place in this world was largely defined by her husband and that if she didn't fight this, then she had nothing at all? It would be so difficult to explain, he would think it sounded ludicrous.

It *did* sound ludicrous. Tess felt uneasy. Somewhere

along the journey between Dublin and Kilkenny, the goalposts in her life had shifted. She wasn't sure how or why, or indeed where they lay now, but everything had changed. It was most unsettling. She felt like she was bobbing along in a world that no longer made sense. Her old life in Dublin no longer seemed relevant or appealing to her, and her new life was not yet defined.

She felt very out of control suddenly, and afraid of the future – a future that might very well not include Peter, her *raison d'être* for sixteen years. Was it fear that was making her hang on to him? Or something more?

"Maybe I do still love him, Jack. I don't know. About *anything* anymore," she said honestly. "But I know that things can't go on like this for me and Peter."

At least that much was making itself clear to her. Something would have to give.

"I'll call you," Jack said awkwardly.

Tess knew that he wouldn't. He wouldn't drop by the house any more either, and there would be no more invitations to the set. They'd had their dance and it was over now. As his jeep sped off, she doubted that she would see Jack Thornton again.

Tess had barely got out of the shower when another car came up the drive. It was Peter. He was early – hours early. He'd said he'd be here at six and it wasn't four yet. Her eyes narrowed further when she saw a woman in the passenger seat beside him. Surely to God he had not brought Jean Ormsby with him? That really would be too much.

But when Carol Taylor stepped out of the passenger

seat, face drawn, Tess knew immediately that it was going to be far, far worse.

The pub in the southside suburbs of Dublin was dark and smoky, even at four o'clock in the afternoon. Oak panelling and wooden floors added to the gloom. Booths were conveniently dotted around the room, affording privacy for illicit lovers and others who did not want to be seen. There were no mirrors or harsh lights to startle or expose and the barmen had degrees in discretion.

The few hardened drinkers at the bar looked up as the door opened and then away. They did not know the new arrival and they did not care.

Roger Croft ordered and got a whiskey, hiding his distaste at the grubby glass. He turned and walked slowly by the booths. At the third booth he stopped. A look of surprise crossed his face.

"Hi."

The jowly, middle-aged man sitting there looked up from his Sunday paper, seeming almost as surprised.

"Oh, hello there. Just waiting for the wife."

Roger smiled. "Shopping, I suppose."

"She'll ruin me yet."

Both men laughed conspiratorially; nudge-nudge wink-wink, aren't women shocking altogether. Never mind that it was a Sunday, and that there were no shops open in this part of town.

"Don't suppose you'd like to join me?" The invitation was carefully indifferent.

Roger looked at his watch doubtfully. "I'm actually

on my way somewhere," he said loudly. "But I suppose I could kill a few minutes . . ."

He slipped into the booth. Both men looked around quickly to gauge the effects of their little pantomime. The other punters did not give them so much as a glance. They were safe.

"So, Roger. What can I do for you?"

Roger looked directly across the table. "It's more a question of what we can do for each other."

Ulick Pearse, Press Officer and chief spin doctor for the opposition party looked suitably puzzled. "I'm afraid I don't understand."

He damned well did understand. Why else had he agreed to meet Roger in this seedy dive on a Sunday afternoon with half an hour's notice?

"I've resigned from the party. I'm running as an Independent." Roger gave it to him straight.

Ulick Pearse gave no indication that he had known this almost as soon as the Government had. "I see. And may I ask why?"

"I'm afraid I can't be specific," Roger said glibly. "There are other parties involved and it's not up to me to reveal details of anyone's private life."

Ulick Pearse said nothing.

"Suffice it to say that I think my reasons will become clear very shortly," Roger added. He was willing to bet that by now, every last Dáil Eireann deputy knew that Peter Fisher was up to his neck in it.

Pearse smiled; a small, upward pull of his lips that revealed very white, very sharp teeth. He was enjoying himself. And why not? It wasn't every day that the Office of Taoiseach was about to become vacant.

"And these reasons . . . are they political?"

"Moral," Roger quickly corrected.

Pearse didn't bother to hide his utter disbelief.

"As you know, I've already spoken out strongly on another moral issue, involving the film. The Kilkenny electorate expect no less of me," Roger murmured.

Pearse looked at him out of lazy, cunning eyes. They had each other's measure all right.

"And you think you'll still win as an Independent?"

"I know I will. No offence, but Bill Mackey's missed the boat on this one."

"We have every confidence in our candidate." Pearse delivered the standard party line quickly and vociferously.

Roger shrugged. If he were in Bill Mackey's shoes right now, he would be bricking it. The problem was that the man had started the race complacently. He and Pearse had thought that the whole thing was a walk-over. It was a fatal mistake, as Roger was about to prove.

He knocked back his whiskey. He had said enough. "If you'll excuse me," he said, rising to go. "I have a TV interview later on."

He saw this hit home with Pearse. Roger was going public and if Pearse was smart, he'd hop on the gravy-train fast.

"Wait," Pearse said. Roger sat down again. Pearse chose his words carefully. "In the extremely unlikely event of our candidate failing to deliver, and in view of certain rumours that have reached my ears regarding the stability of the present Government . . ." He paused delicately. "Our party could well be looking at options for the formation of a new Government in the very near future."

They smiled pleasantly at each other now.

"Would you be interested in talking to us, Roger?"

"I'd be very interested, Ulick."

"Excellent. Why don't we wait until the by-election is over? To see what way the land might lie."

It was crunch time. "No."

"No?"

"I need something a little more concrete."

Pearse was alert. "When you say concrete, you mean . . . ?"

"Money." Roger came straight out with it. "You know how it is yourself, Ulick. I'm now an Independent. And Independents don't have party money behind them."

"Ah."

"Yes. And I have four more weeks of the campaign to fund yet."

"I can see how you might have a problem," Pearse murmured.

"I'll win on free publicity alone, of course, and most of the groundwork is already done," Roger pointed out quickly. "But a little help wouldn't go astray."

Pearse massaged his jaw slowly, a look of careful incredulity twisting his heavy features. "You actually expect our party to fund an opposing candidate against our own?"

Roger didn't bother to reply. Pearse was big enough to work out the percentages for himself. It was a simple matter of hedging his bets. And from what Roger had heard about Pearse and his poker games, he was a gambling man all right.

After an age, Pearse spoke again. "Obviously, this would be highly unorthodox. Unethical, in fact. And it would have to be kept strictly between you and me. But I suppose there are ways and means . . ."

"That's what I thought," Roger agreed.

A hundred miles away, Tess Fisher sat in the sunny kitchen of the house into which she had come as a bride while her husband spoke in halting tones of his affair, the imminent exposure of it by the media in the morning and, finally, the depth of his sorrow at what he had done to her.

"I never meant for any of this to happen, Tess."

She nodded agreeably. "I'm sure you didn't."

"Obviously, I'll take all blame."

"Obviously."

"And I'll do everything I can to protect you and Fiona, you know that?"

"Yes, thank you. And you'll break the news to Fiona. I won't do it."

"Of course I will."

Tess heard Carol Taylor turn on the TV in the living-room. She had made herself scarce early on in the proceedings. Biding her time, Tess thought cynically.

"You're taking this very well, Tess."

Peter was worried. Tess smiled inwardly. How much easier it would be for him if she hit the roof, or chipped one of his teeth or two.

She too was surprised by her lack of anger. The first numbing shock of the news was wearing off now but fury didn't come. She felt completely calm and in control. But that didn't mean that he was going to get away scot-free. He had a few home truths coming.

"That's just it, Peter, isn't it?" she said nicely now. "For sixteen years, I have sat and taken whatever you cared to dish out. Affair after affair. And now I'm supposed to take this on the chin too."

To his credit, he met her eyes squarely. Tess did not spare him. She nodded towards the living-room.

"Don't think I haven't realised why she's here. It's to persuade me to 'take it' in the best possible manner for all concerned."

Peter did not flinch. "Unfortunately, this goes beyond you, Jean and me. Let's not pretend otherwise."

"Let's not." She leaned back in her chair and crossed her arms. "And let's not pretend that your job isn't on the line here. In fact, public opinion on your continued suitability for office depends rather hugely on how I 'take it', doesn't it?"

She had him over a barrel and they both knew it. He watched her carefully now, but she saw no hint of fear in his eyes and she admired him for it despite herself. He was not going to beg her for anything today. He was not going to try to pressurise her. Still, that was Carol Taylor's job, wasn't it?

474

"Tess, I don't expect you to stand by me," he said bluntly. "If it were only for myself, I wouldn't even ask. But there are other things going on."

And he told her about Roger Croft's resignation from the party.

"The Government may well be about to fall, Tess." He paused. "I'm asking you if there's anything you can do to help me limit the damage on at least one front."

Tess hardly heard him. She was stunned over Roger Croft's defection, her keen political instincts rising to the forefront of her mind out of years of habit.

"What are you going to do?"

"I thought we might issue a joint statement tonight, the two of us – "

"About the by-election, Peter."

He was a little taken aback at the abrupt change of subject.

"There's nothing we *can* do. It's four weeks to the election. It's far too late to put forward another candidate. We're just going to have to hope and pray that we can get one of the Independents to come on board."

Tess was lost in thought.

"Tess? Do you think we could agree on some kind of approach for the press?"

She dragged her mind back to the matter at hand. "What exactly did you have in mind?" she asked. "That I drape myself over you and tell the public that you've been a bad boy, but that I forgive you?"

He looked horrified. "I would never ask you to do something like that."

"What then?"

"Tess . . . we have to tell the truth."

She felt that familiar coldness creep over her. "And what might that be?"

"I suppose that our marriage is not working and that we've decided to separate."

To his mind, this marriage was over. And he had taken the liberty of making up her mind for her too. The *arrogance* of him.

"And that you're leaving me for her. Don't forget that bit, Peter. Or were you going to mention it at all?" she asked harshly. He said nothing. She let him squirm for a moment. "No, of course you weren't. That wouldn't go down so well with Joe Public, would it? I'll bet John Graham and your Cabinet cronies nipped that little idea in the bud."

"To hell with John Graham and everybody else," Peter suddenly blazed. "Whatever we tell the press is up to us, Tess. This is our marriage, our lives. Nobody else's."

Fine words. He probably even believed them himself.

"So you've discussed none of this with them?" she asked incredulously.

"No! Well, I mean, of course they know about . . ."

"Your affair," Tess helpfully supplied.

"Yes. But the rest is a matter for you and me. It's nothing to do with them."

She watched him in awe. He really did believe this, she saw. Just like he really believed that he could exist entirely separate from the party machine that had made him what he was.

"So, really, what you want from me is my public blessing," she said slowly.

"Blessing? No."

"What, then?"

"Your understanding, I suppose."

He looked at her so openly, so guilelessly, that she had to rally hard to stop herself from belting him across the face.

"That's quite a lot to ask, Peter."

"I know," he said honestly. "And I don't deserve it. But it's the only way, you must see that."

The only way? He walked off into the sunset with his job and his mistress and she was left with nothing? And she must see that this was 'the only way'? She wanted to scream at him, shake him, both.

"Let me think about it," she said instead.

"Time isn't on our side – "

"Peter!" She took a steadying breath. "Leave me alone for a minute please."

Reluctantly, he got up and went in to Carol Taylor.

Tess sat motionless at the table, every nerve in her body tingling with rage, with a desire to hurt Peter as much as he had just hurt her.

Stop. Stop. Time enough for anger later. She must channel her energy, her emotions.

She had very little time and she must use it well.

She forced her mind onto another level – analytical, rational, perceptive. And with a brutal resolve, she pointed that perception firmly at herself.

She saw a woman who had defined herself largely in

terms of men. Peter, first. She had lived vicariously through him for years, grappling greedily for the meagre crumbs he tossed her from the table of power, fooling herself that she too was somebody, a force to be reckoned with.

In Sheila Burke's eyes perhaps. At a lunch table in Merrion Row with the other self-important wives. But what clout had any of them at the end of the day, when their husbands could take it away on a whim?

And then Jack Thornton. Hollywood legend. What a scream *that* had turned out to be. He had not wanted her for herself, only for the salve she might bring to his battered ego. And when she'd failed that test, he didn't want her either. Because who the hell was Tess Fisher anyway?

It was painful, the realisation that she was in fact a nobody once her alignment with certain people was taken away. It was not enough and never had been, though she had done a damned good job of convincing herself for years that she was content, if not exactly happy.

They expected her to roll over once again for the sake of king and country. But what was in it for her? Nothing. Except dignity, of course, and a chance to hang onto her pride. And when it was all over, dignity and pride were all she would have to keep her company as she fast faded into obscurity and Peter and the party went on to new heights.

She smiled now, amused despite herself. She could always write an exposé book a few years down the line, revealing not only the sordid details of Peter's private life, but that of half the Cabinet too. She would do the rounds of the talk-shows, winning brief notoriety as the scorned woman, before that too faded. Dignity and pride would have gone then, replaced by the pity of the public and the few friends she would have left. Nobodies, like herself.

No. She shook her head sharply. That was no future at all. But unless she took a hand in her own destiny this very afternoon, she didn't see that she had any future worth contemplating at all.

The television was loud when she went into the living-room. Carol Taylor was alone.

"Where's Peter?"

"Upstairs, telling Fiona," Carol replied, turning back to the television. Tess saw that it was the six o'clock news. Roger Croft was in the television studio.

"What's happened?" she asked, seeing Carol's face.

"He's blown the lid on it," Carol said tersely. "He's announced his resignation, citing moral differences between him and a certain party member. He's stopped just short of naming names."

Tess waited.

"I'm afraid he's forced our hand," Carol said quietly. "We'll have to issue a statement as soon as we can."

She turned to Tess, curiously formal. Was she on their side?

Tess looked back at her steadily. "I think we can agree on something."

Carol nodded slowly.

"With certain conditions," she added softly.

If they wanted her to roll over, she would do it on her terms.

Peter was back. "She's not in her room. Fiona."

"Maybe she's gone out," Tess said.

"You mean you don't know?"

Tess started guiltily. "Why should I know? *You* saw her last."

"What?"

Tess suddenly felt sick. "You dropped her home last night, didn't you?"

"No. I though she had gone with you."

They looked at each other, stricken.

Carol Taylor stepped forward. "I saw her leaving the party. She was with Roger Croft."

Chapter Thirty-two

A hand-written invoice for one hundred pounds sat on John Graham's crowded desk. It was from Ulick Pearse. He was looking for his blood money.

"You bastard," Graham said, but there was no humour in it this time.

This time Ulick had gone too far. Roger Croft had been too clever. John Graham had been blind-sided not once, but twice, and it was not a feeling he relished.

Two empty cardboard boxes sat on the floor beside the desk. Ulick had sent them over along with the invoice – his way of telling Graham to clear his desk.

Graham lit another cigarette and stared at the studio photo of Roger Croft which was pinned to the cork-board by the window. His gut tightened into a spasm.

Croft had been his candidate, his boy. Graham had nurtured him much as Betty did one of her tender plants. He had helped the lad along, tried to steer him in the right direction. Only for Graham, dammit, Roger Croft would still be selling women's underwear in the midlands.

And he had turned around and bit the hand that fed him. The little double-crossing shit.

Graham could not believe that he had been so taken in. It was a terrible error in judgement on his part. His legendary powers of perception had let him down badly. But Croft was good, smooth. He had given nothing away – until it was too late. Graham and the Government had been played for fools.

Graham reached down and unlocked the bottom drawer of his filing cabinet. He extracted the thin background file on Roger Croft, the confidential one. After Graham had ordered a second check, a single sheet of paper had been added to the file.

Graham looked at that sheet of paper now. It was a list of dates and times that Roger Croft had been in certain Dublin streets after dark doing certain things that it was not prudent for an election candidate to do.

It was only by sheer luck that Graham's source had discovered Croft's nocturnal activities. Croft was good all right. But Graham was better. And it was time for a little revenge.

He picked up the phone and dialled the number of the friend who had carried out the work, a Garda who occasionally did a little moonlighting for Graham.

"It's me," he murmured. "I've got another job for you."

When he put down the phone, Graham grimly started work on the statement that the Government was officially withdrawing from the film.

Peter had not phoned yet.

Jean couldn't stay still. She roamed from the kitchen into the living-room and back again. Her stomach told her she was starving but the thought of food made her ill. She felt hot and cold at the same time, and kept turning on and off the oil heater like someone demented.

She looked at the phone again. *Ring, damn you.*

It didn't, of course. Her paranoia grew. Maybe he wasn't going to phone at all, maybe he had changed his mind about her, about them. Perhaps he and Tess were right now embroiled in some kind of reconciliation scenario, with him promising never to see Jean again if only Tess would forgive him. Or perhaps Carol Taylor and his Cabinet colleagues had put so much pressure on him that he had caved in. Or perhaps –

Stop, she told herself fiercely. He wouldn't do that. He loved her, hadn't he said so only a short few hours earlier? He had said, had *promised*, that they would be together no matter what. And even if the worst came to the worst, even if he had changed his mind about them, he would still have the decency to phone. Wouldn't he?

She was doubting him, and hating herself for it. And she was angry with him too, she suddenly realised; irrationally and unjustly raging that he had chosen a public life for himself and been successful at it. Had he been an accountant or a shopkeeper, none of this would be happening, because who in this country would give a hoot about his love-life then? She was angry too that just when she needed him most, he was not there with her, but with his wife instead. And that because of him, her reputation, her good name, her very life, were about to be splashed across the national press in the morning.

But at the end of the day the decision to get involved with Peter Fisher had been her own. He had hardly twisted her arm, had he? Bullied her into bed? No, she had jumped right in there all by herself, fooling herself into believing that she knew exactly what she was getting involved in.

She had had no idea, she now realised with a sick start. No idea at all what she was letting herself in for.

She paced faster now as her imagination went into overdrive, filling her overloaded brain with variations on tomorrow's newspaper headlines, none of them flattering. Would the papers actually name her? Would they describe her as Peter Fisher's lover or make her out to be some cheap floozie? Did they know her identity at all?

Of course they did. And even if they didn't, they would make it their business to find out. She would be named and shamed all right.

The quietness of the cottage seemed to close in around her, choking her. Peter had been right when he said that she should not be alone tonight. But who could she call?

Her mother? Hardly. She would be disgusted. Her father, perhaps mercifully, was dead. But Bernice Gannon was very much alive, and all her other friends. Her clients too. All of them would know what she had done, would make some kind of judgement on her.

No, there was no one she could call, no friend she could prevail upon without offering some explanation. She couldn't bear the questions, the justifications she would be forced to mouth.

Ian popped into her mind. None of this would shock him – he was too jaded and cynical. Had he not turned out to be such a ratbag at the end of the day, she might have called him.

The front doorbell rang. Jean was wary. She was expecting nobody. Surely the press hadn't found her yet?

She opened the door, and froze.

Jean Ormsby and Tess Fisher had never formally met, but there was no need for introductions. The world seemed to stand still for an endless moment as the two women silently looked at each other.

Finally, Tess asked quietly, "May I come in?"

Wordlessly, Jean stood aside to let her pass. Half of her was totally shocked; the other half had known all along that Tess Fisher would come here. How could she not?

They stood in the living-room facing each other, the coffee table like some kind of protective barrier between them. They sized each other up. Tess Fisher had come dressed for battle, Jean quickly saw. She wore a simple trouser-suit that reeked of taste and money, in a pale blue colour that reflected the coolness in her eyes. Her hair was freshly styled, her make-up, perfection. She wore no jewellery save her wedding band and engagement ring, both ostentatiously on view as she casually held a Prada clutch-bag. From tip to toe, she looked every inch a Minister's Wife.

Jean, on the other hand, was in bare feet, loose sweat pants, and a T-shirt. It was her regular Sunday gear, the one day of the week that she was able to discard her business suits and relax. She wished for one of those business suits now; it was hard not to feel at a distinct disadvantage when confronted by this immaculate woman.

At least she had one thing going for her: she was on her home turf. It was time to establish that.

"Please, won't you have a seat," she said.

"No, thank you," Tess Fisher said. "This won't take long."

Jean braced herself for the onslaught. She waited for the harsh words and the accusations, knowing that she had no come-back, no excuse.

Except that she loved Peter. And she doubted that Tess Fisher wanted to hear that this evening.

But the onslaught was not forthcoming. Tess Fisher just stood calmly there, fingering that Prada bag.

The spitting-cat routine was not her style, Jean suddenly realised. Tess had not come here tonight to indulge in a bout of name-calling and vilification. There was something else going on. She waited.

"I believe we have something in common," Tess said eventually.

Jean was taken aback by the wry smile on Tess's face.

"Namely, my husband."

"Yes," Jean said, looking Tess in the eye. She would

not hide behind pathetic denials and false protestations. Neither would she offer this woman any phoney apologies.

Tess seemed to appreciate this. "We also have a little media problem in common."

Again, she seemed almost laconic, as if amused by the irony of it all.

"Yes," Jean said again.

Tess Fisher wasn't long in coming to the point. "Look, I don't care that you've been sleeping with my husband."

Jean's face flamed at her bluntness. Tess smiled a little.

"He's done it before, I assure you." Her voice was almost sympathetic now. "And he'll probably do it again, no matter how special he tells you you are."

The words twisted like a knife in Jean. They had been intended to.

"We love each other," she blurted.

Tess shrugged, as though it were a matter of complete indifference to her. Jean felt a stab of anger that Tess thought she was only another one on the list.

"I didn't get involved with him for thrills, you know. In fact, I didn't want to get involved at all. But I love him." Her voice was loud and her heart was beating fast. "I love him," she repeated quietly.

Tess Fisher cocked her head to one side, watching Jean closely, that half-smile on her face again. "You know, I really think you do."

Jean bristled. She was being patronised.

"Then you care about what happens to him in all this," Tess went on briskly.

Jean was a little confused. "Of course."

"You have his interests at heart," Tess stressed.

"Yes."

"Good." Tess smiled pleasantly. "So do I. Which is why you and I have to talk."

Jean waited warily. "Go on."

"We need to protect Peter, of course."

"From the press?"

"No, no. From himself."

Jean digested this, watching the other woman warily.

"Peter, you see, is very idealistic underneath it all," Tess went on conversationally. "Naïve, even. He thinks that people will forgive anything once he tells the truth. Sometimes I wonder whether he's learned anything at all from fifteen years in politics." She gave a little laugh, as though Peter were a loveable but wayward child.

"Take this little problem that we find ourselves with." Her nails tapped the Prada bag. "Peter actually believes that people will see his side of it once he puts it to them fair and square. He expects them to give him their blessing once he explains to them that he couldn't help himself, that he fell in love and that he's now leaving his wife and daughter for his lover."

Her blue eyes bored into Jean. Jean was rooted to the spot.

"He honestly assumes that the public will understand that he cannot live a lie – the same public who elected him over a decade ago on the strength of his morals and his sense of fairness. And he thinks that they will *forgive* him. Imagine!" Her laugh this time was harshly incredulous. "Now, Jean, you and I are a little more worldly, I think."

"What do you mean?"

"We both know that this country is not as liberal as Peter likes to think. People will forgive a mistake, perhaps, so long as that mistake is put right. But they will not countenance his foolish notions of having his cake and eating it." She paused deliberately. "If he is allowed to take that course of action, they will demand his resignation and run him out of town."

Jean felt the last of her world crumbling down around her ears. Tess Fisher watched as her words hit home. She went on relentlessly.

"Peter says he wants out of the political game – I'm sure he's told you that?"

She saw from Jean's face that he had. She nodded.

"He's been saying that for years now. But he wouldn't last five minutes. His whole life is politics, he lives, breathes and eats it. Without it he would die. Do you really want to see that happen? His career ruined and his life shattered?"

Jean could not speak. Anyhow, what was there to say?

"So now you see why we must protect him from himself," Tess said with a finality.

Jean did see all right. She saw with perfect clarity.

"I'm on my way to a press conference with him now," Tess informed her quietly. "I need to know your position."

"You mean, can I assure you that it's over between me and him?" Jean asked, her voice bitter and hard.

Tess Fisher looked equally hard as she played her trump card. "Do you seriously expect me to publicly stand by him if you don't?"

Jean had nothing to better this. If she refused to give Peter up tonight, then Tess would see to it that the public would demand his resignation.

"That's blackmail."

"No," Tess corrected her. "It's a simple matter of choice. You can have Peter, but at the expense of his career. In this life, you can't have it all. And neither can he, even though he's selfish enough to think he can."

Jean would not fold this easily. "And have you offered Peter this choice?"

Tess waved a hand dismissively. "Don't be ridiculous. You know exactly what he would say – that he'll resign, get a divorce, and do the right thing."

"Well then, let him!"

Tess shrugged. "Fine. And in a year's time, probably less, he'll start to miss it all. Every time he picks up an newspaper or meets an old colleague, he'll wonder if he's made the right decision. And unfair as it is, he'll look at you and he'll blame you."

She was right. Jean hated her for it, but she was right.

"I think you've made your point," Jean said, her voice dull and beaten.

"I'm sorry about this – " Tess began.

Jean laughed. "Oh, please."

Tess's face lost some of its hardness. "I'm not enjoying this, you know. Any of it. Do you think it gives me any pleasure to know that Peter would prefer to be with someone else?"

She seemed human now. Almost frail. Jean suddenly saw what it had cost her to come here today, to fight for a husband that didn't love her any more.

"Let him go then." The appeal was direct and simple. "Please. I know I'm in no position to make any demands, but why can't you let us be happy?"

Tess hesitated. She seemed torn. But then she gathered herself again.

"I wish it were that simple."

"But it can be!"

"I'm afraid not. There are other factors."

"What?"

Tess shrugged. "Roger Croft will not be running for the party in the by-election. I'm running for the party instead."

Jean was floored. Tess looked almost apologetic. "So now you see why it has to be this way."

It slowly fell into place for Jean. "The scandal . . . you're going to use it to win, aren't you? Publicly forgiving your husband, publicly forgiving *me* probably. You're going to play happy families."

Tess gave a little self-deprecating laugh. "It's ironic really, isn't it?"

"I think it's rather disgusting, actually," Jean said coldly.

Tess wasn't insulted. "Not really. You see, I've stood

by Peter for sixteen years now. You have no idea what I've put up with, no idea what it's been like living with someone who is public property. Whenever Peter needed me, I was there. And now *I* need *him*." There was a simple dignity about her. "And, frankly, he owes me."

So did Jean, apparently. Her hopes and dreams were about to be sacrificed on the altar of Tess Fisher's ambition.

"I'd like you to leave now, please," Jean said.

"Of course," Tess said.

The phone rang. Both women looked at it, then at each other. Jean picked it up with a terse "Hello". She listened, said "Hold on," and then she quickly covered the mouthpiece with her hand.

"Peter, I suppose," Tess said, a strange look on her face.

"Yes." There was no point in lying.

"I expect he was due to phone earlier," Tess said candidly. Jean's face betrayed her. "I'm afraid he was held up." Tess spoke as though she were a secretary apologising for Peter's tardiness. "We've had a problem with Fiona."

"A problem?"

"She's been missing. But it's all right now."

Jean saw the tiny lines of worry around Tess's eyes and again wondered at the woman's strength in coming here tonight.

"Jean . . ." Tess hesitated. "I wish it didn't have to be this way. For either of us."

492

Then she turned abruptly. "I'll see myself out."

Jean waited until she heard the front door close. Then she took her hand slowly from the receiver and, in halting tones, told Peter that it was over.

Roger was so high after the meeting with Ulick Pearse that he did not want to go straight home to Kilkenny. He'd spent the afternoon in a department store in town, kitting himself out in a couple of new suits for the many television appearances he would be making in the next couple of days. Then an expensive meal at one of the better restaurants, a treat to himself.

It was almost ten o'clock at night when he found himself driving aimlessly through the dark streets of Dublin, stereo blaring. His body was jumpy with adrenaline and his mind racing.

It could not have worked out better, he decided, stopped briefly at a red light and gunning the engine impatiently. He congratulated himself on how he had handled the entire thing. The election was more or less in the bag, and now he had Ulick Pearse eating out of his hand, forced to give Roger anything he cared to ask for in return for supporting a new Government. And Roger intended to ask for plenty. Oh yes. The power of it was almost too much to take in.

Roger laughed aloud. The man in the car in the next lane looked over at him. Roger shot him a filthy look and turned away.

The party had been stupid in turning its back on him. And Peter Fisher even more stupid. If he had treated

Roger with a little respect, none of this might have happened.

Oh, how he was looking forward to publicly condemning Fisher in the morning, the sneaky bastard. He would denounce him from a height, saying that this was yet another example of the immorality and deceit that had characterised successive Governments of late. He would get a stab in at Carol Taylor too. And why stop there? By the time he was through, he would have tarred and feathered the entire cabinet.

Still, he must remember not to sound too self-righteous. People didn't like Holy Joes. The tone should be more disappointed than vengeful. Yes. He must remember to reiterate that his decision to resign from the party had not been taken lightly, but that he felt the people of Kilkenny deserved better, blah-de-blah. Gullible fools, they would swallow the lot and come out for him in droves on polling day.

The red light gave away to green. Roger shot away, rudely cutting up the man who had been staring at him from the car in the next lane. Tyres screeched as the man was forced to brake. Roger laughed again.

He thought of Fiona Fisher now and his smile dimmed a little. Silly and all as she was, perhaps the shock of his rejection coupled with the news of Daddy's affair had been a little harsh.

Still. It was done now. And it was satisfying to think of Peter Fisher trying to wriggle out of *that* one.

He put Fiona from his mind with chilling ease. Now the car was heading towards the quays and the dilapidated buildings that hunched over narrow, mean streets. The orange neon of the few street lamps revealed small groups of two and three, women with skirts too short and eyes that had seen too much. Those eyes followed Roger's car listlessly now as it slid past. They knew it well.

Roger drove on, his headlights on dim. The air stank of the Liffey river and of danger, and he felt excitement rise in him like sap. He knew that he should not be here. As usual, he promised himself that he would head back for town at the next junction, that he was only here to look.

A middle-aged woman took a step towards the car now and Roger speeded up. She did not interest him. He swung into a narrower street, and the scenery immediately improved.

Two teenage boys stood in a doorway, cigarettes bobbing redly in the dark. The blond was cherubic, black greasy roots showing at the scalp. He looked at Roger insolently as the car inched by, cynicism twisting his pasty features into a weary mask.

But oh, the other one was a beauty. He reminded Roger of someone, he couldn't think who. Dark and slim, with narrow hips encased in red jeans. His face all lean lines and soft young skin. Huge brown eyes peered out furtively from under a floppy fringe. He was trying to be tough, but he was frightened all right. Roger could smell it from here. Unlike his friend, the dark boy had not been in the business for long.

He looked directly at Roger as the car went past, and

Roger felt desire flood through him. God, but he was exquisite. And just like Carl Tallon, he abruptly realised. Both had those same dark, lean looks.

Roger watched the boy in the rear-view mirror all the way to the next junction. His foot hovered indecisively over the brake pad. Get out of here now, he told himself. This is insane.

But as always, the risk proved too tempting, the boy too much. Palms sweaty and mouth dry, Roger cut his lights and swung back.

The blond peeled himself away from the doorway. Roger shook his head quickly and fixed the dark boy with a stare. Reluctantly, the boy came around the side of the car and hopped into the passenger seat, tossing his cigarette onto the ground.

"Where can we go?" Roger asked, feasting his eyes on him.

"The park," the boy mumbled, looking straight ahead.

No more words were exchanged until they were through the main gates of the Phoenix Park.

"Down there," the boy said, pointing to an unlit road to the left. A half-mile down the road, Roger pulled in and killed the engine.

"Let your seat back," he said, an old hand at encounters in cars. His breath was coming hard, his desire a solid rock in his trousers.

"Not so fast," the boy said. "Money first."

Roger reached smoothly into his jacket for his wallet. He held out several bills. "Will that cover it?"

The boy looked at the money and slowly counted it.

Roger put a hand on his knee and leaned towards him.

Both of them jumped at a sharp rap on the window. Roger swung around to find a face peering in. It was the man he had cut up at the traffic lights. Oh Christ. To have followed Roger all this way, the guy must be steaming and ready for a little road-rage.

Roger slowly rolled down the window. "Look," he began in a conciliatory tone, "Sorry if I was in a bit of a rush back there."

The man looked from Roger, then to the boy, then to the money in the boy's hand.

"Oh fuck," the boy said heavily.

Roger was confused. Why was the boy looking so resigned?

When he looked back at the man, he found a badge thrust in the window. Realisation hit hard and fast.

"You're under arrest," the man said politely.

"Please," Roger began, his voice sounding very young and frightened. "Please, don't do this to me – "

"Get out of the car, sir, and put your hands on the roof."

"No, you don't understand – you don't know who I am –"

"Get out of the car. Now."

"Please!" Roger was hysterical now, begging. "This will finish me!"

John Graham's moonlighting cop looked grimly at Roger Croft, Independent candidate for Kilkenny. "Oh, you're finished all right."

Chapter Thirty-three

The Aer Lingus flight was packed. Cathy was sure that they were looking at her as she tried to find her seat. They knew, of course, all of them; a young girl alone, pale and frightened, with nothing but a small piece of hand luggage. She felt their judgement like pin-pricks on the back of her neck. Why couldn't she take the ferry like they used to do in the old days, they were saying to themselves? Why did she have to mix with decent folk, people like themselves who were going to London this Friday morning to conduct legitimate business?

She could not eat the breakfast the snooty stewardess placed in front of her with a disapproving look. Instead she buried herself in the in-flight magazine, pricing perfumes and cigarettes that she had no intention of buying. Anything to take her mind off what she was going to do.

Off the flight and on the tube into London. The address and telephone number carefully written on a piece of paper. The money in cash in her bag. Hours and hours to wait yet.

She found a coffee shop. The waitress heard her Irish accent and she guessed too, Cathy was sure. Silly girl, she *was thinking, probably a one-night stand. Cathy slunk to a corner seat, the hot coffee cup grasped in freezing hands.*

Time crawled by, reality biting harder with each passing second. She was going to get rid of Carl's baby. She was nineteen and she was going to have an abortion.

Carl. He'd come with her to the airport this morning. As she'd been about to go through the departure gates, she'd stopped. Suddenly she wanted him to know. She wanted him to stop her.

He got there first.

"Aren't you going to wish me luck?"

He seemed hurt. He thought she had not remembered his big meeting that would secure him a hefty commission and send his career orbiting into the big time. As if he hadn't talked about nothing else for a whole week now. It was his chance of a lifetime.

"Of course. I hope it goes well for you." Her voice had been colourless. He had not noticed, he was on a high.

"And good luck with the agents in England."

She'd told him she was going to London to try and get an English agent.

"Nothing's going to stop us now, is it?" he'd said, smiling.

The moment was gone. Cathy smiled automatically and went.

Her stomach was seized with cramps now. Nerves. It was no big deal, she tried to tell herself. This was the 90s for God's sake, people had choices and options. It wasn't the great big sin it used to be. Women and girls did it every day of the week – hundreds of them, thousands. And her reasons were as good as any, surely. What life could she and Carl give a baby? A

499

baby that neither of them wanted, them with their whole lives
and careers ahead of them? Them that had known each other
only eight short weeks?

No, it was better this way, she assured herself. Carl
wouldn't feel that she had trapped him. He could never turn
around and accuse her of holding him back. Hadn't he made it
clear time and again that his work was the most important
thing in his life?

The cramps were worse now. The waitress was back.
Concerned, offering more coffee. Cathy brushed her off. She
felt dizzy, sick. It would all be over soon and she would be
back in Dublin on Sunday, back to normality. It would all be
over soon. She repeated it like a mantra.

She kept repeating it as she felt herself sliding off the stool
to the floor, as she was being lifted into the ambulance, and at
the hospital where they told her in clinical voices that she had
miscarried.

In the narrow hospital bed, surrounded by strangers, the
irony of the situation overwhelmed her. She started to laugh.
The laughter quickly turned to tears, great sobs that left her
gasping for breath.

Finally a nurse came. She was kind. She did not listen to
Cathy's ramblings that she had been going to get rid of it
anyway. Instead, she brought a phone to the bed and said that
Cathy shouldn't be alone right now.

Cathy rang Carl. It was an effort to keep the choking from
her voice. She asked him to come. He kept asking why. She
couldn't, wouldn't say. He talked about his meeting. She
heard the impatience in his voice.

"Please, Carl."

"Tomorrow evening, I can come then."

He would get his meeting over with first.

Cathy felt a coldness creep over her. In bright, sunny tones, she told him that she was fine after all. She would see him Sunday evening as planned.

She did not cry any more when she put down the phone. She knew that she would never see him again. It was over.

Cathy jumped restlessly to her feet. She was driving herself mad, going over and over it all again. But in the thirty-six hours since the party on Saturday night, she'd had little else to think about. In some ways she was doing it to punish herself. And when it came to self-inflicted punishment, Cathy was an old hand. Nothing Carl could say or do would ever make her feel worse. She'd had plenty of time over the years for guilt-trips and she gone on many.

It was as much guilt as anger at Carl that had made her stay in London. She could not bear to come back to him and pretend that nothing had happened, only to be reminded of it every time she looked into his face. She didn't want to spend every second of the day having "what if" arguments with herself. All she wanted to do was forget. London had seemed to offer a fresh start, where she could put it behind her and start again. She had run away.

On Saturday night, she had run as far as she was going to get. Carl knew now. The look on his face, the way he had spoken to her . . .

She wondered how she could have imagined for one

second that it might have been different. She had been
lulled into a false complacency by his declaration of love.
Some idealistic notion that everything was fine again had
led her to open her trap when she should have kept it shut.

She had lost him for good now. She was as certain of
that as she had ever been of anything.

Cathy felt raw and fragile today, as grey as the Monday
morning she could see through her trailer window.
Summer had decided to bugger off for the day; a cold grey
drizzle had taken its place. She would have to leave the
sanctuary of the trailer at any minute and go to work. She
had never felt less like facing the world. For the first time,
she wished that the film was over.

The set was strangely silent when she finally emerged.
Bodies did not scurry back and forth across the grass like
busy ants. The catering tent was practically deserted. The
only signs of life at all were over by Jack Thornton's trailer,
where a group had gathered, grim-faced.

"Marie?" Cathy found the costume mistress in the
catering tent. "What's going on? Why hasn't work started?"

"You haven't heard then." Marie looked at her
sympathetically.

Cathy felt a fresh burst of paranoia. "Heard what?"

"The film has been pulled, Cathy."

"Pulled?"

"Canned. By Cinerama."

This was some bad joke, surely. "What are you on
about?"

"Perhaps you should talk to your agent." There was
a bitterness in Marie's voice.

"Jean? Why?"

"She's the bloody reason, isn't she?"

"Marie! Will you please tell me what's going on!"

Marie looked at her suspiciously. "You mean you didn't see the TV last night? Or the papers this morning?"

"No. I, um, was feeling a little ill," Cathy mumbled.

Marie produced a newspaper and slapped it on the table in front of Cathy. Cathy's eyes popped.

There was Jean Ormsby on the front page, hand in hand with Peter Fisher, the pair of them looking like love's young dream. The photo seemed to have been taken in a hotel or somewhere. The caption read *Minister Parties on after Film Bash on Saturday Night.*

Underneath was a photo of Tess and Peter Fisher at a press conference last night.

"Jean . . . and Peter Fisher?" She couldn't believe it.

"It would appear so," Marie said tightly.

Cathy skimmed the text. It was awful – full of innuendo and outrage. But at the same time, the facts were clear. Peter Fisher was cheating on his wife with Jean Ormsby.

"Doesn't it seem a bit extreme?" Cathy ventured, not wanting to believe it was true. "For Cinerama to pull the film because of an affair?"

Marie snorted, reached over and turned the page. "That's not all."

On page two was a photo of the party on Saturday night, the crowd laughing and clearly having a good time. The accompanying caption read *High – Evidence of Drugs on set of Thornton's Film.*

Cathy was now flabbergasted. "Drugs? What are they talking about?"

The short article underneath snidely alleged that cocaine had been floating around at the party, without actually offering any proof. But it was enough.

"But the Government . . ." Cathy spluttered. "They'll find another backer, won't they?"

"The Government? Ha!" Marie threw her hands up in disgust. "They're running for cover, shower of spineless bastards that they are. Washed their hands of it all. They don't care about the film, Cathy, they never did. They just used it for their own ends – and used us too. The whole thing was nothing more than a big stunt."

The reality of it started to sink in with Cathy. "It's over, isn't it?"

"Yes. I'm afraid it is," Marie said quietly. "Declan Mahoney is trying to persuade Cinerama to hang in there, but . . ." She shrugged. "If we'd been farther into the shoot, things might be different. They can pull out now without losing much money."

"Is it all about money at the end of the day?" Cathy asked bitterly.

"Yes," Marie said baldly.

They sat there in silence, united in woe.

"At least we've seen the last of *him*," Marie added, jabbing a finger at the newspaper again.

Cathy was in for another surprise as she read that Roger Croft had been arrested for soliciting the night before, just hours after he'd resigned from the party.

"*Ohmigod*," was all she could say.

"It's like the *Titanic* around here," Marie spat. "They're all sinking – the film, the Government, Peter Fisher."

And me, Cathy silently added. She had lost not only Carl, but her career too. And both for the second time around. Why, oh why, had she ever left bloody London?

"Are you okay?" Marie was looking at her, concerned.

"No," Cathy said honestly.

"There'll be other films, Cathy."

Cathy doubted it. And whatever about the film, there would never be another Carl.

Still, she forced an I-Will-Survive smile to her lips. She was good at that.

"Sure."

Marie left. Cathy had no idea how much time passed as she sat there, lost in morbid thought. Nor did she see the old, decrepit Uno creep into the field and drive slowly towards her. A woman in dark glasses and a headscarf alighted.

Cathy looked up eventually as a shadow fell across the table.

"I'm sure I'm the last person you want to see," Jean said. "But I didn't know where else to go."

"I need somewhere to stay for a day or two."

"You can hardly stay *here*," Cathy said rather tartly. She'd managed to get Jean into her trailer without any of the cast or crew noticing. "They'd lynch you. And me too, if they found out I was hiding you."

Jean merely nodded, looking at her hands. Cathy hung back by the door, fighting down sympathy. After all, her agent had just scuppered her film career. And had then shown up looking for refuge. It was a bit of a cheek, really.

Jean seemed to feel this too. "I heard about Cinerama backing out. I'm sorry, Cathy."

"Bit late for that," Cathy couldn't resist saying. "They wouldn't have if the Government hadn't left them high and dry."

"Obviously, I never meant . . ." Jean shrugged, trailing off. "And I wouldn't have shown up here but I thought that maybe you might help me out."

Cathy was deliberately silent.

"The press, they're hounding me," Jean went on in that same, dead voice. "I can't stay at home. And my friends . . ."

"Don't want to know?" Cathy asked archly.

Jean took off her dark glasses. Cathy was shocked by her face. Dark circles rimmed her eyes and her skin looked tight and drawn. Gone was the successful, intimidating businesswoman that Cathy had been so in awe of. This woman looked like a shell.

"I came here because I thought maybe you wouldn't judge me, Cathy."

Cathy was stricken. It was as if she had just kicked a dog when it had already been run over by a juggernaut. What right had she to stand here in condemnation? She, of all people?

"I'm sorry," she said impulsively. "Of course I'll help." She paused, suddenly unsure. "I take it that you and Peter – "

"Over," Jean said in a staccato voice that invited no further comment. She put the glasses on again, hiding her emotions.

"What do you want me to do?" Cathy asked.

"I don't know. I just need a few days to sort things out. And then I'll be out of your hair, I promise."

Cathy shrugged, at a loss. "I don't really have any friends in Dublin I could ask to put you up."

Jean nodded, defeated. Then it hit Cathy.

"My flat. In North Circular Road. I've paid the rent until the end of the month. You could stay there."

"But what about you?"

"What about me?"

"The film is over – you'll be going back there."

"No," Cathy said slowly, the decision making itself as she spoke. "I don't need the flat any more."

"Where are you going?"

"I'll be all right," Cathy assured her, finding the keys and scribbling out the address of the flat. "It's a bit of a dive, mind."

"I don't care. Just so long as nobody can find me."

That was the second time she'd said that.

"The press will soon get tired and start chasing someone else," Cathy said in an attempt to reassure her.

"The press? Oh yes. I suppose so."

Jean rummaged in her handbag. "About the film, Cathy. Here's Bernice Gannon's phone number. I used to work for her. She's offered to represent you and Carl in all this. She'll get some money out of Cinerama for you at any rate. Is he around, by the way? Carl?"

"Carl? I don't know," Cathy was amazed at how normal it came out.

"I need to speak to him."

"I haven't seen him," Cathy went on in that falsely cheerful voice.

"Right. Well, will you tell him that I'll be in contact? About that new project."

Cathy tried not to show her surprise. A new project? Once again, it seemed that Carl's career was orbiting while hers sank without trace. Did nothing in this life ever change?

"I don't think I'll be seeing him." Her voice was stilted. Jean didn't push the matter.

"I'll be in touch, Cathy. And thanks again."

She was gone.

It was amazing really, how fast and final it all was. A lot of the cast and crew didn't even hang around to see what the outcome would be of Jack Thornton and Declan Mahoney's eleventh-hour attempts to stall Cinerama.

Jason Blake had been one of the first to go. Cathy had met him and his gorgeous girlfriend as they had climbed into his limo.

"But Cinerama might change their minds!" she protested.

Jason Blake smiled cynically. "I know Hollywood, Cathy. They won't."

"Please don't go. Declan Mahoney says he'll try to get funding from other studios," she pleaded.

"And I hope he does. But by then I'll be on my next movie."

"You can't give up, not now!" If the star of the whole show were to leave, that really would sound the death knell.

She must have looked pretty desperate because Jason hesitated, then took her in his arms in a brief, hard hug.

"I'm sorry, Cathy. But I've been in this business too long not to recognise when something is dead in the water."

Cathy felt tears well up in her eyes.

"It was lovely working with you," he said. "Maybe we'll do it again sometime, eh?"

She managed a small smile in response to his wink and watched as the limo rolled out of the field, taking her dreams with it.

Several of the more important cast members quickly followed suit, as did the Director of Photography and half the teckies. There was plenty of other work out there and they weren't going to hang around.

"So much for loyalty," Cathy said bitterly to Marie. Marie too was packing up to leave.

"I'm sorry it turned out like this for you," Marie said. "But the rest of us have seen it all before. We still have mortgages to pay."

By evening, the once-bustling set resembled a ghost-town. Half the trailers were gone, as were the catering trucks and the lighting vans. The cameras had been packed up and the microphones taken down. Small, flattened patches in the grass were the only indications that they had ever been there.

There was nobody around. The few cast and crew members who remained had now drifted to the local pub to drown their sorrows. Cathy did not go. She couldn't bear another post-mortem of the scandalous affair between Jean Ormsby and the Minister for Arts. She just wanted to be on her own.

It was dusk when she finally left her trailer and wandered through the field of the film set. She had never heard it so quiet. Even the sheep in the field next door were subdued, sensing that things were badly amiss.

A stray crisp packet blew across the grass in the breeze, and Cathy shivered. The field had a dead feel about it, as though nothing had ever happened here at all.

Like a magnet, the dark farmhouse at the top of the field drew her. Nobody had thought to lock the place up, and she let herself in quietly.

She stood in the middle of the kitchen of what had been Alison's fictional home. A dim work-light had been left on, and it threw shadows across the room. Cathy looked around slowly. Her heart felt pinched. The walls still seemed to reverberate with the drama, the emotion, that she and Jason Blake had invested in the characters of Alison and Richard.

All gone now, she thought. Alison and Richard were dead and buried, finally, after five long years.

So were she and Carl. She knew that he had gone

back to Dublin this morning. Marie had told her. He had not made any attempt to contact her. She wasn't surprised. What was there left to say, except the inevitable recriminations from him and the explanations from her that she knew would sound indefensible? Too much had happened for there to be any hope for them. She should have known this. Saturday night had been a terrible mistake. She should have let old ghosts lie.

But she still loved him. Five years hadn't changed that, no matter how much she had fooled herself. It would just be harder to get over it this time, that was all.

She paused by the door of the farmhouse as she was leaving and looked around for the last time at this place that had become so familiar to her in the last few weeks and marvelled. So much had happened, and yet here she was back at square one. All she had left was a washed-up film career and a heart that had been smashed all over again.

Still, she had been there before and survived. She would just have to do it again.

Chapter Thirty-four

For four long days it had been touch and go. And it wasn't over yet.

They gathered on Thursday night in what had become known as the War Room, John Graham's Press Office on the third floor. None of them had had more than a couple of hours' sleep since Sunday. Bloodshot eyes burned in the backs of their heads as they silently filed in, hands shaking from too many cups of the vending machine's strong, foul coffee.

John Graham had set up a widescreen TV in the corner of the room. Chairs were grouped around it in a semicircle. Peter Fisher had the chilling feeling that he was about to witness an execution.

"What's the round-up after today?" Carol Taylor asked. Her skin was pale and pasty beneath her make-up and she assiduously avoided looking at the TV.

John Graham shrugged. His jacket and tie had been discarded and his fingers were yellow with nicotine. "I'd say it's about forty-forty even," he said in a voice that was hoarse from four days' talking. "With twenty percent undecided."

They talked about it in terms of "Us" and "Them" and the "Undecideds". "Us" was Peter, Tess, the Government, a certain group of liberal media commentators and that section of the Irish public who were prepared to forgive. "Them" was opposition leader Frank Tavey and his party, plus the hostile media and that section of the Irish public who were baying for Peter's blood. The "Undecideds" were still sitting on the fence.

"Better than it was yesterday," Carol said, as though she were discussing the odds on a particular race-horse.

Graham nodded at the TV. "Tonight will decide it one way or the other. It's up to her now."

The war had been fought on the battlefield of the media. It had started on Sunday night, when Peter and Tess Fisher had sat in his rooms in Leinster House and issued a statement in which Peter admitted his affair. Tess had not spoken at all. Her presence by her husband's side was enough. Carol Taylor then issued her own statement in which she revealed that she would not be seeking Peter's resignation.

Then they held their breaths for the reaction on Monday morning.

It was both a blessing and a curse that Roger Croft managed to push them off the front pages of at least two newspapers with his arrest in the Phoenix Park. On the one hand, some of the heat was taken off Peter. On the other, Croft had up to the previous day been the

Government's candidate in the by-election. The second edition of most newspapers did not mince their words.

Government in Double Crisis.

Taylor's Government Embroiled in Two Sex Scandals.

Government Officially Pulls Out from Film..

Frank Tavey immediately called for Peter's resignation. When Cinerama found out that the Government had more or less dumped them, and announced that they too were pulling out, Frank Tavey was back on the airwaves demanding Carol Taylor's resignation too.

Catholic Ireland was in a frenzy. The nation's reporters hadn't had so much news in years. Several papers produced third city editions on that Monday. Radio stations and television networks were choked with wall-to-wall news programmes, with every obscure right-wing commentator in Ireland crawling out of the woodwork to have a go.

They would refer to that day as Black Monday. It seemed that Peter's resignation was inevitable. He offered again. Carol Taylor refused again. They would battle it out for another day and see.

Many of the more moderate voices made themselves heard on Tuesday. They asked some hard questions of the media and its contribution to the scandals that had plagued the film. They drew a sharp distinction between the public and private actions of those in civic life. And they compared the exemplary track record of Carol Taylor's Government to that of various previous Governments which had been racked by financial, planning and cash-for-questions scandals.

Tuesday was also the day that Tess Fisher accompanied her husband on several carefully-planned public outings. She still had not issued any statement, or spoken directly to the media, on John Graham's advice. She refused, however, to take his advice to hold her husband's hand and smile.

"Don't be ridiculous. I will not insult the public by simpering and pretending that everything is okay when it patently is not."

She cut a sober and dignified figure as she stood a measured few feet from Peter. It was exactly the right thing to do.

By Wednesday, support for Peter had taken a small but significant up-swing.

"We just need to hang on for another day," John Graham decided.

Tess Fisher again disagreed. "It's not a question of 'hanging on'. The by-election is in three and a half weeks' time."

"I'm aware of that," John Graham said shortly. Privately, he thought it an act of complete folly on Carol Taylor's part to let Tess Fisher run at all. The woman had absolutely no political or media experience. She didn't even have a job, for God's sake! Just a prominent husband who was even more prominent for all the wrong reasons these days. The only votes she would get on polling day would be sympathy votes, and an election had never been won on the strength of those. Bill Mackey would wipe the floor with her.

"I cannot announce my candidature until we know

whether the public is with us or not," Tess Fisher went on.

At least she had the sense to see *that* much.

"I can't make up the minds of those who are undecided," he pointed out in his most patronising tone.

"No, but I can," Tess Fisher shot back.

He looked at her silently.

"I haven't said a word about this publicly yet."

"We could issue a statement, I suppose – "

"Not worth the paper it's written on," she said succinctly. "They want to hear from me. They want my side of the story, from the heart."

He looked at her impatiently. "What are you suggesting?"

"I want to go on *Newsnight* tomorrow night."

Newsnight? Was the woman for real?

"I want to be interviewed by Derek Long, John. One on one."

Newsnight was the top current affairs programme on Irish television, an arena where political heavyweights slugged it out week after week. Derek Long was one of the toughest and most respected commentators in Ireland.

"No," John Graham said. Derek Long would pulverise her.

"I don't think you have any choice," she said with a small smile.

Carol Taylor agreed. So did Harry Burke, reluctantly, and the rest of the cabinet. But their support was largely based on the fact that it was a last-ditch effort rather than any great faith in Tess Fisher. She was a complete unknown quantity. Only Peter Fisher had shown any support.

"Let her," he had said.

"Am I late?" Geraldine Day now barrelled into the War Room and bagged a chair right in front of the widescreen TV. "It's on at ten, isn't it?"

"You're just in time," Peter said caustically. Geraldine wouldn't miss this one for all the world – Peter's further humiliation at the hands of his own wife. He was surprised that she hadn't brought along popcorn for the show.

Harry Burke now slunk in, and Dan Kilmartin, and the rest of the cabinet. They took their seats and stared blindly at the blank TV. All had an air of despair about them, a hopelessness. None of them expected this Government to see the summer out.

There were no more words spoken as John Graham killed the lights and snapped on the TV. Vacuous ads filled the screen. It was a minute to ten o'clock.

Peter stood at the back of the room, his hands balled into tight fists of tension. Tess would be sitting in the studio now. He found that his nerves were all for her, and not himself. He was almost past caring whether they let him keep his job or not. He was almost past caring about anything.

Oh, he'd gone through the motions all right. All week, he'd watched himself trying to save his career, the film, the Government. He'd given press conferences until his throat was dry. Worked with Declan Mahoney all through Tuesday night to try and convince Cinerama to continue funding the film, even if the Government had withdrawn – a fruitless attempt in the end. He'd spent hours upon hours with Carol Taylor, and more hours with John Graham. And his heart wasn't in any of it.

Ever since Jean had told him in that funny, stilted voice on Sunday night that it was over between them, he felt as though his world had been turned upside down. She had given no explanation. When he'd pressed her, his own voice growing more incredulous and angry by the minute, she'd hung up. When he'd rung back an hour later, sure that she had suffered some momentary insanity, that the fright of the imminent scandal had somehow or other scared her off, he'd got her answering machine. He'd tried all night and she had not picked up the phone.

He didn't give up then. He'd called to her office the next morning. And was told by Patsy, her assistant, that she was on extended leave and that no, she didn't know where she was. Finally, he'd driven to her house only to find it locked-up and dark. Only then did it sink in with him that she was gone.

The betrayal hurt more than anything in his life before. She had run out on him, tossed him aside, after all her wonderful words of love and commitment. Just when he needed her most, she had turned tail and left town.

He had thought that he knew her. He had never once

doubted her strength and backbone. And of course he understood how difficult all this must be for her too, but they had promised each other than they would get through it together. She obviously hadn't meant that, any more than she meant anything else. Perhaps she had never loved him at all, that those were more wonderful words said in the convenience of the moment. Why else had she brought things to a swift and ruthless end at the first cloud on the horizon?

For days he had veered from rage to regret to a terrible sadness. And then, on Wednesday, after days of skilfully dodging and fudging the issue, he had stated publicly for the first time that his affair was over. It was only then that he really believed it himself.

Tess had not crowed. Neither had she looked surprised. He wondered then had she had something to do with Jean's disappearance. If so, she wasn't saying. In fact, she had said remarkably little about the affair at all. There had been no recriminations or angry outbursts. Instead, she taken the ground from under his feet by suggesting that it would be to everyone's advantage all around if she be allowed to run in the by-election.

She had never said out loud that she would not support him if he disagreed. That was not Tess's style. But the implication was there, like a dangerous undercurrent.

It was also crystal clear that she was not fighting for her marriage this time, but herself. Their marriage was over in all but name only, both of them knew that. But it was vital that it remain a marriage nonetheless for their mutual benefit.

"Just for the moment, Peter. And then we'll see," she had said cryptically.

He was less surprised than most by her announcement that she wanted to stand as a candidate. On paper, it looked bad, if not hopeless. Most people in Ireland did not even know her name until now. There was less than four weeks to go to the election. Most worrying of all, she would be running under the banner of "Victim" and that was suicide.

But she had guts. There was no doubt about that. And it was a feat of incredible boldness, cunning even, to come from the back like that and take them all by surprise.

In political terms, it was a daring if risky strategy. Not one that any sane Government would adopt, mind you, but had they any choice?

Harry Burke and Geraldine Day had been the first to throw their hands up in horror, of course. But they didn't know Tess. Peter did. And Carol Taylor seemed to share his quiet faith. Still, everything would depend on how she did in this TV interview tonight.

"Here we go," Geraldine Day said unnecessarily as the opening credits of *Newsnight* filled the TV screen. Peter held his breath.

And now there was Tess, alone at the big round studio table at which four or five people normally sat. She could have chosen a cosy armchair opposite Derek Long but she was too smart for that. Sitting alone at that intimidating table made the statement that she was not afraid. Strike one for Tess.

Strike two she won on appearance. John Graham's advice to trot out her most sombre suit had gone out the window. She wore a simple white blouse, tailored and fashionable, with no suit jacket over it. The result was that she looked fresh, young and open. She did not fidget nor did she reach for her glass of water as Derek Long gave his usual synopsis of the day's news events.

Looking his most ponderous and stuffy, he finally turned to Tess Fisher. He pulled the first punch. "With us in the studio tonight we have Tess Fisher, wife of disgraced Minister for Arts Peter Fisher." He paused delicately to let that sink in, and had opened his mouth to go on when Tess Fisher interrupted him.

"Disgraced by whose standards, Derek?"

Derek Long didn't know where to look. He was supposed to ask the questions, not her.

Peter Fisher almost laughed aloud as he felt himself slowly relax. She would be fine.

As the hour-long interview progressed, she was more than fine. She was great. Derek Long gradually softened and eventually went completely over to her side once he saw that she was not using him or his programme to publicly forgive her husband and make mewling pleas to the public to do the same.

She was strong and confident and she met every question head-on. She admitted that their marriage was not made in heaven, that they weren't sure what the future held but that they were together for now. Again and again she said that; that they were together for now. She admitted to feelings of anger, pain and betrayal over the entire affair. Never once did she lose her dignity. Then she frankly answered questions from the floor. By the time the hour was up, Derek Long and the studio audience were prostrate at her feet.

Then, at the very end of the programme, she quietly announced her intention to run in the by-election. It was another clever move to hold it off until now. There was no time for difficult questions, for Derek Long to put her on the spot. Instead, he had no choice but to wish her good luck, which he did warmly and enthusiastically. She left the studio stage to very warm applause from the audience.

John Graham snapped off the TV. They sat in darkness for a long moment. Then Dan Kilmartin slowly began to clap. He was joined by Carol Taylor, Harry Burke and all the rest.

"She did it," Geraldine Day said, sounding more astonished than pleased.

Peter felt some sense of pleasure for the first time all week. Tess had done it.

Fiona was sitting up in bed watching television when they entered her room.

"I watched you, you were fantastic!" she told Tess. But her welcoming smile vanished as she saw Peter behind Tess. She looked accusingly at Tess. "I told you to come on your own."

"Fiona, please," Tess began.

"It's all right, Tess," Peter intervened. Fiona would not look at him. It had been the same every time he'd visited since she'd been moved from hospital to this discreet and very private rehabilitation clinic that looked more like a stately country home.

"You're going to have to talk to me sooner or later," he said.

"I have nothing to say to you. Full stop."

The words pierced Peter. He racked his brain for some common ground, something that might bridge the gap that seemed to widen with each passing day.

"I've managed to keep it out of the papers," he said.

"What, are you afraid I might embarrass you?" she spat.

"It's not that at all," Peter said quietly. "I just thought you'd prefer if people didn't know."

"Know what? That I tried to top myself?"

This was only bravado, Peter knew. She had been more shaken than any of them by what had happened. And anyway, the amount of ecstasy she had taken wouldn't have killed anyone. But, combined with the amount of alcohol she'd consumed, it had been enough to render her unconscious in an alleyway in Kilkenny, where she'd been discovered last Sunday morning after the press party. She'd been mortified, and terrified, when she'd woken up in hospital. But she still used the suicide-stick to beat Peter.

"Fiona . . ." He tried again.

She wouldn't listen. "Mind you, I couldn't hold a candle to you, Dad. You and your fancy-woman."

It was a curiously quaint term for her to use. But Fiona would not acknowledge Jean Ormsby by name. Still, at least she was talking, which was something. Peter felt hopeful.

"Fiona, I can't tell you how sorry I am. But it's over. I promise you."

For the first time in almost a week, she lifted her head and met his eyes. And Peter felt sick as he registered her disgust, her distaste. Her *dislike* for him.

"Sure, it's over. Until the next one." Her voice was contemptuous. "She wasn't the first, was she?"

Peter was aware of Tess's stillness beside him. He was on his own and she was letting him know it.

"No," he said, unable to lie.

If he'd hoped that telling the truth would in some way heal matters, he was wrong.

"No," Fiona said dully. "So don't stand there telling me that you're *sorry*, and that it's *over*. You're not sorry at all, you never were. You're just sorry you were caught."

"That's not true – "

"What would you know about the truth? You're a liar, a cheat. You've lied for years and years. Why should I believe you now?"

Peter had no answer. His chest felt curiously tight. He tried to tell himself that Fiona wasn't just angry at him; she had been badly duped by Roger Croft in more ways than one. That must hurt. Roger Croft was another person Fiona would not talk about.

"Fiona, please. I'm trying to make it up to you."

The words sounded stupid even as he said them, as though she were a small child he was trying to buy off with the promise of sweets.

"By locking me up in here?" she said, flicking a hand around the room.

The hospital had released her within twenty-four hours. But Peter and Tess had decided that she needed more help than they could give her, hence the rehab clinic.

Her eyes were curiously bright now; involuntarily, Peter took a step forward. When she made no move to stop him, he tentatively perched on the end of her bed. Tess remained quietly at the back of the room.

"I don't know what to say to you, Fiona," he said eventually. "I just don't know."

He wanted to touch her but was afraid. Tears were threatening to spill down her cheeks; only sheer willpower held them back.

"Why did you do it, Dad?"

He felt choked. "I'm sorry."

"Were we not enough for you? Me and Mum?"

He looked at the white bedspread. He could not bear to look in her eyes. Never in his life had he felt so small and worthless.

"I'm sorry," he said again.

Fiona blinked several times; the tears eased away. She was in control again. "I used to think you were great, Dad," she said simply.

"Fiona – "

"Goodbye. I don't want you to come here again."

He had lost her. Eventually, he got up and left the room.

"Your name will be put to the Selection Committee in the morning. They're calling a special meeting."

Tess nodded at this news. They were having a very late supper after their visit to Fiona. Peter did not think that he had ever felt more tired.

"And what if they don't select me?" Tess asked.

"After tonight, they'll select you."

Tess nodded, her only indication that she was pleased with her performance.

"We'll just about make the Close of Nominations tomorrow evening," Peter added.

"And then I have three weeks?" Tess asked.

"Yes."

"It'll be tight." She offered him the shadow of a smile.

"It'll be a bloody miracle, Tess." An answering smile took the sting out of his words. But neither of them were under any illusions about what lay ahead.

"I know that they didn't want me – Geraldine Day and the rest," she said quietly. "Thanks for standing by me, Peter."

"Did I have any choice?" He couldn't help the bitterness that slipped out.

Tess shot him a measured glance. "Did any of us in the circumstances? This way you get to keep your job. And I get to run for election. It's all worked out for the best, really."

Again, he had the suspicion that she had a hand in Jean's disappearance. Then he shrugged. Did it matter really? If Jean had loved him, she would have stayed, no matter what Tess had said or done.

"Perhaps," he said, knowing that his voice was colourless.

Tess hesitated. "Fiona will come around."

"She won't. You saw the way she looked at me. She hates my guts."

"Oh, Peter!"

"She does. And who could blame her?"

"She's young. She has all these notions that people should be perfect. Give her time."

But Peter knew that it would take more than time to heal the rift. Sometimes he wondered how he had managed to make such a hash of his life. In the space of a week, he had lost the two people he loved most in the world – Jean and his daughter. It was time to stop making mistakes.

"What about the future, Tess?"

"What about it?" she asked, but she knew exactly what he meant.

"We don't love each other any more." His voice was low and serious. "Are we going to continue to live a sham? Surely you don't want that?"

"We have a family, Peter. We've stayed together for sixteen years. And we manage to be civil to each other. We have a lot more than some couples I know."

He did not answer. She seemed sad. "Fiona was right. It's not enough for you, is it?

It never was."

"I don't know, Tess. Maybe I should be happy with what I've got. Maybe that's what other people do, instead of always looking for something better. Maybe it doesn't even exist. But I can't do that."

Perhaps for the first time ever, they were talking frankly about their marriage.

"I suppose you want her," she said now.

He did not say that Jean had gone, that it really was over. Even if he never saw her again, he could not stay in this marriage.

"Maybe there are other people for both of us, Tess."

"I don't think so. Not for me, anyway."

"Oh? Not even Jack Thornton?"

On that crazy Sunday afternoon when he and Carol Taylor had driven down to break the news to Tess, they had met Jack Thornton's jeep on the road, speeding in the opposite direction. Peter had found the other evidence in the bedroom, the two wine glasses and the rumpled sheets.

Tess looked him straight in the eye. "No. Jack is not the one for me, Peter."

He believed her. Jack Thornton had left the country with indecent haste, even given the crisis with the film. The only contact Peter had had with him was a sharp phone call last night with the news that Cinerama were refusing to review their position.

"I hope you're happy now, you cheating bastard," had been his parting shot. "You managed to bring us all down with you."

Peter had said nothing. What could he say?

"And you'd better not bring her down with you too," Thornton had gruffly added, slamming down the phone. Peter knew he was referring to Tess. A lot more had gone on between those two than Peter had known. Still, he was scarcely in any position to pull the jealous-husband routine. He was only surprised that she hadn't strayed earlier, given his own behaviour over the years. But that would have been easy. And Tess had never taken the easy option.

"What are we going to do, Tess?" he asked.

She gave a small sigh. "Do we have to do anything?"

"Of course we do."

"Yes, but *now*? Haven't we enough to be getting on with in the next while without giving ourselves more heartache? Haven't we spent sixteen years without doing anything?" She looked at him, her head cocked to one side. "Would it really be so bad to let it go on a little longer?"

She had a point. Besides, what was out there for him if he and Tess separated? A faceless bachelor pad in Dublin, complete with ready-to-cook meals for one? Visits to the cinema with Fiona at weekends, if she ever spoke to him again? And long, lonely nights with only the television for company? At the age of forty-four, was that all he amounted to?

He had imagined it all so differently. He would be leaving not as an end to one thing, but as a start to another. A life with Jean, the woman he loved. A new beginning.

There was no chance of that now. So why not hang in there a little longer if that's what Tess wanted? The alternative was not appealing, and required an energy that he didn't think he had right now.

"Okay," he said, his voice dead to his own ears.

Tess lifted her wine glass. "To us," she said wryly. "It won't be so bad, Peter."

Chapter Thirty-five

"Yes, I *know* the invoice is three weeks overdue," Patsy said earnestly into the phone. "But there's nothing I can do about it."

She rolled her eyes as another barrage of abuse ensued. The door to the agency opened but she didn't look up. She waved a hand half-heartedly in the direction of the chair by the rubber plant.

"Be with you in a minute," she mumbled, turning back to the phone. "No, I'm afraid Jean is away at the moment," she told the caller. "No, I'm afraid I don't know when she'll be back – "

The receiver was snatched from her hand. Her boss was leaning over the desk speaking into the phone.

"This is Jean Orsmby. And there'll be a cheque in the post this evening, okay? Bye now."

She hung up. Patsy looked as though she'd just seen a ghost.

"Jean?"

"The very same. Hello, Patsy."

Patsy was still open-mouthed. In four weeks, there had not been so much as a phone call from Jean. Patsy had almost given up hope of ever seeing her again.

"Where have you been?" she asked, her eyes round as she took in Jean.

Surely this was not the same woman who had slunk into the office nearly a month ago, her hair bundled up and her face thin and white, to announce tersely that she was going away?

If so, she had done a miraculous job of re-inventing herself. She had on one of those gorgeous little suits, but this was not a good copy like her others – this was the genuine article. Versace, Patsy thought enviously, or maybe even Dior. What looked suspiciously like real diamonds studded her ears. Her skin was tanned, her hair shiny and smooth. Energy came off her in bursts. She looked like she had spent a month on an exclusive health farm.

"Away,"Jean merely said, briskly lifting the mountain of post from the corner of Patsy's desk. "Any news?"

"News?" Patsy repeated stupidly. Jean *was* the news, or at least had been for the better part of two weeks. Patsy had spent ages every morning carefully cutting out every newspaper article featuring her boss. There was a file three inches thick now. She wasn't sure why she did it. But maybe Jean mightn't have seen them, wherever she was.

"Phone calls, messages, post?" Jean prompted helpfully. "What's been going on while I've been away?"

Patsy hesitated. Then her round, freckled face crumpled. "We're broke," she blurted. "The rent is overdue, the electricity people are threatening to cut us off, I haven't been paid in a month and there's no money coming in . . ."

"Patsy," Jean intervened sympathetically. "It's okay, I'm back now. I'll take care of everything."

Poor Patsy was not cut out for stress. It had been a terrible thing to do, to leave her in sole charge of the agency, but Jean had had no choice.

Patsy was unappeased. "It's worse than that, Jean."

"What is?"

"Half your clients have left."

"I see."

"Bernice Gannon's done what she can, and so have I, but there's no work coming in for the rest."

"And why is that?" Jean asked slowly.

Patsy looked very unhappy now. "People think. . . what with the press stuff and the film falling through . . ."

"They don't want to touch me with a bargepole?" Jean stated calmly.

Patsy's miserable face was all the confirmation she needed.

"But Cathy Conroy and Carl Tallon are still on the books?" Jean enquired carefully.

"Yes, I think so, but neither of them has been in contact," Patsy said cautiously. "And nobody's offered them any work."

"That doesn't matter. So long as we still have them."

"We do."

533

"Excellent," Jean said with a cheerfulness that clearly unnerved Patsy. "Can you bring their files into my office, please?"

But Patsy hadn't finished yet. "There's something else."

"Oh?"

Patsy reached for a slim file on her desk. She held it out to Jean without meeting her eyes.

"What's this?" Jean asked.

"Three letters from Gorman Finley & Company," Patsy mumbled.

Gorman Finley & Company were solicitors, Jean discovered. They represented Ian Coffey who, it was their understanding, had a claim as an investor to a portion of the profits of the Jean Ormsby Agency. Retrospective and with interest, of course. They would be obliged if she would make her accounts available for inspection at her earliest convenience, after which a cheque to their client would be payable. Thereafter, they would be happy with a twice-yearly payment based on profits.

"He doesn't really own part of the agency, does he?" Patsy cried, unable to contain herself any longer.

"No, he does not," Jean assured her.

"Anyway, we didn't *make* any profit last year," Patsy went on. "But if we ever do, we'll have to pay him, won't we? Not that that's very likely," she added disconsolately.

"Don't make rash assumptions, Patsy," Jean said cryptically.

Jean was taking it all too well in Patsy's opinion. If

she had any sense, she would close the agency before they got deeper into debt.

"What are we going to do?" she asked in a voice filled with dread.

"Leave it to me," Jean said sunnily, sweeping up letters, files, briefcase and handbag, and heading for her office. "Bring me in the newspapers and a coffee, Patsy, would you? A good strong one."

It would take more than a good strong coffee to salvage *this* mess, Patsy thought darkly.

It felt good to be back. As Jean settled herself at her desk it was as if one part of her life slowly slipped back under her control.

Patsy was right, the agency was in disarray. Jean wasn't at all surprised. You didn't walk out on your business for a month and expect it to be in the same state when you got back. Given all that had happened, it was a minor miracle that there was a business left at all, she thought wryly. It wasn't often that an agency's owner was more famous that its clients.

It was the agency that had finally brought her to her senses in Cathy's flat on the North Circular Road, where she had hidden out for days like some kind of sewer rat, dodging the press, Peter and every other living soul. She had wandered about in her nightdress, feverishly reading every word written about her in the newspapers, devouring every scandalous news programme, too frightened to do anything except lick her wounds.

She knew she couldn't go on like this. One morning she refused to read the newspapers and spent the time taking stock of her life instead.

Peter was gone; Tess Fisher had seen to that. Her good name and reputation were shot to bits, thanks to the press. But she still had her agency. And she would not let them take that from her too.

That same morning, she had propped a thank-you note to Cathy on the kitchen table, dropped by the agency, and then caught a taxi to the airport. It was time to fight back.

Patsy arrived in with a coffee and the files on Cathy and Carl.

"Thanks," Jean said, scribbling her name on the first of many cheques. "And here's your wages, plus a large bonus for looking after the place."

Patsy looked at the cheque as though it had already bounced.

"There's money in the account, Patsy," Jean told her gently.

"There's not." Patsy was quite clear on this point.

"There is. Believe me."

Patsy retreated, glancing back at Jean as if she needed to be committed.

Perhaps I do, Jean thought. But certain things had been put in place that should take care of the immediate future, thanks to her sojourn in New York. It was amazing how eager the Americans were for quality material. And willing to pay for it too. She was on her way.

She had one unpleasant task to deal with first. She refused to let herself get angry as she snatched up the phone and dialled. He was simply not worth the energy. But she must make sure that he never had the chance to jeopardise her agency again.

"Hello?"

His voice was raspy and low; Jean knew that he had not yet had his first fix of the day. Good. That should render him a little more amenable.

"Ian, it's Jean," she said curtly, not bothering with any niceties.

"My God," he said. "I thought you'd disappeared off the face of the earth."

Jean said nothing.

"You've been all over the papers," he said unnecessarily. "You and Peter Fisher."

Jean clamped down on her anger. "You should have been too, Ian. You and your druggie friends."

There was a frosty silence now.

"You're half-responsible for the film being canned," she went on ruthlessly. "So don't go pointing fingers at *me*."

"What do you want?" he said sourly, anxious to get off the subject.

"I want you out of my life. Permanently."

"I take it you've received my solicitor's letters."

"Oh yes," Jean said. "I see you've managed to get someone else to do your dirty work for you again."

"I want what's due to me," he blustered.

"You'll get five thousand pounds, Ian, and not a

penny more. And you'll sign a waiver to any further claims on my agency."

"Five grand?" He laughed. "Dream on."

"Take it or leave it."

"And what if I leave it?" he sneered.

"Then I'll ring the police this instant and tell them all about your drug habit, and your pusher mates. You still get your stuff from the same guy, I take it?" Silence. She had him now. "I've got his phone number, Ian – I used to ring him for you when you were too sick to do it yourself, remember? I don't think he'd appreciate the boys in blue breathing down his neck. He might even come after you."

"You wouldn't dare, you bitch."

"Try me." There was a long silence. "Five thousand, Ian."

She could almost hear his brain ticking over. Five thousand would buy a lot of coke.

And coke was the only thing that would chase away the horrors this morning.

"When can I have it?" he asked eventually.

"This afternoon, if you sign the waiver."

He was suspicious now. "How come you got five thousand sitting around the place?"

She ignored him. "Have we a deal?"

"Okay. But if I find out that you've screwed me – "

"Drop dead, Ian."

She hung up. Her hands were steady. His greed, as usual, had got the better of him. Little did he know that the Jean Ormsby Agency was in a rather better position than anybody thought. And it was all hers now.

Her satisfaction was short-lived as she reached for the day's newspapers. Her heart jolted hard against her ribs as she found herself staring straight into Peter Fisher's handsome face. He was on the front page, him and Tess Fisher.

Rattled and confused, she quickly skimmed the text. Of course. The by-election. She had hoped that she would miss it all. But yesterday had been polling day she learned. Today was the count. The photo was of Peter and Tess Fisher walking into their local polling centre to cast their votes.

He looked good, she noted painfully. Relaxed and calm, as if nothing at all had happened. Looking into his eyes, it was hard to believe that he had gone through anything like the heartache she had in the past month.

But maybe she looked that way too. It was a necessary part of survival, hiding your emotions, not wearing your heart on your sleeve. And he was a politician to boot, still trying to live down a scandal. He could hardly appear in public weeping and gnashing his teeth for a lost love.

But did he have to stand so close to Tess Fisher? Hold a hand protectively at the small of her back? There was a tangible camaraderie between the pair, a sense of something shared. A closeness.

Jean's tongue was glued to the roof of her mouth. Was it possible that they were back together? Properly, as husband and wife? Had he really forgotten Jean so quickly, if he had ever loved her in the first place?

He had, she reassured herself adamantly. He had

made dozens of attempts to talk to her in the days after she'd told him it was over. He'd even come to the agency looking for her. Patsy had told her. Even when she'd read in the newspapers that he'd categorically announced that the affair was over, she had still believed that he loved her.

Oh, what did it matter now anyway, she thought dully. After all, she had been the one who'd walked out on him, to his mind. She'd had no choice, but he would never know that. So could she really blame him for having one last stab at making his marriage work, if indeed that was what the photo indicated?

Tess Fisher looked out at her from the page, cool and in control. Neither Jean nor Peter had been any match for her at the end of the day. Jean tried to summon up anger but couldn't. If the shoe had been on the other foot, could Jean be sure that she wouldn't fight for her marriage too? With methods a little less unsavoury perhaps, but nobody could fault Tess Fisher for trying to hang on to what she had.

The Fishers would be the new power couple in town now if she won the election. Today's photo would only be the start of years of media coverage. It would be hard to stomach. But Jean would have to try.

"There'll be someone else for you," Bernice Gannon had said cautiously when Jean had phoned her last week.

Jean had not believed her then and she didn't believe her now. Anyway, she didn't want a man, *any* man. The very thought made her ill. The only one who'd ever mattered was gone. And if she couldn't have him, then she didn't want anybody at all. With a finality, she folded the newspaper on Peter Fisher's face.

Then she went back to work. "Patsy? Get me Carl Tallon on the phone."

Chapter Thirty-six

"You used to do nice rashers. Smoked ones. Now it's all this 'own brand' stuff."

The old boy glared at Cathy out of rheumy eyes. Cathy smiled back with all the brightness she could manage at the end of an eight-hour shift.

"They do smoked ones at the deli counter," she said nicely.

"*Now* she tells me!" He rolled his eyes despairingly at the rest of the blue-rinsed old dears in the queue. Cathy hated him.

"Would you like to exchange these for some smoked ones instead?" she asked, indicating the packet of rashers in his shopping basket. The queue at her checkout was growing ominously long now, the old dears shifting from foot to foot impatiently.

It *would* have to be pension day.

"I'm not walking all the way over to the deli counter, not with my back! I was in the war, you know!"

He had obviously survived, worse luck. Cathy

grabbed the rashers. "Tracy! Can you exchange these for some smoked ones please?" She turned back to the old boy. "How many would you like? Half a pound?"

"Two," he spat. "And make it quick."

Tracy ambled over like a tortoise on valium and languidly took the rashers from Cathy. "Great to be back, eh?" she murmured with a sly wink.

Cathy glared at her retreating back. It was not great to be back. It was terrible.

Nothing much had changed in *Discount Shopping* except the hours, which were longer, and the canteen food, which was worse. Apart from that, Cathy's weeks in London had fallen into the same mind-numbing pattern; four eight-hour shifts a week in the supermarket, with her days off spent hawking her CV around town and trying to gate-crash auditions. She'd even managed to get her old flat back in Brixton. There was a depressing sense of déjà vu about it all.

"There's nothing left for me in Dublin any more," she succinctly told Tracy on her first day back.

Certainly, there was no work. Oh, Cathy Conroy was famous all over town all right, but for the wrong reasons. She was the actress who had starred in the Government's embarrassing flop, the Scarlett O'Hara who had refused to drop her panties. Film and theatre directors were not exactly beating her door down with lucrative offers.

"And what about Carl?" Tracy asked, devouring a Superkings in three long pulls. "He'll think you left because of him again."

Cathy had eventually told her the entire sorry saga.

"I didn't."

That was the truth. He knew everything now. She had nothing left to hide from him, nothing to be afraid of.

"He'll come after you," Tracy declared with all the wisdom of her twenty-three years.

"He won't, Tracy."

"He said he still loved you, didn't he? He'll come after you yet, when he has a chance to calm down."

Cathy brushed this off impatiently. It was ridiculous. He would not come after her and she didn't want him to. They were done with each other, finally. She had to accept that, however hard that might be. And it was hard. She dreamt about him at night, she spent more hours than were sensible thinking about him during the day. It hurt, all of it.

She could not stay in Dublin for her own sanity. And London was what she knew. She might have had no great success in her five years there, but even the failed auditions and the endless shifts in *Discount Shopping* had a sense of familiarity and sameness that she found comforting.

It would do for the moment, she decided. Just until the dust of the last few weeks had settled and she could find the energy to start fighting again.

"That's the spirit!" Tracy had cried. "Don't let the bastards get you down!"

But on some days they did. Like today. She shivered now as the supermarket's swing doors opened behind her, blasting her with ice-cold air.

"Is she killing the damned pig or something?" the old boy growled, looking at his watch. The queue at

Cathy's checkout had stretched all the way back to the dog-food section now.

"I'm sure she's on her way," Cathy said in resignation, searching for a glimpse of Tracy. Another blast of cold air hit the back of her neck.

"Ought to do something about the heating in here," the old boy grumbled.

The doors continued to open and close with no respite. Cathy looked around irritably. She went white. Then pink. Then white again.

Carl Tallon stood patiently just inside the supermarket's entrance. It was he who was activating the electronic doors, which merrily swished back and forth behind him. He seemed unaware of this. His eyes were fixed on Cathy. She was paralysed.

"Oi! Step in properly, you!" the old boy shouted. "We're all freezing to death here!"

Carl Tallon hesitated before taking a step forward, and then resumed his patient wait, never taking his eyes off her.

She swung back to the till, eyes like saucers and heart pounding unpleasantly fast. What was he doing here? What did he want? Hardly a pint of milk and a loaf of bread.

"Two smoked rashers." Tracy was back. She took one look at Cathy's face. "What's wrong?"

"Nothing!" It came out as a screech. She must have made some involuntary movement that gave the game away, because Tracy slowly transferred her gaze to the door.

"That's him, isn't it? Carl?" she asked quietly.

Cathy nodded mutely.

"I don't know what drama is going on here, but can I pay for these rashers or not?" the old boy said querulously to Cathy.

"Oh, be quiet!" Tracy told him sternly. "Can't you see she's upset?"

The old boy was dumbfounded. "Well, yes . . ."

"You ought to be ashamed of yourself!"

"Sorry," he mumbled contritely.

"Now get to the back of the queue!"

Meekly, the old boy took the rashers and shuffled off. The rest of the old dears in the queue were agog now, wondering what on earth was going on.

"I think the checkout girl is ill," one said to another.

"She *does* look a bit off," another agreed. "I hope it's not contagious. I haven't had my flu jab yet."

Tracy put an end to any more speculation by briskly stepping up behind the till.

"Next, please!"

"What are you doing?" Cathy hissed.

"Taking over here. Go and talk to him."

Cathy found herself manhandled from her seat. She rounded on Tracy, furious.

"I do not want to talk to him!"

"If he's come all the way over here to see you, you might have the manners to at least acknowledge his presence," Tracy snapped, fixing Cathy with a look before turning back to the customers. "Next, I said! You ladies are all going to have to turn up your hearing aids."

Cathy slowly turned around. Carl still stood

awkwardly by the door, shoulders hunched in his denim jacket. She had not seen him in over a month and she knew that she must look wary and unsure. It was difficult to see what he felt, if anything. Self-consciously, she tugged at her blue-checked overall. She would have to go over.

The journey seemed to take forever. She stopped a measured five feet from him. She did not greet him.

"What are you doing here?"

"I came to see you."

"But how did you know where. . . ?" she stuttered in incomprehension.

"Patsy told me you were back working here."

"I'm not finished my shift," she said inanely, as if it mattered.

"I'll wait," he said simply.

Cathy was suddenly aware of the din of the supermarket behind them, of the eyes of the checkout queue on them.

"Let's go outside," she said.

It was raining. They were forced to huddle together under the portico. Cathy was intensely aware of his closeness. She saw now that he was nervous; excited even. He fumbled in his jacket, unearthing something.

"I just wanted to give you this."

Clumsily, he pressed a bound manuscript into her hands. She looked at it, baffled.

"It's the first copy of the new play I've been working on," he said, speaking fast. His face was flushed. "It's for you."

"Me?"

"Yeh. Look, it says it right there."

He jabbed a finger at the manuscript. Under the title, she saw printed the words *For Cathy*.

"For you," he reiterated, shifting from foot to foot rapidly.

Cathy looked from him to the manuscript and back again. She really did not know what to say. "Well, um, thanks. Nobody's ever written anything for me before."

He shook his head rapidly. Black hair flew in all directions. "No, no, it's not just a grand gesture, Cathy. The lead character – it's yours."

She really was lost now. "What?"

"I wrote her for you," he insisted.

Cathy's confusion only grew. "I'm . . . flattered, Carl."

This was obviously the wrong thing to say judging from his face. "I didn't write it to flatter you. I want you to play her in the production."

"What production?"

"Oh, sorry – I should have said. Jean was supposed to ring you, you see, and I said no, that I would be seeing you . . ." He waved a hand, impatient with the details, his excitement getting the better of him now. "Anyway, The Phoenix theatre has bought the rights. They said that you'll have to audition, of course, and the director wants to meet you first – "

"The Phoenix?" Cathy interjected in disbelief. "You don't mean . . . not on Broadway?"

"Yes, yes, do you know of any other Phoenix? Now, obviously, you'll need to read the script straight away, Ike *Hanson* will be giving you a call, okay?"

"Ike Hanson?" Cathy parroted stupidly.

"Oh, have you heard of him?" Carl said eagerly.

Had she *heard* of him? Holy cow, he was only the Woody Allen of the theatre world. He was only the most famous theatre director in the *universe* at this moment in time.

"Vaguely," Cathy whispered, certain now that Carl Tallon was suffering from some illness that produced inflated delusions, poor dear. The Phoenix! And Ike Hanson! In his dreams. Next he would be telling her that it was touring the world.

"He's talking about touring it all over the States. Cathy, are you alright?"

"I don't believe you," she blurted.

"I know, isn't it fantastic?" he said, beaming.

"No – Carl – *I mean I really don't believe you.*"

He looked at her suspiciously for a moment. "What?"

Cathy lifted her shoulders helplessly. "All this stuff . . . are you sure?"

He smiled widely now. "I didn't believe it myself at first. I thought Jean had disappeared with the only copy of the play that I had. She was in New York, Cathy. She's sold the rights. And she's waiting for you to call her about the lead part."

Cathy still did not buy it. "There are thousands of actresses in New York. Why would they want me?"

"Because I wrote the part for you. Haven't you listened to a word I've said?"

But Cathy was shaking her head. "You're not the director, Carl."

"Cathy," Carl said levelly, "Jean took over some of the film rushes from *Outsiders*. They want you."

The first rush of euphoria was hitting Cathy. Maybe he wasn't suffering from any delusional illness at all.

"My God."

"I know."

"My God!"

"I know!"

It was a moment before Cathy realised, aghast, that she was on the verge of smiling at him – as if everything was okay, as if their careers were all that mattered at the end of the day. Were they really the same selfish people they had been five years ago? She sobered instantly, shocked at herself.

"Yes, well, we'll have to see, won't we?" she mumbled. "I mightn't get the part."

He looked very serious now too. "You will. You see, I've told them that I won't sign a contract until you're guaranteed the part."

Cathy blinked. "That's a big thing to do, Carl," she said slowly.

From the way he was studying his feet, she knew that this wasn't really about their careers at all.

"Like I said, I wrote the part for you." His eyes locked onto hers. "I was never much good at saying things, Cathy. I never could seem to find the right words at the right time." His grin was twisted. "The only way I was ever able to say anything properly was when I wrote it down. And the play . . . it's my way of saying sorry. For not coming to London that time when you asked me to. And for the things that I said, the night we . . ." He shrugged. "I'm sorry."

Cathy felt so choked that she could hardly get words out. "I should have told you at the time."

He seemed choked too. "Was I really so wrapped up in myself that you felt you couldn't?"

"I don't know," she whispered. "Maybe we both were. I thought it was the easiest thing to do. That's what I can't stand, you know – that I did it because I didn't have the courage to tell you, and I didn't have the courage to go through with it."

He did not offer her any platitudes to ease her conscience and she was glad. She looked at him hesitantly. "I lost the baby, Carl, before . . . that's why I phoned you."

He looked even more crushed. "Oh, Cathy."

"Yes," she agreed sadly.

Without another word, he took her in his arms and held her close, giving her the comfort she had wanted back then. She held herself rigid for a moment, then slowly relaxed against him. She couldn't do anything else.

"We made a terrible mess of everything, didn't we?" she said, her nose buried in his scruffy denim jacket, the jacket she'd given him and which he still wore.

"We did."

She should really get a grip on herself, she thought. Pull herself out of his lovely, warm arms, and tell him that now that everything had been sorted, they could finally be friends. That's what she wanted, wasn't it?

"I love you," she said instead.

She looked at him in horror, the words hanging in the air like stray sparks of electricity. As she waited for his reaction, she felt as if every one of her vital organs had ceased functioning.

"Oh, Cathy," he said again.

Oh, Cathy, *what*? Oh, Cathy, you sad cow? Or – Oh, Cathy, I love you too? Please God let it be the second one, she begged, suddenly realising that nothing had ever been as important in her life.

In a measured voice, he said, "Will you come home with me? To Dublin? Now? Tonight?"

"Home," Cathy repeated slowly. It had a good ring to it, a rightness. "Yes, please."

The reporters had been waiting since dawn. Now, at one in the afternoon, they finally had something to report. Immediately, the cameras for RTE, BBC, ITN and Channel 4 began to roll.

"We've just seen Prime Minister Carol Taylor arrive with Peter Fisher and Tess Fisher here at the count centre in Kilkenny in a show of strength," the BBC correspondent sombrely told viewers. *"Counting has been going on all morning in what has been the most controversial and scandal-ridden by-election in Ireland in memory, but as yet there is no indication of how the votes are falling . . ."*

The RTE reporter had better sources. *"This has turned into a fight between just two candidates, veteran radio star Bill Mackey and the Government's Tess Fisher. When she announced her surprise decision to run just three weeks ago,* on the back of so much scandal, nobody anticipated the extraordinary impact Tess Fisher would have on the Kilkenny electorate . . ."

Channel 4 was less optimistic. *"Tess Fisher is getting the sympathy vote all right, but sources inside say that it will never be enough to close the gap between her and the outright favourite, Bill Mackey."*

"The Government should have had a shoo-in with disgraced candidate Roger Croft," ITN told its viewers, *"but now it's depending for its very survival on Tess Fisher today, a woman who's come from the back of the field and given Bill Mackey a nasty surprise. Whether she can pull it off remains to be seen."*

Inside the count centre, Tess Fisher gave no hint of her emotions. She had been up since five this morning, pacing the kitchen and telling herself that she was mad. And Peter and Carol Taylor were even more cracked for letting her run in the first place. What collective lunacy had led them all to believe that she might actually stand a chance against Bill Mackey, armed with nothing more than a three-week campaign and a marriage that had earned her a permanent position in the gossip columns?

Bill Mackey had smiled at her as she'd walked in. The smile had been genuine, which was worse. He saw her as no more of a threat than the young candidate for the far left, who would be lucky to poll in double-figures.

"It's just an act," Peter reassured her quietly.

"Well, he's pretty damned convincing," she snapped.

He did not retaliate, recognising her nerves for what

they were. She was grateful, and doubly grateful for his permanent presence by her side in the last gruelling three weeks on the campaign trail.

She was only now beginning to appreciate what a true professional he was. On the mornings when she felt she couldn't face another day of electioneering, he would cajole her out of bed with some new and brilliant strategy he'd dreamed up in the dead of night. When she felt she couldn't possibly meet one more constituent, he would meet them with her, turning it into a double-act that worked. He had even sent her home early some evenings while he drove around the city alone, meeting yet more people on her behalf. He was indefatigable when she knew that he must be as exhausted as she.

But more than his hard work, she appreciated his belief in her. It was there in the quiet pep-talks her gave her at the start of each long day, in his insistence that she always go that extra mile no matter how tired and disheartened she became.

"You can do it, Tess," he said a million times a day.

And she believed him. Even when doors were closed in their faces, when voter after voter told her in no uncertain terms that they were voting for Bill Mackey. She still believed him when people accused her of using her marriage crisis for her own ends; even when people demanded answers to the film fiasco, that she did not have. But it was hard to sustain that belief when some women accused her of being a disgrace to her own sex for staying with a cheating man.

Those were the grimmest days. Then on other days,

more women would say that they admired her handling of the whole affair. They would shake her hand and tell her how much they appreciated her dignity and honour through it all, how she had refused to don the mantle of victim. They were proud of her, they said. Hillary Clinton couldn't have done it better.

"We're getting the women's vote," Carol Taylor cautiously announced at an campaign meeting the day *The Kilkenny People* poll confirmed that after her first week on the campaign trail, Tess Fisher had taken ten points from Bill Mackey.

She was right. Sick and tired of male representatives, the women of Kilkenny had flocked to meet Tess first out of curiosity, then conviction. Tess Fisher was a voice they had not heard before. She didn't spout incomprehensible policy at them, she was human; human because her husband had cheated on her and human because she had forgiven him. Like them, she had a child to worry about, a marriage that was not all sunshine and roses, and a face that needed a little help in the morning like every other normal woman.

A second poll a week later confirmed the astonishing fact that Tess Fisher was closing fast on Bill Mackey. Suddenly, she was *A Contender*.

Bolstered, Tess Fisher's campaign gathered strength as it entered its final week. The Government, glimpsing hope on the horizon for the first time in a month, flung its full weight behind her and there had been blanket national media coverage in the days before polling day. Carol Taylor herself had pounded the pavements all last week.

Then yesterday, polling day, and the biggest turnout in the constituency in decades. Everyone had an opinion, it seemed, and they intended to voice it. The first count was expected to be completed in a little over an hour's time.

"How are you, Mum?"

Fiona came from behind, looking healthy and brown. The outdoor job in a local studfarm had suited her. Tess had found time to organise it. Besides, she and Peter were hardly at home these days and Fiona needed some form of supervision. Now she was back in boarding school. Reports were good so far.

"Terrified," she said, throwing an arm affectionately around Fiona's waist.

"You'll win," Fiona said emphatically. "You've worked too hard."

"So has your father," Tess said gently, looking to Peter.

Fiona cut him dead with a look. That familiar pained expression ran across Peter's face.

"I'll go and see if I can find out how much longer they're going to be," Fiona said,

setting off towards the top of the count centre.

"There's nothing I can do, Tess, is there?" Peter asked, looking after Fiona. "She can't keep it up forever, Peter."

But Tess didn't feel optimistic. There had been no softening in Fiona's attitude, no hint of forgiveness. Tess wondered whether she and Peter would ever be close again.

"Tess! *There* you are!"

It was Sheila Burke, elbowing her way through the throng.

"She's here to give you her support," Peter murmured, seeing Tess's face.

Tess knew exactly why she was here, and the reasons were all to do with herself. Harry Burke had been quietly hospitalised yesterday morning. It was undoubtedly the early stages of cirrhosis of the liver. When he came out, he would be in no fit state to continue as Minister for Finance. Sheila Burke was suddenly facing life as an ordinary deputy's wife and this did not sit well with her. She was already desperately shoring up friends and favours. Tess, if she won, would be the most valuable and influential friend Sheila could have.

"Tell me, how are you bearing up?" Sheila gushed, any past insults obviously long forgotten.

"Fine, thank you, Sheila. And how's Harry?"

"Oh, the poor *thing*. He's dreadfully sorry he can't be here, told me to pass on his best wishes and all that. He has every confidence in you, you know."

Liar. He and Geraldine Day would have put more faith in Mickey Mouse.

"Can I do anything? Anything at all?" Sheila asked, fleshy face begging for some sign of conciliation, some indication that she would be part of the golden inner circle should Tess win.

Tess watched her grovel. She was tempted to tell her to get lost. But if she was going to be a politician, then she knew she had to learn how to play the game. And who knew what favours might be needed down the line from whatever sources? Still, it wouldn't hurt to make Sheila suffer a little first.

"A cup of tea wouldn't go astray," she said calmly.

Sheila's face was almost comical in its disbelief. She, Sheila Burke, wife of the Minister for Finance, was being asked to make tea. No, *told* to make tea. And by Tess Fisher, a mousy little nobody from Kilkenny who would not be standing here now only for the fact that her husband had hot pants.

"Tea." She choked the word out.

"Milk with no sugar," Tess confirmed. "If it's not too much bother?"

Sheila knew how to play the game too. There was a price and she would have to pay it.

"No bother at all." She managed a twisted smile and went off.

Tess turned to Peter with a grimace. "I'll spend the rest of my days paying for that if I don't win this bloody election."

At least Jack Thornton's support had been genuine. He'd phoned this morning from LA, to Tess's surprise.

"It's 98 degrees out here and rising. I've got the pool filled up and I'm just calling to know when you're coming to visit."

He was joking she knew.

"As soon as I lose this election."

"You won't. I'm hearing great things this end. I'm rooting for you."

"Thanks. Maybe I'll do a victory lap in California, we can do lunch."

"I'd like that, Tess."

"I'm sorry about the film, Jack."

"Hey, these things happen. I'm back acting now, doing a little shoot-'em-up number with special effects like you wouldn't believe."

"You'll find another movie to direct."

"No frigging way. Too much grief involved. Anyway, acting pays a hell of a lot better and I get more time to lounge around by the pool."

In the background, Tess could hear a female voice calling for him. It sounded suspiciously young and probably belonged to a blonde, if Tess's guess was right.

"You've got company, I won't keep you," she said.

There was an awkward silence. "Good luck, Tess. I mean it."

This time, Tess knew that she would not hear from him again. She wasn't sorry. He had filled an emptiness in her life for a brief period, and she in his, but it was over now.

"Tess? I think they might be going to make an announcement." Peter's face was tense and grey. The three weeks had taken its toll on him too, in more ways than one, Tess knew. There was a certain air of defeat about him, as if everything good in his life was gone and now he was simply enduring – the scandal, the political crisis, his marriage too.

The polling centre's intercom suddenly crackled. The crowd abruptly grew deathly quiet. A sombre voice quietly asked all by-election candidates to make their way to the podium.

"Oh Christ," Peter said.

Tess felt herself go cold. "But the result is not expected for another hour."

She saw Carol Taylor cast a worried glance over. Bill Mackey was as alert as a beagle. This was not good.

"It means that one of the candidates has reached the required quota of votes to be elected, Tess," Peter said in a tight voice. "There's no need to go to transfers. There's a clear victory."

This is it, Tess thought rationally. You've either won or you haven't, it's as simple as that. You can handle it either way.

"You have to go up, Tess," Peter told her, as the other four candidates walked towards the top of the hall. Tess felt oddly detached. Everything seemed to move very slowly. "Tess?"

"Yes. I know."

Face impassive, she left the security of Peter and Carol Taylor and made her way through the crowd. Bill Mackey was already confidently fingering his acceptance speech as she took her place on the vast podium beside him. Never had she felt more frightened as she stood there, waiting for the votes to be announced. In the sea of silent faces, she searched for Peter's but couldn't see him. She was on her own now. But you've always been on your own, she reminded herself. And she felt okay.

The party would go on into the small hours. Half the gathering was already blind drunk. Carol Taylor had even accepted a second glass of champagne, a rare sight indeed.

Miraculously alone for a moment, Tess hung in the shadows by the wall and sipped orange juice. She did not want or need drink. She wanted to savour every last moment of this night. In years to come, she would tell her grandchildren of the night that, against all the odds, she became the first candidate to reach the required quota of votes and was deemed duly elected as the Dáil representative for Kilkenny.

Watching the boisterous crowd, Tess found that she shared none of their euphoria or triumphalism. Peculiarly, her overriding emotion was one of relief. She felt as though she had spent a lifetime as a fullback when, really, she should have been playing centre-field. It had been very chilly indeed in Peter's shadow all these years. She knew that she could never go back.

She watched him now in the centre of the room, surrounded as always by people. He belonged to them. He had never belonged to her in any sense of the word. And she was past accepting second best. Tonight had shown her that she didn't have to anymore.

She still loved him in a fashion – who could resist him? And she would be relying on him in more ways than one as she found her feet in this new world she was suddenly catapulted into. But she did not want him in any other way. And what was the point in prolonging it for either of them?

Suddenly, she knew why she was hanging back here by the wall. She was still tied to Peter Fisher, unable to believe that this was her night and not his, while he was out there in the limelight as usual. She could not embark on the celebrations, or indeed on the new life she had won for herself tonight, until she broke free.

He must have sensed her watching him, because he looked over across the heads of the crowd, eyes questioning.

"Go," she mouthed slowly.

He hesitated, knowing that she meant something else.

"Go, Peter," she said again, offering him a small, crooked smile.

He understood. He nodded slowly, knowing that she was telling him to vacate not just her party, but her life. He looked at her one last time and slipped away out the door.

Tess Fisher took a deep breath, smoothed down her skirt, and then stepped forward into the crowd.

Chapter Thirty-seven

"You have lovely eyes."

He was trying to be romantic, bless him. And why not? This was their third date after all.

"Thank you, David," Jean said. His were lovely too. Chocolate brown with eyelashes that most women would kill for. The rest of him wasn't bad either. He also had an interesting job, an intelligent brain and a great sense of humour.

"Remember that play you really wanted to see?" he said now. "That was sold out?"

"Yes?"

Proudly, he threw an envelope onto the table. "Two tickets. For tonight."

He was also very, very nice, she noted gloomily. So what the hell was wrong with her? What was she behaving as though she'd just climbed out of a deep freezer?

"Great," she said, determined to make more of an effort. She *would* go to the theatre with him tonight. She *would* have a good time. God knows she needed it. After three months of solitude, she was in danger of turning into a nun.

"I'm looking forward to it," she added with a joviality that she didn't quite feel.

"And maybe we'll go for a drink afterwards," he said. "Somewhere quiet."

She took this to mean that he did not particularly like her choice of venue for their date today. The pub was frequented by the theatre crowd, and it was heaving now with the lunchtime rush, a TV blaring in the corner. It was loud and raucous and afforded no opportunity for intimacy.

She hadn't done it on purpose, she told herself. It was simply that it was just around the corner from the office.

"In fact, I've got a very well-stocked drinks cabinet back at my place," he said meaningfully.

Jean laughed too loudly. "Thanks anyway, but I wouldn't dream of depleting it."

She saw his interest grow. Her mother had been right all along, she sadly admitted. Men really did fancy you more if you played hard to get.

Feeling like an old misery guts, she turned to watch the crowd at the bar. She noted that several of them were watching her. Probably marvelling at how she had pulled herself out of the gutter, how she had battled against adversity and scandal to turn her agency around.

She was suddenly shocked at her own cynicism. It wasn't like her. Surely she wasn't turning into one of those embittered, frustrated people who, having been let down by life, couldn't see the good in anything?

No. Despite everything, she still had enthusiasm and energy and nowhere did it show more than in her agency. In the three short months since she had sold Carl Tallon and Cathy Conroy to Broadway, The Jean Ormsby Agency had tripled in size. It was her reason for getting up in the morning, and she was proud of it.

Her personal life would catch up, she told herself. Time was a great healer, wasn't it? Her mother must surely be right there too.

"Coffee?"

"Oh. Yes, please, David." She knew she had been ignoring him, lost in silly self-pity. Determined to at least give things a chance, she offered him a brilliant smile as he stood to go to the bar. He was gratified.

"Don't go away," he said, disappearing into the crowd.

Jean applied herself again to her half-eaten cheese sandwich. She had got thin recently. The noise of the pub ebbed and flowed around her, along with the news on the television. It was muffled but audible.

"Carol Taylor's first cabinet reshuffle since the Kilkenny by-election has been predicable regarding all the main portfolios, although many had expected Peter Fisher to take one of the top jobs."

Jean remained sitting quite calmly, picking at the sandwich. There was no reason to get all emotional. She was well used to hearing about him in the media by now. Not a week went by without some interview with him, or a mention of him in the press. The only time she had allowed herself to get upset was the time she'd read that he and Tess Fisher had separated. But she'd got over it. She'd got over *him*.

And so she scarcely listened as the newscaster droned on. "The big surprise today is Peter Fisher's resignation from the cabinet. He has also announced that when his tenure as a deputy is up in three years' time, he will not be seeking re-election. He has cited personal reasons."

Jean felt a peculiar lightness in her head; a dizziness. It couldn't be true. Peter would never give up politics. He lived for it – hadn't Tess Fisher said so? And hadn't Jean brutally ended things on the strength of that conviction?

It's too late now. Forget it. It's time to move on with your life. He *has*.

She said the words over and over again. She believed herself. But only for seconds.

David arrived back from the bar with the coffees as she got to her feet.

"Where are you going?"

"I've something to do." She spread her hands. "And David . . . you'll have to find someone else to take to the theatre. I'm sorry."

He caught her drift immediately. His face fell a mile. "But I thought . . ."

"I know. And I thought I was over someone. But I'm not. I really am sorry."

She pecked him on the cheek and quickly left.

He was wearing faded old Levis and a checked shirt. She had never seen him dressed like that before and, for a moment, she wasn't sure it was him. Through the doorway, she could see him rearranging cardboard boxes in the little office, face furrowed in concentration. He did not see her at first.

"Peter."

He looked up slowly, dark eyes wary. He didn't seem all that surprised that she was here. He didn't seem all that pleased, either.

"Imelda told me where to find you."

He nodded slowly. Then, a small wave of his hand as he invited her in. "Welcome to my new home." There was irony on his face.

Jean looked around carefully. It was nothing like his palatial corner office in the Arts building on Mespil Road. This office was cramped and vaguely grubby, lit by an unflattering fluorescent light. Metal filing cabinets and a functional desk were the only furniture.

"It's very you," she said.

He smiled a little. "They've taken my Ministerial car away too."

Jean looked at him directly. "The way I understand it, you gave it away yourself."

He looked at her hard. "You understand correctly." If it's any business of yours, he might as well have added.

Silence now as they watched each other under the glare of the fluorescent light.

"Why are you here, Jean?" he asked eventually. There was no bitterness in his voice. He merely sounded tired.

Jean was stung. He was looking at her as though she were just another imposition at the end of a very long day. All her great notions of pouring out her heart seemed ridiculous now. He wasn't interested.

"It doesn't matter," she said levelly. "It was a mistake."

"You must have come for something."

"It was a mistake," she repeated.

"I'll be the judge of that." The weariness was gone from his face now. His eyes flashed. "You can't just waltz in and out of my life as you please, Jean. This time you might have the courtesy to give me some kind of explanation."

She felt a dull shock at his anger. "I did give you an explanation – "

"You did not! You told me it was over and then you skipped town!"

"I did *not* skip town!" She was angry now too, trying to defend a position that she knew looked indefensible. "I had no choice!"

"And what's that supposed to mean?"

She would not tell tales, not now. "Oh, let's just drop it, Peter."

"No. You owe me, Jean. You walked out on me, broke my heart!"

His hurt was written all over his face. She felt sick.

"I didn't mean to! I left because of you!"

"Oh, give me a break."

His incredulity was more than she could take. When she spoke again, her voice was hard and cold. "Your career.

They would have taken it from you if I had stayed."

"And since when have I asked you to worry about my career?"

"*You* didn't." It was out before she could stop it.

"What?"

She said nothing. He was watching her, seeing right through her as always.

"Tess," he said slowly. "It was Tess, wasn't it?"

Jean shrugged defeated. "She only pointed out the truth. That they'd never let you keep your job if we'd stayed together."

"You should have told me."

"Why? What could you have done?"

"Resigned. Like I did today."

"Well, I didn't tell you because I thought it best. And then I left. So there you have it, Peter. Your explanation."

It was all out in the open. He must see now that she didn't abandon him, that she'd been backed into a corner. But he did not look any warmer. It was too late after all, she realised, wondering how it was possible to feel such misery.

"And why are you here now, Jean?" he asked quietly.

She said nothing for the longest time. She should just go. But then again, what had she left to lose? She might as well tell him the truth, for what it was worth.

"I came because I wanted to know if there was still a chance for us, Peter. And I knew that after what happened, I had to be the one to come to you."

He digested this in absolute silence, his eyes fixed on her face. She looked right back. She still loved him and she was not ashamed of that fact. And at least she would always know that she had given it her best shot.

Peter eventually said, "You took your sweet time, didn't you?"

And all the coldness was gone, the anger. He was looking at her with so much love and tenderness that she thought for a moment that she would cry. Instead, she flew around the desk to him. He came to meet her halfway. She buried herself in his arms, holding him so close that she was unsure where her body ended and his began.

"I couldn't before now . . . I almost did when I read that you and Tess had separated."

"Yes," he said.

"Is it true?" She had to be sure.

"We've gone our separate ways. Personally-speaking. Professionally I still see her all the time."

Jean nodded – of course he must, they were fellow-deputies now.

"And how about you?" he asked. "I thought you'd have found someone else."

"I tried . . . but everything changed today, when I heard that you'd resigned."

"I always said that I would some day."

"Peter, why did you step down?"

He pulled away a little, to look down into her face. "It's gone sour for me. I want more," he said simply. "I'll go back and do some consultancy work. Build a house for myself. Maybe grow a few vegetables in the back garden."

Jean smiled. "You? Grow vegetables?"

He smiled too. "Don't sneer. Just because you big-shot agents don't know how to get your hands dirty."

He had been keeping tabs on her career just as she had on his. She wasn't surprised.

"Maybe I want more too," she said.

"Oh, do you? Are you telling me that as an ordinary deputy, I'm not good enough for you any more?"

"You'll do, I suppose."

The banter died. They were suddenly desperately serious. And afraid.

"What do you think, Peter? About starting over? Will it work out?"

He tilted her head up and kissed her then. And it was so right that she felt all her doubts melt away.

He smiled. "There's only one way to find out."

THE END